MARK A. SALTER

SINS

OF THE

TRIBE

A NOVEL

GREENLEAF
BOOK GROUP PRESS

Published by Greenleaf Book Group Press
Austin, Texas
www.gbgpress.com

Distributed by Greenleaf Book Group

For ordering information or special discounts for bulk purchases, please contact Greenleaf Book Group at PO Box 91869, Austin, TX 78709, 512.891.6100.

Design and composition by Greenleaf Book Group
Cover design by Greenleaf Book Group
Cover Image: ©iStockphoto/Dewitt
Author photo by Patrice Kelly Photography

Publisher's Cataloging-in-Publication data is available.

Print ISBN: 978-1-62634-939-1
eBook ISBN: 978-1-62634-940-7

Part of the Tree Neutral® program, which offsets the number of trees consumed in the production and printing of this book by taking proactive steps, such as planting trees in direct proportion to the number of trees used: www.treeneutral.com

TreeNeutral

Printed in the United States of America on acid-free paper

22 23 24 25 26 27   10 9 8 7 6 5 4 3 2 1

First Edition

*Dedicated to the game of college football,
for all its wonders and challenges.*

Wally

....

NEW MEXICO

WHEN I CLOSE my eyes and think of a blade of grass, sweet memories appear, filling me with a purpose abandoned long ago. These memories, independent of my will, multiply and become my thoughts. The blade is uniform in a sea of perfect green and, with one knee on the ground, I place my finger on it, look back to Henry for his nod, then the ball in the grasp of the center's hands. I give a quick command, the ball sails towards me, and my hands take over: catch, place, and spin. Then the sweet thud of Henry's foot sends the ball high over the cresting line and my blade of grass reappears as if the transaction was meaningless.

I think of Dion, Coach Oldham, and the other players and the trust they placed in me and my brother, Henry, even though neither of us belonged. I would've struggled to play small college football. I think of the fans in the stadium and those watching on TV. I feel their intense gaze as we performed our duties, a gaze that penetrated too far and asked for sacrifices without knowing their depths.

Bastille University. *The Bastille University Tribe.* Six-time national champions located on the Florida panhandle near the Georgia and Alabama border, the heart of college football. A place where they'd take your thoughts along with your body if they could. But here in New Mexico, my thoughts are my own. On long drives where the black road converges to a point against a mountainous horizon, or at my aunt's art colony listening to peaceful souls discuss the meaning of their latest creation while I get high, or after I chase the Coach away from the valley and stare at the starlit night—I think of Henry.

The turnoff to my aunt's place was a few miles down the road when I saw the carcass. I pumped the brakes trying to slow my truck, a truck that would never pass inspection. The brakes whined their rusty complaint like they were too tired to make an unplanned stop and I was a good forty yards past the carcass when I came to a halt. This one was big, and I knew the Coach, a Mexican gray wolf, would be happy. The afternoon light was fading, and I reminded myself it was already October. I ran my hand through my long hair and scraggly beard, it was my way of measuring time—I hadn't shaved or cut my hair since everything that happened almost two years ago.

Instead of backing up I decided to walk. I pulled out a garbage bag I kept behind the front seat for just this purpose, stuck it in my jacket pocket, and slipped on my work gloves. The cool High Plains air was rolling in and it gave me a sense of liberation, quite unlike the unending Florida humidity and I gave thanks to no one in particular.

It was a raccoon, the biggest one yet. I looked it over carefully, noting the blunt trauma. The raccoon's head had taken the shot, probably from a front bumper, and it rested in a halo of blackened blood. I used to hate ugliness. I used to close my eyes and wait for it to go away, but over time I was conditioned to look at it for what it was and accept the unchangeable. Like hearing a knee get blown out or the shallow, gasping breaths of a teammate with newly broken ribs. First the pop, then the screams, or worse, the silent swallowing of pain. It wasn't physical pain that emptied them though, it was the pain of knowing they were eliminated from the dance contest like some middle-aged proctor had tapped them on the shoulder with a sad look. Their dreams of going pro, probably marginal to start with, were finished unless they were at Dion's level.

I squatted over the raccoon and tried to see if any whisper of life remained. I hated talking at important times like this, but it was deader than the Tribe's shot at the National Championship two years ago. Nevertheless, I cleared my throat and spoke with a manner of politeness and gravity.

"Professor, I'm very sorry, but the Coach would like to see you."

His body was stiff, I could tell when I picked him up by the tail and lowered him into the plastic bag. The Professor's weight pulled on me like guilt and I soon found myself swinging the bag with the rhythm of my walk as if we were taking a pleasant stroll through the quad. A pickup truck crested the hill, and I knew who it was without confirmation. I put my head down and walked on the gravel, hoping it would pass, but it eased to a stop beside me. It was my Aunt Janie. She rolled down the window and I saw the sad look on her face, like she was watching a recovering alcoholic heading for the bar. She didn't speak and I took a moment before replying to her silence.

"I'm not hurting anybody," I said. "Or anything."

She let another moment pass and I felt her passive disapproval, just an exhale of dry, voiceless air as she checked the rearview mirror for traffic that wasn't there. I loved my aunt even though I barely knew her. When we first met, I looked into her face, trying to imagine the face of my mother, but that had faded quickly and now I saw only her and the gracious deeds she performed on my behalf. She was the only person I could turn to when it all came crashing down.

"Walter," Aunt Janie said. "I need you to stop by tonight. I got another email."

I nodded and painfully waited for her release.

"And do it before you get high."

I nodded again without telling her I'd already read it, then she slowly pulled away. I'd been checking her laptop secretly to see if he wrote again. When I got back to the truck, I placed the Professor in the front corner of the cargo bed and wedged him in with my tool kit to keep him safe. My rifle was jammed in between the passenger seat and the door, the butt of it next to a couple boxes of ammo.

It took a couple of turns for the engine to start and when it did my excitement started to build, I even had butterflies in my gut and was thankful the feeling was as fresh as ever. I could feel the adrenaline pulsing in my veins and the euphoria starting to kick in, like we were running out of the tunnel at Bastille Stadium. As the Professor and I pulled onto the road, I called back to him through the open window.

"Don't worry Professor, we're going to get them sons-a-bitches." I screamed a bloody howl and banged the top of the roof as the old truck strained as hard as it could.

The sun was sinking fast and the Professor and I had to hurry. I drove deeper into the land, the part where I feel like I'm burrowing instead of crossing. It always feels like I can walk out of my trailer and reach out and touch the mesas just south of the colony but to actually get there it's almost a half hour drive over bumpy dirt paths. When I got to the spot in the valley between the mesas, I coasted the truck in and checked the sun. In about forty-five minutes it would dip far enough to cover the valley in the mesas' shade and catching a clear view of the Coach would be tricky.

The Professor's podium was a large flat boulder about five feet high and the Coach always had a tough time scaling it without the risk of a tumble. When I first began to shoot it was only for the thrill of hearing my shot echo through the valley, two or three fading scorches like it was out of a movie. The first day I saw the Coach sniffing around some fallen animal, I drew the sight in and took aim. I didn't know what I was doing. I pulled the trigger and watched through the scope as the shot hit about ten feet away from the Coach. It was like the bullet stung the earth and a cloud of dust burst out of the ground then slowly drifted away, like applause in a faraway stadium.

The Coach had been coming from the scrub brush on the east, so I sat the Professor up as best I could and leaned him against a large rock I'd placed on the podium. I tried to position his head so he'd see the Coach coming but he didn't cooperate, his crushed head drooped to one side in a grotesque manner and I knew he needed a talk. I straightened his head and into those small black eyes I strained for his attention.

"Listen, Professor. He's coming and there's nothing we can do about it, you said so yourself. If I could, I'd raise your paws and stick your middle claw out on each one to let him know how you feel but I can only hold him off for so long. You got me?"

The Professor slumped against the rock with his head draped over again and his fat belly was exposed like a middle-aged man in a skybox waiting for the game to start. A mild wind caused some of his fur to flutter, little black and gray and white strands, beautiful and intricate and it always made me wonder why mother nature would go to such great pains creating life to then allow its destruction in such a cruel manner. The wind blew stronger in response to my thought as if it were trying to carry him away to a better place, but his weight bound him to the podium. His fate was determined, and I had my own work to do.

"One more question, Professor. Have you seen Henry?"

I climbed back in the truck and drove up to my spot, an outcropping of boulders almost a hundred yards away. With my rifle I scaled the boulders to the spot I'd cleared out and settled in lying down on my stomach. The view through my scope let me scan the valley and when I determined the Coach wasn't there yet, I laid down my rifle and pulled out my Tribe flask. The etched arrow on the flask was nearly faded from overuse and the cheap whiskey burned down my throat, but within seconds the bloom of pleasant heat settled over my brain. I took another drink, then propped myself up on my elbows and stared through the scope. It gave me time to think.

The roads I traveled most days, the vistas from atop a high mesa, or this lonely valley open up something inside me. Amid the solitude I can pause the churning feelings inside and draw them into focus, if only for a moment, but the moment is never long enough. I was the one that made it crash, I ruined it, something I had prayed for my entire life, something communal and once pure.

A movement caught my attention, I scanned the valley and the Coach appeared, the Mexican gray wolf. He probably watched me every time I escorted the Professor to his podium. Watching him react to my bullets triggered a lustful relief, but it almost got me kicked out of the colony. The artists were heartbroken when they heard what I was doing. A few of them sat me down and explained how the colony, funded by the good fortune earned during my aunt's time in Silicon Valley, was a sanctuary for gentle beings seeking a peaceful existence in a senselessly violent world, and my shooting at innocent animals violated their communal pact of peace to the point that their artistic souls were blocked from manifesting themselves. As much as I loved my aunt, to me they were a bunch of middle-aged hippies getting high and filling out coloring books. Only Aunt Janie's wisdom made me think, *That wolf is as innocent as Henry.*

The truth is different. That wolf would climb over the dead bodies of his fallen brethren without hesitation in pursuit of fresh meat, just like the real Coach. And after my aunt received the first email, my marksmanship went to hell.

My name is Dion an old friend/former teammate of Wally Hestia. It's very, very important that I contact him, I have tried for two years but now it's super important. There's no trouble, he doesn't have to worry but I need to contact him very soon. Some-one gave me this email and said you may know him or something. Please let him know I gotta talk to him, he can get back to me on this email. Thank u.

Before I was done reading, I could feel something growing out of me like vines trying to reach into the computer, wanting Dion's approval, wanting to be part of the Tribe again.

"Is this a friend of yours?" my aunt said.

I guess I was in shock and didn't notice her question until she asked again. I pulled out my flask, took a long drink, and wiped my mouth.

"He was special, one of the great ones, but he got ruined, too." I looked to Aunt Janie and saw the concern on her face. "It was my fault."

She took my hand in sympathy and we sat in silence.

"You've got to move on, Walter," she said. "You need to find out what he wants."

I didn't respond. I held my head in my hands, waiting for the moment to pass.

"You don't even see the irony of it, do you?" she said.

I lifted my head, wanting her to continue.

"You left and you're free with no responsibilities; you live in a wide-open space with no boundaries. But all you've really done is build yourself a prison." She waited for my response, but none came. "You need to reply to this Dion."

The dashed crosshairs of my scope lined up right on the Coach's temple and a simple squeeze of the trigger would end his life as the

Professor looked down on him. The Coach was a few feet from the podium, sniffing and circling as he tried to determine the best way to scale the boulder. I squeezed the trigger. The bullet hit the side of the podium and the Coach jumped back in fear but didn't yield any further. While he stood there, tongue out, breathing hard, I fired again, and it hit a few feet in front of him. He jumped back and then trotted off into the scrub brush, but I knew he'd be back.

I'd thought I found my own sanctuary here. Looking down the valley on a beautiful afternoon with no connections to the world was enough for me. After I left Bastille—escaped, really—I cut off all connections. I threw away my phone outside the stadium and never went back for my laptop. The only time I'd been on a computer since was when I used my aunt's to delete all my social media and email accounts and to see if that reporter printed the story. But she didn't, another promise of truth that went unfulfilled.

After the first email I drank enough to make my head pound like the marching band was playing off-key just outside my trailer. It was a few days before I responded.

> *I heard you're looking for me, I don't want to be bothered. What's so important and how do I know this is the real Dion McAres?*

The Coach approached the podium, and I could see his determination. I got up on one knee, took careful aim, and squeezed off a shot. It hit behind him.

> *I'm going to Bastille for the Kentucky game. Get there Friday night and call me at the number below. I'll let you know what hotel and I'll get you a room. Click on the attachment to find out why. Dion. TRIBE FOREVER!*

The Coach circled the podium and I stood, not caring if he saw me. I fired off three shots, none close.

The attachment was a picture. My aunt's internet connection was slow, it filled the screen in slow horizontal lines from the top down. I could tell it was the campus right away, the stadium was in the background and there were people tailgating in the distance. Then the top of a football helmet appeared with people standing on both sides of the player. I saw Henry was the player, the people I didn't know. You could take a hundred pictures of Henry while he was in different states of mind and to anyone else, he would look the same. But I could call out every mood he was in; I could tell if he was joyful or sad or panicked. This picture made me cry. He was broken.

The Coach must have come from the far side, he appeared on top of the podium and approached the Professor. Then he stopped and looked in my direction, like he was asking what I was going to do. I fired until the clip was empty, and every shot missed.

> *I forgot to say how to prove its me. You and me are the only ones that know what QB21 means. You have to show up, I'd come and get you if I knew where you were.*

I never shot a single wolf in all my trips to the valley; I didn't have it in me. I sank to the ground and started to sob then covered my ears to hide from the sound of the Coach tearing into the Professor. In a couple of weeks, I'd be at the Kentucky game.

Dion

....

ORCHARD PARK, NEW YORK

THE BALL SPUN towards the ceiling in a perfect spiral and seemed to hang in the air before dropping back into my hands. It was my new ritual: lying on my bed, catching the ball, then closing my eyes and becoming Wally for a moment, trying to imagine what it was like catching the snap, placing the ball, then hearing Henry boom the shit out of it. Watching my boys run onto the field knowing it was a sure thing was like springing a secret weapon on the whole world, and it never got old. They were the most reliable weapon we had, even more reliable than me. And the most innocent. I can imagine being Wally as a holder, but I can never even come close to imagining what he went through.

The ball floated up above me and when it came down, I closed my eyes. I can still see their faces; Wally wanting to be part of the Tribe, Henry not wanting anything other than to be with Wally. The first time I met them is still fresh in my memory: two little white boys, a pair that had no business suiting up for the Tribe. I thought I was special, shielding them from abuse, making sure they felt welcome, but I was just doing it for myself. Through everything that happened, Wally was the only one to act like Bastille meant more than a winning football team and he paid the price for it. I wasn't there for him then, as a matter of fact, I abandoned him when part of it was my fault.

I tossed the ball in the air again, watching the laces spin around as if they were the days flying by. We didn't have much time. I'd searched for him for so long that it became a second job and now that I had made contact, it felt like I'd never hear from him again. The picture of Henry had to make a difference, it just had to.

The ball flew straight up, almost hitting the ceiling, and this time it had a slight wobble, an imperfection. Wally and Henry were perfect. We weren't. We let him down and he took more blame than any man could ever handle, some of it directly from me. We can't erase the past, but we gotta stop this sin from destroying the future. Wally has to believe again, and when he does, so will I.

Wally

....

WEST TEMPLE, GEORGIA FOUR YEARS EARLIER

i.

THEIR OFFENSE OVERLOADED: all three wide receivers and their tight end were lined up to our right, leaving Jameel Williams, their best player, as the lone back and the left side empty. Their quarterback approached the line, pointed at me, and yelled a pre-snap call I'd hear all day. *"The Mike is 16, the Mike is 16."* I was West Temple High's middle linebacker on defense—the Mike, quarterback on offense, and number 16.

It was the first play of the game, and I knew the play they were about to run, something I'd seen on film all week: a toss sweep to Jameel to our left, with both guards pulling. Their quarterback and I held a brief look as he put his mouthguard in and began the sequence with muffled words. He was just a normal kid like me, as opposed to Jameel Williams, who I feared would run over us, by us, and through us all day. Nevertheless, we were going to put a licking on him, at least we had convinced ourselves of that in the days leading up to the game.

"Marshall," I yelled. With a brief glance to my left I saw him nod for my benefit without looking at me. He knew it was coming, too, his job was to hold the edge. Then I yelled "Louie, Louie," to our defensive tackles, which meant penetrate to the left.

Then, when the center snapped the ball, something beautiful happened: Their lead guard pulled the wrong way and met their other guard in a head-on collision behind the center. The center came at me low and fast, and I shot my hands out and popped him on his shoulder pads. Like all mediocre linemen, he stopped moving his feet and I was by him quickly enough to see our defensive tackles bottle up Jameel and just about bring him down. Marshall, our best player, finished him off for a two-yard loss. It was going to be a long game and I loved every second of it.

Game days in high school. They had a special quality that fed me in ways I thought I couldn't live without. Like walking through a doorway into a temporary reality that would soon be shut and sealed again out of necessity. The feeling hummed beneath my skin and started from the time I woke up until I fell asleep, replaying the moments before they became a pale memory. The feeling was better with a win, but still powerful with a loss. Stronger if I played well, but still meaningful if I didn't. It was all war with no death. It was ever-important, without destroying innocence. Everyone cared, but there weren't enough to corrupt. We could perform, create, and destroy; we righteously screamed to claim our victories and howled at our failures; we were unique and unscripted. Instead of existing in quiet desperation, I was alive.

There were thirty-nine game days for me in high school, counting freshman, JV, and then varsity, and it was drawing to a close; the New Brunswick game was the thirty-sixth and also the day I first met someone from the Tribe. If the trail ended there, it would've been enough for me to talk about the rest of my life.

I always woke before dawn and as I laid awake, I listened to the rhythm of Henry's sleep, his innocent breaths barely audible three feet away, a sound that had fended off loneliness since I was five years old. He never woke early or slept late, he waited patiently while I did his homework, and he never left the table until he was told.

I got up and edged my way between our twin beds and reached over the crowded desk, trying to find the window shade's cord without knocking anything over and creating a clatter. Henry wouldn't mind, but my adopted father, the Minister, would raise holy hell if I woke him.

Before we went to bed, I saw the Minister on the screened-in porch, slumped in his overstuffed chair, staring out into darkness. It was eleven thirty when Henry and I got home from work the night before and went through our routine. The side screen door creaked in proportion to the speed at which it was opened and I always pulled it slowly, then waited for Henry to hold it. The main door's knob was barely visible, and I carefully turned it to see if it was locked. When it opened, I stepped into the kitchen as quietly as I could while Henry eased the screen door shut behind us. We stood in the kitchen waiting to hear where he was and with no sound of him, I stepped into the parlor and saw him from behind in his chair out back.

The red glow of his cigarette illuminated the silhouette of the glass in his hand. As he exhaled a plume of smoke, I bent over to look at the bottle of scotch on the counter. It was a good four inches emptier than the night before, so I sent Henry to our room while I braced myself. I'd stopped trying to figure out the reasons for his rage long ago, I just let him land backhands across my face to wear him out and protect Henry. That night was no different.

But the mornings were mine, especially on game days before sunrise. In the pre-dawn darkness, I'd look through my window and imagine a different view before the morning light began its weak coloring of the yard, the goalpost trees, and the forest that led to nowhere. After a few minutes, I laid back down and looked around the room for inspiration, but it was too dark to see.

The poster of Clayton Gilmore, the Tribe's quarterback from the 1979 National Championship team, was hidden in darkness. I couldn't make out the colors and had to use my memory to see Clayton's beautiful green jersey with his white number 12 outlined in bright gold just below *Bastille* on the front of the jersey. His pants were white with gold and green striping down the side. The helmet was the best and it hadn't changed in all these years. It was white, a pure white, with just the right touches. The arrow started at the very back of the helmet and extended over the top to the facemask. Most teams have silly little stripes down the middle of their helmets that don't mean a thing and are just a distraction, but the stripe on the Tribe's helmets ended right on the forehead in a large green arrowhead.

On our bedroom wall there was a classic picture of the Tribe's offense during a game, taken from just the right angle, showing the offensive line, tight end, and quarterback and the first thing you notice is all those arrows on the front of their heads—lined up as if they were coming at the defense's heart. To finish it off, on the right side of the helmet was the *Tribe* in traditional script and on the left side was the player's number.

I admit, there were many sleepless nights spent lying in bed or daydreaming during class or a bus ride to an away game that I'd imagined myself in that helmet with my number 16 on the side. Just like Anthony Duke, number 16, the famous wide receiver on the '85 team that won it all, whose poster looks down on my bed. Next to him is Coach Oldham. For over forty years he's led the Tribe, a hero and the most respected figure in college football, maybe in all of sports. In the poster he's on the sideline wearing his famous green sweatshirt with *"TRIBE"* across the front. He not only coached the Tribe, but had played for them, too, winning our first National Championship in the sixties.

The most recent picture on our wall is brand new, a picture of Dion McAfes, our new quarterback and the latest member of the

Tribe to be profiled by Sports Inc. To be featured on the cover of the country's biggest sports magazine and website is an achievement unto itself and it had been over fifteen years since the last one. But to reach that level as a true freshman after only three games provided much needed hope for the Tribe. The headline said it all: "The Tribe Is Back and in the Hands of Dion." He was only a year older than me, but athletically, we were in different worlds. Dion was six-foot-five and 220 pounds, a five-star recruit with offers from Alabama, Notre Dame, USC, Texas, Florida State, and every other school that ever graced the top twenty. There was a picture of him during his senior year of high school where he was sitting on a floor and beneath him were all the offer letters he'd received. But over his heart was the offer from Bastille and on his head, a Tribe hat. The internet went crazy that day, both for and against.

When the sun appeared, I sat up and reached over to Henry.

"Let's get our chores done so we can get ready for the game. We've got New Brunswick today, and Jameel Williams."

Henry took his time and I waited until he was engaged, then told him to get breakfast. I made both beds and folded Henry's clothes from the night before. He waited for me in the kitchen with an empty bowl in front of him and I filled it with his favorite cereal, then got the milk.

While Henry ate, I went out back to the screened-in patio and took measure of the mess. The Minister had company; there were seven empty beer bottles lined up by the lawn chair and a half-empty bottle of wine by the wicker chair. I collected the bottles, had my own cereal, and straightened up the kitchen.

"Let's go to the Church," I said.

Outside, leaves crunched under our feet as we walked and the smell of smoke from last night's school bonfire hung in the air.

"I wonder if they had a good time," I said. Henry looked at me but didn't speak. "I hope they didn't party too much."

Before we made it to the Church, the morning chill had gotten to Henry. I heard his teeth chatter before he let me know how serious it was.

"I'm cold, I'm cold, I'm cold," Henry said, his voice never changing tone and without inflection.

It was Henry's way of screaming. I gave him my jacket and he wrapped himself in it without putting his arms through the sleeves, but his teeth continued chattering until we got inside. It was my unplanned routine: keeping Henry warm, making sure his helmet was buckled up when he came on the field, telling him it was okay to speak to someone. *Someone is talking to you, Henry,* and he'd see the person as if they'd magically appeared and then he'd look at me again, a sacred reward that filled me and gave me purpose beyond anything I was supposed to subscribe to. He saw the world through me; I was the only one he looked at when called, and when we saw each other, the loneliness that covered me evaporated.

Cleaning the Church would take an hour and a half if I hurried. Henry sat in the front pew, pulled out his phone, and began playing the numbers game that gave him something to do while I went to work. When I finished cleaning, I put on my Tribe hat and we headed for school a mile away. My anxiety was peaking, and Henry's slow movements drove me crazy but there was nothing I could do. The only time he ever moved fast was when he kicked.

Ever since our freshman year Henry had suited up but he never kicked until our junior year. Coach Huey needed every warm body he could to warrant the team's funding and I never had the nerve to tell him how good Henry was. During that junior year we were winless after three games and during the fourth, Lucas, our QB and kicker, broke his ankle just before halftime. We lost 6–0 and Lucas was gone for the year, but I got my first playing time as a QB on varsity. The real shame of it was we did drive the ball three times in the second half inside their twenty—and once inside their thirty—but without Lucas we didn't try any field goals and lost the ball when we couldn't make a first down.

The next day on Saturday afternoon I called Coach Huey and asked if he'd meet me at the field to discuss an urgent matter. While generally a congenial man who knew his football, he was ill-suited for an open conversation about strategy after the shameful burden of going 0–4. The first thing he asked was what in the hell was so important that there was a risk of him missing Bastille's kickoff and I quickly reminded him the game wasn't on for another hour.

That's when Henry, unprompted, approached the ball with three strong steps that caught Coach Huey by surprise. He kicked the ball off a tee for a forty-yard field goal, and it cleared the cross bar by twenty feet. I didn't say a word.

"Henry Nubinski, what in the world?" Coach Huey said. "You kick that ball again."

"Watch this, Coach," I said.

I took the ball over to the left hash and knelt down to hold for a fifty-yard kick. Coach Huey was standing behind us, and when I heard the punching sound of Henry's foot on the ball, that was all the evidence I needed to know it was good.

"Coach," I said, "Lucas is out for the year, and he wasn't that good of a kicker to start with. If Henry's kicking, we win. I know people talk about him, but he's just shy and he knows the rules." Henry didn't miss a single kick the rest of that season and he hadn't missed one this season. I just hoped that he'd get the chance against New Brunswick, the dominant team in our league.

Earlier, when the New Brunswick bus pulled up as we were heading out for warm-ups, they eyed us and we eyed them. They weren't any bigger than us, except for one lineman that seemed too fat to get out of his own way. Then I saw number 5, Jameel Williams, a four-star recruit who had offers from most of the big schools in the south. The program listed him at five-foot-ten, the same height as me, but he weighed 195 pounds, twenty more than I did. I could tell by the way he walked he had more fast-twitch muscles than our whole backfield combined.

After their first play, the two-yard loss, their quarterback cussed out the errant guard and sent him out of the game. On second down Coach Huey, in all his wisdom, called a run blitz through the A gaps and there was nowhere for Jameel to run; I got partial credit for the tackle. On third down they threw long but it was incomplete, not even close. I came out of the game for the punt and sought out Coach Huey.

"Now's the best time, let me do it," I said. I wanted to take a shot down the field on the first play, something I'd lobbied him for all week.

He pulled his headset below his ears, thought for a moment, then turned to me. "Pro right, 383 flow and tell Dyson to play the Z. He's the only one I want you to tell. And get rid of it quick."

I caught up to Dyson before he got to the huddle. "Play the Z and run a fly, I'm going to launch it." Dyson only got about three passes per game and typically dropped the one I threw on target. As we broke the huddle I whispered to Marshall, "I'm going to pull the ball."

New Brunswick was in a 5-2 defense with Jameel, playing strong safety, lined up off the tight end to my left. He began to creep up as if he was an extra linebacker. When the ball was snapped, I turned to my left to hand off to Marshall through the three hole and Jameel bought it. I pulled the ball out of Marshall's belly, and he hit that line like an airboat about to plow through the everglades when Jameel hit him. It was like Marshall hit an unseen piling from an abandoned pier, he didn't just stop, he was *pierced*. But I still had the ball.

New Brunswick's fat lineman was quicker than I thought, and he was half-blocked when he got close, but I ducked under, came up, and launched the ball to Dyson. There was only a fifty-fifty chance the pass was close, and even if it was, Dyson had the same odds of catching it. As soon as I threw it, Jameel crushed me. Cheers from one of the sidelines erupted, but I was hit so hard I couldn't tell which sideline was happy. As Jameel stood up, he looked downfield and then back to me.

"You got lucky, boy," he said.

Still lying on the ground, I replied with a weakened voice. "Damn right, it's not like I'm going to outplay you."

That gave him a quick pause and he helped me up. As we were trotting down the field, watching Dyson score his first TD of the year, I spoke to him.

"A lot of scouts here, light it up."

He looked at me as if I'd violated an unwritten rule. "Ain't you trying to win?"

I shook my head, trying to gain clarity after taking his hit. "We've been talking about you all week; we're going to hit you with everything we've got. And next year when we're watching you on TV, we'll brag about playing against you."

It was as if I'd regained his trust. "True," he said and then headed for his sideline.

After Henry kicked the extra point, we were up 7–0, the only time they'd trailed all season, and I soaked in the moment. The rest of the game is difficult for me to recall, due to the shots I took to the head. I do know that on their next possession, Jameel got enough clearance on his toss sweep to make the corner, and, except for our undersized free safety who tried to tackle him and got knocked out in the process, no one touched him. When we did tackle him, it was due to an overload into the play or a stunt that bottled him up.

There was one play in particular that illustrated the difference between an average high school athlete, like myself, and a top college prospect. They ran a trap play and I had a clean shot at Jameel. I hit him perfectly with my shoulder on his thighs and wrapped up, but he carried me for two steps as if I was a toddler, then twitched his hips and flung me to the side. I watched as he dodged our backup free safety, who wanted no part of him, then ran in for the score. By the end of the third quarter, he'd run for 283 yards, scored five touchdowns, and they were up 41–7.

After the game, Marshall sat next to me in the locker room. "Where do you think that guy will go next year?"

"I don't know, I'm hoping the Tribe will sign him."

"Dyson's having a party, you going?"

I shook my head. "Henry and I are working until eleven."

Coach Huey yelled into the locker room, telling me to turn in my jersey and pants or else I'd have to wash them myself, again. I closed my eyes and took a moment recalling the game. When I opened them, Henry was waiting for me, already showered and ready to go to work.

Wally

....

ii.

DEEP HICKORY SMOKE was all the advertising Papa's BBQ needed; I could walk there with my eyes closed. It was six by the time we went in the back door, and I hung my Tribe hat and put on an apron.

"Nice try today, boys," said Miss Diane. "Wally, help Henry fill the dishwasher before you bus tables."

I gave Miss Diane a nod and a yes ma'am. Henry looked over the stack of plates and began removing the silverware.

"There's no food," Henry said.

"Miss Diane already scraped them, but don't worry, the tables are full."

Henry rinsed the plates and stacked them while I rinsed the silverware. Henry wasn't allowed to attend to the silverware, he'd take each utensil one by one and scrub it clean while dishes piled up behind him. After the first load was in, I put on a new apron and headed to the front.

"I'm hungry," Henry said.

Running that barbecue to those nice people was like looking at heaven through hell's window. When I returned to the kitchen, Miss Diane was waiting for me; she had a sympathetic look.

"You boys are famished, ain't you," she said. "I gave Henry a few ribs and a plate of brisket that got sent back. Go ahead and get a bite."

I loved Miss Diane. After an hour, the pace slowed and Henry had saved plenty. There was even my favorite, Southern-style pork kielbasa. I ate each bite slowly, letting out a pleasurable hum that I found hilarious while Henry stared at me, which only compounded my humor.

"Wally. I need you out here," Miss Diane said.

We had a table in a little alcove near the back and I hadn't noticed it was occupied. A middle-aged Black man wearing both a Tribe hat and polo shirt sat there looking at his phone. He nodded when I approached with water but didn't pay me much attention. I asked Miss Diane if she knew him, but she'd never seen him before. My intuition took over as I picked up a few plates from other tables, sneaking peeks of him the entire time. Then Mr. Wright, a local customer, got my attention and waved me over.

"That fellow in the back, he's a Bastille coach," said Mr. Wright. I could tell he was excited for me. "Go introduce yourself, he was probably at your game today scouting that running back from New Brunswick. You can tell him what it was like tackling that boy."

"I would if I actually tackled him," I said.

I wandered back to the kitchen door and kept stealing glances. When I looked over to Mr. Wright, he nodded in the coach's direction then Miss Diane appeared behind me.

"Go introduce yourself," she said. "We all know how you love the Tribe."

I cracked my neck, screwed up my courage, and approached his table.

"Anything else, sir?" I said. The coach shook his head without looking away from his phone as he studied football scores. I decided to take a chance. "If you don't mind me asking, sir, what did you think of Jameel Williams?" That got his attention.

He looked up at me as if I knew something that I shouldn't. "Pretty fair runner, he had a big day, but I don't think the home team was a good test for him."

I nodded and was about to walk away but couldn't help myself. "What did you think of West Temple? Any future members of the Tribe?"

He sat back a little and took his time answering. "I thought they were going to make a game of it when they scored on that fly route, that was a nice throw."

"Thank you, sir." I tried to hold off a smile.

He sat back and sized me up and I was never so eager to be profiled in my life. He stuck out his hand and I obliged.

"Have a seat young man, my name is Barney Griffin. Are you just sitting down or leaving?"

"I work here, sir. I've got to—" I looked over to Miss Diane. She waved me to sit down, then made a point of turning away to give me privacy.

I settled into the seat as questions started piling in my head.

"You're number 16, right?" said Coach Griffin. "What were you and Jameel talking about after you threw that pass? Is he a trash talker?"

I told him everything from the conversation, what it was like to try and tackle him, how his burst was something none of us had ever seen. It was as if Jameel Williams was my teammate and I was trying to win him an offer. Before I could stop, I relayed my view on every player we faced all season that had a shot to play in college. I offered up stats and he countered with the height and weight of the top tier players and their probable landing spots.

"So, is the Tribe going to offer Jameel?" I said.

Coach Griffin paused with a degree of resignation. "He's a good player, but he'd never start at Bastille. Our backfield is stacked. If you think Williams is hard to tackle, try Jonathan DeVonta, he's six-foot-three, 235 pounds and runs a 4.5 forty. No, I think Mr. Williams will be investing in a winter coat fairly soon."

It took a moment as I ran through the big northern schools. "He's going to Wisconsin, isn't he?"

Coach Griffin looked stunned and leaned in to speak. "That kind of talk can get me fired. I'm not saying it's true, but how did you guess?"

"I would never say anything, Coach Griffin. But it's kind of obvious, Dalton Shaw used to be the Tribe's offensive coordinator. I figured if the Tribe isn't interested, you're doing a favor for a friend, you know, keeping it in the family." The edge of Coach Griffin's concern faded but I wanted his trust. "Believe me, sir, I'm the biggest fan of the Tribe you've ever met, you can ask anybody. I won't say anything."

He must have been lonely because I could tell he enjoyed talking with someone as enthusiastic and steeped in the Tribe as I was. He talked about players I'd followed, all great athletes. His admiration and respect for Coach Oldham was clear; he even said he would've gotten out of the business long ago if it wasn't for him, even though he had higher-paying offers from other schools anxious to harvest our football rich region. He also talked about the Tribe's struggles—since the last National Championship, twelve years ago, the Tribe averaged only eight wins per year and the trend was looking down. That's when they signed Dion McAres and many read it as Coach Oldham's last push for a National Championship before he retired, he was seventy-eight years old.

"What are your plans next year?" said Coach Griffin.

I shrugged, not wanting to answer. "Probably work here and save up for junior college."

"Grades an issue?"

"No, sir, I've got the test scores and grades to get into Bastille."

"I know some good non-scholarship schools that would be interested, we talk all the time."

My response was limp, our plan already set. Henry and I were going to work full time for Miss Diane and live in the studio apartment above the restaurant that looked like an attic with a bathroom. Between the two of us we could afford a beat-up car and get the hell out from under the Minister's thumb, and I wouldn't have to clean the Church or empty his ashtrays or pick up his friends' beer bottles or suffer his backhand across my face.

Getting out from under the Minister had been my life goal since I realized it could happen, but the thought of happily moving away to college and playing DIII football, chasing co-eds, going to frat parties, and getting a degree was a dream I didn't dare entertain. My mood changed as Coach Griffin got up to leave and I played the only real card I had.

"The shame of it is, Coach Griffin, you didn't get to see the best player on the field perform today."

"Why's that, somebody hurt?" he said.

"No, our kicker is the best, but he only kicked an extra point today. If you would've had him last year that field goal attempt that fell short and was returned for a touchdown by Georgia Tech—"

"You mean the kick-six," he said.

"Sorry to bring it up, but it wouldn't have happened."

Coach Griffin sat back down, and I could tell he was sorting through his list of high school kickers. "I'm not familiar with any West Temple kicker and it's my job to know. What are his stats? What camps has he been to?"

"The reason you've never heard of him is that we typically don't get close enough to kick field goals, and regarding kicking camps, he's never been outside of the county. He's never missed an extra point and his field-goal percentage is one hundred percent, with a long of forty-seven yards. Isn't that true, Mr. Wright?" I knew Mr. Wright had been listening and he backed me up. "I'll bring him out, right now."

Henry was in the same spot I'd left him, sorting through plates and bowls. Coach Griffin and I had talked longer than I'd realized, Henry had a full plate of leftovers waiting for me and a stack of pots he hadn't touched yet. I tried to straighten him up and was about to tell him of his pending interview, but I knew it was useless.

When I presented Henry to Coach Griffin, the context put him in a new light. Henry was pale and seemed disaffected, he looked to a spot on the floor next to Coach Griffin and his arms seemed skinnier than usual as they hung untouched by the short sleeves of his dirty t-shirt. I wanted to stand closer to Henry without seeming awkward; I hated seeing him in a naked light. If Coach Griffin had just chuckled, said goodbye, and walked out of the door, I would've been satisfied that I'd tried.

Coach Griffin bent over slightly trying to lock eyes, but Henry shifted his gaze.

"What's your longest kick, son?"

"It's okay, Henry," I said.

"Forty-seven yards against Central. There was a ten mile-an-hour crosswind." Henry spoke as if he was reciting homework.

Mr. Wright and I subtly exchanged prideful glances, but Coach Griffin was a quick study.

"You don't mind the other players trying to block the kick? You ever get tackled?"

"Wally told me to ignore them. I got knocked over once. Wally said it was okay."

Coach Griffin looked through the window and gauged the light.

"Any interest in kicking a few balls right now?"

"We're working right now, Miss Diane pays us," Henry said.

Permission was granted from Miss Diane followed by Mr. Wright's declaration of his secret desire to bus tables and wash dishes. Ten minutes later, we were on the field with the headlights of Coach Griffin's car aiding the dwindling light. I pulled out Henry's kicking shoes and four worn balls from my bag.

"Whenever you're ready, Henry, kick one from the twenty in the center, then from each hash," said Coach Griffin.

It was child's play, I thought. Henry's first kick went through, the kick from the right hash was perfect but from the left hash it wobbled and barely made it through.

"No, no, that was your fault," said Coach Griffin, looking at me. "You held it wrong and didn't give him a spot to aim at. Look here, I'll show you."

Coach Griffin coached me up, right on the spot. "Count the other nine players in the huddle, then find a spot seven yards back from the ball, then pick the *exact* spot and place your finger on it so the kicker can line up. And when I mean pick a spot, I mean pick a blade of grass. Then you look to your kicker, wait for his nod, then turn to the center and call the snap. You catch, place, and spin to get the laces out, then stare right through the ball until your blade reappears. Got it?" Coach Griffin knelt down and went through the process. "Go ahead and kick it, son."

Henry was lined up with his head focused on the ball and his body cocked. Then he relaxed and his attention drifted away.

"What's wrong?" said Coach Griffin.

I slowly approached. "He only kicks when I hold."

Coach Griffin shrugged and tossed me the ball. "Did you understand what I said?"

"I got it, sir."

Henry kicked from the left hash at the twenty again and the ball spun perfectly. I ran down past the end zone and retrieved the four balls as fast as I could, I didn't want Coach Griffin to try and strike up a conversation. I returned out of breath.

"Can I pick the spot?" Coach Griffin nodded and with a thrill in my spine I thought, *It's showtime*.

The grass in the middle of the field was worse than before the game, it was almost dirt at the forty, the equivalent of a fifty-yard try. I set up and Henry unleashed his leg, and that ball flew with a slower spin as if it had to pace itself during its long and perfect flight.

"Now, Henry," I said, sprinted to the left hash, and set up like the clock was running out. He followed at speed, the only time he ever ran. Another command and we sprinted to the right hash and it was like a mirror image of the last, good by ten yards. I went to fetch the balls again, but Coach Griffin stopped me and jogged over to his car as we stood catching our breath.

"How's your foot?" I said.

"Are we getting ice cream after this?"

"Yeah, after we finish the dishes."

When Coach Griffin returned, he emptied a bag of footballs onto the ground, college balls, all inflated hard with Tribe logos on them. I picked one up and held it with the reverence of a gem.

"I'm going to arrange the balls on the field, and I'd like you two to take your time and try each one," said Coach Griffin. He started to set the balls on the hash marks, starting at the thirty.

"Sir, if you don't mind, we can do better than that," I said.

The locations I picked were outside of the rules and would embarrass a normal kicker. Henry unleashed each kick in succession, we were running to the next spot before the previous kick, perfect and always plenty long, hit the ground. The first spot was at the intersection of the goal line and the sideline, only thirty yards in distance, but the gap in the goalposts looked as if it was only a foot wide from that angle. Further up the sideline, we hit from the twenty, then again at the forty where the numbers would normally be. Then Henry made it from each hash on the fifty, the equivalent of a sixty-yard field goal. We went through the drill again starting at the other sideline while Coach Griffin caught the balls to make sure they went through. We were both sweating in the cold air when we finished and I sent Henry to sit on the bench while I helped Coach Griffin collect the balls. Coach Griffin was in awe.

"I've never seen anything like it," he said. He stopped to get my full attention. "I don't mean to be rude, but is he okay?"

I looked back to Henry, sitting fifty yards away, looking at his phone as darkness closed in. "Nothing's wrong with him, he's just shy, very shy." Coach Griffin didn't look convinced, and I continued. "He's always taken normal classes and gotten As and Bs, he works, does his chores, and never gets in trouble. He's just a little different."

Coach Griffin looked over to Henry and shook his head. "You're right, we would've beaten Georgia Tech last year with him. He doesn't get nervous by the rush?"

"It's like they're not even there."

He gave us a ride back to Papa's and gave me his card.

"I can't guarantee anything, son, but I'll bring it up. I'm going to need to see him in a game, probably with another coach." Then he gave me two footballs. "It's the damndest thing how I lose these balls all the time."

Wally

....

iii.

AT PRACTICE ON Monday, I told Marshall and Dyson about Henry's impromptu tryout.

"A Bastille scout in West Temple?" said Dyson.

"He was scouting that New Brunswick running back. And besides, you've seen Henry kick, the guy was amazed."

"You better tell Coach Huey," Marshall said. "If they're serious they'll call him."

When I told Coach Huey, he let out a pained laugh like he'd burned a steak. "Do you know what this makes me look like? I've got a kicker the Tribe wants, and I barely use him, I'll look like an idiot." He was quiet for a moment in contemplation. "These next three games, any time it's fourth down and we're on the forty or closer, we're kicking."

"How about the forty-five?"

The next week we played at Scottsdale High, Henry kicked three field goals and we lost 13–9. But the kicks were thirty-eight, forty-seven, and fifty-two yards. Marshall, Dyson, and I scanned the crowd for Coach Griffin but he wasn't there.

The week after that we won a shootout at Clark Valley, 36–33, and Henry kicked three extra points and five field goals, the longest was fifty-three yards. This time, it seemed our whole team, except Henry, was looking out for the absent Coach Griffin. I emailed him after the game with the stats and waited patiently for his reply but didn't hear back.

On the following Monday, the Minister sent me a text as practice ended telling me to get home, I had a visitor. I didn't mention it to anyone, and I barely showered after practice in my rush to get home. Getting caught up in the excitement affected my thinking, I was a block from school when I realized I'd left Henry behind and had to return. Weeds shot up through the cracks in our front walk and I felt embarrassed as I approached the front door. Then it dawned on me the Minister was probably inside talking to Coach Griffin. I closed my eyes and cringed at the things he'd say.

I took a deep breath and opened the door. The parlor was quiet, and disappointment overwhelmed me. After we stepped in, I noticed a woman sitting on the couch—no Minister and no Coach Griffin. We stared at each other for an uncomfortable moment as if one of us was in the wrong house.

She gracefully stood and approached a couple of steps. "I suppose you don't remember me, there's no way you could, really," she said.

"Hello, ma'am." She extended her hand, which I delicately shook. "I'm Wally and this is my brother Henry." Silence took over again until I spoke. "Is there something we can help you with?"

She seemed pleasant and pained at the same time and I started to wonder if I was in some kind of trouble. I sent Henry to our room as she sat back down on the couch. I could tell she wasn't from West Temple or any rural town; her jacket was brand new, and her purse had some funny design on it. I gave her time, letting her know she had my attention.

"I'm here to tell you some very sad news. But first, I should introduce myself. My name is Janie Hestia, and I'm your aunt." She paused for a moment. "Do you remember the last time you saw your mother?"

I shook my head and looked down as a feeling I couldn't control started welling up inside me—something buried deep that time and Henry and football had covered in thin layers with each passing day and game and season. But the feeling was stronger than the accumulated dust of my life, I squinted hard and used my fingers to hold my eyes shut as shudders of a long-lost pain pounded my skin from the inside, demanding release.

She came to my side and tried to comfort me. "I've been looking for you for a long, long time. I was there when you were born, I helped take care of you." She cradled my head as my sobs came forth in waves I couldn't control. After the pain started to ebb, I opened my eyes. Henry was in the dark hallway and I nodded to him, letting him know I was okay. He returned to our room.

"Have you seen her?" I said.

Aunt Janie's eyes nearly closed and her own tears spilled out. "I'm sorry. I'm so sorry, but she's gone."

The pain started to come back; a rippling emotion of abandonment that made me close my eyes again. When my new Aunt Janie put her arms around me, I held on. Minutes passed and when the rhythm of my breaths returned and my eyes stopped watering, she asked if we could go for a walk.

"By the way, did you meet the Minister?" I said.

"Is that what you call him? That actually makes me happy." I was so glad she knew. "I should've looked here first, but my sister swore she was taking care of you long after she left Georgia. I've been to half a dozen states over the years looking for you." She paused and looked at me, and I felt the same bond I had with Henry. "Take me to your favorite place," she said.

In the light of dusk, we made the long walk to the football field. As best I could, I told her about my life, which was Henry and football and rooting for the Tribe, and it took a couple of turns to convince her I wasn't a star quarterback. Learning about my mother didn't take long, Aunt Janie didn't know much. Drugs, alcohol, a series of bad men, and made-up stories of me were all she had. Aunt Janie lived a different life. College, then business school and a career that landed her out West. She had her own challenges as a woman in Silicon Valley, she told me, and when her company had been bought out the previous year, she'd been able to retire to New Mexico to start her second life. That's when she doubled her efforts in looking for me, knowing I was about to reach college-age.

"I can pay for any school you'd like to attend. In fact, the University of New Mexico is close, you can go there," she said. Her excitement started to grow. "If you want, come with me now; you can finish high school out there and leave that son of a bitch behind."

For a moment her offer gave me peace and I drank it in.

"There's a chance for me to do something here," I said. "If you're serious about helping me pay for college—"

"I'm dead serious, and I'll pay for all of it, plus spending money." Her emotions began to well up again and she gently held my face. "I should have quit years ago and found you. I'm so sorry."

"I appreciate it, but I could never leave Henry."

She gave me a moment then asked what I wanted to do.

"You see, the school I've always dreamed about is Bastille University."

"Wow, can you get in?"

"I think so, and there's something else. There's a chance—I mean a real outside chance—I could play football for them. But not on scholarship, I'd have to pay for it myself."

Aunt Janie held herself back in astonishment. "Jesus Christ, Walter. I don't know anything about football, but I sure know about the Tribe. There's a couple of Bastille alumni from my old company, and one of them had a picture in his office of their coach. Oldham, right? I thought you said you weren't a star?"

"It's not me. Henry's the talent."

Something about her changed. I could see it in the dim light. "I want you to figure out what you want and pursue it with everything you have. Your mother was a sad story, but you don't have her issues. I didn't know what you'd be like before today; I didn't know what I would find. But you've raised yourself into something special, and if you want to play for this team there's nothing holding you back."

We took our time walking back home as I pointed out the meaningless landmarks of my life and the rutted path I'd grown to live by. A few times I had to dry my eyes. The pure, sweet feeling she triggered overcame my normal defenses and I let her see me as I was. She stayed at the new hotel by the highway and came to practice every day. At Papa's, she got to know Miss Diane and Mr. Wright while Henry and I worked. She was supposed to fly back to New Mexico on Thursday but extended her stay to see me play.

The day of my thirty-ninth and final high school game was at home, and as happy as I was to have Aunt Janie at the game, I hadn't heard from Coach Griffin. When the bus from King's Prep arrived, we took the field for warm-ups. Coach Huey said he would keep an eye out for anyone from the Tribe and let me know.

Our bleachers were filled with people we knew, the visitor's bleachers had a handful of people that all looked like parents. If a betting man followed our level of football, King's Prep would've been favored by at least ten points, but something happened to me since my aunt's visit and the talk of the Tribe's interest in Henry. I started to believe I could play.

We received the kickoff and on the first drive I ran Marshall to the left twice in a row and on third and three I called a roll out pass right to our tight end and we gained thirty yards. My confidence was so high, Coach Huey let me continue calling my own plays.

We scored a touchdown on that drive, and I had to remind myself that if anyone from Bastille showed up, my fate would be determined by field goals. We traded touchdowns in the second then they ran a punt back just before halftime.

When we came out for the second half, I saw them immediately. Coach Griffin and another gentleman with a Tribe hat were standing on the track just behind the fence on our side. The water station was close to them, and when I sauntered over before kick-off Coach Griffin nodded to me.

"We're late, traffic. Let's see what the kid's got."

In the huddle, our boys were fired up and bound and determined to give Henry his chance.

"Don't forget, do not cross their forty-yard line, run out of bounds if you have to," I said.

Marshall forgot. But he faked a pretty good hamstring injury when he realized he was at their twenty-two-yard line and dropped to the ground like Jameel Williams hit him. Three plays later, Henry kicked a thirty-nine-yarder. We had another chance when King's Prep fumbled deep in their end and, through a series of intentional offsides and a hold, Henry hit a forty-three-yard field goal. Our defense held and we were up 20–14 when we drove to their forty-two and faced fourth and eight with under a minute left. A fifty-nine-yard attempt was long enough to show Henry's capability and I settled in knowing it was a sure thing. I found a blade of grass and put my finger on it. I looked to Henry and he gave me the nod. Then I looked to the center and gave the command.

Just before the ball sailed towards me, a thought flashed through my mind: Would Henry ever know? I knew he felt emotions, but would he ever be able to express the joy we felt, the camaraderie, the sweet victory, or the devastating loss? Would he ever know what I was trying to pull off? Did he even want me to? He had to; it was our way out.

After I heard Henry's foot go through the ball and saw my blade of grass reappear, I knew it was good. I simply stood up without looking at the ball and looked in Henry's eyes with gratitude. Then I watched Coach Huey jump and pump his fist as if we'd won the league, and noticed Coach Griffin smiling as the other Tribe coach scribbled in his notebook.

Wally

....

iv.

THE SOUTHERN PLAINS of Georgia rolled by and with each passing mile I could feel the twigs and branches of West Temple falling away. As we passed each town, I imagined it had a high school quarterback better than me, yet, here I was, on a three-hour drive to the almighty Bastille University. The euphoria that set in when Coach Griffin called had evolved into a sinking feeling as the visit approached. Instead of recruiting pitches, I heard disclaimers to lower our expectations. Just a visit, Henry and I were two of the many stones to be overturned.

Even if Henry failed to measure up, we would at least get an inside look at the greatest college football program and maybe even meet Coach Oldham. Henry sat in front as the Minister drove while I sat in back alternating between boredom and anxiety.

"You know," said the Minister, "I'm thankful to the Good Lord that I played soccer my senior year at the behest of the head coach. I quickly took to it and led our team in goals, but it is from that blessed experience that I learned the fundamentals of kicking, and, through Providence, was able to pass it on to Henry."

The only thing he ever taught Henry was fearful obedience with the back of his hand. I'd seen him prepare his sermons on Saturday nights with a glass of scotch in one hand and notes in the other. He'd develop his speech until he slurred, and he was doing the same now.

Bastille University, Exit 35. It wasn't a normal highway sign, although it was clearly installed by the state. Next to the words was the logo of the University: the outline of their famous academic tower and a caricature of the stadium that looked like the Colosseum in Rome. My mood picked up.

The Tribe. *The Bastille University Tribe.* Nothing like it in all the world. All those that comprised the larger Tribe, like me, who pledged our undying love were rewarded in ways that transcended the poor fools rooting for their corrupt schools. The typical state schools were propped up by the government and only through their massive enrollments were they able to put forward enough enthusiasts to make it seem like they were legitimate. Only the Ivies approached the academic integrity of Bastille and they had the common sense to keep their football programs at a modest level, even though I knew I wasn't good enough to play for them.

But sometimes I'd miss the point, Bastille was never negative. *TRIBE FOREVER!* Bastille has always been the greatest program with the largest national following. I've been told you can travel to any major, secondary, or tertiary city in these United States and be within ten miles of a sports bar whose main menu on fall Saturdays is the Tribe. The Tribe is honorable, kind, and victorious. Values and sportsmanship are upheld in common with the essence of our nation and in doing so are woven into the fabric of this great land.

However, there was one regrettable incident long ago, before I was born, that landed us at a crossroads, and if not for the wisdom and leadership of Coach Oldham, maybe we'd be like all the rest. Back in 1978, a brawl erupted outside of Bastille Stadium after the Florida State game between some Tribe loyalists and the visiting Seminole fans. The ruckus carried on longer than your usual flare up and by the time it was over, all of Bastille's campus security were there as well as the city of Bastille's police force. Even though we won the game, Coach Oldham declared it the darkest day in

Tribe history. The university brass offered up the usual crafted statements about sportsmanship and honor, but it was Coach Oldham who laid down the law. He held a press conference on Monday afternoon to address the issue and by the time he was finished, everyone partial to the Tribe—so it was reported—felt like Coach was talking to them, specifically. He broke down the partisan hatred, and in its place, a new definition emerged of what it meant to be part of the Tribe and what it meant to be one of the brethren that compose college football. Coach Oldham was lauded coast to coast for his ethical leadership, even by the Florida State coach, but Coach Oldham turned it around and said he was simply inspired by the sportsmanship of Florida State that he had observed over the years.

From that day on it was a sin to disrespect opponents and their fans and it became a point of pride to welcome visiting teams and their patrons with the utmost Southern hospitality. Visiting fans were greeted on their way to the stadium with wishes of good luck, handshakes, and tailgate food and drink. The whole spectacle brought a new dimension to the Tribe and elevated Coach Oldham to an esteemed level that he never seemed comfortable with, which added to it even more. On top of all that, Coach Oldham won a whole lot of games and national championships.

But we've always had our fun and worn our outward signs of loyalty with pride. Every school has logo adorned t-shirts, caps, jerseys, shot glasses, mugs, keyrings, flags, tailgate tents, coolers, tables, grills, and collapsible chairs. Dozens of websites offer team inspired trinkets, such as cufflinks, lighters, coasters, golf balls, barbecue sets, cornhole games, and lawn gnomes. All schools have sold these wares, but we outsold entire conferences.

Newborns get swaddled in hospital-approved Tribe blankets, weddings take place on the fifty-yard line and are consummated in a skybox, and the recently deceased enter the next life in

Tribe-decorated caskets or urns, depending on final wishes. Sweatshirts, knit hats, and PJs are obvious, but I was most impressed when I saw a Tribe-inspired line of lingerie. It wasn't the logical combination of the Tribe and lingerie—a perfect melding of triumph and excitement—that surprised me, it was how the Tribe's logo was made clearly recognizable, even with such little material to work with. Unfortunately, I never came across any of this in high school, which only fed my desire to attend the school in person.

And the best way to watch a game was in person, or so I'd heard. RVs arrived on Friday afternoons because they wouldn't let them in on Thursday. By Friday night, the campus bloomed with activity: pep rallies in the quad, the marching band in the baseball stadium, booster club dinners and socials, and cheerleader and circus performances in the basketball arena. The city of Bastille's town square would get closed to traffic and people would take to the streets amid live music and beer tents. At midnight, they sang the alma mater in the quad with everyone swaying arm-in-arm and at seven a.m., you could smell bacon and eggs cooking in the sea of tents surrounding the stadium. Fans of the visiting team report that it's their favorite away-game destination, except for the game itself, of course. The abundance is overwhelming; you could enter the parking lot in your underwear and be fed, clothed, and drunk by the time you made it all the way around the stadium.

But for all of this madness and excitement, there was one thing each and every member of the Tribe had in their power that was used to bond, inspire, and intimidate—*Raising the Arrow*. Extend your right arm to the sky with your fingers straight up and cap it with your left hand like you're signaling time-out, except close your fingers to an angle and the arrow is raised. Raise the arrow and scream the cry of the Tribe, a loud, vicious sound that's held for as long as you can. When you come across someone with a Tribe t-shirt, you raise the arrow to communicate your common bond.

When your life crosses a milestone, like a wedding or the birth of a child, you make sure at least one picture captures you raising the arrow. When a goal is achieved, like buying your first home or scaling Mount Everest, you raise the arrow. Texas has its Hook 'em Horns and Miami has the hand-signaled U, but neither of those meant anything beyond the individual. At Bastille Stadium, with the entire crowd raising the arrow and screaming the cry, an unfair advantage was affected that not even Coach Oldham could stop.

Most other teams make their noise at kickoff, raising their yells in anticipation that climaxes when the kicker actually kicks the ball. At Bastille, the noise grows to a deafening level and continues after the kick, at which point the collective arrows would slowly drop with the arc of the ball until they were all pointed at the kick returner and just before he caught the ball, a collective *BOOM* would be fired at the player as the arrows were released in a direct shot. The practice resulted in a couple of turnovers per year. Barry Otto, the NFL Hall of Famer who went to Michigan, was asked after his induction what was the most nervous he'd ever been. Without hesitation, he said his sophomore year when Michigan played at Bastille and he received the opening kickoff. Right before he was about to catch it, the *BOOM* rattled his senses enough to distract him and resulted in a turnover at the Michigan fifteen.

There was also a positive application of raising the arrow. If a Bastille player makes a game changing play, he's rewarded with the intensity of 90,000 fans. With coordination unseen, the crowd raises the arrows, and the noise builds and the Tribe player, humbled by the attention, pulls his hands across his chest as if he was ripping open his jersey and pads to expose his heart to receive the *BOOM* from the crowd, filling him with glory.

The image of the multitudes with their arms raised into arrows is a part of the University. When I received the school application in the mail, a glossy brochure was included with pictures taken from field level looking up at an angle into the stands to show a rising field of arms raised in arrows. I couldn't imagine what it felt like to be the beneficiary of it.

We pulled into the University's main entrance and drove beneath the famous steel archway that had *Bastille University* in metal script and beyond that was Prisoners' Fountain shooting fifty feet in the air. The combination of the two was one of the standard views they showed on TV after coming back from commercials and I turned back to see where the camera's probably set up. The three of us were silent as the car slowly made its way through campus and found the stadium.

When I got out of the car, I stood in awe. Even the Minister was humbled. The sand-colored walls rose fifteen stories high with pointed arch windows on each level. It wasn't just a stadium; you could see that when they showed aerial views on TV. Normal stadiums end at the farthest ring of seats, but Bastille Stadium had an outer ring of buildings attached that held administrative offices and classrooms. It seems that when the University needed to expand, it expanded from its heart.

We followed the main walk to the entrance on the south end zone, a glass entryway that spanned ten stories. Henry stopped and looked up at a window washing crew dangling on their platform far above. Inside, the plush green carpeted hallway was wide enough to practice long snaps for punts and the ceiling had to be three stories high. We stopped in front of the bookstore, but I didn't see a single book, just beautiful arrangements of Tribe clothes and memorabilia. I wandered in and softly touched the sweatshirts and t-shirts and miniature helmets.

On the far side, jerseys of the most prominent past and current players were arrayed high on the wall like they were the skins of warrior angels waiting for ascension. I found Henry standing outside the bookstore staring at a map of the stadium's interior. He lifted his finger and pointed to a notation, letting me know the weight of our circumstance. The words said, "You Are Here."

Coach Griffin met us at the inner entrance to the stadium. "Players and Authorized Personnel Only," the sign read.

"Welcome to Bastille," he said as he introduced himself to the Minister. When he shook my hand, I sensed a touch of anxiety in his face and voice; I wasn't the only one nervous about Henry's formal audition.

"Let's take a quick tour of the stadium," Coach Griffin said.

The Minister took over the conversation and Henry and I slowed our pace until we were out of earshot. The inner concourse walls were white painted cinder block and high above was the reverse contour of the stadium seating supported by heavy metal infrastructure. As we walked, I tried to imagine what it sounded like when the Tribe scored and the tens of thousands of fans above screamed and stamped their feet in celebration. We came to the locker room door and Coach Griffin swiped his key card.

The lights came on in sequence, one by one, and after the fifth light I thought it would mark the end of the room, but the lights kept illuminating around the curve of the stadium. I was struck by the simplicity and solemn grace: the deep green and white carpet, the spacious locker stalls composed of heavy lacquered wood, whiteboards spaced out every ten lockers or so, and the trainer's room behind me. A long arrow on the carpet started at our end, and I followed its curve with the shape of the room until it ended in the large arrowhead at the double doors.

I turned around to Coach Griffin. "Is the tunnel through here?"

"Sure is. Let's go out to the field."

The tunnel is where they gathered and held strong as their energy spilled over and the crowd howled. Just before the Tribe ran out, cheerleaders would line up on the field, the flag bearers would sway their poles, the smoke machines would pump their mist, and the fireworks around the top rim of the stadium would explode high into the air. Loud music would be overtaken by the crowd and the PA announcer's voice would be indecipherable. As we walked through the sacred tunnel, I ran my fingers along the wall trying to feel traces of energy still echoing off the walls. We walked out to midfield and I turned around slowly, taking in the views and building a panoramic imprint in my mind.

A player jogged out to meet us, I could tell by his size and clothes. The size of his frame was unnatural by any common standard and he wore a Tribe hoodie, Tribe sweatpants, and, when he got close, I saw that even his flip-flops were Tribe logoed.

"Coach Griffin, I'm sorry I'm late," he said.

"You're not late, son, we're early," said Coach Griffin. "This is Henry Nabinksi, Wally Hestia, and Henry's father. This here is Jeremy Stills, the boys' host for the weekend."

Jeremy was a big white lineman with curly blond hair and a face that looked like it sunburned easily. After the stadium tour, we met in a conference room on the press level to discuss academics and financial aid, but the Minister kept hijacking the conversation.

"Any chance we can meet Coach Oldham," the Minister said as the meeting broke.

"I'm sorry, Coach would love to stop by, but he's tied up in important University matters," Coach Griffin said. "You can pick the boys up anytime tomorrow afternoon."

On our way out, the Minister whispered to me, "Take the bus back."

We were left in the care of Jeremy. "Let's drop your stuff at the dorm, then we'll tour the Performance Center." He gathered his backpack, which had arrows on three sides with his name and number, 76, on the top.

It wasn't a dorm like I had imagined, it was a luxury apartment. A full kitchen with a microwave, a Keurig, and granite countertops;

two bedrooms, each bigger than our tiny room at home with a full desk and a laptop; a flat screen TV in the main room with a video game setup and a leather couch that looked brand new; a shared bathroom with a walk-in tiled shower and separate sinks. The carpet in the main room had the Tribe arrow and the color scheme throughout was green, gold, and white.

"If you're on scholarship or an invited walk-on, you get to live in one of these," Jeremy said. "Wait till you see the Performance Center."

The walk from the dorm to the facility was about a block away, manicured and landscaped with tall hedges to separate the football players and students from mingling unnecessarily. The facility was a three-story building with minimal outward indication of what it held inside, like it didn't want to draw attention. Jeremy used his key card to get in.

"We spend most of our time here, we only use the stadium locker room on game days," Jeremy said.

The tour of the Bastille University Football Performance Center was as impressive as the stadium. One hundred and thirty thousand square feet devoted to the betterment of the program. The lobby was steel and glass with etched logos of the Tribe's arrow. Jeremy showed us the weight room, it had machines I'd never seen before and a dozen Olympic platforms with rubber-coated weights. The locker room had stalls that looked like closets for each player with more drawers and shelving than we had in our entire house. The meeting rooms were labeled for each position group and the auditorium sat well over a hundred in large, cushioned seats. The players' lounge was on the second floor, accessible by an escalator—two pool tables and ping pong tables, a dozen flat screens, lounge chairs, video game consoles, and Gatorade machines. It was more than I could take in.

"Are you hungry? They're serving dinner," Jeremy said.

The dining hall was a combination of a futuristic restaurant and a food emporium. Rows of apples, oranges, pre-cut pineapple, and grapes were on display. The food buffet line was nearly empty, the servers stood behind their stations looking bored. Signs adorned the walls exhorting the benefits of fruits, vegetables, and lean meats. I got in line and loaded up with mashed potatoes, okra, and a strip steak. Henry followed, getting the same as me, as always.

"What do you think?" Jeremy said.

I hadn't said more than two words since we were introduced. "I can't believe I'm here."

"Yeah, it's a special place. Once I set foot on campus it was a no-brainer." Jeremy said. "I had full-scholarship offers from Syracuse, Boston College, and Maryland, but my parents knew this is where I wanted to go."

"You're a walk-on? You don't have a scholarship?"

"An invited walk-on, there's a big difference. An invited walk-on means they want you, but they don't have any more scholarships. Just a walk-on means you'll get crushed in practice for a few days before they cut you."

About a half dozen players entered the dining room and I tried to see if I recognized any of them. Then, out of the corner of my eye, I saw two more and I knew who it was without a direct look. Dion McAres. His big, shaggy, mohawked Afro extended his height by three inches, a look other people were starting to copy. I'd seen his face on TV and websites, during live games and interviews. You knew there wasn't a stitch of doubt in him, he was all confidence, and yet his humble words deflected adulation onto teammates and coaches and the larger Tribe itself, to the point that critics said it was disingenuous. He was always calm unless he wanted to be excited, and then everyone followed. Jeremy noticed my stare and turned to glance.

"Yeah, that's him," he said then turned back. "Did they talk to you about a scholarship?"

I shook my head and gave a sarcastic half grunt. "My brother is the talent, not me. Coach Griffin thinks I could play DIII ball. I'm just his holder."

"If you guys are brothers, how come you have different last names?"

"I was adopted. Doesn't matter, we've been together since we were five. So, how do you like it here?"

"I love it. Got in a few games last year as a redshirt freshman. I'm not going to beat out Andre Decker, he's the best center in the country, but after he leaves I'll have a chance to start. If I do, they'll give me a scholarship for my junior and senior years. I'm the long snapper, too, that's why I'm your host this weekend. Before your brother kicks tomorrow, you need to catch some of my snaps to get used to it." He looked at Henry. "You going to kick tomorrow?"

"Henry, Jeremy's talking to you," I said.

Without looking at Jeremy, Henry spoke. "Wally says I need to kick for Coach Griffin again, maybe even Coach Oldham." In this new setting, his monotone voice seemed flatter than usual, I looked to Jeremy to see his reaction.

"Not real social, is he?" Jeremy said.

I shook my head and put my arm around the back of Henry's chair as I looked for clues in Jeremy's face to see where he would take this.

"I heard he can kick, though," Jeremy said. "Evan will love it, he's nearly perfect under forty but any longer and he's a wreck."

I felt relieved as Jeremy told me the importance of taking the hardest courses over the summer, allowing for a lightened load during the fall. Even then, in-season was marked by fifteen-hour days, each minute planned out and monitored to comply with

NCAA rules and adherence to the Tribe's work ethic. Henry nudged me.

"Do they have ice cream here?" I said.

"No, just frozen yogurt," Jeremy said. "It's over by the Gatorade."

"Henry, see those guys over there? It's just past them," I said. "Fifteen-hour days?"

Jeremy continued about academic counselors and tutors, off-limit frat houses known for drugs, the dress code for away games and how to make up for missed classes, acceptable booster inter-actions and how to politely decline perks that violate NCAA code, bars to avoid and parties that are can't-miss, how to avoid cover charges, and media policy for upperclassmen.

I glanced over to check on Henry but focused on Dion and the other player he came in with, they were deep in conversation. Beyond them was a table of more players and further on Henry stood in front of the frozen yogurt machine. One of the players stood next to Henry, talking to him. He glanced over to his group with a smile on his face as if he was about to laugh. The other players watched intently, tensed with unvented laughter. I stood up in fear, then quickly made my way over.

By the time I got there, Henry was alone again, holding an empty Styrofoam cup. I overheard the player who had talked to him tell the group, "Now that motherfucker puts the *special* in special teams."

They broke up laughing, even though they tried to cover it up. I took the cup from Henry's hand and filled it with chocolate frozen yogurt.

"There are a lot of choices," Henry said.

"You always get chocolate."

The laughter behind me subsided but I could feel the stares on my back. As I led Henry back to our table the heat of embarrassment filled my face. Then Dion spoke, his voice clear and recognizable.

"That's bullshit. Don't belong here."

My heart sank, I wanted to leave before my love for Bastille soured. I'd tell Jeremy we had to go, we'd get our bags from the dorm and find the bus station. Tomorrow we'd show up for work at Papa's and tell them it didn't work out. I couldn't imagine showing my face to anyone else, or Coach Oldham.

"What's wrong?" Jeremy said.

I shook my head and watched Henry eat his frozen yogurt, he was a slow eater and I hated him for it. "Hurry up, Henry. We've got to go." I closed my eyes to help the moments pass and heard Jeremy rise from his chair, I wanted to leave before he became part of it, too. Then I heard him sit down again. When I opened my eyes and looked up, I was split with despair. Dion McAres was sitting in front of me, the famous face and hair, the intense look, staring at me and I knew I didn't belong.

"I hope you heard what I said." He looked offended and I shrank with fear, thinking Henry would tell him about his picture on our wall at home. "What those idiots said was bullshit. It's not Bastille." My self-loathing broke and Dion started to smile, like he'd put out a fire.

"My name is Dion." He extended his hand to shake, and I obliged as relief poured through me. I started to tell him my name, but he cut me off. "I know who you are. Wally, right? And this is the man, Henry."

Henry surprised me, he stood and made eye contact as Dion's large hand swallowed his.

"Now, them boys over there," Dion said. "They bust each other without mercy, they can't help themselves." He turned to the table of players who were all watching and let out a quick whistle. The offending player quickly made his way over.

"Yo, I'm sorry, man. It's just inside this building, we a bunch of rude motherfuckers."

Dion nodded to him, then with a quick turn of his head, sent him away. "Hey, Garr, come on over here," Dion said.

The player who had been in conversation with Dion joined us. When he sat, I worried for the chair, he was the biggest person I'd ever seen. He was muscular but not like a body builder. He was as tall as Dion but two coats of muscle thicker. Jeremy looked normal by comparison.

"This is Garr Johnstone, five-star recruit, number one defensive tackle in the country, number two overall," Dion said.

"You a recruit, too?" said Garr. His voice was so deep, it was felt more than heard.

"Kind of, not like you, though. My brother, Henry, is a kicker."

"You got a position?" Dion said.

"I played QB in high school, I hold for Henry."

"Damn, boy. Then you play QB here behind me, then. Don't come here without a position." He looked to Henry. "Henry Nubinski, 'the Nuber.' I heard you can kick a seventy-yarder? That true?"

Henry spoke without my prompting. "My longest kick was fifty-nine yards against King's Prep. My longest in practice with Wally is seventy yards. I can kick it from the sidelines but that's not allowed."

Dion smiled and looked to Garr. "See what you going to miss if you become a Seminole or an Aggie?"

"Come on, man, you said there'd be no hard sell."

It was hard to imagine Garr walking the halls of a high school.

Dion stood. "All right, we've got to go, you boys have a good visit," Dion said. "Jeremy, you taking them out tonight?"

"Absolutely, wherever they want to go."

I could see the effect that Dion had on Jeremy, and we sat in silence until Dion and Garr left the dining hall.

"That was pretty cool," Jeremy said.

The next morning, pre-dawn, felt like a game day and I wondered if I'd ever experience another one again. I pulled a chair up to the dorm's window and stared into the dark, imagining the hopeless view from our bedroom window back in West Temple. But as the early light of dawn appeared, it began to unveil a view I never thought I'd see. The top windows of the Bastille tower reflected a golden light as its dark silhouette slowly appeared against the deep blue morning sky. In the distance, the top of the sand-colored walls of the stadium emerged, then other buildings and structures that comprised the university began to bloom in the morning sun. There was promise and life beyond my limited existence, but the only one I wanted depended on Henry.

At nine o'clock we had breakfast at the dining hall, at ten we toured the campus with Jeremy. By eleven, we had changed into Tribe workout clothes and were led to the practice fields. They were bordered by the Performance Center and twenty-foot-high fences covered with tarps.

"While Henry gets acclimated, I want to see you throw a few balls," Coach Griffin said.

An unknown player ran pass patterns as I heaved decent balls to him. I caught a glimpse of the top story of the Performance Center and could've sworn I saw Coach Oldham watching but I didn't dare look up. After a dozen passes, Coach Griffin called Jeremy and Henry over.

"Wally, take a couple of snaps and then go through the kicks we discussed," said Coach Griffin.

"I'll do three quarters speed, then ramp it up," Jeremy said.

Jeremy's snaps were faster than anything I'd caught in high school, but after a few I was ready. I knew Coach Oldham was watching, I imagined we had ten minutes or less to make an impression. Blade of grass, Henry's nod, Jeremy's hands on the ball, my call. The ball whistled at me and slapped my hands, I placed, Henry kicked, and the blade returned. No other noises. Three kicks then back up further, three kicks then move to the hash, then the other hash. We moved quickly like clockwork, never missing, never stopping, and I relished in the power of Henry's leg.

"Let's do it again," Coach Griffin said. "Start at the ten in the middle, then each hash, then move back ten yards until Henry's kicking from the fifty. And this time, we're adding some distractions."

"Coach Griffin," I said. "I hope this isn't a problem, but he can only kick thirty a day."

Coach Griffin paused, then turned to Henry. "How many kicks so far?"

"Nine," said Henry.

"No problem," said Coach Griffin. "Thanks for letting me know."

On the next snap, music exploded from unseen speakers and I nearly bobbled it, but Henry kicked without awareness. A few other players were on the field and Coach Griffin lined them up in front of Jeremy, waving and screaming. It became a game as other players offered to rush from the edge. Coach Griffin used a bullhorn from behind us, but the only noise I accepted was the sweet thud of Henry's foot. One after another, each ball sailed through the goalposts like a flight soaring above stormy weather.

"Damn, boy. I'm going to get you this time." An edge rusher flew by, not wanting to block—he didn't have a helmet on—but was sure he could rattle us. Vile taunts came, the volume of music varied and peaked on Henry's approach, and the bullhorn amplified unkind words about West Temple and those that came from it. Henry hit from the fifty in the middle, the left hash, and then the right hash, the equivalent of sixty-yard kicks. Then the music stopped and the players looked to a spot behind us.

"You're right, Barney. I've never seen anything like it."

I could pick out that voice in the middle of a tornado. I'd heard it in calm interviews and on AM radio with bad reception while cleaning the Church. I turned around. He was smaller than I'd imagined and a little frail.

"My name's John Oldham, it's a pleasure to meet you, Wally, Henry." He shook our hands and told the other players they were free to go back to their workouts.

"Where'd you learn to kick a football, young man?"

I nodded to Henry.

"Wally taught me in our backyard," Henry said.

Coach Oldham spoke to Henry as he slowly led us to the far side of the field to a set of modest bleachers. I stayed at a respectful distance and was thankful Henry answered innocent questions without my approval. I had coached him up to respond by saying "yes, sir." They talked for about ten minutes while Coach Griffin and I threw a ball back and forth, the whole time I stole glances at their conversation. Then it was my turn.

"Wally," Coach Oldham said. "Can you spend a few minutes with me?"

I took a deep breath and jogged over as Coach Griffin led Henry for a walk around the practice fields.

"Your brother has quite the leg, I'm very impressed." He took his hat off and ran his fingers through his gray hair. "Very impressed."

"Thank you, sir." I struggled to compose myself.

Coach Oldham took his time and settled onto the bleachers, then invited me to sit. "Coach Griffin talked to your coach and a few others in West Temple, you're an impressive young man, you should feel proud."

I nodded in appreciation.

"Wally, your brother has the talent to help us, there's no denying that. I do have one scholarship available, and I would say Henry's kicking warrants it. As for yourself, I can offer you a spot as an invited walk-on. That means you'll be on the team and live in the players' dorm. We can get you financial aid, but you'd have to have the resources to pay for part of it. I can offer you that, but I'm hesitant, I'm not sure this is the right thing to do."

"I understand, Coach." I hesitated a moment. "Can I ask why?"

"I think a better idea is to make a few calls to some small school programs, I'd be happy to do it on your behalf. Places with top-notch academics like Bastille, but programs that will give you the chance to play. Regardless of the level, it's still college football and can be a great experience for you."

"I don't know, sir, it's not something I've thought about."

"Or you could attend Bastille as a student and have Henry stay in West Temple. I swear, the best way to enjoy this program is from the stands."

"I don't know what we're going to do, but Henry and I have to stay together. I'm not leaving him with his father."

"Yes, I've heard a little about him, too. Do you have the resources?"

"There's a way I can make it work."

"You really want to come here, don't you?"

"I would do anything to be a part of this."

"Then let's address the elephant in the room." He turned to face me. "What's wrong with him?"

Coach Griffin was talking to Henry. As I looked over to them, I could tell Henry was suffering in his lonely world in the presence of a stranger without me. I didn't want to lie.

"He's undiagnosed." I had never said that in my life. Coach Oldham nodded, then leaned back and waited for me to continue. "He does his own schoolwork with a little help from me, he's never had any special classes. He doesn't communicate well, but that's never held him back."

"But you've carried him, haven't you? I'd like to hear your story."

I closed my eyes and hidden memories emerged from dark corners. I'm not sure of the words that made it from my mind to his ears; I'm not sure what's true and what's been contorted by time and desperation.

On a hard pew in the back of a church, I stared at an envelope with swirling pen marks on the front foreign to me. I couldn't read, I was only five. A loud voice held everyone's attention and I couldn't tell if it was good or evil. When the service was over and the people left, I kept my eyes closed and head down and waited, not knowing the reason. When I opened my eyes, the Church was dark and empty, save for colored light coming through stained-glass windows. I curled up on the pew, held the envelope tight, and fell asleep.

I woke when the organist, an old woman, returned. She had forgotten something, and, on her way back out, she nearly passed me by. I remember being hungry and hoped she had food in her purse, but we just stared at each other for the longest time until I handed her the envelope. A half hour later, the man with the voice I heard was sitting next to me.

"I'm the Minister, how are you?" he said in a manner that tried to make me comfortable.

After he opened the envelope and read the page inside, he didn't seem very happy. He must've read that page five or six times, and with each reading he became more agitated while I just sat in silence. After a while, he tore the page to shreds.

"We're going to have to find you a home, boy. In the meantime, you come with me." Any conveyance of comfort in his voice was gone.

He took me to his house and led me to a bedroom in the back. A woman, his wife I supposed, asked who I was and said kind words as she tried to approach, but the Minister wouldn't let her. I looked around to take in my surroundings and then I noticed him.

He was a sickly looking boy sitting at his desk, looking straight out the window, and not moving like he was a mannequin. Even though I was bigger than him, I could tell we were the same age. I walked up and bent over to look at him eye to eye, but he didn't budge except for a few blinks.

"What's your name," I said in a whisper.

"Henry."

"My name is Wally." I sat there looking at him for the longest time until he turned to me. Then we stared at each other, it was mesmerizing as we took each other in knowing we both had found safety.

The next day after the Minister left the house, his wife, Henry's mother, sat me down to talk. She asked me my age, where I'd come from, and what my favorite food was. It was good news to her that Henry was only six months older than me. She told me that I could sleep with Henry and that they'd get twin beds soon so we could each have our own. Henry's clothes didn't fit me, and we ended up at the local discount store where she bought blue jeans, a few shirts, and a Tribe sweatshirt; it was the most beautiful thing I'd ever seen. Then she took me over to the school and while we were waiting, she leaned down to me and spoke.

"I completely forgot to ask, what's your last name?"

By now I'd taken a liking to her, and I answered right away. "Hestia, my name is Wally Hestia."

Her smile withdrew slowly and her eyes tightened in anger, I got really afraid. We left the school without talking to anyone and she sent Henry and me to his room. I heard her on the telephone screaming and carrying on with a lot of bad words. Being hated is meaningless when you're unaware of what it means; the only thing you can think of is survival. I quickly figured out that they didn't care for Henry very much and left him to his own devices, which meant wetting the bed and walking into storms of foul moods.

It wasn't long before I could tell when he needed to use the toilet or when the Minister and his wife were in a rage. I'd lead him to the bathroom or sneak us both outdoors when it was best to avoid them. When they drank a little, we'd come out; when they drank a lot, we'd hide. But they mostly drank a lot, and I couldn't always predict when to hide and I'd feel terrible when one of them took the belt to us.

The only saving grace was the Tribe. After a couple of years, I learned that on Saturday mornings in the fall, the best course of action was to clean up their mess from the night before, make coffee, ride our bikes to the bakery for doughnuts, and have the sports section ready for a noon kickoff. It was like being part of a real family for those three hours. Then one day, she was gone, and the Minister took it out on us.

By the time we were ten, we were like unwanted pets. We got caught sniffing around outside of the barbecue restaurant in the village but the woman that owned the place took pity and started feeding us leftovers. After a while she found odd jobs for us to do and paid us in corn bread and ice cream. The only time we spent with the Minister was learning how to clean the Church, taking his whoopings, and watching the Tribe.

And then one Saturday after the Tribe kicked a long field goal in the rain just before halftime, I noticed Henry was gone. I looked through the house and went back to our room and then I heard it. He was in the backyard kicking this round gym ball we had over the goalpost trees—two trees with long, horizontal branches that met in the middle and formed a rough goalpost. I watched from our room for most of the second half while the Minister called for me to join him. But I was mesmerized by Henry. He kicked it over and over without showing joy if he made it or frustration if he didn't. It was soothing to watch, and he did it again the next day after services and the next day after school. Within a few weeks, he couldn't miss, but our yard was small and it wasn't much of a challenge.

After the Tribe's season was over, I took him and an old football I'd found to the high school field to test his skills. He missed on the first number of kicks, but I could tell he was learning from each one. His calm concentration, or lack of distraction, was like an escape for me. When he did connect from twenty yards out, I was sold and took it upon myself to lead his way. I looked up videos and articles on the internet and we studied them together. I kept the limit to thirty a day to keep his foot from getting injured, but still, thirty kicks a day every day for years starts to add up. By the time we were fourteen and playing on the freshmen team, he could hit from forty. During our sophomore year, he made one from fifty-three yards, but no one would believe me. His legs really filled out our junior year and he made one from sixty. When our main kicker went down, I told Coach Huey.

I tried to fill in more details of game specifics, especially the long kicks at the end of our senior year, but Coach Oldham waved me off, he'd heard the rest from Coach Griffin. It was like I came out of a trance. Bright green grass lay before us and a sense of peace came over me. Then Coach Oldham turned to me, and I could tell he'd made up his mind.

"This is what I have to offer: a scholarship for Henry and an invited walk-on spot for you, but there are conditions.

"Both of you have to succeed academically," he continued. "If Henry can't handle the schoolwork, he can't stay enrolled in the University. If he can, then he kicks and you hold. If it works, both of you can be on the team all four years, as long as it doesn't ruin you."

I could barely breathe, and probably stared a little too long. "Coach, I can't thank you enough, this is the greatest thing that's ever happened to us." But I had to ask. "If you don't mind, sir, what do you mean about getting ruined, do you mean the team accepting us?"

"Don't worry about your teammates, they'll accept you. Look around, it's everything else."

Samantha

....

THE SEATBELT SIGN lit up and I checked my phone before I had to put it in airplane mode. Sure enough, Abbey had sent another text.

> *I can't thank you enough for being here last night. Jerry and I will get through this, good luck covering the Bastille game. Love you.*

Looking up, I saw that I had enough time to reply.

> *Love you, too. I'll be back Sunday night and I'll stop over. Don't give up hope, it will happen.*

The sight of the two of them sitting on their couch, their eyes red and puffy from crying, had broken my heart. They had tried for years, and this time we all thought it was going to happen. Somehow, I'd known as soon as my phone rang and I'd seen her caller ID that she'd miscarried again. I took a deep breath, braced myself, and drove over to their apartment right away, I didn't even knock when I got there.

I'd held on to her like I had held on to my mother when my father died, and I had felt the pain in her sobs and wringing body. Jerry had been so sweet and delicate with her, but he was emptied out, too. If there was ever a couple who deserved a child, it was them.

I should be there with her, we'd been through everything together, but now I was off to the great Bastille University to cover the Oklahoma game; two powerhouses that couldn't see past the scoreboard regardless of the damage and exploitation needed to get their W. I didn't know how much longer I could do this: the maniacal fan bases, the pompous coaches, the grabbing hands. I couldn't tell what was worse, the hypocritical bullies justifying their sadistic tactics by saying football was critical to the success of America or the homespun coaches that spent more time building up their saintly images than actually coaching, like Bastille's Old-ham. They all use these kids, then cry at the slightest provocation as if their game is the most important thing in the world. And I have to watch, wait, and ask pretty little questions that I've asked a million times while a coach stands at the lectern with the self-importance of a man who moves the chess pieces of global power.

And then they complain. Abbey and Jerry have real pain, and I couldn't cry with them. It's embarrassing and I'm lesser for it, but at least Abbey understands, she was there, she was there for all of it.

The plane taxied out to the runway, and I stared off at distant clouds, waiting for the memory to play in my head. I wish I could cry; I'm too hard to feel anymore and I don't know if I ever will. I haven't cried since my father died, and even before that. I guess I don't really remember the last time I did.

I do remember the rec basketball game, when I was on the team with Abbey, we were twelve years old. I could play, she could barely dribble and the only way we could be on the same team was by rigging the system. I guess corruption starts at a young age. Abbey's mom's boyfriend was one of the rec coaches and he knew I was good. After he cornered me at the evaluations, I knew I shouldn't get mixed up with him, but Abbey and I couldn't bear the thought of playing against each other.

"It's easy," he said. "Just have your dad be the assistant coach and you're automatically on my team." His goatee and stubble made me nervous, and, after that, he kept nagging me. He even called my dad and let him know he didn't have to attend a single practice; it was just in name only. I begged my dad and he finally caved, even though we both knew there was something strange about this guy.

We won a couple of games but then faced this team with two sisters who both played elite-level travel basketball. As the game went on and their lead grew, our coach started yelling louder and louder until just about everyone in the stands was looking at him across the floor. The older sister had post moves, quick feet, and a good shot, but I was good enough to slow her down. Our real weak spot was Abbey; she guarded the younger sister and was no match. That girl could play. She would get a pass from her sister at full speed and drive the lane, and Abbey couldn't touch her. At halftime we were down by eighteen and our coach laid into Abbey, telling her to set her feet in the lane and take a charge.

The third quarter was fine; the sisters had to sit due to playing time rules and we brought the deficit to under ten. The sparse crowd of parents and a few relatives even got into it as we started the fourth quarter. Sure enough, on their first possession the younger sister got the ball at the top of the key and flew by as Abbey jumped out of the way in fear. As I was taking the ball out, I heard our coach slam his clipboard on the floor and call a time-out. There was sweat coming off him, we were all a little nervous and didn't want to get close.

"Abbey," he said. "If you don't step in the lane and take a charge, I swear to God I'll bench you."

Abbey's lip started to pucker and I put my arm around her as we walked back out on the floor. She asked me what she should do.

"Are you kidding? Stay out of her way, you'll get killed. This is supposed to be fun, remember?"

The game clock wore down and they built their lead well into double digits again when the older sister fed the younger one the ball on a pretty good give-and-go. She was in full stride when she hit the lane. Abbey stepped out of the way, raised her palms with a shrug, and smiled. The ref laughed, the sisters laughed, and so did everybody in the stands. Except our coach, of course. He called a time-out and was steaming mad as we walked towards the bench. I looked over to my dad across the floor and he looked at me with a bit of concern. Then our coach got us gathered around him so he could chew out Abbey in relative privacy. He was ready to burst, but so was I.

"I thought I told you to take a goddamn charge!" he said. Abbey sat there looking down at her lap, fidgeting her fingers. Then he lifted her chin and I could see tears forming in her eyes. "Oh, Jesus Christ," he said. "Stop being such a—"

I could see the word forming in his mouth, his lips pushed out to the very edge as he tried to hold back from saying our culture's second most popular word.

"A what?" I said. "A pussy?"

He turned to me with a rage I wouldn't see again until I became a sportswriter.

"That's right, coach," I said. "She's got a pussy, why don't you have a heart?"

That just enraged him further, he took his clipboard and smashed it on the bench, breaking it in two pieces. It was dead silent in the gym; I remember the sound of the broken piece hitting the floor. He came up and stood over me with his finger in my face, telling me how I better watch my mouth or I was in for it. But I just stood there with my hands on my hips, staring right back at him, repeating my line. I must've said it two or three times and each one egged him on beyond his breaking point. But I wouldn't budge, I knew my dad would be there any second. Then the coach took his eyes off me, he looked up at somebody his own size and I knew it was time.

"I don't feel safe," I said.

Then a whistle blew right behind me, and I turned and saw the ref all fired up.

"You're out of control," the ref said to our coach. "You're done, leave the gym."

The crowd burst into applause, including the parents on our side, and that's when I noticed. My dad was the only one not applauding, he was slumped a bit and I could see disappointment in his face dragging him down further.

Later that night, my parents sat me down and told me—Dad was sick with leukemia. It crushed him that he was too weak to protect me. They'd kept quiet for a number of months to keep my childhood innocent for as long as they could, but at that moment they regretted not telling me. They both broke down in tears like I'd never seen and then brought me into their hug. I just held on as tight as I could while they cried their eyes out, and it was at that moment I steeled myself off or else I would've drowned. I've never cried since.

Before I went to bed that night, I wrote to the rec league director and explained everything that had happened that day, telling him it was his responsibility to ensure our safety and well-being from overbearing coaches. I wrote about my dad and how he'd been such a great father and if it wasn't for his illness he would've coached, and he certainly would've stood up for his daughter and taught our coach a lesson. I also wrote how my dad was a great example and how he never used intimidation and that we should rely on the good virtues of the community to respond to this unfortunate situation and make sure it didn't happen again.

Before I sent the note, I shared it with my dad to make sure the spelling was right, and his reaction welded something to my heart:

I hadn't realized how writing could ease someone's pain and give hope. That was the day I knew I'd become a writer.

Dad died a few months later. I just held on to my mom while she cried enough for the both of us under an outpouring of support from the community. It was like a special gift you didn't want but needed to survive. I thought our community was special, that they'd never let one of their own fall through the cracks.

That's why I was shocked when the next rec basketball season began and our old coach had a new team. He gave me a real stare and a half-snicker, and I knew it was his way of enjoying my pain. He was a goddamn bully, and I couldn't believe they let him coach again. I asked the director at the next game and all he said was they were short of coaches. I can still see it to this day, him walking the sidelines, complaining about the refs, bitching at his players, and cheering louder than anybody as his team ran up the score against us. I'll never forget it.

The plane's engines roared and we started moving down the runway. *We'll see*, I thought. It was going to be a different year; somebody's going to have a reason to cry.

Wally

....

BASTILLE

i.

THE LOCKER ROOM door swung open, flooding us with the noise of the sold-out stadium for the season opener. The seven o'clock game was televised nationally, I was a long way from West Temple. Eighth ranked Oklahoma was taking the field and our crowd sounded their disapproval; we were four-point underdogs, ranked seventeenth in the country. During pre-season, we focused on Oklahoma and their big running back, Tyquan Ray. The scout team ran every Oklahoma play from the year before until our defense reacted instinctively to near perfection. But during pre-game warm-ups, when I saw their offensive line and Tyquan Ray in the flesh in those famous crimson and cream uniforms, I got worried. They were big and pissed-off and looked nothing like our scout team.

When the locker room door closed the quiet din of preparation returned. I leaned over to Henry.

"Put your helmet on," I whispered.

All through camp, I waited for someone to tap my shoulder and tell me a mistake had been made, that they appreciated our effort but we didn't belong. I'd never seen so many tattoos and dreadlocks, that much speed and athleticism, or all that size and aggression.

During stretches the first day of practice, Henry and I were in the back, and I realized that any one of them would've been the best player at West Temple or on any team we played. I felt like a harmless ranch dog dodging between the legs of thoroughbreds and spent most of my time making sure Henry didn't get trampled.

Henry pulled his helmet on, buckled the strap, and put his mouthpiece in. He looked like a twelve-year-old that got the uniform for Christmas and was wearing it to the game, and I wondered what the hell I had gotten him into. I stole glances at him, then closed my eyes, etching the memory deep. My heart skipped when I first saw mine: the arrow extending over the front to the large arrowhead, the Tribe in script on the right, my number 16 on the left.

"Bring it in." I looked up and saw Coach Oldham in the middle with Coach Dixon, our defensive coordinator. The press had said for years, to mixed reactions, that Coach Dixon was the heir apparent, and being on the inside confirmed it. Dixon was a former linebacker and captain for Coach Oldham, and even though he was now forty-something, he looked like he could still play. After six years in the NFL, he'd come home to Bastille. His authority over the program was evident by the deference he received from other coaches, even on the offensive side, and the manner in which he injected his voice into all elements of the program. His smiles were few, but you knew he was on your side. If he complimented your play, you'd mention it to a friend.

I asked Jeremy why the entire Tribe Nation wasn't behind Coach Dixon as the next head coach. Jeremy looked at me like I was a pup.

"You mean Kareem Dixon? A Black man with a Muslim first name in the Deep South? It's a mystery."

Coach Oldham stood in the center with the team surrounding him on one knee. He didn't try to inspire or incite higher intensity; it was already done. "Do not let your excitement overtake your judgment." When he was through, he looked over to Coach Dixon. "Kareem, anything else?"

Coach Dixon looked us over slowly, we all believed he could kick the shit out of any coach in college football. "Compete, compete, compete. If you do that, you'll get your chance to explode. Go ahead, Dion."

The coaches left the locker room and we all stood around Dion. The year before he arrived, the Tribe won five and lost seven. Last year, his first, we won eight, which could have been nine if not for the kick-six against Georgia Tech. He pulled his helmet over his wild mohawk, and we waited for his prompts. Each time we responded in unison, it sent chills through us.

"TRIBE FOREVER!"

"TRIBE FOREVER!"

"TRIBE FOREVER!"

As Dion led us out, the clacking sound of our spikes on cement sounded like a marching war machine but the roaring stadium noise soon drowned it out as we entered the tunnel. The crowd had raised their arrows, their shrieks piercing and harmonizing in a constant pulse. Henry and I were in the back with the assistant coaches, and I held on to his shoulder pads and felt the energy affect the team. Guys were jumping on the balls of their feet, making their own noise, the bottled-up energy flooded the tunnel and only Henry wasn't affected. The smell of dirt and grass, sweat and fresh uniforms hung in the humid air as the walls seemed to shake with angry vibrations. My childhood was spent dreaming of the Tribe. Just once I had wanted to run through that tunnel and into the maelstrom of 90,000 screaming fans. But now, I was terrified.

Then someone tapped my shoulder and when I turned it was Coach Oldham. He leaned close and spoke into the earhole of my helmet. "Enjoy it, this is a special moment for you." I was shocked and as he passed me by, my own wild screams added to the noise.

Then we were released, and it was like the field was a vacuum and our energy shot us forth into a bath of constant noise louder than what I'd felt in the tunnel. When Dion and the others out front approached midfield, the arrows were shot and the *BOOM* was leveled as the fireworks went off above the stadium. Television didn't do it justice.

After the national anthem and coin toss, our kickoff team huddled on the sideline and then took the field. The entire crowd, except for the few Oklahoma fans, raised the collective arrow and the shrieking began again. Our starting kicker, Evan, held his arm high waiting for the ref's signal as the noise slowly intensified. Henry stood next to me watching silently.

The kick sailed high, turning end over end through the thick air still littered with stagnant smoke from the fireworks. Just before the ball landed in the returner's arms, the arrows were released with the *BOOM* and right on cue the Oklahoma returner bobbled the ball which sent the crowd into a further frenzy. He didn't fumble but we tackled him at the eighteen.

I could see Marshall in my mind watching the game at Dyson's house. Mr. Wright, Miss Diane, and Aunt Janie would be watching and looking for Henry and me on the sideline. I wanted to creep closer, but something held me back. I didn't want to get close to that goddamn field.

A year ago, I played nearly every down and was proud to be a West Temple Panther. After we were offered by Coach Oldham, I focused on Bastille so much that my senior year went by without being memorialized with parties and lazy days. I toned down my outward zeal for the Tribe, since I wasn't even the top player at West Temple. Henry was the star of my story; I was one step ahead of being an equipment manager.

After graduation, the countdown began in earnest. We enrolled in the summer session at Bastille, taking two classes. The Minister barely acknowledged our impending departure except for mentioning that, upon our return—which he believed would be before October—we were to get full time jobs and find alternative living arrangements.

The first morning after our arrival, I woke after dawn and looked out on the campus and our new life in disbelief. I wasn't religious, the Minister had ruined me on that long ago, but still I wanted to thank a higher power for our good fortune and the world that was opening up before us. The only thing I could think of was closing my eyes and thanking the Tribe and all who believed in Her.

That night, there was a knock on our door. Marcus James stood before me, a starting wide receiver and a high school teammate of Dion's.

"Let's go, boy," he said. "Dion needs another body to throw to."

Without a word, I followed. The air was thick with humidity and I was sweating before we passed the end of the dorm.

"Get dressed and get some gloves," Marcus said.

The manicured practice field looked like a fairway with stripes and I tried to imagine the activity and struggle that would take place in August. But now it was quiet, the only movement was the faint circling of insects around the lights above.

There were two others besides Marcus and me, Tony Gio and Eddie Mason, both freshmen receivers, and when Dion walked onto the field they stopped talking. We ran the routes Dion called, one after another. The spirals were tight and arrived sooner than I expected, and I dropped the first two. I didn't know how long Dion wanted to throw and didn't ask. I lost count of the routes well after a dozen.

"You all right?" Dion said.

Sweat poured off my head as I bent over to suck in air. "I'm good." I was going to run routes until he was satisfied.

Eddie was long and lean; I was amazed at his burst. Grass flew from his spikes when he took off and his dreadlocks bounced like mad snakes. I wondered how out of place I looked. Tony didn't drop a single pass and after each catch, he'd pull the ball in tight, then plant a foot and turn up field. He was only an inch taller than me, but his solid build was made to absorb shots over the middle.

The passes kept coming and I lost track of time. The balls seemed to get heavier, causing me to drop more than I caught. My speed slowed and my legs started to burn. I ran a deep post and Dion launched it farther than I could reach. I stopped mid-route and watched the ball arc high above me and land twenty yards beyond, then roll into darkness.

"We good," Dion said.

When I got to the ball, I dropped to one knee to catch my breath. I didn't want to hold them up, but the relief kept me planted. When I looked up everyone was gone. I collected the ball and slowly made my way back.

The locker room was dim, I dropped into my chair and looked up at the label bearing my last name.

"Thanks for running." Marcus sat down a few lockers from me. "I think he's worn out the rest of the receivers."

"Anytime; whenever you want."

"I've seen you before, you're the brother of that kicker, right?"

"I'm Wally. We were here the weekend Garr Johnstone was being recruited." I hesitated for a moment. "I can't believe he chose A&M."

Marcus let out a half grunt. "I can, but don't mention it to Dion. Arkansas A&M, not my kind of place, or Garr's."

"You know him from before?"

"Yeah, we all grew up together in Pahokee, like two streets away from each other. Garr's a year younger than me and Dion, but they're tight, like brothers. Both of them had to play up in the older leagues when we were kids because they were bigger than everybody. Then Garr ends up at a different high school and I'll be goddamned if he didn't chase me and Dion all over the field three years in a row. I thought for sure we had him. Garr's going to start every game until he retires, he'd be a first rounder if they could draft him today."

"Why'd he choose Arkansas A&M? Not the most glamorous program."

"Come on, why do you think?" Marcus held his hand up, rubbing his index finger and thumb together in the sign for money. "Same reason he didn't come to our high school. He wanted to come here, but a man's got to do what he's got to do. Thank God we don't play them this year. They were top twenty last year, with Garr they're going to make some noise."

All summer long, everywhere he went, Dion was watched. The Tribe was sick of five-win seasons, being relegated to the type of team that struggled to make it to a bowl game. They wanted a top-twenty team and once the Dion-led Tribe delivered they wanted a top-ten team, and if we were going to make that kind of effort it might as well be top-four and a playoff team. Over the din of the crowd at Vic's Pizza I heard students arguing the odds of whether we'd make the playoffs. In a barbershop, old men debated the likelihood of Dion winning the Heisman. At the supermarket a middle-aged woman responded to the cashier with, "Tribe Forever."

They had been waiting for this day since last December, and when Dion stepped out onto the field after Oklahoma punted, the crowd swelled with anticipation. I pulled on the headset I got to wear as a backup QB and listened to the nervous chatter of the coaches.

First play from our twenty-eight-yard line: Handoff to Jonathan DeVonta to the right side, gain of four.

Second and six: A pass to our tight end on a drag route, good for eight.

First down from our own forty: Inside trap to Jonathan, but Oklahoma stunted into it, loss of three.

Second and thirteen from our thirty-seven: We signaled in a middle screen, but Dion called an audible and the coaches went nuts.

"Jesus Christ, they're baiting Dion. They're going man on the left and they're going to roll the safety."

"Coach, can we get a time-out?"

"The Mike is going to blitz, goddamn it all."

Their middle linebacker blitzed; the screen would've gone for twenty. The pocket collapsed before Dion could set up, but it was like he didn't care. He rolled wide to his left, planted his feet, and threw deep to our best receiver, Tarik Fields, who used his 4.4 speed to run a fly. Dion took a hard hit; he never saw the ball clear two sets of defensive hands and land in Tarik's gloves. We were up 6–0 and a full-throated roar poured over the field like a wave of elated anger.

After the extra point Oklahoma started from their own twenty and chipped away at our defense. On one sweep to our side, it sounded like a stampede as a handful of our defenders chased down their runner and crashed in a pile right before us. By halftime we were up 17–13, but it felt like we were behind. They had run the ball for over a hundred yards, and we were only ahead because of two missed Oklahoma field goals.

We traded touchdowns in the third quarter but our guys looked worn down. I navigated the sideline and followed the play calls on the headset as I tried to stay out of the way. Then I turned to Henry and my heart sunk—he was sitting on the bench staring at his phone. I hustled over to him.

"Henry, give me that, you can't bring it out here." He looked at me like he knew he'd done something wrong. "This isn't like high school; we'll get in trouble." When I handed the phone to one of the trainers, I heard the crowd noise evaporate in disappointment.

I looked to the field and saw Tyquan Ray run by our sideline in a blur, I'd never seen anyone that big run that fast.

We were down 27–24, and I could see hints of dejection in some of our players until Dion walked by, pumping our guys up. We started to come alive again when Dion drove us to their forty, then he connected on a pass at the Oklahoma ten to Marcus James, but he fumbled when he got hit and the energy went out of the crowd again.

Oklahoma continued to pound our defense into the fourth quarter. Five yards on a trap play, then nine on a toss sweep. No matter what stunts or run blitzes we used, we couldn't stop them. We all knew why. Our defensive backfield was inexperienced and their QB had a cannon arm, forcing us to play deep with little run support from our strong safety. We had to rely on our defensive line to keep Tyquan Ray in check, but our guys were worn down. After an Oklahoma holding penalty, they were faced with fourth and eight and punted. When the defense came off the field, I heard Coach Oldham over the headphones.

"I'm putting Carter in the box for good, this kid's killing us," he said. Carter Schultz was our strong safety, he played at least fifteen yards off the ball until then.

I was within earshot when Coach Oldham got the defense together. I didn't want to get too close, but I had to hear what he was going to say. Then Coach Oldham looked at me.

"Wally, stand in front of that camera." A reporter and a cameraman were getting too close, I positioned myself in front of them and shook my head. Then I turned to listen to Coach Oldham, he was urgent and had to talk louder than usual.

"We're putting eight in the box. Carter, line up five yards off the ball over this Ray kid and you put a hat on him every time he touches the ball, that's enough of this. Where are my corners? All right, they're going to line up the receivers wide, use an outside technique and funnel them in. Do not let them run the sidelines, their QB has a gun. Melvin, where are you?" Melvin Richardson was our free safety and a true freshman; he looked as nervous as I had before the game, a look that hadn't improved. "Okay, Melvin, line up an extra ten yards deep, don't worry about run support unless you're the only one left. As soon as they see eight in the box, they're going to test you young guys, got it?"

After another one of our drives stalled, the defense headed back onto the field and Oklahoma saw it immediately. They still ran Tyquan on a fullback lead over the right tackle, and Carter met him just as he passed the line of scrimmage. Even though Carter was outweighed by thirty pounds, he showed no fear and met Tyquan in the hole at full speed, it seemed like the pop echoed throughout the stadium. Gain of one.

Oklahoma didn't bother running it again, on second down they took their shot. After the ball was snapped, they faked it to Tyquan and our entire sideline screamed out "pass" and I watched Melvin backpedal. The field seemed too big for him to patrol it. I didn't see their QB throw, there were too many players in front of me, but I saw the ball sail high and straight towards us. There was no way Melvin was going to make it. The crowd rose as I inched closer to the field and saw our cornerback chasing their receiver; he'd already been beaten. I wanted Melvin to head up field more to get a better angle on the receiver so he wouldn't score after he caught it but, instead, he was headed for the spot right in front of me. Relative to Dion's passes, the ball floated in the air a fraction of a second longer, and as the receiver raised his hands to make the catch, Melvin leapt from yards away and extended himself into the path of the ball. He caught, cradled, and dragged his feet before he went out of bounds. It was the most athletic thing I'd ever seen.

We cleared out of the way as he slid out of bounds. Then he stood and held the ball up to show he had control and the ref immediately signaled we had possession. I got Henry out of the way as Melvin was mobbed by other players with screams and slaps to his helmet.

"You got the arrow!"

"Do it, baby, they're waiting!"

I looked up to the crowd, they'd raised the arrow and the screaming had commenced. It was terrifying and hypnotic.

"Yeah, yeah, take your helmet off and rip it open." The offensive linemen were urging him on, they never got the arrow.

As Melvin popped off his helmet and stepped forward into clear space, I looked around and saw the entire stadium taking part. He waited the prescribed interval as the screaming built and I saw tens of thousands of hands raised in arrows just like in the university brochure. Then he did it. Melvin raised his hands to his chest and ripped them apart like he was exposing his heart. All those thousands of arrows quickly dropped in unison in the direction of Melvin's heart, then they ripped their right arms back and sounded the *BOOM*. Melvin fell back into the arms of waiting teammates a changed young man.

After the commercial break, our offense took the field with just over three minutes remaining. Dion fed Jonathan DeVonta the ball three straight plays and they had to measure for a first down. From our own forty, Dion dropped back and threw a perfect pass to Tarik, a game-winner. Half of us on the sideline dropped to our knees in disappointment when he dropped it. After two more runs to Jonathan, Dion ran a naked bootleg and barely crossed the fifty without going out of bounds.

Then Coach Griffin yanked my arm. "Warm up Henry."

His words passed through me like bullets, I didn't move.

"Let's go, warm him up."

Henry followed me to the practice netting where Evan was also warming up, no one talked. In between practice kicks I looked up to the scoreboard to see the down and distance. First and ten from their forty-nine-yard line. I didn't want to go out there. I looked back to Henry as he lined up for another practice kick. To him, it was as if we were in our backyard. Second and seven from the forty-six and the clock running.

Someone from the stands yelled, "You've got to make it, Evan, send it to overtime."

Please, Dion, I thought. *Please get it to at least the twenty.* From the twenty on in, probably even the twenty-five, Evan would kick. Third and three from the forty-two. I looked up to Henry, but he shook his head, he was ready.

Oklahoma called a time-out. Coach Oldham called us over to stand by him, and the closer I got, the more nauseated I felt.

"If we don't make the first down, I'm sending you boys out there. Are you ready?"

I nodded quickly, almost in twitches, as Jeremy slapped the back of my helmet.

It was a simple handoff to Jonathan, and I thought he had it. Then, an Oklahoma player pumped his arm. Fourth and one from the forty.

"Go." It was all Coach Oldham said.

There were forty seconds and the clock was ticking. I couldn't breathe as we ran onto the field, it was like falling off a building in a dream. I was floating and disoriented and couldn't feel the ground. My helmet seemed too big, it rattled as I ran, distorting my vision. I shouldn't be here, I'm not prepared, I'm not good enough. *The* Dion McAres offered a hand slap in encouragement, and I almost missed it; the exchange was a blur. When I got to huddle, I couldn't speak. The linemen were breathing hard, like I'd entered a pen of live bulls. There were spots of blood on their white pants, they all looked to me, waiting, until one of the linemen spoke.

"Call the fucking play, already."

"Wally, call a field goal," Jeremy said.

"Yeah, yeah. Field goal on set," I said.

"What the fuck is set? Is that first sound?" one of them said.

"Set is first sound, San Fran, San Fran," Jeremy said.

As I broke the huddle, I realized I'd forgotten to count the players. It was too late, there were twenty-eight seconds left. My hands were numb, I shook them to get some feeling back but it was useless. I picked a blade of grass, placed my shaking finger on it, and raised my other hand to Jeremy. Twenty-two seconds left. My up hand was shaking, my fingers were empty plastic tubes that would explode when the ball flew through them. I looked to Henry and he nodded. I looked to the ball in Jeremy's hands and was about to call out, "Set." There was quick movement to the right and the whistle blew.

Oklahoma jumped offside. The ref placed the ball on the thirty-five, called a first down and Dion came back onto the field as we ran off. Henry and I stood by Coach Oldham with Evan, waiting to see which kicker he'd go with.

"We're taking a shot," Coach Oldham said.

Oklahoma stacked the line; we were outnumbered up front. Dion took the snap and rolled to his right as two Sooners chased after him. No one was open when Dion let go of the ball, I thought he was throwing it out of bounds. It sailed high towards the sidelines, and, at the last second, Tarik's hands rose above the defender's, and he caught it at the eight. The defensive back fell as Tarik stopped himself from going out of bounds, it was a quick couple of steps to the end zone.

Wally

....

ii.

MY FAVORITE MOMENTS surprised me; simple fragments of solitude nestled in the heart of Bastille. There wasn't a lot of time, I didn't know how the real players did it. Every hour was accounted for, and if they had free time, especially Dion, they watched film. Even if they didn't, they'd come out of practice worn down like they'd been in a fight. Not the best way to settle in for hours studying collegiate level concepts, especially when some of them had struggled to get through high school.

When I found a few quiet moments, a subtle pleasure filled me. Sometimes I hung out in Tony and Eddie's dorm room, watching them play video games. Other times I took in moments by myself, like sitting in Masters Library, trying to study but realizing I was daydreaming about the life I was actually living. The main hall of the gothic library was stories high and made me feel small, and at the same time, part of something important. After Henry would fall asleep, I'd walk through campus as if I was furthering my integration into the sculpted and manicured and exclusive organism. I was trying to soak it up before reality set in: Henry didn't belong in college, and I didn't belong on the field.

I laid in bed the night after the Oklahoma game horrified by what I'd been through; running out onto the field during a live game was the most traumatic moment of my life. Like a frayed hole in an old shirt, my nerves showed through in practice the week after the Oklahoma game. When Henry lined up to kick in practice, my lead hand shook, and I was more worried everyone had seen it than I was about the snap. The ball grazed my hand and bounced away.

It felt like the whole team was watching as I muffed the next one by overcompensating. The sound of annoyed groans only made me sweat harder, I had to wipe my hands on my pants. On the third try, I reached for the ball instead of letting it come to me and lost my placement. It wasn't where Henry expected and the kick never elevated, it smacked Jeremy in the rear and everyone cracked up. I looked over to Coach Oldham, he gave a quick shake of his head and Coach Griffin blew his whistle to end practice.

Coach Oldham didn't call on us to kick against Kent State, a game we won handily 43–13 in the blistering heat, but my problems continued in practice the next week. Coach Griffin began keeping track of the snaps I handled properly instead of Henry's accuracy; Henry never missed when I placed the ball correctly. By Friday, my success rate had climbed to seventy-five percent, and with each snap I held my breath and gritted my teeth hard enough that I was chewing through my mouthpiece.

"Coach Oldham believes in you," Coach Griffin said. "But we've got to figure this out before the conference schedule starts."

His words had the opposite effect; Coach Oldham knew I didn't belong and every morning I looked at my phone with apprehension, waiting for a call or a text asking Henry and me to see Coach Oldham so he could dismiss us.

We didn't get on the field when we traveled to Colorado State but did see Aunt Janie in the parking lot after the game. The next week in practice I was worse. Before practice, during practice, and at the crucial moment when I got in position to place the ball, I imagined all the different ways I could screw up. Success required the equivalent emotional effort of scaling a mountain and it was wearing me out. Then I overheard Coach Oldham.

"Barney, you've got to fix this now. Henry is a difference maker and we're not able to use him."

When I heard that I wished I would've kept my mouth shut the night Coach Griffin walked into the restaurant. Tony and Eddie tried counselling me at night, but their conflicting ideas led to arguments that didn't require my presence. Jeremy snapped balls to me in the dorm hallway and after a dozen perfect catches he turned to me.

"We're fixed, right?" he said.

"We're good."

On the first try the next day the ball deflected off my clumsy hands right into Henry's. He caught it and the team sarcastically cheered and I was humiliated. Dion stared at me, and I couldn't tell if it was threatening or sympathetic.

▼ ▼ ▼

On Thursday, I had an appointment with Professor Bertrand, our academic advisor. The first meeting took place while we were still in camp and took all of five minutes—I told him we had to be at practice. I don't know if he could tell I was lying, I didn't want to expose Henry. But the way he spoke made me comfortable. "Come back anytime," he said. "You don't need a reason, but you do need a friend. Or at least someone who's paid to be your friend." He snickered at his own joke at a level slightly unwarranted, which was funny in its own right.

As I entered Professor Bertrand's office, he held up a finger like he was trying to finish a deep thought as he stared into his book. I couldn't tell his age; he had to be late forties, maybe early fifties. Just a short, balding professor who was a little overweight. He snapped his book shut and asked me how I liked it so far. A goofy smile came across his face as he nodded to coax an answer out of me. He was funny; I tried to hold back a chuckle and kept it to a grin.

"I love it."

"I knew it," he said as he clenched his fist in victory. "This is a very special place, take full advantage of it."

His small office was cramped and overflowed with books and magazines and stacks of unorganized papers.

"Now, let's get serious. How's it going? Are you keeping up with the classwork?"

"It's a lot harder than high school."

"That's understandable, the first semester is always the hardest. Do you have a plan?"

I paused a moment, like it was a trick question. "Not really."

"What if I told you of a sure-fire, fool-proof method to earn straight As throughout your entire college career—would you be interested?" His eyes lit up as he talked, and I found myself smiling again to hold off laughter.

"Of course, does it cost anything?"

"No, I'm serious. My proprietary four-step program is fail-safe, easy to implement, and completely within your control. I've offered this secret program to every student I've ever advised, and yet, few are able to incorporate my sage wisdom. Are you ready?" I nodded with genuine interest. He held up a finger. "Number one: Go to class. Not just a class, every class, do not skip. Easy, right?"

I nodded.

"Number two, and this one is big: Sit in the front row." He leaned in as he spoke for emphasis. "The benefits of seat selection are astounding. You won't be distracted by others; out of courtesy to your professor you won't play with your phone; you'll focus on the material being discussed; the cool kids will think you're a nerd and not ask you to get high after class; your professor will get to know your face and have a glimmer of hope for you; and you might actually learn something. As they say, geography is destiny."

"That actually makes a lot of sense."

"Three, possibly the most important: As soon as class is over, proceed directly to a quiet place and review the material. The distractions here are plentiful, mainly, the opposite sex, weed, and video games. What people don't realize is that material learned via lecture has a very short shelf life. If you immediately review it, its chances of survival improve by a factor of ten. If there's homework, get the ball rolling. If you get behind, you'll never get an A. Finally, get to know your professors as needed. These are the people that can help you the most and if you take their life's work seriously, they'll take you seriously."

He waited for me to respond, but he could see it in my face. "That's incredible, I'm going to try it."

"Don't just try, do it. Now, how's your brother doing?"

The question caught me off guard, I mumbled he was fine and changed the subject. He knew. After a few minutes, I got up to leave.

"Before you go, Wally, I need to share something with you. It's about my role as your advisor."

I sat back down.

"I don't typically advise athletes; this is a special favor to John." He could tell I didn't know who John was. "Your coach, John Oldham. He thinks highly of you and your brother, in fact, I think he was delighted to give you this opportunity, but he also loves the integrity of the institution. He asked for my view on your brother and, at the end of the semester, I'm to tell him if Henry really belongs. Your brother doesn't have to come see me if he chooses not to, but I will be looking at his grades. If he happens to be a painfully shy person that performs academically, then everything is fine. As for you, I encourage you to come by as often as you like.

As wonderful as this university is, it's also large and having some-one help you navigate it can be invaluable."

As I walked out of his office, I figured we'd be back in West Temple for good by Christmas. At least we'd beat the Minister's prediction.

We traveled to Ole Miss for the beginning of our conference schedule and were tied at the half, seven all, but their only TD was on a punt return. In the second half, we blew them out and won 35–16. There were a couple of times we could've kicked but Coach Oldham didn't send us in.

We were 4–0 and the energy on campus and around town started to build. "Is Bastille Back?" was the headline on Sports Inc.'s college football section.

What's Dion like?

People would see my football backpack, and the question popped up frequently.

"He's a good guy and a great leader," was my standard answer.

Can you get me his autograph?

I visited Professor Bertrand again. His academic strategy had had an immediate impact, and I wanted to tell him.

"Have you thought about what you'd like to major in?" he asked.

"I don't even know where to start."

He took a moment to gather his thoughts. "I'm going to give you four things to think about, they're objectives for your college career, if you will. Are you ready?"

I nodded.

"First, get straight As." He waited for my reaction, but I was still. "You only have this opportunity once, if you get straight As you get choices in life. Less so if you get Bs, and with Cs you're told what to do."

The thought scared me. I thought of the Minister.

"Second, expose yourself to as much as possible. This is a major university with every academic topic and activity you can imagine. I promise that if you do, you'll come across something that inspires you, besides football of course. The third thing, enjoy yourself and make as many friends as possible, but do it in that order."

I took a moment to absorb his words, I felt like writing them down, as I waited for the last. "What about the fourth?" I said.

"Oh, of course, I nearly forgot. It's probably the most over-looked aspect of college: Make sure you take advantage of the non-academic education."

I waited a moment then asked, "I'm not sure what you mean."

The Professor sat back and I studied his face, trying to assess how naïve I was in his eyes.

"For most students, college is the first time they're exposed to the multiple currents that comprise the world, things like the full spectrum of ethnicities, religion, sexual orientation, politics, and the great American sub-cultures. Other things, too, such as competing academic schools of thought, the business and politics of universities, and the effect of big-time college sports. Now, the multitude of all these currents concentrated in one place is itself rare, and each current is interesting enough. However, when these currents collide, that's where your real education takes place."

I found myself thinking up reasons to visit the Professor and I tried to pass his lessons on to Henry.

"We've got to make this work, Henry."

He didn't respond as he stared at his phone; I knew he was playing his numbers game. I settled in for a long night of home-work not knowing which to start with, his or mine.

▼ ▼ ▼

A week later, a text came at 6:15 a.m. from Coach Oldham's admin: *Could you please stop by at 7:30 to meet with Coach Oldham?* It was sent to both Henry and me. My stomach turned over; this was it, we were done.

Henry and I sat in chairs in front of his desk as Coach Oldham looked at a page that Randy, the Director of Football Operations, our DFO, reviewed with him. I still wasn't used to the fact that Coach Oldham knew us and called us by name. For the rest of my life, people would find out I played for Bastille and they'd ask what he was like. He was the rare person who was common and larger-than-life at the same time.

His modest office wasn't much larger than Coach Griffin's. I always imagined his office would be a grand spectacle, like a museum in progress with memorabilia adorning the walls. The only decoration was his framed degree from Bastille and a few pictures from decades ago.

After Randy left, Coach Oldham addressed us. "Gentlemen, thanks for coming in this early. There's something I need to discuss with you."

I bowed my head, knowing what he was going to say.

"Is there something wrong, Wally?"

As I looked up to him, I reminded myself it might be the last time we spoke. "Coach, I just want to thank you for this opportunity and I'm sorry I've let you down."

"It sounds like you're about to quit on me."

"No, sir, I would never quit the Tribe. I just thought—"

"Look, we've got Alabama at their place in a little over a week and we're going to need every point we can get." He paused a moment. "I think I know what your problem is. Bastille is a large stage, but you do belong here. You belong on this team. I think everybody in the stadium knew you were terrified when you went on the field against Oklahoma and that was my fault, you weren't ready. But I have faith in you, just relax and get prepared. However, this isn't the reason I called you in today."

I sat back in relief and looked to Henry in fear as I mentally begged him to not pull out his phone in front of Coach Oldham.

"I wanted to see how you're doing academically. Professor Bertrand says you're doing great, but he hasn't seen you yet, Henry."

I looked to Henry afraid of what he was going to say. A moment passed and Henry turned to me. "Henry, tell Coach how school is going." Henry turned back to Coach Oldham and blinked his eyes. I couldn't tell if he was looking at Coach or staring in his general direction. "Henry?"

Finally, Henry spoke. "I go to every class, I sit in the front row, and I do my homework right after."

"He's doing great, sir. I don't think he'll be on the Dean's list, but he's passing all his courses."

Coach Oldham looked relieved; I hadn't noticed the tension. "Good. I can deal with a botched snap; I can't deal with academic fraud."

▼ ▼ ▼

Dion and Coach Oldham were talking on the field before practice, it was still strange seeing them in real life. Then Coach Oldham looked over to me, nodded to Dion and patted him on the arm. I had become Dion's pet: I caught return passes for him in pre-practice warm-ups every day and before games. I'd studied the playbook like it was the Rosetta Stone and knew it better than everybody. Sometimes Dion asked me private questions about unfamiliar defensive fronts. But I imagined he'd run out of patience with my holding issues and had let Coach Oldham know it was time to move on.

"Yo, Wally, you've got to settle a bet with me and Tarik," Dion said as I handed him the ball. "Remember against Ole Miss when we had the bubble screen called and they blitzed the corner on the left and rolled the safety? Tarik was in the slot on the left and motioned to the right and he says I should have given him the sign to run the post since the safety cleared."

"First of all, Tarik should never be in the slot," I said.

"True that. It's like locking a thoroughbred in a phone booth."

"Any time they bring the corner, they're desperate. Besides, the linemen aren't going to know, and they'll be bailing out before you set up to throw. And even if you did get the ball off, some of them might be more than three yards past the line. Giving him the sign doesn't work on screens."

"That's what I told him," Dion said. He yelled over to Tarik. "You hear that, T? My boy says you was wrong."

"Umm, Dion, don't say it like that, I don't want to piss him off."

Dion turned to me. "Good point." He looked to Tarik and spoke with an English accent. "Tarik my good fellow, our esteemed colleague, Walter, respectfully disagrees with your position regarding said bubble screen, the issue we debated over tea this afternoon."

Marcus started cracking up, slapping his leg. "Ever since he seen that movie, man."

"Nobody's going to fuck with you," Dion said. "Not with me around. But you need to explain it to him, he's afraid to look stupid in front of the coaches." Dion looked over to me. "He don't know any of the running plays."

Marcus's return throw was off target, I reached and caught it with one hand.

"Don't tell me you can't catch," Dion said. "Your head is messed up. That's okay, I've got a little something planned for you today."

Thirty minutes later, Dion ran the offense against the full scout team. As he approached the center, one of the linemen called out, "Pic, pic."

"Cone, cone, cone," said two other linemen simultaneously.

Tarik motioned to the right, the center snapped the ball, and Dion threw the bubble screen. Whistles blew and Coach Oldham shook his head, while the offensive line coach called out our tight end.

Next play was a counter to Jonathan with our center, Andre Decker, predicted go in the first round, pulling lead. As Dion approached the line, the chatter began.

"The Mike is 50," Dion said.

"Cone, cone."

This time Dion answered. "Pic, pic, pic."

On the following play, Jonathan shifted to the slot, the center snapped the ball, and Dion took a seven-step drop. He waited an extra moment then threw deep to Tarik.

"Dion," Coach Oldham yelled, "You're not going to have that kind of time. Look him deep then find the tight end crossing. Jonathan will find a hole in the flat if it's not there."

They lined up for the next play: "Pic, pic, pic."

Before Dion got under center he yelled out, "San Fran, San Fran."

I put on my helmet; I didn't want anyone to see the smirk on my face. After the Oklahoma game I asked Jeremy what the line calls were.

"There's not many," he said. "A 'gut' is when a defensive lineman shades and the call tells the guard to block down and the tackle swings underneath to block the Mike. A 'gap' is when someone on the defense, like a safety or a linebacker, steps into a gap and the O-lineman that calls it has to block him and the next offensive lineman over picks up the guy he originally had. There's a few others, but we don't use them much."

"But what about all that pic and cone stuff? And San Fran? You called that in the huddle during the Oklahoma game."

Jeremy laughed. "That's when we forget the snap count. It's the funniest thing, we spend all this time memorizing plays and rule sets, but we can never remember the snap count. As soon as the QB calls the play you start thinking of your assignment, when you approach the line, you pick out your guy and by the time you get in your stance, half the guys have forgotten the count. Pic means it's on one, cone means it's on two. If you don't know, you call out 'pic, pic' and whoever knows, usually Dion, will call back 'pic, pic.' If the snap is on two, someone will say 'cone, cone.'

"What's San Fran?"

"That's if it's on first sound. Get it? The first letters of first sound are FS but some dyslexic flipped it around and started using San Fran for the code," he said.

"What if the snap is on three?" I said.

"No one snaps it on three, we can't count that high during games. The funny thing is, the defense never gets the whole pic/cone thing, not even our own defense in practice. I mean all season long they don't. If they ask, we just tell them it's a split adjustment, which isn't a thing once you're lined up."

The walk through was almost finished, it was time for Evan and Henry to kick. Coach Griffin called out fourth down and Jeremy, Evan, and his holder ran out onto the field. After they went through his series of kicks, it was our turn, and I was filled with dread. Then Dion called everyone in.

"If you're not in the play get over here, defense on this side, offense on the other," Dion said. "We're going to fix Wally's little problem right here and now." Hoots and jeers rose as they closed in on either side of the kicking formation. Then Dion continued. "We're going to make some noise and spook this shit out of Wally's head. Offense, you say 'Nu' and defense you reply with 'Ber.' Melvin and JD, you guys get close to Wally and get inside his head with whatever you can think of." Eddie and Tony volunteered to help with the taunts, then Dion directed the rest of the team until they found their rhythm.

Nu-Ber, Nu-Ber, Nu-Ber.

"Wally, don't call the snap until I say," Dion said.

Coach Oldham and Griffin were off to the side, watching like anthropologists. The chant got louder and my harassers began their work in earnest. They called me vile names and threatened physical acts I'd never considered.

Nu-Ber! Nu-Ber! Nu-Ber!

The volume increased and I could feel them inching closer. Jeremy was half turned waiting for Dion's signal. I began to sweat more from my nerves than the heat.

NU-BER! NU-BER! NU-BER!

Then it hit me, anxiety began draining me of control and my hands started to shake.

NU-BER! NU-BER! NU-BER!

The taunts from my four tormentors were personal, I could hear it in their voices that they meant it and they were right. Panic rose in my head like water in a submerged car, I couldn't breathe and was about to bail out.

Dion was behind me, he began speaking directly into the earhole of my helmet in a voice only I could hear. "Listen to them, boy," said Dion. "They hate you, all of them, they hate you."

NU-BER! NU-BER! NU-BER!

"They hate you so much, they want to rip you to pieces and feed you to gators." The chants and taunts rang in my ears. "Everyone does."

NU-BER! NU-BER! NU-BER!

"But not these guys, this is your team. Everyone outside of Bastille hates you. They hate me, too, and I love it. They hate all of us."

NU-BER! NU-BER! NU-BER!

I strained to hear his voice.

"But inside these walls, you're one of us and we need you."

NU-BER! NU-BER! NU-BER!

"Now block out the noise."

Dion must've signaled to Jeremy, he quickly turned and locked the ball in his hands as the rest of the offensive line tensed in position. I called for the ball and it flew back. I caught, placed, and spun, then Henry's foot drove it high and when it cleared the line I jumped up and pumped my arm as my taunters mobbed me.

"Very good," said Coach Oldham. "Now let's get Henry some work."

I caught every snap and Henry's final kick of sixty yards left everyone in awe. When we got back to the dorm, it felt like I'd safely swam to shore. I didn't know if it would last, but Dion had reached me and I wanted the feeling to remain. But a pile of books stood on the table and I was behind.

"Henry, can you at least try to do the homework? I'll correct it, but I can't do it all."

He looked up from his phone then came over to the table. I opened his textbook to the right chapter and slid it in front of him. I went to my bedroom to read and when I returned thirty minutes later, the book was opened to the same spot and Henry was in the same position. I closed my eyes and dropped into the chair.

"I'll do it," I said.

Wally

....

iii.

HENRY AND I sat on the bench as the Duke QB threw a desperate pass with seconds left. The Thursday night game was closer than we expected but it was never in question. The pass was a wobbler and fell incomplete as time ran out. Henry and I didn't make it onto the field.

When I woke up Friday morning, it felt like an impromptu holiday; we were schedule-free and able to enjoy the luxury of idle time. In the dining hall, Jeremy nodded to me as I walked by the offensive line table, the one closest to the buffet. Big Andre Decker slapped my hand and called out to Henry, "The Nuber!"

A dozen others repeated it without looking up from their food and Henry responded as they'd trained him to.

"I am the Nuber."

From what I could tell, Henry and I were the only ones to go to class. Sometimes I laid awake at night and thought about what it would be like if my own skills warranted my presence at Bastille, and I had a normal roommate. Instead of being the buffer for Henry, I could be myself and chase girls and drink beer and bask in the glow of the Tribe; I wondered if it would always be this way. I mentioned this to Professor Bertrand and his answer surprised me.

"Most people go through life always wondering what it would be like if things were different or they'd made another decision long ago than the one that put them on the path they were suffering. My answer to that: They would've found a different way to screw up their lives, revisionists always imagine the other path would've been perfect. Just live the life you're in as best as you can."

His answer gave me peace; Henry gave me purpose.

We spent the afternoon in the library where I studied in between sessions of reading online articles about the Tribe's 5–0 start and hype for the Alabama game. We each had a philosophy essay to write, which meant I had to write both, something I'd try to start in our dorm after dinner.

Instead, I watched the sports channels, waiting for news about next week's game. I went out to get ice cream at Henry's request at eight but didn't get back until after nine. The end of a movie was on when I returned, which we watched until I realized it was ten. I switched off the TV and pulled up the topics for the philosophy essay.

> "Using a current situation in politics, business, or culture, explore and contrast the different facets of Consequentialism vs. Kant's categorical imperatives."

I pulled out the textbook and tried to make myself read but drifted off to sleep. I woke to the sound of laughter in the hallway, followed by a few large bodies bumping against the walls. Consequentialism, I'd already forgotten the definition. I felt myself dozing off again.

"Edward, come out to play."

It was a voice from down the hall speaking in a high tone, almost singing.

Henry was still on his phone playing his numbers game. "Henry, put your phone down and start your homework."

"Edward, where are you?" The voice was closer.

I looked to Henry. "Who's Edward?"

Without looking from his phone, Henry replied, "Eddie doesn't go by Edward and his dorm room isn't on our floor."

The footsteps and bumps against the wall continued up the hallway. Then the sound of a large fist pounding our door startled me, there were giggles and unintelligible words.

"Edward, get your ass out here, now." There were other voices and more hands rapping our door. "Don't make me come in—" whoever it was broke down in laughter. Another voice struggled through giggles: "Dion requests the honor of your presence, you little fucking Edwards."

I closed my laptop and looked at the light around the doorframe seeping in from the hallway, it was partially blocked by the shadows of feet. I approached the door and rested my hand on the knob as my heart sounded in my ears. I spoke quietly: "There's no Edward here, who's out there?"

"Just come on out, we ain't going to hurt you. Or your Edward." They cracked up again.

I opened the door and it was our top three defensive linemen whose first names I didn't know. Even the coaches used their nicknames, "Pokey," "Simba," and "Malibu." Within seconds, Henry and I were escorted to Dion's room on the top floor as the three of them staggered and giggled. Dion's door was open and a cloud of smoke drifted out into the hall. When we entered, Henry's presence was noted.

"The Nuber!"

"Nuber!"

"The Nuber's here!"

There had to be over a dozen players, Black and white, in a room littered with empty beer cans, pizza boxes, and a couple of bongs. The chant began.

"Nuber! Nuber! Nuber!" It went on until a whistle broke the rhythm.

The crowd cleared a narrow alley, at the end Dion was sitting on a large leather chair elevated by a two-foot-high platform with Jonathan DeVonta sitting next to him. A plume of smoke hung over his head. He raised a finger to his lips and shushed the crowd, his eyelids looked heavy. Everyone stopped yelling, only the sounds of a few straggling giggles were audible.

"I would like to hear the Nuber announce his presence with authority," Dion said.

The players leaned in watching Henry closely as he stood in silence. Then he spoke as if it were just him and me in the room.

"I am the Nuber."

The crowd erupted, the "Nuber" chant came back, and I wrapped an arm around Henry and reminded the guys not to touch him.

"Nuber, get your ass over here," Dion said as he told Pokey to get out of the chair next to him. "Now, for you, Wally, it's time we see you do your best Edward, the Nuber don't have to." Dion slurred his words. "Malibu, Simba, E-40 our boy, pronto."

Simba approached me with two oversized cans of beer, forty ounces each, fresh from Dion's fridge. Malibu staggered over with a roll of duct tape in his hands, Simba started to talk but let out a large belch, first.

"This here is a little game called 'Edward Forty Hands,' self-explanatory." At least that's what I thought he said as he swayed to keep balance.

Dion took a hit from a bong then looked at me as he motioned it towards Henry. I shook my head and mouthed the words "please no." Dion nodded, put the bong down and stood with a beer raised. "Here's to my boy who ran routes all summer, knows the playbook better than anybody, and takes care of our secret weapon that we going to use against them Tide motherfuckers. Wally, Wally, Wally!"

The rest of the crowd joined in until Pokey yelled, "No, goddammit, he's Edward you dumbasses."

After Simba placed one of the forty-ounce beers in my right palm, Malibu started wrapping duct tape until the beer and my hand were one. I was shocked by the sharp sting of cold in my right hand, but it was slightly mitigated by the pain in my left hand after the other beer was secured.

"Edward! Edward! Edward!"

Pokey was the mean one, he popped the tabs of the cans and looked down at me through bloodshot eyes. "Go, boy. We cut the tape when you finish."

It was fair and accurate to say that I was an inexperienced drinker, and this was mainly due to three factors: I grew up in the house of a minister who preached against the evils of alcohol, I directly witnessed the results of these evils as they ran roughshod over the Minister, and finally, with Henry to watch after, the opportunity rarely presented itself. But, like every other endeavor I came upon at Bastille, I threw my heart into it.

They chanted my new name as I chugged the beer in my right hand. Simba informed me of the need for weight and temperature balance in slurred words that had to be decoded and I switched to the left. The trifecta of the beer's carbonation, temperature, and alcohol made my eyes water, which the howling upperclassmen took as a sign of weakness. I told them they were tears of joy and they were all a bunch of pussies, which they loved.

I tried to settle into a bearable pace but after ten minutes I was sloshed and had trouble expressing myself. When Dion got Henry to repeat "I am the Nuber," I laughed so hard beer shot out of my nose, which to many was the highlight of the evening. After twenty minutes, my hands were numb and there was still more beer in the cans than I'd ever had in one sitting. Nearly forty minutes in, I finished them off and staggered in the middle of the room.

"He's going to blow!" someone said.

Jeremy took me by the arm and the back of my shirt and led me to an open window. When my stomach compressed against the windowsill, the beer I'd fought so hard to consume was ejected into the night air.

An hour later, I was nearly coherent and found myself talking to Dion.

"My first party at Bastille," I said.

"You never go out?" Dion said. I shook my head. "Me neither, I hardly leave campus anymore except for games and to see my guy."

"Your guy?" I said.

Dion held his hand up and rubbed his index finger and thumb together.

▼ ▼ ▼

Coach Dixon's whistle blew hard and quick, triggering additional pain. I lifted my hands from my knees and sprinted for the far goal line as sweat collected in my eyes. *Come in last,* I thought, *but not by much.*

"The first ten were to get all that alcohol out of your body," yelled Coach Dixon. "The next ten are to get you in shape for Alabama."

Every fiber in me was empty and sending panicked signals begging for relief. My squinting eyes, blurred by sweat that magnified the sun, kept focused on the hazy goal line far away as my mind desperately counted down the passing yards. Less than twelve hours before, my brain had reeled with the happy chaos of alcohol and the approval of Dion.

QBs, tight ends, and linebackers ran sprints together and if I beat anyone, Coach Dixon would be all over them. I was the

slowest of the group and thought I was the most hungover. Scott
Matthews and Jake Sanfilippo, our two starting middle linebackers, both seniors, were inseparable and did everything together;
they even vomited side by side after the fifth hundred-yard sprint.

"You two show up to my practice hungover and puking?"
Coach Dixon said. "And you come in last?"

They both glared at me as Scott wiped his mouth. I knew my
role. After the last sprint, half the team dropped to the ground
in moans.

After standing under a cool shower for twice the normal time
and getting lunch with Henry, I fell asleep on our couch. An hour
later I woke and the first thing I saw was the stack of textbooks on
the table. I rolled over; I couldn't do it. But I couldn't sleep, Henry
played the TV too loud.

"I'm going to Tony and Eddie's room, are you okay by yourself?" I said. Henry nodded without taking his eyes off the TV, but
I hesitated at the door, my view lingering until he turned to me,
then I knew it was okay to leave him.

When I walked in, Tony and Eddie were seated in front of their
TV, playing a combat video game I never understood. They were
perched on their chairs as their fingers constantly twitched the con-
trollers until one of them was eliminated and stomped away in
defeat. Then the cycle would start over with taunts and laughs,
their eyes never leaving the screen.

"What up, Wally. Where's Henry?" Tony said without looking
at me.

"Watching TV." I took a seat off to the side and noticed a silver
flask with the Tribe logo etched on the front. It was beautiful and
I picked it up. "Where did you get this?"

"He stole it," Eddie said. "Can you believe that? A rich, white
boy on a full ride stole it right out of the bookstore."

"I didn't steal it, you dreadlocked hipster wannabe. It was

damaged goods and I found it. I was doing them a favor. And I'm not rich."

"It was damaged because you knocked it on the floor. And your daddy played here, he got a Bastille education, and you're not rich?" Eddie looked to me. "You ever meet Mr. Gio?" I shook my head. "He's one hard motherfucker, let me tell you. That's why our boy here can run them crossing patterns."

"You going out tonight?" Tony said. "Almost had you. You're going down this time."

"You little Italian mafia boy, you ain't beat me in the last three games. I am the *truth*," Eddie said.

"Not after last night," I said. "I've got to study."

"You're the truth?" Tony said. "You study enough for the whole team, enjoy it while you can."

"It's not just my classes, Henry needs a ton of help," I said.

"Not only am I the truth, I am the *source* of all truth," Eddie said.

"Bullshit," Tony said. "There are only three sources of the truth: little kids, drunk people, and yoga pants. Use the tutors, Wally, that's what we got them for."

"I can't, if they work with Henry, they'll see how bad it is," I said.

"You said he was fine," Eddie said. "How much help does he need? How did he pass the SATs?"

"You don't want to know; I shouldn't talk about it."

"There, you're dead," Tony said. "Does Coach Oldham know?"

"Not even close, boy," Eddie said.

I covered my face with my hands. "Oh, God. I can't believe what I did."

"Hold up, pause it," Eddie said.

Tony made a grunting noise, then growled. "Too late, I win."

"Check it out, Tony," Eddie said. "Wally, what's up, man?"

I dropped my hands; both were staring at me. "I really screwed up. I did something bad." They waited for me to continue. "You can't say anything. I lied to Coach Oldham, right to his face. I told him Henry was doing fine in school."

"That ain't good," Tony said. "We ain't going to say a word, bro, but I thought you said he was doing the work on his own."

I shook my head. "I've done his work ever since we were in grade school, but it was easy, we always had the same classes."

"He can't do any of it?" Eddie said. "How does he pass his tests?"

"I do his homework and show him what to memorize. But we've only got one class together, it's like I'm taking eight classes."

"What about the tutors?" Tony said.

"You know how Oldham runs this place. They'd tell him in a minute and it would be over."

"What's he taking?" Eddie said. "I know he's got geometry, I'm taking that, too."

"We both have philosophy, so that's not too bad," I said. "The other two are astronomy and eastern religion."

"I can help him with that one, I'm taking it, too," Tony said. "My mom's a Buddhist."

"Get the fuck out," Eddie said. "They got Buddhists in Tennessee?"

"Mid-life crisis," Tony said. "Anyway, let's do this: I'll work with him on eastern religion, Eddie will help with the math class, you're already doing philosophy with him, so the only extra class is astronomy."

"I can't ask you guys to do that."

"Bullshit, we're here to get educated," Eddie said. "We ain't going to let you down. Besides, the Tribe can't lose the Nuber."

"What if Coach Oldham finds out?"

"Come on, seriously?" Tony said. "He'd be proud we're all

helping each other out." Tony turned back to the TV. "Next game, boy, you're going down."

▼ ▼ ▼

I squatted down and placed my hand on the grass of Bryant-Denny Stadium as the Alabama faithful sang their song, I didn't think I'd ever get *Rammer Jammer Yellowhammer* out of my head. The place was almost as hallowed as Bastille Stadium, but instead of the arrow, there were a lot of scripted As on crimson shirts accompanied with houndstooth accents. Alabama was ranked number one in the country and we were tenth, a big enough matchup of marquee programs with star players that the network hosted their famous morning long pre-game show on the Alabama campus. We were lined up to receive the 5:30 kickoff and Dion was working our sideline like we were already down by twenty.

"This one is for JD, we ain't going to let him down today."

Our guys responded in kind, doing their best to keep focused as the crowd noise grew. Marcus James received the kick two yards deep into the end zone, broke two tackles before he got to the twenty, and headed for an alley near our sideline. Their kicker forced him out at the forty-five.

It was running back by committee and Dion handed off to Julius, a sophomore, but when he turned the far corner he was blown up. Their linebacker shed a glancing block and met him at the line, I saw the bottom of Julius's cleats as he was upended. It was a highlight-reel hit and the Alabama linebacker stood over Julius, triggering the ref to throw a flag for taunting. The linebacker hung his head as he trotted off the field into the waiting glare of Alabama's famous coach. The penalty put us at their twenty-eight-yard line and our guys gained confidence in inverse proportion to the ebbing crowd noise. Dion audibled out of a trap play and threw a strike to Tarik on a post, but one of their safeties tipped it and the ball bounced off the crossbar. On second down we ran a toss sweep to Marlon, our third string running back, but our fullback missed his block, a loss of two. They blitzed on third down and Dion threw it away. Then Coach Oldham signaled for Evan to kick a forty-seven-yarder.

As soon as the ball cleared the line, I could tell he missed it. The ball's spin was off axis and curved to the left like a hooked golf shot. Dion clapped his hands to keep the bench alive. "That's all right, we going to run up and down this field all night, baby." He'd been clapping that way since the previous Sunday's practice.

That practice seemed longer than six days ago. When I woke up that morning, my head was pounding; I ended up going out with Tony and Eddie. Henry was standing in the doorway of my room ready to go to practice, his silent impatience always caused a crisis the few times it had happened. I threw on some clothes, found a snack bar, and headed for the Performance Center without going to the dining hall.

We weren't late, it was quarter to ten when Henry and I took our seats in the back of the auditorium, only a few guys were there. I closed my eyes, settled into the deep chair, and tried to sleep a few more minutes before the meeting. Clusters of guys came in, I opened my eyes, took a look, and then tried to doze off. The next time I opened them it was ten fifteen and the room was only half full. Through blurry eyes, I began to take notice.

Instead of sitting in their usual seats, talking and horsing around while we waited, guys were talking quietly in small huddled groups.

"Henry, what's going on?" I said.

"Coach Oldham is late."

I got up and wandered to the back by the doors.

"They ain't got no motive yet, don't know." It was Melvin Richardson, he noticed me listening and I asked him what was going on. "You ain't heard? JD's mom and older sister, man. They got murdered last night up in Atlanta."

Jonathan DeVonta, our starting running back, the guy that got teased for being a mama's boy. The year before, on the eve of the Georgia Tech game, his mom and her friends brought a spread of Jonathan's favorite food to the hotel, enough to feed the team. I heard about it during camp when Pokey and Simba complained about our dining hall food and wanted to know when JD's mama was going to come down to feed us. Then they argued who she liked more.

The rest of the team was in the hallway, and they began to make their way in when Coach Dixon arrived. He stepped up to the podium and waited for us to get seated amid an uncomfortable silence.

"For those of you that haven't heard, there was a horrible tragedy last night." Coach Dixon didn't choke up, but he took his time. "JD's mom and sister lost their lives last night to senseless violence." With his hands on the podium Coach Dixon lowered his head and the room was silent for a long moment.

"We all love JD and now is the time to show that love. On the field, he's one of the greatest players in the country but that's not why we love him. Off the field he's one of our pillars, he's the kind of young man you build teams and communities with. Now, he's going to need our community. Coach Oldham went to see him this morning and found out he was on his way to the bus station to head back to Atlanta. Coach called me and said he's driving JD himself and we should go about our business. He'll let us know when we can reach out to him."

Coach Dixon looked down and let the silence of grief fill the room. Henry was staring straight ahead, and I wondered what he felt. When I looked up, Coach Dixon wiped tears from his eyes. "I don't know how I can ask you, at this moment, to focus on football.

One of our brothers is in agony right now." He wiped his eyes again and opened the manila folder to review the practice schedule.

Dion, sitting with his head down in the front center seat, raised his hand until Coach Dixon acknowledged him. Dion stood and turned to all of us, his face in anguish, tears rolling freely down his face. For the first time to me, he looked like just a nineteen-year-old kid.

It seemed he didn't know what to say, at first. Then he spoke. "Y'all stand up, everybody, join hands." Everyone in the front row followed Dion's lead and faced the rest of us as we stood and joined hands. "Raise them up." We did as told, and Dion led us in prayer, our hands encumbered and unable to stop the falling tears.

On Sunday night, Coach Oldham returned, and we met again.

"I know some of you are particularly close to Jonathan, and your texts and phone calls have given him strength in his time of need," Coach Oldham said. "Services are this Tuesday, if you'd like to attend, we will look into travel arrangements."

Dion stood and raised his hand and Coach Oldham offered him the floor. Dion turned around and looked at us. "Every motherfucker in this room is going." He looked back to Coach Oldham. "Sorry about the cuss word."

Coach Oldham, a man who never swore, shrugged his shoulders. "Fuck it," he said.

We all laughed; it was the first time anyone had since we'd heard the news.

"All right, boys," Dion said. "We got Alabama this week, let's get to work."

We were like machines in practice on Monday, running and hitting with precision but without intensity. After practice Coach Oldham mentioned it.

"That's a throw away practice. If you want to win this game, come to practice on Wednesday ready to go."

By my estimation, we spent ten hours travelling by bus on Tuesday. We all wore our Tribe blazers and ties and most of us stood outside the small white clapboard church during the ceremony. At the end we walked up the aisle single file, made the sign of the cross, and respectfully walked out. Jonathan's three younger brothers and younger sister sat at his side. As we passed by, some nodded, some touched his shoulder, and others hugged him. Dion had been first, and Jonathan wouldn't let him go, so he stayed by his side. The mourner's stared at us as we passed, I could see their gratitude for the respect and support we offered Jonathan.

On Wednesday, Coach Oldham gave special attention to our second- and third-string running backs. "Julius, Marlon, this is your chance, we need you. Defense, let them know you're there." The practice was vicious, Thursday's was fast, on Friday we flew out in the morning for Tuscaloosa.

After Evan's missed kick, Alabama took over at their own thirty and the first thing I noticed was their movement off the line and their lack of mistakes. In previous games when momentum was against us, our guys dug a little deeper until we were in control again. But against Alabama with their crowd howling nonstop, we felt overmatched.

"Make a play, somebody's got to make a play," someone said.

They drove down to our ten and on third and eight they missed on a corner route and settled for a field goal.

During the ensuing kick-off I stood next to Dion. "Their Willie linebacker, number 33, let me know if he's bailing," he said to me.

It was clear that Alabama wasn't going to let Dion beat him with his arm. They subbed in an extra defensive back on first down and then another on second and third—it was like the field was littered with defensive backs in red. JD would've made a difference; it was rare when one defender could bring him down, the same wasn't true for Julius and Marlon. We chipped away with two- and three-yard runs and an underneath pass and got a first down. Dion threw a long pass to Tarik but there were two Alabama defenders fighting him for the ball and it fell incomplete. I kept my eye on their Willie linebacker and, sure enough, at the first sign of movement away he scraped the line and shot through play side gaps or pursued underneath. On a run to our left, one of their defensive backs got his bell rung and there was an injury time-out. Third and eight.

Dion came over to the sideline to talk with Coach Oldham and when he was about to turn and jog back out onto the field, he glanced at me. With my hands close to my chest, I flashed three fingers with each hand and then raised my thumb to signal 33 was bailing.

We had three-man route called but Dion audibled back to the same exact play we'd just run, an off-tackle to the left, and I felt like I was the only one in the stadium who knew what he was going to do. Andre snapped the ball, Dion went to handoff, then he pulled the ball and sprinted to the right, into the area where 33 was supposed to have backside contain. He ran for twenty-three yards, by far his longest run of the season. As I hustled down the sideline behind the team, I heard Pokey yelling at his defensive teammates.

"You see that? Our boy can make plays, you see that? Next possession, a turnover or three and out."

Dion drove us down to their fifteen and on fourth and three Evan went back onto the field. He had to make it; I didn't know how I'd react in a live game. Evan made the thirty-two-yarder but if it was two yards longer it would've been wide right, two words I hate to hear.

The rest of the half was brutal, I'd never seen such intense hitting in my life as Alabama rotated in wave after wave of fresh defensive linemen. Except for Andre Decker, our offensive linemen weren't getting any movement on runs, and on passes they looked like they got a group rate on roller skates. Dion took a beating, and we were down 17–3 at the half.

"Just a little time, that's all I need," Dion said in the locker room during halftime as he slapped the linemen's shoulder pads. Instead of sweat and red faces on the linemen like in the first five games, they had the look of a group trying to hold on.

"Max protect," Coach Oldham said to the offense. "Julius and Marlon, sell out, we've got to keep Dion upright."

Right before we kicked off for the second half, I put the headphones on and heard the new plan.

"You're sure about this," said Coach Dixon.

"Absolutely," Coach Oldham said. "First rule in the book, put the ball into the hands of your best player."

This was going to be Dion's game, and his play was beyond anything I'd ever seen. With failing protection, he'd keep his eyes upfield and deliver a pass as waves of crimson battered him. On a roll out with two defenders in front and one chasing, he pump faked, dodged, and turned a six-yard loss into a seven-yard gain and a first down. When he came off the field after throwing a TD, he bypassed congratulations and went to the bench where the trainers examined his ribs. With an oxygen mask on, he'd fist bump players that approached and after Pokey nailed their running back and caused a fumble that Simba recovered, he popped the mask off, checked with Coach Oldham, then trotted onto the field.

A toss sweep left towards our sideline, Marlon carrying the ball. He tried to cut up field but was tripped and a Pokey-sized defensive tackle speared him in the ribs. Our guys screamed for a penalty and got it, but it wasn't much consolation. I'll never forget the sound of his shallow, gasping breaths as he held his ribs while he was gently guided to the bench. Our head trainer did a quick examination, then looked at our running back coach and shock his head, then called for the cart to take him to the locker room.

They scored on the next series to make it 24–10, then Coach Griffin came over to me.

"For the rest of the game, next time we cross the fifty, warm up Henry," he said. Waves of anxiety shot through me; I took deep breaths to keep it at bay.

Then I looked to see where the ball was and that's when I saw it, something I'll never forget. A defensive lineman stunted, our left guard made the switch and drove through him, then they fell on the knee of one of our guys that was in a vulnerable position. The pop was barely audible through the crowd noise, but still grotesque. After the pass fell incomplete, Dion immediately waved in panic to our bench.

The trainers ran out as Dion and a few others knelt beside our injured player, his hands desperately clutching grass. Minutes passed as they examined him then I heard a coach over the headset.

"Fuck, it's Andre. We've got to get Dion to take a couple of snaps from Jeremy."

More time passed and everyone on the field had taken a knee. Coach Oldham jogged out and knelt beside Andre while the trainers urgently cut the pants leg of the damaged knee. The medical cart was driven onto the field, and after more time they stabilized his leg and lifted him onto the cart. When they drove him away, Dion came to our sideline and took a few snaps from Jeremy.

Our guys didn't have it. Dion was sacked twice in a row, and we punted as the third quarter ended. When they got the ball, Coach Dixon dialed up the blitzes. On a roll out to their sideline we chased their QB and well after he threw it out of bounds Pokey nailed him with a vicious late hit. After the penalty, Coach Oldham took Pokey out of the game and he took a seat on the bench right next to me. I didn't want to get up and walk away, like I was avoiding him, but I didn't dare say anything. He sat next to me, breathing hard, as Coach Oldham tried to calm him down.

"Not now, not ever, Pokey. I understand your frustration, but that's not the Bastille way."

Pokey nodded his head.

"I can't put you back out there until you've got it together," Coach Oldham said and waited a beat. "Okay, let me know." Coach Oldham started to walk away.

"I'm good," Pokey said. Coach Oldham turned back. "Tribe Forever," Pokey said as he stood and put his helmet on.

"Good, next series you're back in," Coach Oldham said.

On offense, all our timing and choreography fell apart. On pass plays, Dion dodged defenders like he was in the middle of a freeway then he'd run or launch a deep pass or run the line of scrimmage trying to find an open receiver. When we crossed the fifty, I warmed up Henry as my hands shook. I couldn't see the action on the field, and I was looking to see the down and distance when Dion landed out of bounds up field with two Tide players on top of him. He took a moment to get up before heading back to the field. Our backup QB was pulling for him to stay in the game more than anyone.

Then we scored on a fade to Tarik in the corner to make it 24–17.

The Alabama fans howled in disgust. In a lull I heard one yell, "What do we have to do to stop this guy?"

Carter Schultz picked off a pass at midfield and I buckled up my helmet.

"Henry, do you need to warm up?" I said.

He shook his head. After two no-huddle plays Coach Griffin snapped at us to get to the sideline.

"Come on, Wally, pay attention. You and Henry need to be next to me on every third down in their territory."

As I was nodding to him Coach Oldham called my name. "Go." It was already fourth down from their forty-two-yard line. A fifty-nine-yarder.

My head was foggy as I ran onto the field, just like against Oklahoma. As I passed by Dion, he held a hand out in encouragement and I responded. I could see the pain in his face, and it burnt something into me, clearing the fog. When I got to the huddle, I counted out nine players, I made ten and Henry was eleven.

"Field goal on first sound."

I found my blade of grass and gave Henry another second. I looked to him and he nodded. I looked to the ball in Jeremy's hands. *Do this goddammit*, I told myself.

"Set."

The ball flew towards me and I didn't think, all those reps took over. I was an expert in my narrow field: My hands caught the ball like it was receiving a passed note, I placed it on my blade of grass and turned the laces towards the goal. Henry's foot, unseen to me, only heard, passed through and sent the ball on its flight. As it passed over the line, I took note of the linemen in their collective battle, like a ten-foot wave about to crash down on us. But instead of water that would wash through, they fell onto each other as some turned to watch the ball. After it went through, one of their edge rushers spoke to Henry out of earshot of the ref.

"You got lucky, bitch."

I collected Henry and reminded the guys to not congratulate him with head slaps. As we approached the sideline, I fought the urge to scream in joy. Coach Oldham was talking over the headset in preparation for their next possession when he cast a glance towards me with a quick head nod. I felt divine relief. If I could've, I would've dropped to my knees to thank the Tribe and all Her wonders.

Dion approached us on the bench and slapped my helmet. "Feels good, don't it? That kick's going to be the difference."

Our defense held and when Dion took the field, I heard the lamentations of the Alabama faithful behind me. This was Dion's game, the only reason we had a shot to win it.

A minute thirty left. Two passes over the middle for first downs and then he ran it for fourteen out of bounds. Forty seconds left. A roll out to the right, no one open, he threw it out of bounds. Thirty-two seconds left. Second and ten, Dion rolled to the left, holding the ball as defenders closed in, all our receivers rolled with him into a crowd down the sideline. Except for Julius. He was alone in the middle of the field at the line of scrimmage waving his arms. It was Dion's target all along. He spun backwards, planted his foot and threw a strike to Julius with only one defender near him. The ball landed in Julius's hands, but he'd turned his head to see where the defender was, and it popped into the air. Julius reached back to secure it, but it was gone. The Alabama dimeback picked it clean and was in a full sprint towards our end zone before any of us reacted.

▼ ▼ ▼

The professor's wood door had a large opaque glass pane, I couldn't tell who he was meeting with. It was the first time I had to wait. I looked at my phone, it was 2:05, I would probably only get a few minutes with him before I had to collect Henry and get to practice. I sat back down to finish the text I was sending.

> *Thanks Aunt Janie for watching, pretty scary going out there but Henry made the kick. Thanks again for the spending money and everything else you've done for us.*

I opened the Sports Inc. app on my phone and tapped the Bastille icon, but it was Tuesday, the cycle had moved on and there was nothing new about the Alabama game, just analysis about the upcoming Louisville game. "Can Bastille Reset, Or Was It a Mirage?" The story was written by Samantha Yardley, and if I could've deleted the article, and everything else she'd ever written,

I would have. Then, my mind drifted back to the Alabama game and the practices leading up to it.

"You don't have much time, but you've got more time than you think," Coach Oldham said during practice the week before. The same thing that had happened in the Alabama game had happened during practice a few days before: A receiver in the moment of locking the ball into his hands thought he had it and turned to locate the defenders. But he turned away too soon, and the ball bounced off his hands. "Your hands don't catch the ball, your eyes do," Coach said. And just like the play in practice, Julius, in high-pitched intensity that few will ever know, committed a sin in a fraction of a second, a sin with a small time frame that was long enough to allow a spotlight of shame to shine on him that would endure until he redeemed himself in the eyes of the larger Tribe.

But not the Tribe in the locker room after the game. Dion's locker was next to mine, I had to move my stool over to give him and the ice bags attached to his knees, ribs, and throwing shoulder room. As soon as he sat down, he saw Julius across the room with his back to us, clutching his hanging head. I couldn't help trying to hear if he was crying. Dion stood up through pain and hobbled over to him as we all watched. He took a knee and spoke into Julius's ear then put his arm around him with their heads touching. Other guys approached Julius and offered quiet words or a pat on the shoulder. Coach Dixon went over to Julius and knelt on the other side of him.

I didn't see Coach Oldham enter the room, I only noticed when the sounds of shedding equipment and quiet conversation stopped. He looked over the room for a long moment, then made his way into the center, offering private words to some of the players as he passed. He had a peaceful look on his face.

"Kareem, I'd say that was a pretty fair team we just played," he said.

"That's right, Coach."

Coach Oldham took his time, congratulating players for key plays. "We lost to a fine Alabama team in their place. Our season's not over; if we win our division, there's a very good chance we'll meet them in the conference championship. In the meantime, I would like to address one individual, Julius."

We all waited, then Dion told Julius to stand.

"You will not let an unlucky bounce define you. You and Marlon played a great game on limited practice, filling in for Jonathan is not an easy thing. Even then, we ran for over a hundred yards against the toughest defense in the country. I will defend your play, your work ethic, and the young man you are in front of the college football world. Is that clear?"

Julius nodded as Coach Dixon patted his shoulder.

"We've got Louisville next week, put some time into your studies and be ready for practice Monday. I'm going to talk to the press and then check on Andre and Marlon."

He spent a few more minutes addressing individual players and, like children, they waited for their dose of approval. Part of me wanted the same treatment, but I knew my place.

Coach Oldham had performed the same in press conferences for decades, handing out praise to the team as a whole, attaching player names to big plays. He never called out the refs—*They're human, too*—he never blamed bad luck or the weather—*The other team has the same challenges*—and, Jeremy's favorite, he never blamed a loss on execution.

"Watch," Jeremy said. "When a coach blames it on execution, it's their way of saying his plan was perfect but the players screwed it up and it's not his fault."

I watched the press conference online the next day after I heard about the scandal. It was boring until an unheard question provoked something in Coach Oldham. He turned his head, focused on the reporter, and in an aggressive manner, asked the question to be repeated. The camera turned to the reporter, and I recognized her immediately, it was the reporter who was nosing around our bench during the Oklahoma game. I turned up the volume.

"Coach Oldham, do you think the reason you lost the game is because you had the team skip practice on Tuesday?" Her name was Samantha Yardley.

Coach Oldham looked flustered and angry. "First of all, the reason we lost isn't due to one missed practice."

"If one practice isn't going to make a difference then why not do it every week? Why have so many pre-season practices? Why not let the players have more time to study or get a job?"

"Your question is out of line." His anger was building.

"I don't think it is. Last week you said the Alabama game was the biggest game for the program in years and everything possible was being done in preparation. Yet, twenty percent of your practice time was lost, and you never addressed it with the media? Can you tell us why?"

Coach Oldham stared at her as a PR staffer tried to whisper something in his ear.

"You know exactly why we didn't practice on Tuesday and it's disgusting you're making an issue of it now. One of our players tragically lost family members last week and I decided to take the team to the funeral services in support of him. When young men come to Bastille, I tell their parents how difficult it is to play a sport, attend school, and begin life on their own. I also tell them that their sons will be part of a group that will support them academically, collegially, and emotionally. If that support means putting a football game at risk, then that's what I'm going to do. Imagine being the player that suffered such a horrible loss, and now he's hearing, through your harmful words, that he's the reason we lost a football game because we chose to provide emotional support."

"The school offers a lot of support to players; did you think it was necessary to put the game at risk? There are a lot of people that depend on the success of the program, do you think it's appropriate to sacrifice their needs?"

"Who are you talking about? Whose life or livelihood depends on us beating the number one team in the nation?" Coach Oldham waited for her to answer. "We're done here."

The press conference became its own story for a day, but it lived on in social media and internet forums. "He's there to win, not to coddle a bunch of entitled jocks!" "This is why Coach O is loved by everybody." "If this is the reason we don't make the playoffs, he has to go. He's wasting Dion's talent!"

As I waited for the Professor, I skimmed through her work, looking for other controversial articles. The professor's door opened, and a young professor looked at me as he walked out. He scoffed in disregard when he saw my backpack.

"Congratulations, young man," Professor Bertrand said. "I saw your big play; my wife and I never cheered that loud for a field goal before. How did it feel?"

"Is there something wrong with that guy that was just here? He gave me a dirty look when he saw my backpack," I said.

The professor's mood changed. "Don't worry, it's a sad story. He's having trouble getting traction here." He looked away and I could see concern on his face.

"It happened so fast I can barely remember it," I said.

"Oh, yes, the kick. Sorry about the loss, but you guys are still—"

"We're five and one, we can still make the playoffs. Did you hear about the press conference? I mean that reporter, why would someone do that?"

The professor sat, he seemed distant as I pulled up a chair.

"Sometimes I feel like it's just a game and everything is fine," he said. "Other times it seems—" His voice trailed off but I waited. "It's too destructive."

I sat in silence for a moment. "You mean like Andre and Marlon getting hurt?"

"Oh, my. Yes, that, too." He shook his head and was quiet for a moment. "After the game, my wife and I were having a glass of wine, and as we sat there, we had this sense of melancholy, something that's rare for us. I don't think it was about losing the game, I mean, we want you guys to win but it's not life or death for us. I remember sitting there as this one play ran over and over again in my head like I was watching the replay, probably because they ran the replay a dozen times." He looked up at me. "It was the play where your lineman had his knee broken in two. I can't imagine the amount of force needed to cause such harm to an athlete that big. Anyway, while I'm staring off into space, my wife gets my attention and asks me the strangest question. She said 'Tell me what I'm describing: Physical specimens are selected from the masses, they're housed, fed, and trained physically and mentally. They then perform with the risk of great physical harm all for entertainment and gambling.' I looked at her like it was a dumb question."

"What did you say?"

"I said she was cynically describing college football. Then she shook her head and said 'No, I just described dogfighting.'"

I didn't respond at first. "Do you think that, too?"

The Professor exhaled as his eyes drifted away. "It's hard to argue, but my thoughts run a little deeper. I don't know if you'd agree or take offense. Either way, I'm troubled by the pressure John is under, that question in the press conference was deplorable, that's the part that bothers me. Pressures like that, if unchecked, can be corrosive."

"What do you think about football?" I said. "You don't like it, do you?"

The Professor smiled. "I actually think there's a very strong need for it, I just don't think the higher education system is where it should take place, although it's the most obvious. I don't know how John handles it."

"I thought everyone loved him?"

The Professor shook his head and let out a sardonic chuckle.

"Let's see, where do I start? He's won all these national championships, he's been a paragon of virtue in a field that's susceptible to unsavory characters, his players graduate, some go on to the NFL, and all of them revere him."

"So, what's the issue?"

The Professor took his time. "Remember the non-academic education I mentioned to you? The colliding currents of life? This is a prime example. They—Bastille, the students, the fan base, the alumni, the administration—they want more."

"How can they?" I said. "He's done everything, he's why Bastille is special."

"A few years ago, when the team only won five games there were calls for him to retire. Did you know he only makes about $500,000 a year? Most people would kill for that money but there are coaches in the country who make more than ten times that. Even schools that couldn't come close to Bastille pay their coaches more."

"What's wrong with that?"

"His assistant coaches leave all the time, he can't keep them here when they're offered more money for the same jobs. Yet, Bastille is the place where young coaches come to get groomed by John. The fans scream about this, but he thinks he's overpaid to start with, he doesn't think coaching a recreational game warrants a king's ransom. Next, the boosters want access to him, and the school brass wants to use him as a fundraising tool. Golf tournaments, banquets, appearances—he doesn't do any of it and the big money people, both inside the school and out, feel like he's not fulfilling an important part of his job. I even heard the invisible boosters, the kind that don't write the big checks, resent him even more. A friend of mine outside of the school shared with me something I couldn't believe. He said each big-time football school has hundreds of boosters that are fed with names of recruits and their job is to *welcome* the potential player with cash and favors of all sorts in a way that can't be traced to the school. And John refuses to let that happen."

"Garr Johnstone," I said.

"Who?"

"There's a guy at Arkansas A&M who grew up with Dion and he wanted to come here but the word is that A&M gave him all kinds of money. The guy's unbelievable, he's leading the nation in sacks as a true freshman."

"See what I mean? John doesn't have a TV show, he lives in a modest house, and he doesn't sacrifice the academic mission of the school by recruiting players who can't make it academically. Talk about the integrity of the school, don't even mention the Sky Bowl to him."

"What's wrong with the Sky Bowl? It's only been around two years," I said.

"It rubs him the wrong way. Apparently, it's for the top teams that don't make the playoffs and a Las Vegas boondoggle for team fans on New Year's Day. I heard they pay the schools so much money and hype it and over produce it that it's more of a money-grab spectacle than a football game. And Bastille, with its national following, is a natural. Did you know that alumni donations skyrocket when the football team wins and plays in a major bowl? John's old-school; he once told me that, in retrospect, he would've been happier as a high school coach."

"I don't understand," I said. "Coach Oldham is the greatest, why can't they appreciate him?"

The Professor stared at me, his eyes almost squinting like I'd missed an important question on one of his exams. "Because it's not about John. It's not about you or your brother or your famous quarterback, Dion, or anyone else on the team."

"Then what's it about?" I said.

"It's about the irresistible and undeniable urge for tribal domination." The Professor paused a moment knowing I'd need time to absorb his words. "And I don't mean the Bastille University Tribe. Everything is tribal, Wally, tribalism is the strongest dynamic in humanity; stronger than morality, kindness, rationality, even sovereign constitutions—unless of course a nation defines its tribe by that constitution."

"I'm not sure I follow," I said.

"That's okay. Let's go a little further. But first, do you know what my topic of professorship is?"

"No, I'm not sure," I said.

"It's a combination of philosophy and anthropology, it's a new area I'm researching called Evolutionary Philosophy. Do you really want to hear more about this?"

"Yes," I said as I stowed my backpack beneath my chair.

"Okay, here goes. The human species, really all organic species, has one overriding drive. What do you think that is?"

"I don't know, happiness, love?"

The Professor politely shook his head. "No, survival. The survival instinct is the most powerful thing in any of us, in fact, in all biological organisms, and it's been groomed over millions of years by evolution through an uncountable number of generations trying to survive through brutal conditions. Funny thing about people: Most believe in evolution but they don't believe it's still going on—a strange conceit, don't you think? Or worse, they would deny that the factors that provided their existence are not only still deep within them, they'd never believe these factors are the primary cause behind every decision they make. We all think we're self-aware, self-driven by our objective intellect, but we're not. We're closer to being robots driven by our evolutionary roots with just a sprinkling of free will and intellect. It's a self-reinforcing dynamic; those that didn't have a strong survival instinct perished, as did their bloodline. You and I are only here because thousands of generations have weeded out all those except for the ones that somehow figured out how to survive long enough to reproduce."

"We don't control ourselves? I'm not sure I can get my head around that," I said.

"Understandable, but here's an example: Obesity is a plague upon the modern world, and I'm pretty sure the afflicted have not willingly chosen to become that way. Do you know why it happens? Because in the modern world, food is cheap and plentiful, and the majority can't help themselves. Turning down food requires one to defy not only hunger in the moment but also the screaming orders of your cumulative ancestors, ancestors who lived on the edge of starvation and whose urges are built into every cell of your being. It's remarkable the situation isn't worse.

"Another example: Sex, the obvious purpose of which is to reproduce. If sex was boring or painful, the species would've died off long ago and maybe some branches of the species did. But for us, the homo sapiens, it's a really big deal, and without it we'd never be here. It's no wonder sex is one of the leading topics of art and commercial exploitation, and the cause of so much misery. Infidelity, sex trafficking, sexual assault—all horrible events caused by the deep-seated urges built into our DNA that some can't or refuse to control.

"But here's the problem with survival: Across the vast majority of human history, acquiring resources like food was hard and dangerous, and once acquired those resources were even harder to protect. To make it worse, throughout antiquity, families themselves were made even more vulnerable by the reproductive cycle and for all of this there was only one solution. So, how did our

forebears survive? Through the protection of tribes. Are you following me so far?"

"Yeah, I guess. But I don't see how it relates to college football,
though," I said.

The Professor smiled. "We'll get to that. Now it's not lost on me
that my academic pursuits take place at an institution the very nick-
name of which is the Tribe. The point is that tribes are critical to
survival; in fact, survival is only accessible through tribes. However,
simply being tribal isn't good enough. The survival of the tribe itself
is paramount; if a tribe perishes, so do its members. Have you ever
heard of the Indus Valley Civilization or the Mycenaeans?"

"No."

"Exactly. They were destroyed by war and famine. Therefore,
right or wrong, moral or immoral, rule number one is the tribe
must survive, and the only way to survive is to dominate. Look
around, tribes are everywhere, the wealthy join country clubs, the
working class join unions. Poor urban kids join gangs and rich
suburban kids join frats and sororities. Of course, the most prominent tribes of our day are defined by religion and ethnicity and
it's tearing our national civility apart. Think of an inner-city child
born into horrible conditions. For him, a street gang may be the
only path to survival, at least in the moment.

"It used to be straightforward, you were born into a tribe and
that was that. You'd work at the direction of your father or the
tribal elder and it was all you ever knew. Then, the world indus-
trialized, and over time, mental power became more important
than manual labor. However, this caused a problem: Your local
tribe isn't capable of providing high-level education. Therefore, we
needed a new solution, and someone came up with the bright idea
to create an academy to train all the young minds, young minds
at the age of impression, the age when affiliations and connections
are hardwired into their brains, when they're looking to become
part of something larger than themselves—universities."

"I've never thought of it this way. So, universities are tribes, too?"

"Yes, universities are tribes and keep one thing in mind: Universities have the same hunger for survival as the lowliest bacteria. So, what do they do to survive, to keep enrollment up? They build four-year summer camps with de facto professional football teams and amenities to die for, and by the way let's not allow that academic training to get in the way. When the football team wins, applications and alumni donations skyrocket, because everyone, without knowing why, is driven by these deep urges to be part of the dominant tribe. That means the pressure on John Oldham to win would drive any other coach to do so at any cost and the powers that be here at Bastille can't understand why he won't. John will be fine, he's got too long of a history here; it's the university I'm worried about."

▼ ▼ ▼

Dion took a seven-step drop and threw deep to Tarik. We watched as the ball ascended above the enclosed walls of the practice field, it seemed small against the backdrop of blue sky, then it gracefully fell into Tarik's hands far down the field. Someone tapped my shoulder.

"They want you."

I looked over to the defense's field and immediately knew why. Trainers were huddled around a player and a bullhorn called out my name as Coach Dixon directed the defense and the offensive scout team to the other end of their field. The scout team QB must've been injured. My nerves lit up almost like the first time Henry and I ran onto the field against Oklahoma. As much as I was listed as a QB, I only threw during drills; to be the scout team QB would be a badge of honor. I pulled my helmet on and began running over. Someone gave me a yellow pinny to wear and after I put it on, Mac, the grad assistant, pulled me into the huddle.

"FSU runs shotgun, you take the snap and if it's a handoff or pass you run the play. If it's a designed run, Eddie takes it."

The FSU QB was a dual-threat player; their offense was designed around his runs as much as his throws and to prep our starting defense an extra QB was used. I would catch the snap with Eddie standing beside me with a ball already in his hands, and the QB not running the play immediately knelt down, then got out of the way.

"Eddie, this is you," Mac said as he held the play diagram up for the scout team offense. "Hestia, call the snap."

"On one, on one." I was glad I didn't have to run the first play. After I caught the snap, I knelt, then backed out of the way as Eddie ran to the right and was violently swallowed up by the first team defense. After Pokey got off him at the bottom of the pile, I saw Eddie with one eye looking out of the earhole of his helmet.

Coach Mac held the next play up, a fly pattern to the left receiver. Eddie and I stood side-by-side as I called out the signals. The ball flew into my hands on a wobble and when I looked up, I saw nothing but the green jerseys of the defense collapsing the pocket. I went to throw then clutched it, stepped up, and tried to release but Simba's raised arm blocked mine in mid-throw. The ball fell to the ground about tens yards away.

"Jesus Christ, Hestia, get the goddamn ball off," yelled one of the coaches. "Simba, we're running out of freaking quarterbacks, don't hit him."

"Just release it," said Mac. "We just want to give the defense something to react to. Can you throw an out?"

I nodded and said yes while trying to hold my composure. But Mac was wrong. Unless you were an immediate star like Dion or Melvin Richardson everybody did time on the scout team and just giving the defense something to react to would ensure you never left it.

When you make a play on the scout team you don't celebrate. The best you can hope for is a fellow scout teamer's quiet recognition or a defensive coach taking notice when he watched the practice film that night and mentioned it to your position coach. Ascending from the scout team to special teams or the twos was earned from grinding away at practice against the starters.

Can I throw an out? "Absolutely," I said. After throwing in drills and working out with a program designed to improve arm strength my passing skills had improved. But throwing a five yard out to a small window near the sideline called for the ball to travel nearly thirty yards.

I called the signals, caught the snap, and glanced to my left as the grunts and sound of contact approached. Then I turned my body to the right, set my feet in the direction of the receiver, and let it loose. I'd never thrown a pass like that in my life, it sailed with purpose and minimal arc, and was in the air before Tony made his cut. He had a fraction of a second to locate the ball then he snatched it with his hands and turned up field. Our starting cornerback committed when he saw the ball in flight and went for the interception, but he was too late. Tony ran for another fifteen yards before Melvin pushed him out of bounds.

Coach Dixon wasn't pleased, he yelled his displeasure to the cornerback. "You're in man-to-man coverage with no help, don't you gamble with my defense."

Mac gave my helmet a light slap. "Nice pill."

When Tony got back to the huddle he nodded with a subtle grin.

"Next play, Tony, you're the Z—motion left, zone run right," Mac said.

From then on, I was the scout team QB. Instead of being an appendage to Henry's talent, I had my own place, and when I looked over to Henry, he was staring at me. I held his look for a moment as his eyes filled me with quiet pride.

▼ ▼ ▼

"Here it is," Tony said as he tossed the five-page essay on my desk.

"I can't believe you're doing this; you and Eddie are saving us."

Tony chuckled. "Funny thing is, Henry's going to get a better grade than me. Let's go, just one beer."

A moment before I had wanted to sleep. But now, with Henry asleep and my mind too tired for more philosophy, I found the energy to explore. I wanted to be asked who I was. *You're the backup holder?* I wasn't embarrassed, but I felt exposed the few times I was asked. *I'm the scout team QB.* I'd say it with a degree of resignation, but it marked territory for me. I checked on Henry and debated whether I should leave him, then he turned over in his sleep like it was his way of approving.

Tony and Eddie led me to the strip and we walked among the Thursday night crowd, passing by worn down retailers that served the university population. Vic's Pizza and Gail's Coffee, the major burger chains, a few tiny sit-down restaurants and dive bars. A tattered awning, a lamp post with fliers for live bands, black water puddled in small crevices by a street drain, a light stanchion intact, its twin on the other side of an entrance with broken glass. We waited in line at the Parthenon, one of the hotspots, until Marcus James slapped me on the shoulder.

"Come on, boy, you making us look bad," he said.

We followed him to the front of the line and, with a few quick words, entered into a scene of sensory overload and deprivation. I could feel the thumping music in my chest and had to lean close to Tony's ear to speak. The bar had two tiers, the upper level with a railing encircling the space, allowing revelers to look down on the dance floor. At first, all I could see in the darkness were glow sticks wrapped around necks and arms, heads thumping on the dance floor, their rhythm matched by the upper-level partiers, half watching and half dancing. Girls in tiny denim shorts, their rear ends hanging out the bottom, their G-strings showing on top. Bros, dudes, preppies, gangbanger posers, and Tribe faithfuls watched them with glee, bumping, high-fiving, doing shots, and chugging beer. Girls struggled through the crowd not wanting to be touched, unless they did, but I could never tell.

We waited a half hour to get a drink then a waving arm caught my eye. It was Marcus in the corner with a few guys from the team. Tony, Eddie, and I patiently squeezed between bodies showing bar respect, the only protocol preventing chaos. A divider separated Marcus and the others from the crowd, the kind of divider you see at airport security. I reached to the clasp to undo it and a hand pressed against my chest.

"Players only." The bouncer was as big as Jeremy.

"We're players, ask Marcus." I had to yell into his ear.

Marcus waved his arm and the bouncer let us through. Beneath the upper tier it was quieter by a few degrees. On the far side of the table was a familiar face but I couldn't place it. He was huge, but not like the bouncer or a lineman, just obese with a full beard and a hand full of cash. He pointed to me as he spoke into Marcus's ear. Marcus quickly replied, then the guy waved me over.

When I got close, his fat, sweaty hand wrapped around the back of my neck. He shouted to the bartender, "Three shots of Wild Turkey and three beers." Then he turned to me. "Fucking cool, you're the holder for that kid with the leg, holy shit is he good." He told me his name, but I couldn't understand him. Henry had kicked four more times since the Alabama game, all longer than forty-five yards; he was five for five and I had nothing more than normal butterflies. The Wild Turkey was placed in front of us in little plastic Tribe shot glasses. Tony, Eddie, and I toasted, thanked our impromptu host, and downed the shots. The intense vapors rose through my sinuses and almost made my eyes water. Someone poked the back of my shoulder, I turned and saw it was Jake Sanfilippo and Scott Matthews, together as usual.

"Don't fuck around, you shouldn't even be here."

I didn't have the nerve to ask them why they were, but I wondered if they knew who the fat guy was and asked.

"Friend of the program," Scott said. "Your basic jock-sniffer. He's got a lot of money though; owns the biggest car dealership in Bastille."

Marcus was talking to a group of girls leaning over the divider, yelling back and forth, the words unintelligible. He tapped our fat host on the shoulder and pointed at the girls, then our host waved the money in his hand for them to see. One girl shrugged in confusion until our host showed them what he wanted. He motioned with his hands that he wanted them to flash us, but the girls waved us off, then lingered, acting coy. A few of the bros around them made an issue of it, encouraging them until they were surrounded. Even Jake and Scott broke off their conversation to join in, yelling for them to take it off. Then chants started, the music seemed louder, and the alcohol hit my brain.

"Take it off! Take it off! Take it off!"

The girls huddled, then turned to us. At once they lifted their shirts. Two of them flashed only their bras, but the one on the end hadn't heard the plan and gave us the full view. The corner crowd went wild with cheers and the bouncer uncoupled the divider and let them in. More beers and shots arrived, but I gave my shot to the clueless one who'd given us the full flash. I kept the beer.

"What's your name?" she said. I told her but I could tell she couldn't hear. "Are you on the team?" she asked with slurred words.

"I'm the scout team QB," I yelled.

"You're a scout? Like a boy scout?" She tilted her head and swayed as she talked, I couldn't tell if she was dancing or drunk. Someone passed behind me and I put my arm around her waist to steady her, then shook my head.

"Yeah, I'm a boy scout." Then I shouted into her ear. "Yes, I'm on the team."

She took my hand and told me she wanted to dance, something I was less experienced in than drinking. She bumped the table and beer cans fell, the others rebuked her, but she ignored them and I gave a mild defense as we made our way around the table.

"Thanks for the beers," I said to our host.

He nodded, then a sneer came over him as his face reddened. "Fucking kill Florida State, I hate those Seminole bastards." Then I remembered him.

It was Andre's jersey guy that was up front near the players entrance for every home game. Our walk from the Performance Center to the stadium wearing ties and our Tribe blazers was one of our traditions and every game he was there with his face painted wearing Andre's number 51 jersey. I stared at him an extra beat and nodded my head, then turned to the girl, who was dragging me to the dance floor with her G-string arrayed above the top of her denim shorts. I was in high hopes.

The dance floor was packed and within a minute someone pinched the back of my ear. It was her boyfriend, I thought, or a bouncer noticing she was too drunk. I turned and it was Jake Sanfilippo and Scott Matthews, they had Tony and Eddie with them.

"Out now, Dixon sends around the grad assistants at eleven."

An hour had passed since I had left the dorm; I paused a moment in disappointment.

"Now, or you're on your own."

I followed them to the back of the club, then turned to see if the girl was following me, but she'd been absorbed back into the rhythmic mass of bodies. We emptied out into an alley and stood listening to muffled thumping music while Jake checked around the corner. When he deemed it clear, Tony, Eddie, and I stuck together as we jogged down a side street, then turned right to head back to campus.

"We can't go back to the dorms, the RAs will be waiting for us," Tony said.

We followed him as we passed the west side of campus, and I was grateful for the cool fall weather. Past the CVS, the freshmen dorms, then the Wellness Center. We wound our way through the quad, by Masters Library, past the campus bookstore, and came out on the north side to frat row. Tony ascended the stairs of the second house, I didn't know which frat it was. Someone in the front room saw Tony and pointed up the stairs. We walked up to the third floor, then out onto a rooftop patio. A group of six people were there.

Their conversation came alive when they saw us, and Tony became the center of attention even though there weren't any girls. I stood in the back until one of the frat boys approached me.

"So, you, like, practice against the first team D? What's that like? I mean fucking Pokey is a beast."

"First rule of the scout team, get rid of the ball quickly," I said.

The guy laughed and carried on about how he'd get killed, which I thought was accurate.

"You going to the game?" I said.

"Absolutely, we're going to get lit before, you guys miss out on the best part, dude."

A red Solo cup was handed to me, and I filled it from the keg but it was half foam. One of them complained the keg was out, another said to call a pledge to replace it. A bar in the basement was mentioned and one by one they left until it was just the three of us.

"Look what one of them fine fraternity brothers gave me," Eddie said. He produced a joint, then looked around for a lighter. I'd never tried it. Eddie lit it, took a hit, and passed it to Tony. After he took a hit, he held it out to me.

"Don't have to if you don't want to," Tony said. "But it definitely relaxes you. Maybe you should indulge before you have to hold." Eddie cracked up. "I'll coach you through it."

The acrid smell was unmistakable, and I coughed the first time I inhaled. The joint made its rounds a couple of times before Eddie butted it out and threw it over the railing. The backyard was nearly barren, empty kegs were lined up along the back fence. A light breeze blew, and I could see the Bastille Tower through shifting limbs of trees behind the house. Tony raised his flask and offered a toast.

"Not a bad start to the season, I just wish I could get off the scout team," Tony said.

"Me, too," Eddie said.

I laughed a little. "I still can't believe I'm here. The scout team is good enough for me." They chuckled, then Tony held the flask up again.

"To Wally, you made it buddy." We sipped from the flask like it was a chalice.

"If it wasn't for you guys, Henry and I would be done. I can't thank you enough."

Eddie held the flask up a moment longer, the back patio's light reflected off the etched arrow giving the moment a solemn feel.

"You made it, brother," Eddie said.

I nodded and said thanks. It would take a while to soak in.

Wally

....

iv.

ALL THE EYES of the players, coaches, and fans followed the path of the military aircraft. They appeared as dots above the horizon in the blue sky, then quickly flew over at a low enough altitude that I could clearly see the landing gear hatches on the jet I was focused on. Then they disappeared, leaving a roar and exhaust in their wake. As the jets passed, the crowd's wild applause filled in and I couldn't tell which was louder.

Florida State, the mighty Seminoles, just an hour drive from our campus. When they received the kick, the arrows flew in unison and we tackled their return man at the twelve. In the locker room right before we came out the intensity was higher than I'd ever seen, and I knew we were going to win. The fans were just as intense, although something troubled me. More fans had lined our pathway from the Performance Center to the stadium than at previous home games, and in places it was like walking through an angry mob. Then I saw him, the fat guy from the Parthenon, all dressed up in his Tribe jersey, face paint, and Tribe-colored pants in wild stripes that looked like pajama bottoms, with a beer in hand.

It was like a small pebble was overturned and out of place in the mosaic of my thoughts, but I couldn't see where, I could only feel it. The feeling hung in my head as I dressed for the game. In between catching snaps for Henry's kicks during warm-ups, I tried to identify it, then admonished myself for getting distracted before such an important time. Then, back in the locker room before we came out for good, it hit me. Pokey passed by us, number 93. The fat guy outside the stadium, the overspending denizen of the access-restricted corner table at the Parthenon, provider of shots and beers, the gatekeeper for the drunk girl I'd wanted, was wearing a new jersey—Pokey's number 93, not Andre's 51. I didn't know why it was important to me; I couldn't mention it to anyone, they'd think I was weird. Then I thought further, maybe it would bother them, too; maybe there was an underlying hidden truth barely exposed, like a single dangling string in the form of a newly acquired jersey. Andre didn't matter anymore, he was tossed away the second he couldn't contribute. I turned away the thought; we were about to run through the tunnel again, a ritual that was as exhilarating as ever, something more important than some obscure truth.

Our defense looked like the best in the country, better than Alabama's. FSU went three and out on their first drive, they even threw an out on third and six, but our cornerback played it perfectly from his nickel corner position against their slot receiver and broke up the pass. I was filled with quiet pride, it made me feel like I was a part of the action since I'd tested him all week in practice on the same play.

When we got the ball, we watched with the expectation of seeing Dion put on a clinic. Tony, Eddie, and I had begun running projections through the rest of the season to compare Dion's numbers to previous Heisman winners. After three plays we were on FSU's doorstep, and it felt like we'd blow them out. On the next play protection broke down, but Dion dodged and stepped up to drill a pass to Tarik in the end zone, then we all went flat. Interception, the FSU free safety must've read Dion's eyes all the way.

When Dion came to the sideline, I tried to gauge his mindset to see if he was troubled, but there wasn't a change. As time was running out in the second quarter, we ran a stop and go to our tight end, but somehow Dion forgot the route after our tight end had turned up field. The FSU linebacker caught it like he was the intended receiver, and we went into halftime down 7–3.

I didn't know what to expect in the locker room, the offense was somber and listened to Coach Oldham break down our mistakes like he'd already studied the game film. As we headed out for the second half, our defense acted as if they had the chance to win the game and pay back Dion for bailing them out over the past two years.

By the fourth quarter, it was clear it wasn't Dion's day: He was ten of twenty for ninety-eight yards and three interceptions. Nobody had received the arrow and after Dion's fourth pick, which they ran to our thirty, the surrender cobras started to appear in the stands.

Then something happened. After two holding penalties, FSU punted and Melvin Richardson, the guy who, I had to remind myself, was just a freshman, caught the punt and found a seam. Coach Griffin was in front of me while the punt was in the air and he kept repeating "fair catch, fair catch" as if Melvin had a radio receiver in his helmet. It looked for sure he was bottled up as two Seminoles broke their sprint and waited for him to catch it, but with a quick deke to the left then a spin between them, he broke to our sideline and the stampede was on. After outrunning a few more, a Seminole dove at his legs and got a hold of his ankle but Melvin twisted through it and no one else could catch him. Before the extra point to tie the game, Melvin stood in the end zone and got his second arrow of the season while we went crazy on the sidelines.

After the kickoff, FSU had the ball deep in their end and we thought they'd kneel and go to overtime. But on first and ten Jake Sanfilippo tipped a pass on a blitz, and Scott Matthews made a diving interception. I was kneeling on the sideline and saw that the ball never touched the ground.

"Goddamn, those guys do everything together," said Jeremy.

Evan was mobbed after he kicked a thirty-yarder to win it and we were 9–1.

▼ ▼ ▼

The used strips of athletic tape from my ankles laid crumpled beneath my stool. I still had my game pants on as I balled up the tape and tossed it towards the large plastic garbage can in the center of the locker room. I missed, and the tape rolled to the other side in front of an empty locker. That's a problem they never considered when they built this place, I thought.

The locker was empty, it was JD's, he didn't return after the loss of his mother and sister. A few stalls up was Andre Decker's empty locker. Across the way, Marlon's was unused, but he sat on a stool in front of it in his street clothes. Five starters in total were gone for the year due to injury, as well as three of the second teamers. We hadn't heard the extent of the damage to our tight end, he'd make six starters lost.

They called targeting on the FSU strong safety for drilling him as he reached for a pass. The hit shocked us, but we were relieved when he popped up and took two steps. Then he started to wobble on the third. He tried to take a knee, but ended up sprawled on the field. They didn't even bother bringing him to the sideline, they carted him off and he sat on the back payload of the cart with his head slumped over like a robot someone had turned off. I didn't bother to count the scout team players injured in practice. The locker stalls were wide to start with and as the number of empty stalls grew, the open spaces were unavoidable reminders.

I walked over to retrieve the tape then returned to my locker next to Henry. Coach Oldham had taken a seat in front of Dion, two lockers over. Immediately after the game, Coach Oldham told us how proud he was.

"Gritty."

"FSU is one of the best, as always."

"My pride in you is immeasurable, not because we won, it's the way you played."

He acknowledged Evan's game-winning kick, the interception by Scott Matthews, and the defensive line's five sacks. Then he approached Dion while I was picking up the balled tape; I debated whether to give them privacy but my curiosity won out.

"It wasn't your day, Dion, but we got the win, move on," Coach Oldham said. "We'll look at the film and figure it out."

Dion was visibly upset, he only nodded in response.

"I appreciate you congratulating the defense's performance and supporting the team while you struggled, but if they see you moping, they're going to think you only care about yourself. That's an unhealthy dynamic and you know it."

Dion raised his head, took a deep breath, then nodded. "Let's get ready for South Carolina. Tribe forever."

"Tribe forever," Coach said.

Dion stood and walked to the defensive area of the locker room addressing players on the way with thanks and congratulations. Coach Oldham started to walk by Henry and me, then he stopped.

"Wally, nice work on the scout team this week, Kareem was very impressed. Henry, you keep ready."

I nodded and said thanks, then, as he walked away, I turned to Henry with a smile that I struggled to keep modest while Henry stared at me. "Did you hear that?" I said.

Henry repeated Coach's words verbatim in his flat tone and I struggled to not laugh. But Coach Oldham's compliment was something I'd hold on to like an heirloom.

I was half dressed when the media entered the locker room, a flood of rumpled reporters and on-air types wearing ties and pampered hair. I buttoned my shirt. Some I recognized as local, and a few were from national outlets. In all, there were over two dozen and at least half went directly to Dion's locker. Some held their phones to record the conversation as they jockeyed for position, crowding me out of my space. Henry stood to leave but I told him to sit, I wanted to listen. The questions were predictable, what surprised me was their tone—they knew Dion was troubled by his play and they asked questions in a respectful manner.

Q: *How do you feel about your play today?*

Dion: *It wasn't my day; I made some bad reads, then I couldn't get in rhythm. Our defense gets all the credit for this one.*

Q: *Did your receiver run the wrong route on the second interception?*

Dion: *That was completely my fault, Justin ran the right route, it was a mental error on my part.*

Q: *What did Florida State do to get you out of your rhythm?*

Dion: *They're a great team, one of the best defenses in the country. I think they did just about every- thing right.*

As I listened, I thought about how I would answer but couldn't improve on Dion's replies. I knew he wasn't fragile, but at times, I could see a fraying of his patience with people outside the pro- gram. Either fans who wanted pictures with him smiling like it was the highlight of his day or questioning him so they could say they had an intimate football conversation with the great Dion McAres. After ten minutes, the reporters seemed to have what they needed, and the relaxed mood gave me relief. Some drifted away, but most hung around as the conversation lightened; they laughed about something, but I didn't hear what was said. Then another reporter joined, she wedged into the crowd, nearly sticking her rear end in my face. I moved my stool to make room.

"Dion, do you think you've blown your chances for the Heisman?"

Everyone turned to the reporter, it was Samantha Yardley. I looked at Dion, he was glaring at her. None of the reporters spoke, a few looked to Samantha and then back to Dion.

"I'm not concerned," said Dion.

"But you're one of the front runners, at least until today. How would you explain away today's performance to the voters?" she said.

"I wouldn't, my job is to play, not explain," said Dion.

"I know Coach Oldham never discusses the Heisman, but the athletic department has launched a PR campaign. How do you feel about letting Bastille down?"

Dion didn't respond, but his eyes narrowed and his jaw started to clench.

"A PR campaign?" someone asked. "How much is the school spending on this?"

"How come Coach Oldham won't discuss this?" asked another.

"There's no campaign," Dion said. He began to say more but was flustered.

"Seriously, how do you even think about the Heisman after today?" Samantha said.

There was a small gap of silence. No one else would've asked these questions, but they all wanted to hear the answers. And Dion didn't have anything to say. I couldn't help myself.

"It's not in the playbook," I said loudly as I finished buttoning my shirt. My words shocked me; they came out before I had a chance to stop. All the reporters turned towards me. I saw a skinny one with his shirt buttons in the wrong buttonholes, a fat one with nose hairs hanging out of his nostrils, and one who must have had bad eyesight. He raised his glasses and squinted in my direction. Samantha Yardley was inches from me.

"The Heisman's not mentioned anywhere in the playbook. It's not mentioned in the weekly game plan, either." I glanced at Dion, I couldn't tell if he was horrified or relieved. "It's not even in any of our classes, imagine that."

Samantha Yardley turned completely towards me, as if she'd found a new target. "Would you like to expand on that a little more? What's your name?"

They were all looking at me, their phones and cameras had shifted in my direction. Dion raised a hand to his mouth, and I could tell he was smiling while I could barely breathe. It was like stepping into a sword fight in my underwear.

"My name? John Q. Nobody. I'll spell it, capital 'N-o-b-o-d-y.'" I even looked down to her phone as if she was typing my name. "There's no campaign, just an intern sending out tweets. Dion never talks about it, and it's not in the playbook."

A few of the reporters began to snicker and I got the sense they enjoyed seeing her embarrassed. Ms. Yardley coolly lowered her phone and looked up at the nameplate on my locker. The rest of the reporters began walking away, a few with smirks on their faces. I picked up my backpack and led Henry out of the locker room.

Hours later, after I'd become a brief internet sensation, Coach Griffin called to remind me about respecting the press. I could tell he wasn't mad; I think he was holding back a laugh, which meant Coach Oldham wasn't mad. As soon as I hung up Jeremy pounded on our door—I was summoned to Dion's room, and upon arrival,

I was jumped by Eddie, Tony, and Pokey. Their laughing mockery was fine, their friendly punches were too enthusiastic. Then Dion broke it up and took me out into the hall.

"That was funny, but don't do it again. You can't speak for me," he said.

"I'm sorry, I just thought she was out of line."

"Fuck it, we won. Come on in, my girls are hosting a party later on at their sorority."

▼ ▼ ▼

"How do you do it?" the Professor asked. The question was serious, his eyes portrayed honesty. Mrs. Bertrand took a sip of wine, and their son, Milo Jr., a student at Bastille, waited with his fork midway to his mouth. The Professor wasn't mocking or sarcastic, curiosity was his happiest pleasure. They wanted to hear the secrets, mechanisms, and protocols born of necessity and refined with ingenuity that allowed us to practice, hit, study, bond, rest, play, heal, keep humble, never fear, intimidate, and do it all without letting the incessant and intrusive attention, combined with the constantly startling hype, distract us. The moment I first stepped on campus I could feel it, but after we beat South Carolina, the attention increased in a way that couldn't be centrally planned: It came from the nucleus of every cell of every Tribe partisan.

"I was scared to death the first time I went out there, I still get scared. Guys like Dion, I have no idea how they do it."

"Bastille National Champions don't just get a trophy," the Professor said. "They get a permanent pass to Valhalla."

"Where's that," I said.

He laughed in response. "It's a concept not a place."

Earlier in the week he had invited us, but I told him Henry had to study. "A home cooked meal," he'd said. I knew Henry was in our dorm playing his numbers game. Meeting Mrs. Bertrand scared me; the left-wing, bleeding heart. Dogfighting, she'd said. But I was in too good of a mood when I arrived; Dion had his best game.

Their apartment wasn't much larger than our dorm, but it was older. Instead of granite counters they had laminate. Instead of Tribe-themed walls and new carpets, theirs were neutral; the carpets were clean but frayed. The TV was dated, I could tell by its size and depth; it was turned off, with no NFL game playing as a backdrop during Sunday dinner.

"Tell me, Wally, have you decided on a major?" Mrs. Bertrand said.

"No, ma'am. The closest I have to a major is following the Professor's advice."

She smiled, patted the Professor's arm, and started picking up dishes. I did the same.

"No, you're our guest." Their son, Milo Jr., helped his mother, he was a 4.0 student.

"Organic chemistry, now that's a major that will get you out of a place like this," the Professor said as his eyes followed his son's path into the narrow kitchen.

Then he looked at me. "In two years, when I get tenured, we're buying a place. A nice little ranch house we can fix up. John even insisted that he be invited to the housewarming."

"I've kind of wondered, how do you know him?" I said.

The Professor looked over to his wife and son, immersed in washing the dishes.

"Now you're really taking me back. Years ago, I gave a presentation on a paper I'd published, it's something we all do here, it's open to everyone which means we get about ten people. John attends these a lot, it's kind of a thing for all of us to have him attend and he was interested in my topic. Afterwards we talked for an hour or so and became friends after that."

"You like Bastille, don't you?" I said.

Professor Bertrand removed his glasses and leaned back in his limited space. "I really do." He nodded, as if he was confirming his own good fortune. "It took me years to figure out my life and now that I've found it, it's better than I thought it would be. It took a lot of sacrifice, though."

"What kind of sacrifice?"

"I came here for undergrad and probably got as much out of this place as anyone, I really loved it. Except for my major, it was accounting. Good education though and I got a good job right out of school. Then, after a few years, I went up north and got my MBA. I should've known then."

"Known what?"

"That I didn't love it. In fact, I hated it. Nevertheless, I soldiered on. The good news: I met Mary at a book reading. At first, I thought she was some kind of left-wing do-gooder, but I was hooked immediately. After we married something happened, something terrible—my career started to suck the life out of me." He paused a moment. "I realized that I didn't garner any satisfaction from my work, it was a grind that would never end, that it would always be about money and nothing more. Now, for many, that's exactly what they want and good for them, the wheels of commerce are what affords cultures the wherewithal for things like universities. But not for me, I was miserable. From the outside we had the perfect life. I had a good job, we had a child, Mary worked at a non-profit that she was passionate about, and we had a nice house. Standard-issue suburban housing with a mortgage to take care of during the week and landscaping to enslave me on the weekends. I'm sorry, maybe this is too much."

"No, I want to hear," I said.

"After years of this and a well-developed habit of self-medicating with wine, Mary brought it all to an end. We had been discussing my unhappiness for quite some time and then one Friday night we had a long, difficult conversation. To be frank, I probably wasn't much fun to live with and I thought she was tiring of me. But then she really crawled inside my head, trying to beat it out of me to figure out what I wanted to do with the rest of my life. I was in tears, telling her I didn't know and that I couldn't go on. Then, she said it was enough and walked away, I thought she was done.

"She called to me from the office where our bookshelves were. 'It's right there,' she said as she pointed to the books. I had quite a collection of great fiction, non-fiction about culture, politics, religion, and my favorite, philosophy. That night, we decided I was going to quit the corporate world and pursue academia, a path I often alluded to but lacked the courage to take seriously. I'll never forget the beautiful feeling of my own self-oppression lifting from my shoulders. It took a year before I actually applied, and then another before we pulled up stakes and traded in a comfortable life for one of intellectual stimulation and poverty. I've never been happier. I wake up every day with my heart full of love for my wife and inspiration for my work. Two years. In two years, I'll be a tenured professor. This is why, my friend, you need to find out who you are in these college years and be true to yourself."

The Professor got up to help with the dishes while I remained seated. I didn't know there were people like this in the world, and I was wrong about Mrs. Bertrand, she was strong and kind, like Aunt Janie. There was no mention of dogfighting, no probing questions about the program. She asked about my background then offered comfort. "Anytime you and your brother would like to come. Are you going home for the holidays? If not—" If a storm with high winds blew through, they'd huddle close and survive, then help neighbors. She served others, running a women's shelter. "Half my time is spent raising money," she'd said. "The singular skill of a university president," the Professor said. And the Professor taught;

it was like an aura arose when he witnessed safe passage of ideas to new minds. They returned with dessert and more questions.

"Is Dion a good guy? Are they mean?"

"Yes and no."

I woke from the attention, turning to their son. "What's it like? How hard do you study? Do you go out? Have you been to the Parthenon?" I studied to play, a means to an end. Milo Jr. was learning topics I'd never heard of, topics that drove the world. "Do you sit in the front row?" Milo Jr. laughed. "I got that speech, too," he said.

"How are your grades, if you don't mind my asking," said Mrs. Bertrand.

I looked to the Professor.

"I never discuss it, that would be a violation of privacy," he said.

"All As and one B," I said.

"I told you, Mary," the Professor said. "This is why I wanted you to meet him." Then he looked to me. "I know you'll never be the star of the team but you and your brother's story is inspirational. It makes me believe in what college football can do for someone; you two are special."

At 8:30 I sensed it was time to go. I left offering thanks, promises to return, and an invitation to Milo Jr. to hang out and meet some of the players.

"You're a fine young man," said the Professor. He hugged me. "Next time, bring Henry; just come as you are, no worries."

"I will, he's studying this time, he's making it work."

The Professor tilted his head like he'd been proven wrong and was glad of it.

On the walk home, I found myself pausing in thought as I sat on a bench in the quad. The Professor and his family living in their small apartment; I wanted them to have a grand house, something in line with their virtues. The thought, or disappointment, was tricky. I stood up to get away. This is my home, now. In the far

corner of the quad, behind the statue, I'd made out with a sophomore girl after the Florida State game, then went to her room. Up
ahead was the path I took to my Tuesday/Thursday classes. My
favorite junk food was Vic's pizza on the strip.

I cut through an alley and walked by the Tribe store then
turned back and stood in front of its plate glass windows. The
t-shirts, caps, sweatshirts, collectibles, trinkets, and everything else
that held Tribe colors for value were quietly sleeping for the night.
I looked at my reflected image in the window like I was part of the
merchandise, nestled comfortably in my dream home.

I belonged. Practices were my games, the scout team my team.
Before the South Carolina game, I slung dozens of balls each practice. I let them fly and quietly drank in my wins. Even the hits.
On a roll out the receivers were covered, no options through the
air. I ran past the line, dodged a linebacker, and found myself flying through the air. Carter Schultz hit me, technically speaking, he
cleaned me out, knocking off my helmet. But when I was hit and
the split second after, I didn't feel pain, just a sense of soaring. Success or failure wasn't in mind; I was playing for the Tribe. When I
hit the ground and rolled over, pain shot through me like an electric
shock. Then Carter leaned over me. "You okay?" A blink to see if
I could see. A breath to see if I could breathe. A move to register
pain. "You okay?" he said again. No thoughts, an empty shell, I
could think of only one thing. "Tribe forever." Carter smiled, then
laughed. Then his face turned serious. "Don't do that shit again,
now get out of here." *I belong*, I thought.

Then, something else came to mind like an uninvited guest:
Henry didn't.

I sat on a bench in front of the Tribe store and looked at my
reflection again. This time it felt like I was on trial. I lied to them,
the two people I had yearned for my entire life; one I had known
of, one I hadn't. Coach Oldham and the Professor. Aunt Janie

would've paid for any school, and I could've gotten an apartment and brought Henry with me and loved my Tribe from afar. "An inspirational story," the Professor said. I was a fraud.

If my deceit was uncovered and Henry was exposed, the embarrassment Coach Oldham would suffer would stain the end of his career and Henry would be the reason, something he didn't deserve. And I'd lose the Professor; I couldn't bear his compliments—*an inspirational story*—when I'd been cheating for Henry the entire time. I finally belonged to the only pure organization in life and our presence was the only thing impure. I bent over and clutched my head; I had to tell both of them. I'd tell them after the season.

▼ ▼ ▼

Georgia Tech at 3:30 eastern on Friday afternoon, the day after Thanksgiving. I'd watched this game for years at Papa's BBQ while I worked. Miss Diane didn't mind, everyone in the restaurant watched, too.

The walk from the Performance Center took longer than usual, the crowd lining our steps was bigger than before the FSU game. "This is what it was like the last time we won it all," said Randy, our DFO. Henry and I were near the end, the part of the line where people would question if we were players if we weren't wearing our Tribe blazers.

I didn't expect what happened next. "Nuber!" "It's the Nuber!" People called out to him, some stuck their fists out for bumps, but Henry didn't respond. I took a few quick glances; it was like they were kids at a parade begging firemen for candy.

"I am the Nuber," Henry said. Only I could hear him through the crowd noise.

In the locker room: superstitions, rituals, and habits. I could describe each players' routine. Pokey sat at his locker in street clothes until Coach Dixon walked by looking surprised that he hadn't dressed yet. "Let's go, Poke, don't you make me wait." Jeremy changed into shorts and a Tribe t-shirt, then disappeared into the restroom. Thumping rap music came on and somebody complained. "Too bad, country boy. We won last time we played this." Dion sat at his locker in street clothes, softly nodding his head in time to the music playing through his headphones as he studied the play script. Jake and Scott dressed into their football pants and undershirts, then left to walk the field. The whiteboard with the pre-game schedule was on the far wall, and even though I knew it by heart, I walked over, checked the clock, and marked time, waiting thirty minutes before kickers and punters went out for warm-ups to get dressed. When I got back to my locker, Dion was fully dressed. I don't know how he did it so fast. I wondered if he waited for me to check the board to start getting dressed, but I doubt it. When I started changing, Henry stopped playing his numbers game on his phone, handed it to me and took off his shirt.

Warm-ups: Henry and Evan took turns launching kicks, Coach Griffin prescribed each distance despite us knowing the routine in our sleep. The rest of the team on the field, stretches, individual, ones versus ones in non-contact, the return to the locker room, then Coach Oldham's brief words. I still looked at him like he was saintly flesh, he even had a pale aura that set him apart. Then Coach Dixon, then Dion, then it was time. The pressure in the tunnel made it hard to breathe, the crowd started the scream and raised the arrows. We took the field amid screams, flying arrows, *BOOMS*, fireworks, and jets.

Dion was on his game; quick throws into tight windows, audibles away from pressure, throwing it away when forced. On a third and one from our forty-nine he feathered a catchable ball to our tight end, but he lost control when a Georgia Tech linebacker stripped it away. Groans on our sideline until Dion came off the field. "We got this, just keep playing, they can't stop us."

What a strange game, I thought. Tech's misdirection offense was a misnomer, its power was precision, not confusion. They held the ball for eight minutes and scored on a four-yard jet sweep that had everyone fooled. "We talked about this!" Coach Dixon's veins appeared on his bald head as he shouted over the crowd noise to the assembled defense. "This is assignment football, almost every play they have four options, do not leave your assignment." It was hard for our defense, it's not like they were purposely ignoring Coach Dixon and trying to take the game into their own hands. Their whole football life they'd been taught one thing: swarm. But Tech wanted us to swarm on defense, they kept their options open deep into each play. Attack the QB on an option and he'd pitch to the running back. Cover the QB and the running back and they'd hand it off on a backdoor counter to the fullback. Stack the line and string it out, and their QB would take a step back as he's running the option and float a wobbler to the tight end, who'd been ignored all game.

The wobbler floated down, this time into their little-used wide receiver's hands as he crossed our goal line. We were down 21–17 with three minutes left in the half.

"Dion, the defense is worn, I don't want them back on the field this half," Coach Oldham said. Grunts and short runs, I was bent over with my hands on my knees, looking down the line of scrimmage, watching helmets arrayed inches from each other, then colliding, grass flying back from spikes.

"Get him ready," Coach Griffin said.

Dion worked the ball down to their forty-four. A time-out with seventeen seconds left. "Go."

We ran out, I counted players, then called the field goal. We broke the huddle with a clap and then I noticed, they'd been chanting it since we ran out.

"Nu-Ber! Nu-Ber! Nu-Ber!" The crowd on our sideline yelled "Nu" and the crowd on the other responded with "Ber." I picked my blade of grass and looked for Henry's nod as the chants continued. Sixty-one yards, it would be a Bastille record. The chants reached new heights, I was afraid Henry would be distracted or say his line in response or the line wouldn't hear my call. The play clock ticked down, I looked to the ball cradled in Jeremy's hands.

"Set!"

The ball was perfect, it spun towards my extended hand, I caught, placed, and spun. Henry's foot swung through at a speed too fast to see and once it cleared the line, I stood to watch its perfect flight.

Georgia Tech wouldn't let up through the second half. They were like a machine, executing finely designed plays while our guys faced uncertainty every down, like trying to guess the correct door and knowing we'd eventually make the wrong choice. Halfway through the fourth, we tied it on a simple post to Tarik, a forty-yard pass.

Then I saw Jeremy half bent-over, shaking his left hand, then compressing it. Our offensive line coach readied the backup center, but Jeremy waved him off. We traded possessions and had one more chance with a minute fifteen to go. Dion threw for fifteen, Julius ran for eight, and Tarik dropped one that would've put us at their twenty. A pass to our tight end, then a spike and one more to Marcus on the sideline. "Go," said Coach Oldham.

It was my huddle now. As Henry found his spot and the crowd chanted his name, I counted the players in the huddle, their hands on their knees, all but one. Jeremy's left hand was out of position, just the heel of his palm rested on his knee with his fingers held away and slightly shaking. A drop of blood fell from the tip of his gloved index finger through one of the little holes to allow for ventilation.

"You okay?" I said. His nod worried me. *Call time-out,* I thought, we had one left. But it wasn't my place to go to the sideline and tell Coach Oldham and Coach Griffin, request a new long snapper that wasn't warmed up and whose nerves would be like mine when I'd run out onto the field against Oklahoma. He'd snapped to Dion since it first happened. I took comfort and broke the huddle. The chants grew, I looked to Henry, then to the ball. Jeremy's hands fully enclosed it, even the damaged finger.

"Set!"

I didn't have a chance. The ball skimmed the ground, then hit grass, tumbling end over end past Henry and me. I sprung after it in full sprint screaming, "Fire! Fire! Fire!"

We never practiced the fire drill, there was never enough time, and it was unspoken that practicing failure only induced it. But it was simple. The linemen block to the right, the left end runs a crossing pattern, while the kicker wheels backside and finds space in the middle.

The ball was still rolling when I went to pick it up, and with my back to the play, I had no idea what was happening. As I reached down, a Georgia Tech player flew by, he wanted a clean scoop to run the open field in front of him, but he misread the bounce. Without dropping to my knees, I picked the ball and turned to the right to look for an open receiver, then three guys in white smothered me. I covered up to prevent a fumble as their hits drove me into the ground and their arms dug at mine, trying to cause a fumble. Even after I opened my eyes there was little light; I was encapsulated, just the sounds of Georgia Tech players celebrating. As someone helped me up, I saw Henry standing downfield by himself.

We lost. We lost in a hurtful, shameful manner. I sat on my stool in the locker room, stunned and embarrassed. After the botched snap the game went to overtime. On the first play Dion gunned a pass to Tarik, like he'd had enough, and we were up by seven. Then Tech ground out a series of plays; it was like dying by a thousand cuts. They scored and lined up for the extra point. I know they didn't know me and didn't do this for effect, but it seemed they were rubbing it in my face. At the snap, their holder caught the ball, placed it, then picked it up and rolled to his right. A Georgia Tech special teamer snuck through and was wide open in the end zone and their holder floated it to him. They went for two and stunned us.

Henry and I walked back to the dorms in the dark with a few other guys. The crowd was gone, the parking lot empty, the yellow lines marking parking spaces that hours ago had been filled with tailgaters were littered with party refuse. I kicked an empty beer can. It was the silence that bothered me, like the Tribe had stopped breathing. I didn't speak, I tried to take solace in Coach Oldham's words.

"We've had a great season; you've done everything you've been asked to do."

"We're ten and two, you've got a bright future."

"A New Year's Day bowl game."

He huddled with Jeremy, whose hand was bandaged and iced. Red eyes and sorrow, his shoulder pads still on, his jersey stained with grass and dirt and blood. Dion and other players approached and consoled, and I took my turn paying respect.

The media was subdued, even Samantha Yardley. When she approached, Dion looked at me and shook his head in warning. I stuffed my backpack and listened to the questions. She didn't say a word, just held her phone out to record Dion's comments. Her face looked worn, and I stared too long. She turned my way, held my look, then gave me a slight nod. I nodded back and breathed easier. When the rest of the reporters dissolved away, she left, then turned back to Dion.

"Just one more question," she said. Dion nodded. "Do you think it would've made a difference if you had Garr Johnstone?"

I could tell the question caught Dion off guard. "No, he's a great player, but no."

She paused as if out of gas, then tried again. "I know you guys were childhood friends and he was heavily recruited by Bastille. As a true freshman at Arkansas A&M, Garr leads the nation in sacks and tackles for loss, he's a lock to be a first-team All-American. You don't think he would've helped against an offense like Georgia Tech? Do you think he'd be a starter at Bastille?"

I closed my eyes and waited for Dion's answer.

He took a deep breath. "Garr Johnstone couldn't start for Bastille, because he chose to go somewhere else."

I let Dion's answer roll around in my head a few times. It was perfect.

We had dinner at nine. By ten I was with Eddie and Tony at a frat house. At eleven a frat boy got our attention. "Can you believe this shit?" He held up his phone, it had the app for Sports Inc. The headline read, "McAres: Johnstone Couldn't Start for the Tribe."

I closed my eyes and saw Henry standing downfield by himself, as if we were separated; the idea bothered me more than the truth about him. I shook off the thought, I felt like I was leaving the fight. On Monday we'd quit; I'd tell Coach Oldham the truth about Henry, and the two of us would head back to West Temple.

Wally

....

FAREWELL

BOOM.

BOOM, BOOM.

The tympani rang out, the sound hard and circular, echoing with hints of rain. I looked to the sky, wishing it would.

The tympani sounded the rhythm again. Loud, determined, then silence, painful silence. It sounded a third time, its volume lowered like it was dying. Then trumpets, the sound of determination, rising above, proud, then sorrowful—sorrowful and sweet. I ran through heavy rain over wet sidewalk, breathing too hard to vent or cry out in the awful morning. The Professor would know.

Memory is distorted, chronology absent, like someone spliced intersections in the wrong places. All at once, the end. It happened. I looked up into the darkened stadium, unable to tell how many were in attendance, if any. Money fell, sticking in helmets. The soulful cried, we had to move forward alone without our graceful past.

Henry's eyes, still and dry, his mind unable to process, except for his quiet screaming.

"Wally, Wally, Wally."

All the doors were open, like jail cells offering freedom, but no one left, just me. Dion looked at me, sighed, then turned away.

Breathe. Think. But I couldn't, tears rolled, everyone's did. Everyone except Henry, but I know he was lost, too. He's the one that showed me. "COACH OLDHAM DEAD." Sports Inc.'s website used all caps.

The music continued then ended before I was ready to stop listening, just like I wasn't ready to stop playing for Coach Oldham. The haunting music, it took me days before I learned what it was, something called *Fanfare for the Common Man*. I liked that. We filed into the stadium, few lights were on, they'd set up a stage in one end zone. Esteemed mourners spoke of his virtues while the jumbotron displayed his portrait. I was in a foul mood; they'd done it all wrong. I thought Coach would hate it, my thought was confirmed when I saw Coach Dixon. I knew he hated it, too.

Other than the music, there was no reason for the production, but like the Professor said, the school couldn't help itself, that was its business. Rumor was the clergy fought over the leading role, conveniently overlooking one fact—he wasn't religious. It didn't stop them. Celebrities and politicians offered to appear, then added offers of favors to be rendered in the future, the righteous spotlight too mesmerizing to withstand.

I woke Sunday morning, not wanting to move anything beyond my eyes; it would be too painful. Even though we had a bowl game to play, which one we didn't know yet, the season was over. The ceiling of my bedroom, I tried to focus, too blurry, just like the night before. After we lost to Georgia Tech Friday night, we bitched about the game and we bitched about Samantha Yardley. Then we drank. We drank to freedom; we drank to our success. A New Year's Day bowl, the Tribe hadn't had one in years. Surely, we were headed to Orlando, someone said. Not Vegas? Not Vegas. No hookers and blow? We laughed. They've got that in Orlando. They've got that here.

Study, no watching the Saturday games, study. A trip by Dion's room. "I should've let you shut that bitch up, again," he'd said. Then Tony and Eddie's room. Weed. A drink. A game's on, time passed in a steady stream, then another game. Feed Henry, I was buzzed but he didn't seem to mind. A nap, a wakeup call, the Parthenon. Thumping music and shots; I was free. The girls, a redhead in uniform, tiny shorts, and cleavage. We danced until we both were sweaty, she bought me drinks, I bought her shots, we made out in the corner then went to her apartment. After we were done, I returned to the club. Still crowded, but anonymous to me, the faces shifting faster than I could register. Then Eddie, we're leaving, frat row. Two a.m., then three. I forgot about Henry. *He didn't forget to run his pattern on the botched kick*, I thought, *he'll be fine.* At five in the morning, I returned and checked on him, kneeling beside his bed, listening to him breathe. I sat and fell asleep leaning against his dresser. At first light, I crawled into my own and listened to an early morning thunderstorm.

At eleven, I woke and used the bathroom, then looked in on Henry. He was gone, maybe he'd bring me back food from the dining hall. I fell asleep for another hour until I felt Henry standing above me.

"Wally, Wally, Wally."

When I heard those words, I rolled over in panic and looked at him through squinting eyes. Then I opened my eyes in fear, I could see horror in his face in a way no one else could. He stood above me holding his tablet. I slowly sat up and received it.

"COACH OLDHAM DEAD."

He died in his sleep with his wife next to him. Panic filled me, emptying everything else; I thought the room was going to disappear, leaving us homeless. I dressed quickly and walked the halls of the dorms, then headed to the floor above. Jeremy's door was open and I stood in the doorway. He was sitting at his desk with the same red eyes from the locker room after the Tech game. He didn't speak, we looked at each other for a moment in silence then he looked away. I didn't hear much and none of the usual; no laughing, no swearing, no music. I strained to hear crying but heard silence instead. I panicked.

I took the stairs and ran to the ground floor, bursting open the door and stepping into cold rain. It soaked me, I looked up, heavy drops fell on my face and into my eyes. I ran past the Performance Center, past the science building, past the student dorms where only freshmen lived. The campus was empty, and I ran at full speed, nearly slipping on corners. Glass buildings and stone structures looked ugly and cold. The doors were locked, it was Sunday, maybe another way in. A side door was propped open an inch, I stepped in out of the rain and bent over to catch my breath as water dripped onto the floor, like blood draining from my body. Up the stairs, two flights, then the hallway, it was dark except for one door. Light spilled out from the Professor's office, and I nearly slid by. I stood in his doorway, panting, still dripping, and he turned to me. He was sad, too.

"I'm so sorry, Wally," he said. "I know how much he meant to you."

Cold air and wet clothes wicked the heat from my body and I started to shiver, then to sob. He approached and hugged me. Moving papers from a chair so I could sit, he wrapped a blanket around me.

Later, we met as a team. Coach Dixon spoke words of comfort, but it felt like a conveyor started carrying us to into a dark tunnel. A petition was signed by all the players pleading to the administration to hire Dixon as head coach. It was sent to the press and published on social media; former players took up the cause, the handful who were in the NFL and thousands who weren't. The press tried to interview Dion, he took a breath, bit his lip, and walked away. They criticized him, but he couldn't speak. Practices were muted, dull, and unorganized at first. Then, in homage, we took it seriously—a pale therapy.

We traveled west a few days after Christmas, Henry passed all his classes with straight Cs. We landed in Las Vegas for the Sky Bowl, the money too much for the administration to turn down. The game was useless, we lost to Colorado by twenty-two points. No one cared, the week after Coach Oldham died, they made the announcement: Boone Castritt was named head coach.

The only thing I remember about the Sky Bowl was a TV time-out. Skygirls and Skyboys with air cannons that shot t-shirts into the crowd ran behind our bench, behind Colorado's, and around the end zones of the new retractable dome stadium. Instead of t-shirts, though, they launched small bundles of dollar bills that bloomed at their apex and fluttered down into the crowd. People screamed to be the target, jumping, waving, pleading. In the second quarter a Skyboy tripped, and his cannon fired directly over our bench. "Don't touch it, don't touch any of it!" said a man in a suit.

We all stepped away as money floated down, all of us except Henry. He stood at the fifty-yard line, staring up at the falling money as the Skygirls and Skyboys frantically collected it. Then Henry held out his overturned helmet, catching the dollar bills as they descended upon him like snowflakes. We all laughed, then cheered him on as he wandered out onto the field holding his helmet, catching money. When the falling had stopped and the money was collected, Henry approached me holding his helmet out, he'd collected seven dollars. Then the man in the suit hurried to us and pulled the money out of Henry's helmet. I swear I saw him stuffing it in his pockets as he walked away.

Wally

....

THE NEW BASTILLE

i.

Tribehondo@GarrBeast: As an outsider, what do you think of the human race? Dion's gonna run up the score on your fat ass next season.

Aggie4life@Tribehondo: If I wanted to kill myself I'd climb up Dion McAres' ego and jump down to his IQ. McAres won't live through the game.

THE BASTILLE FLAG above the Performance Center fluttered in the strong breeze like it was the only living thing on campus and I stared at it from our dorm in a passive state. Classes were a week off and we had nowhere to go. We spent less than a day back in West Temple; Marshall and Dyson had left town, and Papa's BBQ went out of business. The only familiarity was the back of the Minister's hand as he called us out for our achievements like they were a direct threat to his own relevance.

I hated myself for letting him beat us. When we were young, I had no choice. As I grew, I realized the imprint in my mind was beyond my control and we suffered his antics with dread that was more chemical reaction than will. But I could control where we were, and before he woke up the next day, Henry and I were on the bus back to Bastille.

There was no one to tell and nowhere to go. I tried to rationalize not quitting by thinking it would disappoint Aunt Janie and the Professor, but the truth was different: I was hooked, and when we received notice of the first team meeting with our new coach it gave me a point on the horizon to stare at through the Bastille flag. Then it was time for the meeting, and it felt like a safety bar had been lowered over us, locking us in.

Henry and I took our usual seats in the top row of the team meeting room and as the room filled, I took notice of the pace and volume of people entering. There were far more than at the end of the last season but nearly twenty guys were injured then. Not in attendance: Evan, Carter Schultz, Scott Matthews, Jake Sanfilippo, Simba, Malibu, and the other seniors.

The new guys were easy to identify even if I didn't see their faces; they didn't head for a seat immediately, they lingered as they looked for an open seat that would be theirs for good. About half still belonged in high school, but somehow they graduated in December so they could enroll early and take part in the full off-season. The rest were transfers from junior colleges, jucos, a source that was new to Bastille, and they were easy to pick out. They had a layer of muscle difficult for a high school senior to achieve without an extra year or two in a juco program. Their demeanor conveyed a level of disregard, not the fresh hope of someone who'd never left home before.

Someone spoke in my ear loud enough for Eddie to hear. "Dion just told Sports Inc. that he doesn't deserve to start anymore, he's going to backup Wally Hestia, the true star of the Tribe." It was Tony. Eddie held his hand to his mouth as he giggled in delight.

"It's about time," I said.

"Henry, are you ready?" Tony said. Henry didn't look up from his phone. "The Nuber!" Tony said with quiet exuberance.

Henry looked up at nothing. "I am the Nuber." Then he dropped his view back to his phone.

Tony and Eddie exchanged high fives as they giggled. "I love it, Henry, and I love you, buddy. That never gets old."

An angry voice called out from the front of the room, telling us to take our seats. Players hurried in from the hallway, confused and looking at the clock that indicated we had another five minutes.

"Goddammit, take a fucking seat now, I don't care if it's on the floor." The speaker was tall, thin, and bald, his voice pierced the din with a quick cadence that made me feel like there wasn't a speck of self-doubt in him. Players quickly sat in the closest open space and waited for him to continue.

"My name is Sly Ellington, I'm the new Director of Football Operations. I'll make this easy, if you're not five minutes early, you're late, and you don't want to be late, trust me. Next, if I call you, text you, or slap you upside the head there's only two reasons to not respond immediately: The first is that you're talking to Coach Castritt and the second is that you're dead. Clear? Good, maybe you guys aren't that stupid after all."

Sly was completely different than Randy, our old DFO. Randy made us feel like he was everyone's personal valet; there wasn't an issue he couldn't help with, there wasn't a time he wasn't available, and we were only a small part of his job. I had no idea where he went, I don't even remember seeing him on the plane after the Sky Bowl.

Sly looked up and waved in the assistant coaches, there had to be twice as many as Coach Oldham had. They descended the side auditorium stairs of the meeting room in line wearing identical Tribe polo shirts. Coach Dixon, the only holdover from Coach Oldham's staff, was in the middle. They came to a stop and stood against the far wall. Coach Dixon used to speak as much as Coach Oldham, he always wore a pullover windbreaker or a sleeveless workout shirt, but now, with his matching polo shirt amid the horde of new coaches—I stopped counting after twenty—he looked like just another coach.

Sly continued. "For everything directly related to football and training, you turn to one of these gentlemen. For everything else in your life, you turn to me." As he spoke, he turned his index finger towards himself revealing a disturbing grin. "If you have any issues, and I mean any, you turn to me. Here are some examples: academics, nutrition, tutors, intrusive fans, out-of-line boosters, women—both young and old—professors, administrators, law enforcement—both campus and city—and journalists, especially journalists, or anyone else who will take your focus off the reason you're here. Now let's talk about off-the-field distractions. No matter where you are, what time it is, or what situation you find yourself in, you call me. Not mommy or daddy, not your girlfriend, never a lawyer, you call me. Is that clear?"

We all responded with obedient silence. As Sly continued I looked over to Coach Dixon, his arms were folded, his face hard. I wondered why he was still here; every other assistant from Coach Oldham's staff went on to other programs, drawing on Coach O's vast network across the country. I swallowed hard and listened to Sly give us instructions on our new way of life.

There were a lot of changes, and Sly was at the center of each. Everyone was scheduled to meet with the new team nutritionist, the rumor was that we'd have to log our food intake and sleep patterns into some database. A new workout program for each player was introduced, we all received new academic advisors that reported to Sly then he gave us an overview of academic courses that were now available online. All our contacts and social media feeds had to be logged into another database as well as our daily schedule. I looked for Dion in the front row; he had the same look as Coach Dixon.

"Now, for those of you who haven't met him, I'd like to introduce our new leader, Coach Castritt."

I didn't notice Coach Castritt sitting in front, I would've recognized him immediately. He'd been Coach of the Year in the Big 12 and the Pac 12, won the Rose Bowl twice, plus the Fiesta as well as a of bunch other bowl games. He'd been on the sidelines for decades until he'd retired two years before and taken a network studio job. His natural charisma and hardened persona made him a perfect fit for television and the media was surprised when he took over for us. "This is the only job I'd come out of retirement for," he said at the introductory press conference.

As much as we'd grown accustomed to Coach Oldham's celebrity, Coach Castritt's was different. Coach O was homespun, he avoided attention; Coach Castritt was made for it, lights popped up wherever he went. His celebrity was ubiquitous, I saw pictures of him with politicians, movie stars, and icons of every sport. He was a former lineman at Texas and he played in the NFL for seven years. His dark hair, broad, jowled face, and oversized frame were unmistakable; you could pick him out of a crowd just by looking at his silhouette.

Coach Castritt stood at the podium and took a deep breath, his nostrils flaring, his face bitter. He slowly scanned the room, making eye contact with each one of us, but it was more than that. I held my breath as his view swept over Henry and me. He remained silent; an awkward surprise that became unsettling. There wasn't even the sound of guys stirring in their seats; not a cough, not a breath, only focus on our new coach, a focus the tension of which grew with each passing moment. As we waited, I wanted to glance at the others and see if their reaction was the same, but I didn't dare take my eyes off Coach Castritt.

Then, a single pair of hands started clapping. It was Sly. The assistant coaches caught on and joined in, but we didn't until Sly stood, turned to us, and clapped until we understood. We responded in kind, clapping as the volume increased as if we were making up for our unsophisticated silence. It went on, and I could feel my palms turn red. There wasn't a natural conclusion, the awkward feeling returned as we continued clapping and the silence seemed long ago. Someone noticed Sly giving another obvious hint, the hint to stand. Like a wave starting at the front of the room and ascending to the back, we stood, our applause even louder, like we were trying to find an out-of-reach peak.

Then, someone in the middle let out a celebratory scream like we'd won an important game. It was a new guy, he had to be a juco transfer. He was huge with blond hair in a ponytail and tattoos covering both arms. He raised a fist as he jumped up and down and let out a blood-curdling scream and a subtle smile crossed Coach Castritt's face. More screams came, they punctuated the applause until the screams themselves battled the clapping hands for attention. Heads bobbed up and down in front, guys were bouncing on their feet, clapping and screaming. I turned to Henry to make sure he was taking part and was struck with amazement: His phone was in his pocket and his hands were clapping as loud as anyone.

A rhythm took over and I could feel adrenaline pour into my veins. The clapping was louder, tight, and in time with the voices that turned from screams into guttural woofs at a volume that had never been reached in the auditorium before. We peaked like animals, held in place by thin awareness as euphoria filled us. Moments ago, our bodies were calm, even dead compared to the state we'd entered. And all Coach Castritt did was stand in front of us.

And then it stopped. Coach Castritt raised his hands and we instinctively knew. "Be seated," he said and we all sat with a collective thump. Coach Castritt took his time, he didn't have notes; it was like he was giving us a moment to absorb who was before us. Finally, he spoke.

"Attitude," he said as his familiar baritone voice carved hard through the echoes. "Of all the attributes you need to be successful in my program, attitude is the most important." He paused again letting his words sink in. "There are seven key factors for an elite program and the most important is attitude. If you don't have the right one, we fail. If you have the right attitude, we will have the opportunity for the ultimate success."

As Coach Castritt spoke I had to remind myself that I wasn't watching this on television.

"The first key factor is talent. There will be some incoming freshmen over the summer, but other than that, the talent in this room is what we have. The second is training and conditioning—if you don't train and develop your talent with an attitude of wild hunger, you're not going to make it."

Coach Castritt listed out the other key factors giving examples and directives for each. Fundamentals, the offensive and defensive scheme, game planning, and execution. "You'll notice I don't count luck as a key factor because we can't control it. The only way to address uncontrollable factors, such as luck, is to be better than our opponents even when they have luck on their side. How do we do this? Attitude, the only thing that you can control and is the source for how well all the other factors play into our success. I'll tell you this, gentlemen, you may be in this room due to talent, but you'll only stay because of attitude."

I felt hope in his words, attitude was the only thing I've ever had. By the end of Coach Castritt's talk, grief was no longer our dominant emotion, although I couldn't define the new one. It was like wearing new clothes you hadn't yet seen in the mirror. When he released us, half the team headed directly for the weight room.

At dinner that night, all we talked about was Coach Castritt. Our reservations had been eased, until Jeremy mentioned the mandatory drug tests; he'd been the only one to read all the new team rules.

"How long does it take to get it out of your system?" Eddie asked.

"Two weeks if you hydrate," Jeremy said. "Thirty days, max. I looked it up."

"Two weeks? When's the first test?"

"Half the team will get busted."

"The Nuber will be the only one left."

"There's a lot of new guys," I said.

"Don't bring it up," Eddie said.

I looked at Eddie, trying to understand his concern.

"Eighty-five," he said. "We got eighty-five scholarships to work with. Eleven seniors are leaving but they're bringing in nine jucos from God knows where and a whole bunch of freshmen. There ain't enough room on the boat if you get my drift."

The next morning, I woke with one thought: *I've got to get in front of Coach Castritt.* After my workout I stopped by the football office but didn't enter, the foyer was crowded and my intuition told me to try later. Then it became a routine; after working out I'd pass by and each time there was a crowd—one time a network crew had arrived for an interview, another time there were men and women in power suits anxiously waiting. Even when the foyer was clear, the sound of voices approaching around the corner spooked me. Then I received a text from Sly: *Stop by at 2:30 today.* I had just gotten out of the shower after working out and had fifteen minutes.

Sly didn't look up when I knocked on his open door, just a signal with his finger. I sat for several minutes as he typed away on his computer, then he took a call. It must've been from a booster, the tone of his voice was accommodating; access to Coach Castritt was promised, a number was written down. When he was ready for me, he focused with attention I suddenly didn't want.

"Tell me about your brother," he said.

I hesitated, not knowing what to say. "He's a great kicker, he was perfect last year with a long of—"

"I know his stats," Sly said with a trace of impatience. "Tell me about *him*." He folded his arms and leaned back in his chair.

"We're really close, I mean, we've been together forever." I could tell Sly wasn't satisfied. "He's doing fine in school, everybody likes him. He's just super shy."

"He's special, isn't he? Has he ever been diagnosed?"

I looked down and shook my head. "No, sir."

"And don't give me that bullshit about him doing fine in school. I know you and your pals carried him last year." He stared at me, waiting for admission.

"That's not true, I helped with some things. You don't know that."

Sly quickly leaned forward, his glare held my attention in a way I didn't dare shake. "First of all, I know everything. If not in the moment, then soon enough. Second, there's not a goddamn chance your brother would survive a single class here and we both know it. Let me get this right, he only kicks when you hold? Is that how you got yourself on this team?"

I felt exposed. "The reason he's never been diagnosed, our father, his father—"

"You're adopted, right?" he said.

I nodded. "Are you going to kick us off the team?"

Sly chuckled softly in a mocking tone. "Let's see. He was perfect last season with a long of sixty-one yards from the left hash and you held every time without screwing up. You're a walk-on and you played scout team QB last year. You have a 3.9 GPA, a spotless record and have never missed a workout. I think we can make room for a couple of boy scouts."

"Then what do you want to know?"

"You've already answered it for me, but there is one hitch. You can't do his homework for him anymore and you can't take the same classes. There's too many snoops around here, there's already been rumors." I must've look astonished. "You're a kid, you don't know how this works. He's already been assigned new classes and he has his own tutor. Can he get to classes on his own?"

I started to panic. "You can't separate us, he'll—"

Sly held his hand up and I knew not to say another word. "Now, can he get to his classes on his own?"

I took a breath and looked down. "Not the first couple of times. When he's in a routine he's fine," I said.

"Good, we'll have him escorted for the first week." Sly looked back to his computer and began typing. After a few moments he looked back to me. "We're done, get the fuck out."

I picked up my backpack and withdrew from his office. The foyer was empty, save for the new receptionist and a young woman. The receptionist gave me a quick smile, but I was distracted by the girl waiting at the front desk, she was beautiful. Instead of leaving I took a seat, pretending I had further business. I pulled out my phone and opened the Sports Inc. app. When I first walked through the foyer to meet with Sly, I was preoccupied, I hadn't noticed the changes.

A large, green marble arrowhead spanned the length of the floor. It was new, the arrow was inlaid into white marble, trimmed in yellow, and its shine made me squint. Glass and chrome and dark, polished wood. The rumor was three offices were merged into one to accommodate Coach Castritt, they even added a private bathroom. They must've done it while we were at the Sky Bowl; I never saw a construction worker, a paint brush, or a speck of dust.

She shifted her weight and I slowly looked up from my phone, my eyes discretely following the path over the marble floor until her black high heels came into view. I'd never seen her before; I couldn't stop stealing glances. My view ascended her legs, perfectly shaped, encased in tan stockings, then her skirt. When she leaned onto the front desk, her hips shifted, filling out her skirt in a way I'd never seen.

"There she is." The familiar voice froze me, I didn't look. "Cyrus, this here is Nicole, she's your hostess for the weekend," Coach Castritt said. Cyrus Mathison, a juco All-American linebacker had offers from top programs a year ago, but had needed a stint in junior college to get his grades up.

"Now, Cyrus, I'd like you to take your time and really immerse yourself in all things Bastille. Nicole is our top hostess; she'll show you around this weekend and make sure you see everything we have to offer. You have my number; we'll meet again tomorrow morning. Coach Dixon will be here, too."

I tried to keep my head down, but I couldn't help myself. I watched Cyrus and Nicole exit the foyer; Coach Castritt did, too. Then he turned to me, holding my stare. His pleasant demeanor was vacant, a near-scowl replacing it. I struggled to talk but words wouldn't come. When he turned back towards his office, I dropped my head and exhaled, then got up to leave.

In the middle of the quad, Nicole was standing with Cyrus the recruit, looking at a piece of paper. She pointed to Masters Library, then looked back to the paper. It wasn't on my way, but I couldn't help myself. As I got closer, I saw it was a campus map, she was giving him the layout. I approached and introduced myself and I could tell they both recognized me from the football offices.

Nicole smiled and ran her fingers through her silky auburn hair, positioning it behind her ear. I was stunned. Bastille had its share of hot girls, but I'd never seen anything like her, and I reminded myself to look at her eyes, not her large chest. She smiled and chatted, including me in the conversation like they'd been waiting for me all along.

"We're looking for the new multi-media center; I think it's by the Student Union and the big fountain," she said. Then she introduced Cyrus, he was at least six-foot-four and had to weigh 250 pounds. He looked me over then asked if I was on the team; he seemed disappointed when I said yes.

"It just so happens I'm going right by there." She mouthed "thank you" out of Cyrus's view. I continued, "The fountain is called Prisoners' Fountain, the water signifies flowing knowledge, and if you come to Bastille, you'll imprison it in your mind."

"That is so cool," said Nicole. Cyrus didn't respond. I made it up, I had no idea where they got the name, but I didn't think Cyrus was the type to investigate.

I led them through the student union, the dining hall where students ate, and over to the multi-media center. "You've got to see Masters Library, even if you don't study there, the architecture is amazing."

"I just love beautiful architecture," Nicole said.

"Seriously, man, what about classes and shit?" Cyrus said.

I thought about it for a moment and then gave it a dismissive shrug. Cyrus seemed relieved and turned his attention back to Nicole's chest.

"I just love it here," she said. "There's no place like Bastille."

"I agree," I said. "What year are you in?"

She paused. "I'm kind of between majors right now."

"That's the thing, the school has so much to offer that the hardest part is figuring out what to major in," I said.

"That's absolutely right," Nicole said.

I described my favorite parts of campus, the best places to study, and the weekend hotspots. "I just love the Parthenon," she said. Mostly she listened, asked a few questions, and giggled at my attempt at a joke. Cyrus seemed distant, then agitated; he didn't try to hide looking at her like she was prey.

"One more thing, Cyrus. The women here are all smart, beautiful, and classy," I said then looked at Nicole. "Some more than others."

"Thank you, so much, you are so sweet." She touched my hand as Cyrus's eyes fell to her chest again. He ignored me when I said goodbye but I didn't care, I was looking at the spot on my hand where she touched me.

▼ ▼ ▼

For the first time in my life I was free, and I didn't like it; Henry's new routine took shape almost immediately after I met with Sly. It was almost a naked feeling, and any enjoyment was eaten away worrying about Henry. After my workouts, I'd play video games with Tony and Eddie or hang out with normal students listening to Tony talk up the girls or throw them passes as they worked on their routes. Sometimes I'd run routes for Dion. Henry and I would talk at night before he went to sleep.

"Do you like your classes?" I said.

"Yes," Henry said. "Craig tells me what to do." I asked Craig about him and learned more about Craig's background than Henry's new routine. He'd majored in sports management and wanted to be an athletic director. I asked him how Henry was doing.

"It's like I'm an undergrad all over again," Craig said.

"Isn't Henry learning anything?" I said.

"It's easier if I do it myself, but it's risky. If anyone outside the program knew what we're doing we'd be in deep shit. That's just for this semester, though. Sly's working on a different approach."

Later that night, watching TV, I looked at Henry staring at his phone. I could still feel the connection, but I was troubled that I couldn't tell his mood.

"Do you miss spending time with me?" I asked.

Henry looked up. "Yes. I want to get pizza at Vic's," he said.

"We'll go tomorrow after our workout."

▼ ▼ ▼

Even during the afternoon lull, Vic's was still half full. We took a seat in a booth at the far end and looked at the menu on the paper place mat in front of us. I pulled my wallet out to check our cash, just a few dollars. "One slice, Henry, one slice of cheese pizza."

A waitress approached. "I'm just going to get a slice from the counter," I said. Truth was, I didn't have tip money and felt bad about taking up a table. At the counter there was one slice on the pan, big, but dried up. The waitress was back at our table, and I thought Henry must be ordering a soda. When I got to the booth someone was in my seat and my jaw must've been open as I sat next to Henry, I couldn't believe it was her. I slid the slice of pizza in front of Henry and stared.

"Now, that looks appetizing," she said. It was sarcastic, but I didn't think it was directed at me. Samantha Yardley of Sports Inc. wore her hair pulled back in a ponytail, covered by a baseball cap, and a light jacket. She took her time looking over the menu, completely unaware.

"It's Henry, right? You said onions, sausage, pepperoni, and extra cheese?" She looked to the waitress. "A large, please. One check."

I sat back in the booth trying to pour all my hatred and disbelief into her without speaking. She unfolded a napkin and placed it in her lap.

"Lighten up, Mr. Nobody. That's John Q. Nobody, right?" she said. "I have to admit, I caught a lot of shit about that. So, tell me Henry, how is school going?"

"You've got some nerve coming here and sitting down with us," I said.

She was looking in Henry's direction then turned to me. "I didn't come here looking for you, I'm in town for the basketball game, tomorrow. Don't get your hopes up, Duke is going to smoke your boys."

"You can't buy us pizza, it's against NCAA rules," I said.

"Please." She dismissed my comment. "Look at it this way, I'm probably not going to finish it. Then, it'll be garbage. Garbage is free. I don't think the NCAA is watching."

"Right, then you'll write an article telling how you personally saw us violating the rules," I said.

"I'm after bigger fish, don't worry."

"Then why are you bothering us?"

She rested her chin on her hand as she looked at me. Her face seemed worn; she was probably younger than she looked.

"Let's just say I'm looking for sources for a story I'm doing."

"How can you even talk to me after what you did to Dion?"

Henry pulled out his phone and started playing his numbers game; he wouldn't hear a word.

"Don't give me that bullshit, Dion and all you guys know what you're getting into." She pointed to Henry. "What's going on with him? Is he even here?" She looked to Henry. "Henry, do you know a lot of people would be interested in hearing your story? Henry?"

I almost panicked. "You want to write about Henry? There's no way."

He looked up to her, then me. I nodded letting him know it was okay to focus on his phone.

"Wow." She sat back in the booth. "Seriously, I'd really like to get to know you guys."

I wanted to send Henry to another table; I wanted to humiliate her. "There's no way in the world you're getting close to us; I'll call our DFO and you'll get banned."

"You mean Sly, that scumbag? Castritt's fixer? I could tell you stories about those two."

"You don't even get it. What you did to Dion and Garr was disgusting, they grew up together and now there's nothing but bad blood, and you created it out of nothing." I sensed a pause in her, I was surprised. The day after her quote had been published, Garr responded.

> *GarrBeast @TribeMcAres: Nice loss to GT, maybe*
> *a little D would save your ass*

Dion responded the same day.

> *TribeMcAres @GarrBeast: Just keepin it real, my*
> *boys are all we need*

> *GarrBeast @TribeMcAres: You gonna need more*
> *than that when I whip your ass next year*

The internet picked up on it immediately. It seemed the world knew their intertwined life story and playing out their torn friendship on social media enhanced the drama. After Coach Oldham died, it got worse.

> *GarrBeast @TribeMcAres: What you gonna do*
> *without your tribe daddy? Suck your thumb? RIP*
> *Coach O*

> *TribeMcAres @GarrBeast: Coach O was the greatest*
> *coach in history, never be another one like him. No*
> *matter who takes over we always play for coach O*
> *at the great Bastille, not some podunk farmer college*

It was like a flash flood had rolled through two campuses and their fan bases; Arkansas A&M had never been a rival until the Twitter war took over. The athletic directors of both schools stepped in and let Dion and Garr know it had gone far enough, but the partisans of each side kept the feud burning outside campus walls.

"You have to admit, what you did was awful," I said.

She looked away for a moment then settled back in. "It's part of the game, you have no idea what they want. I promise, let me get to know you guys and I'll write something great about you."

"That's why you sat down with us? You can't, I'm not talking to you about my brother, ever. Even if I wanted to, you'd have to tell the world about what you did to Dion before I agreed."

She shook her head in a mocking way. "First of all, I don't need your permission. I can go to West Temple and ask all the questions I want. Just this little non-conversation with him and your defensiveness is enough, so don't tell me what I can and can't do. Believe me, you're not the reason I'm here. It's not Bastille's basketball team, either."

I looked over to Henry, he was absorbed in his phone. Other patrons in the dining room didn't pay us any attention, but I looked around anyway.

"Don't worry," she said. "No one knows it's me and I'm not sure they know who you are. It'd be nice to keep it that way, wouldn't it? I mean, given the condition of your brother."

"What do you want?" I said.

"Castrict. He's a son of a bitch. This is the story: Let's compare the old Bastille to the new. You've lived through a season with Oldham."

"That's another thing," I said. "Why did you go after Coach O?"

"I'll explain it when you're older. For now, think about it, the Bastille program is about to go through the biggest change in its history. I'll admit, I was a bitch to Oldham and—"

"And a bitch to Dion."

"Obviously. But the man was a saint. Wouldn't it be interesting to see the differences? You know about Castritt, don't you?"

"Sure, coach of the year at two different schools, all those bowl games then he was on TV."

She smiled with the delight of deep secrets. "You have no idea what you're in store for. He's the ultimate CEO coach, he loves the few, hates the many. He'll drive the living shit out of everyone in the program until he gets what he wants. Coach Oldham made, what? A half million a year and felt so awful about it he and his wife gave most of it back to the school. Castritt's salary is six million, before incentives. But, since that's not enough, the boosters are buying him a three-million-dollar house. I didn't even know there are houses that expensive down here."

"That's insane, how can we pay him that much?"

"Are you kidding? Half his salary is paid by the boosters out of their little kitty. Don't worry, the One Tribe Club has over a quarter billion in assets; they can afford it. He's been on TV the last two years; do you want to know why he left football? At his last school he was given a multimillion-dollar severance package and when we looked into it, both he and the school said they mutually parted ways on good terms. You know why? The rumor is that he was banging the wife of the school president. It was too uncomfortable for him to stay and too embarrassing to say why."

I looked on in disbelief.

"If he likes you, and there won't be many, you're fine. If he doesn't, you're screwed. Has he found his first victim?"

"No."

"It'll be soon. Let me guess, he's opened the doors and brought in a ton of jucos and new freshmen. I'll bet some of the vets are a little worried. Has he rolled out the drug test?" I nodded. "That's beautiful, almost genius. Declaring to the world his virtuous outlook by doing everything he can to prevent his players from using drugs, when, in fact, it's a convenient way to get rid of marginal players. Not a single starter will get busted, just the guys he doesn't like that are using up a valuable scholarship. You better tell your buddies to knock off the weed. Then again, Castritt will get them one way or another."

"I don't believe you, he's not Coach Oldham but he's not like you're saying. If he was, Bastille wouldn't have hired him."

She leaned in with a condescending smile. "You are adorable, where were you when I was in college?" I didn't respond. "Look, I'm sorry about the past, I've got my own pressures, but this is a real issue. Oldham deserved every bit of praise for doing things the right way and Castritt is going to use this place to enrich his name and his wallet and destroy everything that gets in his way. If you help me, I'll never reveal the source, but I've got to have someone on the inside."

The pizza arrived, Samantha paid, and then asked for a box. She took a single slice.

"This is still my team, you're asking me to be a traitor."

"No, I'm not. Just let me know what the reality is. This is big, you never know, maybe someday I can help you. That's how this works, think about it." She stood and started to walk away.

"Before you go, one thing." I waited until she got close. "Maybe I'll do it, just to show you're wrong, but first, you have to do something. You have to tell the world what really happened with Dion; you have to say that you twisted his words."

She nodded with a smile and looked away for a moment. "It won't do any good, but, yes, I'll see if they'll let me. But that means you help me with this or the world's going to learn about you and your brother."

▼ ▼ ▼

The gray bar was a foot above me as I laid flat on the bench. Bench presses, the football litmus test. Rap music thumped away as I tried to focus: breathe deep, unrack the bar, drop it smoothly, and pour all my strength into my hands, arms, and chest. The day before Eddie and I watched Cyrus and another new linebacker, Hunter Devlin, each bench 405 pounds for a set of three. I was shooting for a new personal max—205 pounds.

Eddie spotted me, helped as I unracked the bar, and waited as I stared at it suspended above my head. My feet were planted and my back was arched as the bar descended with control. As soon as it touched my chest, I drove it up, trying to keep my butt on the bench. It went up cleaner than I expected.

"Strong, do another," Eddie said.

It came down again and I drove it with my eyes closed but this time it wasn't as clean. But it was all me.

"One more," Eddie said.

The drop, the drive, the struggle; the ascent was too easy. I opened my eyes and saw Eddie's hands helping, probably accounting for ten of the pounds, but it was all the difference in the world.

"Nice," Eddie said. I racked the bar and sat up, proud and embarrassed.

"New max?" Eddie said.

"Yeah, don't say it too loud. Pokey warms up with more than that."

"I can't do much more," he said.

"But you run a 4.5 forty."

I wiped off the bench and we headed to the far end for the quick lifts: hanging power cleans, snatches, power shrugs, and push presses. We'd already done speed work, upper body, and core exercises. I was thankful it wasn't leg day. We had to wait, the platforms for the quick lifts were all in use; Jeremy and another offensive lineman had just started their power cleans and I watched without looking obvious.

Jeremy stood on the platform taking deep breaths with his eyes closed and his hands pure white with chalk. He took another breath and lowered to one knee in front of the bar. Straps dangled from his wrists, he took his time affixing each to the bar, then clenching, rotating, and tightening. I added up the weight, 275 pounds not counting the clips.

He got into position: a full squat over the bar, his arms extending straight down, his back arched and his eyes staring forward and bulging from internal pressure. Then he slowly rose in a dead-lift, the bar hanging just above his knees. Veins rose in relief from his neck and his pale complexion turned red, making his curly blond hair seem almost bright yellow. There wasn't a relaxed muscle in him. Then he popped it. In a motion that was almost too quick to see, he exploded straight up. The bar moved maybe two feet, but Jeremy introduced enough kinetic energy into the weight to allow him to drop back into a full squat and catch it with his hands at shoulder level. With a final grunt he finished the lift, a full front squat to a standing position. Then he did it four more times.

"Damn," said Eddie. "That shit's for real."

"I know. I like to wait until these guys clear out before I lift my *tens* of pounds," I said.

Eddie laughed. "You seen Pokey squat the other day. I couldn't count the number of plates he had on the bar, we all just stopped and looked. Them new linebackers, too. Hunter something and Cyrus something."

"I met Cyrus, not real sociable. I can't believe they already got him in school," I said.

"Yeah, shit's different around here now," Eddie said.

"What do you mean?"

"You watch. Some stuff is better, some is worse, but it's definitely different. Know who's pissed off the most?" Eddie said. "Dion. Matter of fact, we were going to ask you to check it out, you being his boy and all."

"I've barely seen him."

"You track him down. Something ain't right."

It was another hour before we finished and I sat with a towel around my neck in front of my locker. Eddie was right, there was something different about Dion. His gait and his tone seemed clipped, it was that way ever since Coach Oldham died, and I'd assigned it to grief. I looked over to Dion's locker, it was empty.

A few more days passed and I only caught glimpses of Dion—at the dining hall, walking across campus, leaving the Performance Center with his head down. On Friday I worked out earlier than usual and when I returned to the locker room, I saw his street clothes hanging in his locker. I went back to the weight room to see if I missed him then the indoor practice field, but he wasn't there, either. I didn't want to go up to the third floor, the coaches' floor, but the meeting rooms were there. I passed by the coaches' offices with my head down trying to avoid contact and I almost ran into our new offensive coordinator.

"Fucking watch out," he said.

After he passed, I took note of the room he'd exited, the quarterback's meeting room. I approached slowly trying to hear Dion's voice, but it was silent. I stopped just shy of the doorframe and tried to breathe quietly, then took another step.

In the dark, Dion sat in the front seat, looking up at the screen that showed a play diagram, his silhouette not moving. A new diagram appeared every few seconds. I knocked on the door. Dion turned and held my stare for a moment, then nodded and I knew it was okay to enter. He continued flipping through plays and instead of talking I followed along. He went through twenty plays or so, then he stopped.

"You seeing it?" Dion said.

I nodded as I spoke: "Yeah, but what about the route trees?"

"Ain't no trees. Just options. I'll start from the beginning," he said.

As Dion flipped through the plays I leaned in and took note. Running this offense would be foreign to Dion, the equivalent of asking him to read a book in a different language. Instead of placing Dion at the center with all success dependent on him, he'd be a small cog with a limited role. It wasn't an offense with the complexity that only he could handle—multiple pass routes that gave him at least four different targets to throw to—it was an offense that required him to run the option, something he'd never done. The passing offense was simplistic, high school level; sprint draws where he'd run to one side with a single receiver as the target.

"Any seven step drops?" I said.

Dion shook his head. "Nope, this is like Nebraska in the '90s." He continued flipping through the plays, then reached the end and started again. In the darkened room I could see the small reflection of the plays on his eyes. He blinked occasionally as if to wipe them away.

"This can't be the whole offense," I said. "Castritt knows what you can do."

"Already met with him. Like oil and water, man, and I don't know why."

He kept flipping through the plays then, after some time, he turned off the projector. We sat in the darkened room, Dion's head was down, and I kept silent.

"Name one QB that's ever played for him that made it in the NFL," Dion said. My silence answered his question.

"Maybe Dixon can talk to him," I said.

Dion let out a bitter chuckle. "They already hate each other."

"There's got to be a way, people won't stand for it."

"My last year," Dion said. "I'm playing this year and I'm gone. With this offense, shit, I'll be a mid-rounder, maybe worse. Run, Dion, run."

▼ ▼ ▼

The bullhorn sounded from across the indoor practice field, far enough away that it should've been nothing more than a nuisance. Instead, all of us, well over a hundred, strained to listen as we gasped for air.

"You were ten and three last year, and if it wasn't for a handful of lucky plays, you would've been seven and six." Coach Castritt's voice, electric through the bullhorn, was our pulse. With my eyes closed and body shedding sweat, I waited for the next whistle. It came, sharp and quick, triggering a drive of energy we were told existed but didn't believe. Don't come in last.

Speed didn't matter, effort did. I sprinted the fifty-three yards across the field, touched the white sideline, then sprinted back. I'd lost count after a dozen. The sharp whistle blew for the linemen, their feet pounding the turf was like a dull static.

"There he is, that sonofabitch, that's twice you're doing this to me!" Castritt said.

At the far end of the field a body was slumped onto the turf, the sprint half accomplished. The dim lights and sweat in my eyes prevented me from making out who it was, I hoped it wasn't Jeremy.

"Send that lard ass to the shed! You show up to my workouts out of shape, hungover, or both, and you'll spend the whole goddamn season in there."

This was Castritt's second visit to voluntary conditioning. The strength coaches pushed us the other times, and when they sensed resistance Castritt was invoked. "Just wait until he runs conditioning, you'd be wishing you worked harder now." They were right.

"Everybody stop and look, watch him head for the shed," Coach Castritt said. I still couldn't tell who it was, but a feeling welled up: I was grateful it wasn't me. "The only time success comes before work is in the dictionary," Castritt screamed. "But half of you probably don't even know what a dictionary is."

We ran one more sprint and it was over. Some collapsed, some took a knee, I laid down on the artificial turf and closed my eyes and I heard him one more time. "Championship teams don't rely on luck, they outwork everyone else." I don't know how long I laid there; we were oblivious to each other. A string of my own words played through my head, filling empty cells: *I can outwork anyone.*

After a minute, I opened my eyes and sat up and made the walk to the locker room, which seemed longer than usual. I turned the dial on my locker to seven, then reversed to twenty-two, then back again to thirteen. It wouldn't open. I tried it again. In the open portion of my locker someone else's jeans and shirt were hung, and strange shoes were in the bottom with someone else's Tribe backpack. I tried the combination a third time, it didn't work. I reached down to the backpack to see the name, and, just as I touched it, a forearm struck me from behind pinning me to the locker. A hand jammed my head against the locker's frame, I couldn't move.

"What the fuck are you doing in my locker, bitch?" Someone snickered off to the side.

"This was my locker, it used to be," I said.

I was pushed to the side, then fell over a chair. The sparse movement in the locker room stopped, I could feel everyone looking at me. Hunter Devlin stood above me with his hands on his hips, his glare was hard, and I knew to stay down. The snickering to my left had turned into a taunting laugh; it was Cyrus.

"Yo, bitch, find someplace else, like another sport, you pussy," Cyrus said. I turned to him and caught a glance before looking down and gathering myself. Hunter Devlin, the juco transfer, stood over me. After another moment when he knew I wouldn't challenge, tension released and he tied his long blond hair in a ponytail as I stared at the tattoos that covered both his arms.

"That's enough!" I looked over my shoulder, Sly happened by and intervened. "Hestia, get your ass up, your locker is over here." I stood without looking at them, trying to ignore their quiet giggles. Sly waited for me at the far end of the locker room.

"You and your brother are sharing a locker, we're over capacity," Sly said. "Here's the combo, and don't fuck with those guys."

Cyrus Mathison and Hunter Devlin, our two new inside linebackers. Dion was the only one they showed deference to, the rest of us were judged and abused in their presence. If Dion was present, I breathed easier and stayed close. If he wasn't and I crossed paths with Cyrus or Hunter, I braced for taunts and planned an exit. It was a miracle they didn't bother Henry, but I'd happily absorb their abuse for him.

Our old linebackers, Scott Matthews and Jake Sanfilippo, were seniors, they had played their last game. Neither expected to get drafted and they weren't invited to the NFL combine, but they kept on training for pro day just to say they got a look. The scouts showed up, but they were only interested in a defensive back. Andre Decker watched as he stood with the aid of his crutches, he was damaged goods. Almost as a courtesy they watched Evan kick and put Scott and Jake through a workout. Coach Dixon spoke on their behalf, talking up their football smarts and high motors in a vain effort to offset their forty times and bench reps. Cyrus and Hunter stood off to the side whispering and smiling at the performance. As the workout went on, their voices rose.

"They may not be big, but they're slow," said Hunter. Cyrus cracked up and they exchanged high fives. Coach Dixon shot them a look and they eventually left.

▼ ▼ ▼

"I can't stand them," Tony said. He looked over his shoulder at the far table in the dining hall where Hunter and Cyrus sat, laughing too loud, commenting on everyone that passed.

"Spring practice is going to be a bitch if I'm the scout team again," said Eddie. "You sure you want to be the scout team QB again?"

"Absolutely, QBs are off limits," I said. "Henry, hurry up, I've got to meet the Professor."

"Not what I hear," Tony said. "Full contact on the scout team, even the QBs."

"I've got to go, but I don't want Henry to get abused. Can one of you walk him out?"

"They're leaving," said Eddie. A sigh of relief came over the table, we didn't look at each other.

Even if I sprinted across campus, I'd be late. The Professor wouldn't mind, he didn't wear a watch, but I wanted to show courtesy. Even so, I waited another minute to let Hunter and Cyrus clear out.

Outside, I hurried to a jog then a car pulled up next to me. The windows were tinted and I didn't pay attention until one rolled down.

"You need a ride?" Her voice brought me to a standstill. Nicole removed her sunglasses and unlocked the door. "You look like you're in a hurry."

I tried not to stutter. "A ride would be great."

Like unspoiled land, her car was precious and I sat carefully, buckling the seatbelt gently. Her smile made me look away. I thanked her weakly and told her where I was headed. To her, a casual moment, a costless favor; to me, a moment of grace.

"I'll never figure out the campus streets, there are more gates and one-way streets than I've ever seen," she said.

"Make a right up here."

"Are you looking forward to spring practice? I heard the team is going to be awesome this year, I can't wait," she said.

"There's a lot of new players, we'll see," I said.

"Will that hurt your chances to play?"

I let out an embarrassed laugh. "Not really, I just hold for field goals and extra points. I'm not like the rest of these guys."

She glanced at me and I didn't know what to make of it. When she looked to the left, I closed my eyes in shame. *Ask her something! Where does she live? Who does she hang out with? Was she in a sorority?* The distance was too short, I could see the Professor's building a block ahead. I had only one chance, a moment that would pass and be gone forever. She pulled into an empty spot and turned to me as the engine hummed. I breathed in another soft wisp of her perfume. This was my chance, *say anything.*

"So, how many miles do you have on this car?" I said. She seemed puzzled. "I mean it's a really nice car."

She looked at the odometer then back at me. "Twenty-two thousand. Thanks, I don't drive it much. Is this the right place?"

As her car pulled away, the sweet pulse of nerves in my stomach evaporated. I closed my eyes and tried to smell her perfume, but it was gone, and my memory was no help. I turned towards the building and rubbed the back of my hand on the spot she touched when she said goodbye.

The Professor was seated on a bench next to his building, his arms relaxed, his legs crossed. He reached his hand into a brown paper bag, retrieved a wrapped sandwich, opened it, and took a bite. Masters Library was in the distance, its Gothic architecture framed the Professor, portraying him in his element. The same scene in a public park, without knowledge of who he was, would've made me feel like I'd come across someone without purpose, maybe retired or out of work. I wouldn't see the peace he carried, the indifference to status. I took my time enjoying his subtle pleasure, it was something I wanted to feel but not ruin. I called to him when I was ten feet away.

"Well, well. My former advisee still has time for me," he said.

"More like the other way around."

His red sweater was buttoned to the top, only the white collar of his buttoned-down shirt was exposed. Tan shoes made of faux leather and blue corduroy pants; it was like someone dressed him in the morning for school. Only his hair moved in the light breeze. He offered me a sandwich.

"I told Mary we were meeting for lunch, she made you a sandwich. Do you like egg salad?"

I said that I did, but I didn't, and when I took a bite, the Professor laughed.

"Don't worry, I hate egg salad, too."

He offered me an apple, then small talk: He asked about my coursework, how the team was doing, the weather. Then silence. The Professor looked at nothing in particular, while I waited for the reason for my visit. I tried to ask him about his classes but I could tell he wasn't interested. After an uncomfortable silence he turned to me, his demeanor serious.

"I may have made a mistake asking you here today, I did it out of impulse. Nevertheless, I'm always glad to see you. Do you think you'll have time to stop by for dinner some evening?"

"Professor, is there something on your mind?"

He shook his head. "I'm sorry, in my zeal to get to the truth I've overlooked the bounds of propriety. I don't want to put you in a difficult spot."

"Is it a favor? I'll do anything. You've helped me so much."

He took a deep breath and leaned forward with his hands clasped. "I appreciate your offer. It's a simple question, really, something I've asked in the past." He paused as if to give me a chance to opt out. When I didn't move, he continued. "How's your brother doing academically?"

It was a question I didn't expect, but it should've been obvious, and I hesitated, trying to gather my thoughts. "He's struggling, but he's getting by. I help him, you know, like a tutor. I'm the only one that can really reach him, but he's doing the work." Lying to the Professor was easier than I thought, but I knew living with it would be harder.

The Professor seemed relieved; he patted my arm in support. "All right. You see, I don't mind football. I realize it's a significant part of the university and it's not going away, but it can't distort the larger mission here, there's too much at stake. I'm glad to hear your brother is performing, in fact I'm relieved beyond description that he's not the problem. The problem is what's being injected into the integrity of our academics going forward. There's a proposal for a new curriculum, a specialized program for rudimentary students. It's one thing if they cherry-pick courses from established programs, but quite another if entire majors are created that undermine the foundation of who we are. If this new curriculum is established, it will be a hollowing-out that will only expand."

"Is this new thing that bad?"

"By my estimation, a middle schooler wouldn't be challenged."

"I know it's not right, but who does it hurt if they let a few athletes take it. You don't know how hard they push us, and some of these guys couldn't do the work if they had nothing else going on."

"I know, it's the fundamental conflict of these major sports. At least one of them. But academic fraud comes with significant penalty, and I believe this new coaching staff hasn't had enough time yet to sink its teeth into the nooks and crannies of the school in order to work the system. They're not yet able to push guys through with a friendly phone call or a strategically subtle application of pressure; that was never done under John, and the academic staff here wouldn't accept it. Therefore, the easy answer is to lower the bar entirely by creating a curriculum sanctioned by the university that can shepherd through players. It's a brazen move, but these guys are pros."

"What are you going to do?"

"Let the process run its course. I've been asked to sit on a committee to review the curriculum. If it's as bad as I fear, we'll have to vote it down. You see it's not just a player we're talking about, it's the integrity of the institution. First, it's one player, then more, then other students. It will be like an aggressive can-cer that erodes what makes Bastille special. Nobel winners were trained here. Some of our nation's top leaders in business, politics, and law; people that shape our culture. Some, when interviewed, point back to their formative years at Bastille where the bar was so high, they didn't think they could make it, but then they did and they were special because of it. Do you realize the world is at a perpetual fork in the road? Everyone believes we're on an inevitable march towards classical liberal democracy, technologi-cal innovation, and economic productivity. But the truth is we're always on the precipice of sliding back into chaos. The only thing that binds us to the right path, the dynamic that provides com-munal enlightenment is education, the development of the mind. This is what I care about, and I'm compelled to do my part." I didn't know what to say, there was an awkward silence. "So, how is this new coach?"

I was relieved he changed the topic; I took a deep breath and felt my body sag. "It's definitely different. Under Coach Oldham, you felt like you were part of something special, now it's—I don't know how to say it."

"A tad evil?" the Professor said. I nodded in response. "There's been rumors about this new guy. Remember our discussion about tribalism? Just remember, it's all about becoming the dominant tribe, and one culture's sin is another culture's virtue. Tribes are all about victory, and if they achieve it, they'll look back and assess what means were required, point to them and then say—'that's our moral code.'"

▼ ▼ ▼

Thunder struck in the distance, I hurried to a jog to avoid the com-ing storm but knew I wouldn't make it. It was late and I worried about Henry, he'd been alone all night. The thunder sounded again, and I was surprised I'd heard it; a subtle cry against hard wind. At first, I thought it was an animal. I stopped before I reached the corner of the dorm and waited for a break in the gust.

"Please help." It froze me. Sobs followed, convulsing sobs; I stopped and retraced two steps. In the corner, through unkempt bushes, I saw parts of a small silhouette, maybe someone's head, rocking and heaving. My first reaction: run. I drew a shallow breath; my feet wouldn't move and my heart pounded. I reached into the bushes to clear a path as thorns dug into my hands and my feet sank into mud.

"Is someone there?" I pulled the sleeve of my sweatshirt over my hand and parted the tangled branches. In pale light I saw dark hair of a girl's head clenched to her knees, her body balled together, the only movement was the vibrations of her convulsions. Through sobs she pled, "Help me."

I moved in further. "Are you okay?" She didn't react, her body shook. I reached out and touched her arm and she recoiled in fear.

"You're not one of them, are you?" she said.

"I'm not, I'm not. Did someone hurt you?"

She continued to cry. I rose slightly to see if anyone was close then I crouched back down.

"It's going to rain, you can come inside."

She looked up through branches and screamed. "No!" Her eyes were red and nearly closed, her face was taut, I'd never seen terror in anyone's face before. "Don't take me in there."

My eyes adjusted to the light, she had a swollen lip and I noticed scratches on her hands.

"I won't hurt you, I'm not one of them. It's going to rain, I'll call security," I said.

She screamed again. "Not security! No police, they said they'd kill me." She buried her head deeper into her knees, sobbing and shuddering.

I didn't know what to do. "Can I call a friend? I don't have a car, I'll walk you."

Her convulsions took over, she couldn't speak, and I gave her time.

"I've called and no one answers." Her words were nearly inaudible. "I want to go home, please take me home."

"Where's home? I'll take you; do you live on campus?"

"Not here, not this place. I want to go home."

She wound herself tighter as it started to rain. I took off my sweatshirt. "Cover yourself with this, it'll keep you dry."

I placed the sweatshirt over her head and she seemed to exhale for a moment. She pulled the sweatshirt off to position it better and saw the front—"Bastille Football."

She lost it again. "You're one of them!"

She pushed it away into the bushes and mud, I knew I'd never wear it again. Rain fell, I felt weak and began to shiver.

"I'm not one of them. Let me help."

She raised her head; her face was ashen white and I could see in her eyes she'd been dehumanized. It was a small window of acceptance and I made the call as we stared at each other across a terrible void.

"Professor, I need your help, we need Mrs. Bertrand's help." My voice shook as I spoke. He'd been asleep, but he quickly became aware and I heard him wake his wife as I tried to explain.

"We'll be right there," he said.

"He's good, his wife can help." The girl reached out and held my hand; her touch breached something deep inside me and my own tears began to flow.

I don't know how much time passed, it was infinite in the way a memory will never leave and then they were there. Mrs. Bertrand ran over to us, I could barely stand as I got out of her way. The Professor stood back and motioned me over.

"Do you know anything?"

I shook my head and wiped my eyes.

"We're going to take her to the hospital, why wouldn't she let you call the police?"

I wiped my nose on my bare arm. "I don't know, she said somebody told her they'd kill her." I turned towards Mrs. Bertrand; I could barely see them through the bushes, but I could tell the girl's arms were wrapped around Mrs. Bertrand.

"This is going to be awful," The Professor said. "I'm glad you called, Wally, it was the right thing to do."

We waited, standing in light rain; I called Henry and told him to go to sleep. Maybe it was something in my voice, he hesitated, then agreed. After a few minutes Mrs. Bertrand helped the girl stand, the Professor and I hurried over to clear a path from the bushes as they disentangled from thorny branches.

"I'm going to take her in the car. I'm sorry, Milo, you two are going to have to walk," Mrs. Bertrand said.

"Of course, we'll see you there," the Professor said. He turned to me. "We only have the one car. It's a couple of miles, I need you to come with me. Sooner or later the police will be brought in, and they'll want to speak with you. Do you need a jacket or something?"

I shook my head. "I'm fine."

"Okay, tell me everything you know."

I told him, which wasn't anything. The rain had nearly stopped but the air was damp, streetlights filled opaque spaces without illumination. I found myself opening up to the Professor about the team's new atmosphere; the dangerous character of the coaches and new players, how the new currency was brutality. He nodded like a doctor observing dangerous symptoms.

"It's still Bastille, though," I said.

"I hope so."

It was nearly a half hour before the Professor and I made it to the hospital, we walked down a small, crooked street over broken sidewalk. Inside, the Professor led me down a quiet hallway, away from the bustle of the emergency room. It was poorly lit and felt like walking the halls of an asylum, but it offered secluded privacy. In a small waiting room damp air drew out the smell of mold, there were a few mismatched plastic chairs. I took a seat while the Professor carefully opened the inner door, then disappeared. He came back carrying two towels, I dried myself and used it for warmth.

"Mary will be out in a minute," the Professor said. He wiped his face with the towel then closed his eyes. His face seemed worn, his body sagged.

"She was raped, Wally. Brutally. This is going to be terrible for all involved, even you." I nodded and didn't speak. "Don't be offended, but Mary had to ask if it was you, the girl said no. The poor young woman is hysterical, but Mary's calmed her down and the police are on their way. Her father is en route, also. The police are going to ask you where you were tonight."

My words came out quickly. "I was watching film with Dion and another quarterback, Cooper, he's new. It was late, you have to badge in and out of the Performance Center, plus there's video cameras." I could feel myself starting to panic.

The Professor raised his hands. "Wally, I believe you, so does Mary, so will the police. But you were the only one that saw her. I recommend, if they ask, to provide a DNA sample to completely clear yourself."

"Yes, sir."

More than an hour ago I was in a great mood; Samantha had called.

"Okay, Mr. Nobody. I did my part, I just tweeted out that Dion was misquoted about Garr after the Tech game. I really took a hit with my people for doing this."

I was stunned, I didn't think she'd come through. I thanked her but she didn't seem moved.

"So, tell me, what's it like there?" she said.

I had forgotten about our deal. "Nothing's changed, there's a lot of new guys. We're still grieving about Coach Oldham."

"Bullshit. You owe me, and I'm going to get a story out of that place one way or another." She hung up.

I didn't care, I ran up to Dion's room but he wasn't there, then headed to the Performance Center and found him in the QB room watching film with Cooper. He seemed relieved when I told him but it wasn't the reaction I expected. "We'll see," he said. I took a seat as they replayed the Alabama game.

My feet were wet, my socks were still soaked from the rain, and it kept me from sleeping. Every time I shifted in my chair a chill rose alerting my senses, reminding me where I was. I lost track of time and it felt like hours, the silent wait occasionally interrupted by a soft, pained cry from the girl or Mrs. Bertrand's voice providing comfort. I looked to the Professor.

"No police?" I said.

"Not yet."

Classes were out of the question, they were Friday classes, a few hours off. Exposed overhead pipes, old and discolored, gurgled with sound either coming or going. This wasn't a place anyone would choose to come. I rolled the towel up and propped it against the wall to rest my head.

Headlights swept across a side door I hadn't noticed, the Professor and I both sat up and exchanged glances. A moment passed then a knock on the door. It opened and a man appeared, not the police, just a middle-aged man. The Professor quickly got up.

"She's through here, sir. I'm Milo Bertrand, your daughter is with my wife, Mary, she's a social worker."

The man, the girl's father, glanced at me without changing his look, a frozen look, it echoed the look the girl had when our eyes first met in the bushes. I moved to stand but the Professor gave me a quick wave and they disappeared behind the inner door.

Then I heard his sobs and wisps of pain from his daughter. Mrs. Bertrand's voice was strong and reassuring. After a few minutes the Professor and Mrs. Bertrand came into the waiting room, and the Professor hugged her as she wiped tears from her face. They waited, passing the moments discussing meaningless things, like logistics of the interrupted day, and when the police would show, they asked how I was doing.

"I'm fine," I said.

Mrs. Bertrand went back in, and I heard a muffled conversation filled with loss. I looked to the Professor; he raised his hands slightly asking me for patience.

"I'm going to call the police again." He walked out onto the street for better reception.

I nodded and sat back in my chair. At least her father was there, he'd provide her strength, he'd take her home. I'd go back to the dorm and sleep, then eat, then wait for the eruption when the police investigated, when the media found out, when Coach Castritt tore the team apart.

The inner door opened and the father slowly came out, his face stricken in anguish and out of respect I stood without knowing what to say. He raised his head, then charged. It was a weak punch to my jaw, then he tackled me and we fell over chairs.

"You son of a bitch, you scumbags!" He straddled me, hitting my covered face with harmless punches. He continued screaming and hitting while I absorbed and didn't fight back; I'd taken beatings for lesser causes.

The Professor entered quickly followed by a police officer, they pulled him off of me. The father took a seat with his head in his hands, his cries sounding a deeper anguish as the police officer motioned for me to join him outside.

We stood under a streetlight as he pulled out a small notebook and pencil. A crackled voice sounded over his radio, he responded with a code then looked at me.

"Okay, first of all, do you want to press charges," he said. I must've looked puzzled. He nodded his head towards the door. "You were assaulted, do you want to press charges?"

I shook my head. "No, his daughter was raped, he's upset."

The officer took my statement but there wasn't much I could provide. He asked me to spell my name and write down my contact information.

"You're on the team, right? How we looking this year?"

I hesitated before answering. "I don't know, we'll find out in spring practice." It seemed to satisfy him and he said I was free to go.

"One more thing," the officer said. "When Arkansas A&M comes to town, that son of a bitch Garr Johnstone better stay in his hotel, or I'll bust his ass."

I nodded and watched him slowly make his way into the side door. It was deep in the night, the part where it becomes the new day. I decided I'd go to class, I'd be fine, and began walking back to school. A parked car was ahead, and I was startled when the driver window descended.

"Hestia, get in, I'll give you a lift back to school." It was Sly. He was silent until we were on the main thoroughfare. "First of all," Sly said, "I thought I made it clear you're supposed to call me whenever a situation comes up. Don't fuck up again. Now, tell me everything you know."

Wally

....

ii.

ArkA&Mlover@Bastille84: Great, a thought crossed your mind, must've been a long and lonely journey. McAres is a soft whiner, Garr is a monster and will destroy him in his pompous house.

Arrowshot9@ArkA&Mlover: Isn't it dangerous to use your entire vocabulary in a single sentence? When Garr Johnstone leaves Ark. A&M and travels to Bastille to play, the avg. IQ of both places drop. Johnstone is a thug, McAres is a superstar.

A WHITE BIRD circled high above; I couldn't take my eyes off of it as I laid on my back holding the ball. The crisp spring air held the bird aloft, it was probably looking for food and wondering why we were killing each other. The sharp whistle blew, I quickly turned and rose, digging my spikes into the grass, generating torque, launching myself into my opponent; a flash of the other player, bigger than me, hard contact, helmet to helmet, blackness. I spun, churning my legs, opening my eyes; an arm crossed my face, both arms wrapped around me at the hips. I was picked up and driven into the ground. Raucous taunts and jeers that were unintelligible poured into my ears, they didn't matter, finally the whistle. I looked to see where I was—just beyond the midpoint, I'd gained a half yard. A small but important victory. Dion slapped my helmet when I got back to the end of the line.

Each day of spring practice we started with the nutcracker drill. "This will be a physical football team!" Coach Castritt screamed through his bullhorn from his elevated perch. Hunter and Cyrus screamed in support from the beginning, their bloodlust poured out at every chance. It was different than last year's fall training camp. Then: tight choreography, precise timing, hitting for effect, saving the worst for the other team. Now: a weeding out, survival of the violent, opportunities to blow someone up were sought out, and, if achieved, were celebrated, while the victim carried humiliation until their redemption came.

I took part and felt something awakening in me. "Run through him!" Coach Castritt said. He didn't just say it, he screamed. Marcus James had popped up and easily evaded the tackler with a quick move, a violation of the spirit of the drill. The ball wasn't important, the new culture was. Castritt made them do it over again, and, the next time, Marcus was crushed, losing his helmet in the process. The team went wild, like youngsters eagerly sopping up a reckless new norm.

The practice script wasn't that different than the year before except for the nutcracker drill. However, by the third practice I noticed the difference—everything was screamed; bilious, red-hot, accusing, full-throat. If you were the last one running to the next drill, you were screamed at; if you made a mistake, more of the same. If you destroyed your opponent in a drill, your reward was manic congratulations delivered at high volume that an outsider would recoil from. Technique was taught but not with the precision under Coach Oldham; it was subordinated with purpose for one thing: violence. I could tell right away violence was like money, it covered a lot of mistakes and the more we had, the better we'd be.

But there were lulls for me. I didn't get any reps outside of the scout team and during the lulls, thoughts surfaced delivering hard truths. Her name was Julie and I couldn't stop thinking about her in the weeks that followed the attack. The Professor told me she was a sophomore and she'd left school. Although we'd never met and probably didn't have any classes together, I felt her absence. It troubled me. I'd see an empty seat in a class and remind myself it wasn't her seat but then I'd think further; somewhere on campus there was an empty seat, it was undeniable. But it had been denied. The police didn't ask to speak to me again, and it wasn't mentioned in the local paper or the campus news. Coach Castritt didn't mention it in team meetings and when I thought of approaching Sly to ask if he knew anything, good sense overtook and I kept my silence.

Dion was next. The whistle blew and in one motion Dion was up and moving, a quick feint to his right, then a head-on collision through Cyrus and it was over as we screamed. New synapses were forming, new paths of excitement fed through violent domination.

Then Tony tapped my helmet and pointed to the front of the line. Henry was on his back waiting to go next. I ran through a couple of players to the front, buckling my helmet as I went. Henry was staring straight up with a calm look on his face.

"Kickers don't do this drill," I said as I pulled him up and pushed him aside.

Hoots and taunts were called out. "Take his spot, asshole."

"He wants you, Hunter!"

"Kick his ass, Dev!"

It dawned on me, who I'd be facing. It was Hunter Devlin: six-foot-four, 245 pounds, a 4.5 forty, and long blond hair as if being tough wasn't enough, he also wanted to be pretty. I didn't stand a chance. The whistle blew. I know that I made it up, I know that I turned, I even felt my left foot plant and my right take the first step. Then he hit me, cradling me up like meaningless refuse, driving me back, planting me into the turf, my head snapping against the ground, my body reacting in crisis to the coming pain.

"You coming for me? I'm going to fucking kill you, bitch."

I could barely hear him through the screaming celebration. I closed my eyes to let moments pass, then more. When I opened them, a trainer was kneeling over me staring into my unfocused eyes.

"Let's go, you're out," he said. Minutes later, I found myself sitting on the first row of the bleachers next to Henry. The trainer came over and asked a question I couldn't answer then he looked over to one of the coaches. "Concussed, he's out."

Breathe in, breathe out. The bird, I wanted to see the bird again. I lifted my head to the sky, but the sun was too bright, I squinted then looked to the ground covering my eyes. My head throbbed as more time passed.

"We're at the Performance Center," Henry said. I gave him a strange look. "We're in Bastille." I looked at him through squinting eyes. "The trainer asked if you knew where you were. You didn't know. We're in Bastille. You've got blood on your face."

I wiped my cheek and it came back red but nothing serious. I dropped my head into my hands and closed my eyes to let time fade. *Julie.* Somewhere on the field in front of me was a criminal. Voices sounded as people approached, mad voices, one in particular. Then they were quiet, the only sound was movement, contact, running, and the whistles of practice in the distance.

"Jesus H. Christ, where the hell do you think we are?"

I looked up and through squinting eyes I saw Coach Castritt; it was the first time he'd spoken to me. My gaze went too long, Henry answered for me.

"No one knows," Henry said. "The trainer wanted to know, he asked Wally, but Wally didn't know. I know. We're at the Performance Center. In Bastille."

I watched them in a detached manner as if it was a TV show.

Coach Castritt slowly approached us and bent over with his hands on his knees. I couldn't hold his stare, my eyes drifted down to his belly hanging over his belt, it was huge. My jaw hurt from the hit I'd taken, I rubbed it with my mouth hanging open as I looked back up to him.

"Where in world did Oldham find you two?" Castritt said.

While still looking at Castritt, I began to slowly shake my head. "Don't answer, Henry." It was too late.

"West Temple, Georgia. I'm a kicker, Wally holds for me. I am the Nuber."

"What the hell kind of program was Oldham running?" He looked at Henry. "I heard you were special, but not this special. We're kicking at the end of practice; I want to see what you can do. And wipe that goddamn grin off your face."

Forty-five minutes later with my ears ringing and my eyes sensitive to light, we lined up for field goals.

"What's the count," I said. I'd lost count of his kicks; I couldn't do the math.

"Seven extra points and fourteen field goals," Henry said. "Nine more."

The Nuber chants started; it felt like last season. I'd held so many times I could do it in my sleep, or at least the state I was in. I concentrated on my blade of grass, looked back to Henry then called for the snap. Henry hit from forty, then fifty, then fifty-five. Our vets who'd seen Henry kick before howled in delight, each kick nearly perfect. Gasps came from some of the new coaches.

"Stop that goddamn chant," Castritt said. "Defense, I want a full speed rush. If you can distract him only the offense runs sprints. Everyone else get in here and make it loud, we're going to do this from each hash."

We were surrounded and the screams unnerved me, but when I looked back to Henry, he was unaffected, as if he was waiting in line for dinner. Corners flew by after the ball left his foot, almost colliding. Defensive linemen strained through cracks with out-stretched arms. Henry hit all three kicks from the right hash.

"Move to the left hash," Castritt said.

It got serious. After Henry hit from forty, a scuffle broke out among the linemen. After he hit from fifty, the screams turned to threats. When he kicked it through from fifty-five, it grew quiet.

"One last chance," Castritt said. "If the Nuber can hit from sixty, no sprints for anybody."

Cheers went up immediately; they all knew it was a lock except for Henry and me. As the team lined up, I remained standing, still dazed, not knowing who to tell.

"What the hell's the matter with you?" Castritt screamed.

"He hit his limit, thirty kicks a day. He won't kick," I said.

"He'll goddamn kick if I tell him to kick."

I didn't like the way Castritt came towards us. I'd seen him yank facemasks and jerseys and get nose-to-nose with players, screaming out punishment. I stepped in front of Henry.

"You can't touch him," I said.

Castritt's face turned red. "You don't tell me what I can and can't do, you son of a bitch!" His face peered down into my face-mask as his words streamed into me like speeding lava, not even the Minister had ever screamed at me like that. I kept Henry behind me as I stared at the red veins in his eyes, inches from me. When he was done, he spit on the ground and turned away.

"We're running double sprints. Helmets on."

It was brutal. After practice I sat at my locker, afraid to turn my back to open space. Hunter, Cyrus, and Pokey sat across the room staring, then Hunter slowly raised his middle finger towards us, and I knew I had to wait until they showered and left.

"Hestia, get your ass over here and bring your brother," said Sly.

He led us up to the coach's floor and told us to take our spikes off before we entered the foyer. We waited over a half an hour before we were called in. Castritt sat behind his desk, and when he saw me, a bitter scowl came across his face. Then he turned to Henry with a calm look.

"What's the longest you've kicked against a live defense?"

"Sixty-five yards last year in practice. I can make it from seventy," Henry said.

"Have you ever missed?"

"Not since high school. That's when Coach Griffin taught Wally how to hold. I never miss."

"Thirty kicks a day?" Castritt said. "Sly, tell the Nuber's position coach to set up his practice schedule and game-day warm-ups so he doesn't kick more than thirty times." He looked back to Henry. "You're free to go." Henry left without any prompt from me; he didn't even look at me.

We were alone and the scowl returned, I seemed to get smaller in his presence. "First of all, you're not a QB, not on my team. The only time you'll take a snap is on the scout team, and scout team QBs aren't off limits." He paused a moment as if to hear the air hissing out of me. "You're just a holder, that's how you'll be listed in the program. Strange thing about holders, did you know that out of every sport—football, basketball, baseball, and even goddamn ice hockey—there's only one position where a player starts off on his knee: the holder. It's like he's already surrendered. That's you, you're not a QB." Then he leaned towards me. "If you ever challenge me again, I'll ruin you. And your brother." He held my stare for another moment then turned towards his computer. I knew it was time to leave, I didn't want him to tell me to get the fuck out. Coach Dixon was in the foyer and on my way out he patted me on the shoulder.

"Hang in there," he said.

▾ ▾ ▾

The Professor slumped in shame when I appeared in the doorway. I almost didn't recognize him; he wore a suit and tie like he was on his way to a business meeting.

"I'm so sorry, I completely forgot. Can you stop by tomorrow?" he said.

"We have the spring game tomorrow, how about Monday? If I'm still on the team," I said.

The Professor stopped what he was doing and took a seat. "What's wrong? Has something happened?"

"Coach Castritt is different; a lot of guys are nervous about tomorrow. If he could, he'd get rid of me in a second."

"I don't understand, I didn't think that was at issue," he said.

"I'll let you go, it's just that tomorrow's more like a final tryout for a lot of guys. Spring practice was brutal. It doesn't matter, it looks like you're going somewhere."

"I'm sorry, Wally, I really do have to leave," the Professor said as he finished packing his briefcase. "This is about the new curriculum issue; it's very important." Then he looked up. "You know what? There's not a single person from the athletic department on the committee, but everyone is scared to death to even mention sports. The outrage amongst the academic types is through the roof, but we're all a bunch of chickens in the face of the administration."

"How do you know it's for the football program?"

"Oh, we know." The Professor chuckled as he spoke. "There's not a single department that supports it, just a few key untouchable administrators, the ones in charge of fundraising. Trust me, their job is a lot easier if the team is winning. However, there is one person that I don't know that we all believe is associated with the team. He sits in the back and doesn't say a word."

"Is he tall, thin, and bald?" I said.

"Yes, and he looks mean, too."

"That's Sly Ellington, he's our Director of Football Operations."

"Director of what? Is that like a coach?"

"No, he's Castritt's right hand man for everything off the field. He's the guy that drove me back from the hospital that night."

"That's another thing that disgusts me. Not a single thing has been done. Stop by Monday and we'll catch up."

▼ ▼ ▼

"Garr Johnstone Can't Read This—Tribe Forever!"

The words were painted on a bedsheet and hung from the upper deck. I turned again to read it but my eyes took note of the tens of thousands of people packing the stadium, all for the spring game, an intra-squad scrimmage.

"Sly, get somebody to take that down," Dion said as he pointed to the hanging bedsheet.

Throughout the scrimmage, I stole glances at the bedsheet sign. About an hour in, I realized it wasn't coming down.

I looked back to the field and saw Dion look to his left, to Tarik. He held the look for an extra beat, and I knew, I *knew* it was wrong. The play called for Dion to catch the shotgun snap, fake a handoff to the back through the B gap, sprint to his left with the slot receiver trailing in the pitch position, and then either throw to the dragging tight end, keep it, or pitch.

Instead, he faked the handoff and dropped a few steps. The trailing slot receiver was confused, he slowed his run with his palms up and a lost look on his face. The linemen weren't set up to hold pass protection and defenders leaked in but didn't hit as Dion uncorked a bullet to Tarik. The crowd cheered when Tarik gathered it and trotted into the end zone. Castritt blew his whistle and slammed his headset to the ground.

"How many goddamn times do I have to tell you, run the fucking play as I called it," Castritt screamed. Dion looked down the field and clapped as Tarik made his way back. "Do you hear me?" Castritt said as he took the field.

Then Dion popped his helmet off and let it fall without regard, his restraint broke. "T's got man coverage, the defense is in cover one, and the safety is creeping. It's an automatic six points."

Castritt turned to the bench and screamed, his face red and bulging. "Cooper, get your ass in there." Then he turned back to Dion and approached until they were face to face. We couldn't hear what was said, only angry gestures by Castritt as Dion stood stoically. Then Dion picked up his helmet and walked to the sideline with Castritt following him. "Anybody else want to tell me how to run this goddamn team?"

It happened all through spring practice. While watching film of Dion's improvised plays, the remnants of Coach Oldham's days, success would be celebrated with quietly charged comments: "nice," "they can't stop you," "keep it up." But if Castritt was in the room, the comments were absent.

"That's not the goddamn way the play was designed." Then Castritt would give a reason why it wouldn't work, or point out there'd be a risk of a turnover or the intended play was used to set up a different one on the next series. Dion watched without emotion. After a while he reclined, near the end of spring practice I wasn't sure he was listening.

Dion went back in on the next series. A counter option to the right but he pitched too early, a three-yard loss. Then a sprint draw to the left but he waited too long and had to throw it out of bounds. On every play his timing was out of sync, and when he came to the sideline, he didn't have anything to say. Our offensive coordinator sat with him on the bench reviewing what had happened and Dion listened and nodded, then walked away when the conversation was over like he had other thoughts on his mind. After the scrimmage in the locker room the media cornered him as usual and I was within earshot.

"I was a little rusty, but we're getting there."

"We're practicing against the best defense in the country, they made the offense look bad today."

"It's completely different, I'll always miss him."

They didn't stay long and by the time I got out of the shower the locker room was nearly empty. Dion didn't speak, just the sound of the equipment manager collecting gear, a quiet conversation a few lockers over, the heavy silence of the stadium above us. After Dion left, I sat on my stool trying to remember the feelings of last season. Someone approached, my disappointment must have been obvious.

"Don't look so excited to see me," Samantha said. Then she turned to Henry. "Nice kicks today. Looks like you're going to be the only way Bastille scores this year." She turned back to me, but I avoided eye contact. "I thought you said nothing's changed here. What's going on between Dion and Castritt?"

"Nothing, just a new offense. It takes time."

"Bullshit."

"All I have to do is tell Sly you're looking for dirt and he'll ban you from Bastille. This is still my team."

"Sly? I don't think so. Someday you're going to need me, don't be naïve."

▼ ▼ ▼

In dim light Jeremy's head stuck above the crowd outside the Parthenon, his curly blond hair made him easy to pick out. Spring practice was over, it was time to go out. Eddie called to me as I navigated the crowd amid thumping music pouring into the street.

"Where's Tony?" I said.

"He ain't feeling it after today. Three drops," Eddie said.

"They were bad passes, they can't hold it against him," I said.

"One was, one hit him right in the chest and the last would've been a circus catch. He went over to frat row. Least he got some balls thrown his way. I got ten plays, eight were runs and the other two the QB didn't even look my way. Fuck it, time to drink."

"How long to get in?" I said.

"Don't know, the place is packed."

I turned to gauge the depth of the crowd waiting to get in and something caught my eye. Silver thinning hair of someone walking briskly on the sidewalk across the street. Jeremy waved, inviting us up front to skip the line. As I circled the crowd, I saw the man again from a distance as he looked over his shoulder, it was enough to trigger familiarity. I couldn't determine if he stood out because of his age or something about his movement. Another middle-aged man stood in the doorway of the coffee shop, he seemed normal and I paused. Something was off.

"You coming in?" Jeremy said.

"Go ahead, I've got to check something out," I said.

I broke from the crowd and immediately regretted missing my chance to skip the line. The heat and humidity were like summer, and I began to sweat before I broke into a jog. After the first block I stood at the intersection, chiding myself for chasing ghosts. I turned around and considered my options. Then, to my left up an empty side street I saw him again but only his silhouette. After he turned the corner, it felt like he was never there, I was left staring at bugs swirling in the streetlight. I followed.

At a deserted corner I saw him again; he was a block ahead, walking with an unsteady gate. He continued on behind the Parthenon, then another two blocks, then he disappeared into a parking lot. I lost track until I saw him at the far end of the lot, sitting on a grass berm wet from earlier rain. I approached slowly, making little sound, barely breathing. He brought his hands to his face in anguish. I remembered who it was. When I was twenty feet away, I spoke.

"Mr. Feldman, is that you?"

He turned towards me abruptly, his hands still close to his face, his eyes straining to see me in the shadows. I was nervous as I stepped closer, but he still didn't know who I was.

"Mr. Feldman, it's me, Wally Hestia." I spoke cautiously. "I'm the one that helped. I helped your daughter. We met at the hospital." I paused to see if he remembered. "Are you okay?"

He closed his eyes, and his hands covered his face again as his body heaved in silent convulsions. I didn't know what to do. I sat on the grass and felt water seep into my skin.

"Can I—"

"He raped my daughter," he said. His voice was pitched and cracking. "He raped her, and no one will do anything about it."

My hands clutched the grass at my side, I looked at him as if he'd fallen into a well.

"I'm so sorry, sir, I don't know who did it."

He slightly turned his head towards me, his face was taut and pained. "She dreamed of going to Bastille since she was in middle school, it was all she cared about. Now she's broken and she'll never come back. I know who did it."

Sweat beaded on his head then ran down his face in a rivulet. He repositioned himself and reached in his jacket pocket. He pulled out a gun and I froze.

My heart sounded in my ears and a chill came over me. I wiped my forehead clean. "Sir, you can't do that, it'll only make things worse. Please."

"I'm going to kill that son of a bitch; I'm going to blow his balls off. I don't care what happens, I'm going to kill him."

"But, sir—"

"I know who did it; I don't know his name but she told me what he looks like. He's got long blond hair and a lot of tattoos."

I knew instantly it was Hunter Devlin. I'd seen him entering the Parthenon a few minutes ago. I could've offered up his dorm room number or told Mr. Feldman his schedule.

"Sir, there are four or five guys like that on the team, you can't kill them all. We'll go to the police."

"I've already talked to the police, they said she'd have to come in, but she won't. My daughter's broken and they won't do anything."

"Sir, you're scaring me, please put it away."

He cradled the gun, turning it over slowly. Then he looked at me again. "How can you live with yourself? How can you be on a team with people like that?"

My throat was tense, I couldn't speak without letting emotions escape. "It used to be different. I hate it now; I don't even know what they're doing to my brother. Please put the gun away."

Traffic noise a block away was the only sound, I listened and tried to stay still. He put his hand on my shoulder and I felt myself shudder in relief. "I'm so sorry what I did to you that night, please forgive me. But if you had any morals, you'd get the hell away from here."

"You don't deserve what happened. You don't deserve what they'll do to you if you shoot somebody."

Headlights swept through the parking lot, then different lights: red and blue and white, flashing in sequence over and over, neither of us moved.

"Jesus Christ, oh God," said Mr. Feldman.

"Give me your jacket, if they find the gun it'll be bad."

We stood as he took off his jacket and handed it to me. I rolled the gun in it and stuck it underneath my arm. A spotlight struck us, and we winced in the light, then I heard footsteps approach and started to panic.

"Everything all right? What are you two doing?"

Mr. Feldman's shallow breaths were the only sound, I was afraid he was going to run.

"It's my car, it broke down," I said.

The police officer looked around. "Where's your car?"

"This is my uncle, I called him to help. But then I called a tow truck, and they already came. I just waited for him." Sweat formed on my arm, I could feel the jacket slipping.

He looked to Mr. Feldman. "Where's your car?"

Mr. Feldman tensed up; I closed my eyes hoping he'd speak. His voice was weak. "It's over—"

"I gave him bad directions, he parked on University," I said.

"Okay," said the police officer. He seemed satisfied then he looked at my arm. "What's that?"

I looked at the jacket, afraid metal was sticking out. I enclosed my hand around it and held it up slightly. "Just my jacket, I thought it was going to rain."

The officer approached with his eyes focused on me. "I've seen you before." I tried to hold steady. "You play for the Tribe, right?"

I nodded as I replied. "Yeah, backup QB and holder for the Nuber."

"The Nuber? Goddamn. Does he ever miss?"

"No, sir. He's the greatest kicker in the country."

"That's awesome. I work security on game days, we're all fighting to get the in-stadium assignment for Arkansas A&M. We've got to crush those bastards."

As the officer drove away, Mr. Feldman let out an audible sigh and wiped his forehead. Then he bent over and shuddered.

"What am I doing?" he said.

"Mr. Feldman, I'll help, I'll do whatever I can. But not this way."

After a few moments we walked to his car in silence; I didn't offer the gun back and he didn't ask. Behind the wheel of his car, he rubbed his eyes; he looked frail.

"I don't know what to do," he said. Then he looked to his jacket still rolled up and stuck under my arm. "Please get rid of that thing. My God, what am I doing?" His voice trailed off.

I woke the next morning without movement. Mr. Feldman's jacket was on the top shelf of my closet with the gun rolled up inside. On the walk home there had been a couple of places to dump it; a drainage pond that was always full, a dumpster that reeked, I even thought about dropping it into a campus post box. But it was on my closet shelf, and I stared at it as an exotic sense of power settled inside me. I'll throw it away later, I thought. It was time to call Sly.

My phone sat neatly in front of me, Sly's name appearing bright. My finger was an inch above the phone icon, all I had to do was press it. If I did what I was told, I'd be rewarded in subtle ways that had more power over me than anything I could do for myself. Sly would summon me to his office where I'd hand over the gun and tell what happened. Then the police would be called, they'd visit Mr. Feldman and he'd crack and fall further.

My finger slowly circled Sly's name, once pressed the path would be set. I made the right call. It rang twice before he answered.

"Professor, this is Wally. Everything is okay, but something happened last night that I need to tell you about."

▼ ▼ ▼

The Professor and Mrs. Bertrand asked me to wait for Milo Jr. to leave the apartment. Their calm concern made me feel safe, and when we were alone, I told them about Mr. Feldman.

"Does anyone on the team fit that description?" Mrs. Bertrand said.

"It's a guy named Hunter Devlin," I said. "I know it's him."

"How can you be sure?" the Professor said.

"There are four guys with tattoos and hair like that. Two of them are offensive linemen and I saw them at the Performance Center working out that night. They're good guys, too. The other is a defensive back, but—" my voice trailed off.

"What?"

"He's gay. No one talks about it."

They discussed what to do and agreed Mrs. Bertrand would contact the case officer.

"You're not going to get Mr. Feldman in trouble, are you?" I said.

"No, I'll call Mr. Feldman today and ask for the description, then relay it onto the police. I won't mention last night," said Mrs. Bertrand.

"But Mr. Feldman said he already gave the police the description," I said.

"The more voices, the better," the Professor said. "By the way, what did you do with the gun?"

I paused a moment. "I threw it out."

I took my time walking back then found myself taking a longer route. Hunter Devlin. I'd looked into his background after our first encounter when he pinned my head to my old locker. An All-State linebacker from North Carolina. I could relate a little bit; I read a story about his abusive father who drove him relentlessly in football—inhumane training, verbal and physical abuse, until finally the father was arrested for child abuse when Hunter was fifteen years old. During high school, Hunter was arrested twice for assault, plus his grades were atrocious and every school avoided him, forcing him to spend two years at a juco, where he was a first team All-American both years. After spending time in the cocoon of a rural juco under the equivalent of house arrest he was deemed clean enough by Castritt and a few other programs. His tutors did most of his classwork at Bastille, and, the rumor was, he wasn't planning on attending any classes in the fall. He'd play one year at Bastille and enter the NFL draft.

The strip was ahead, I decided to go to the coffee shop. I had lied. Twice, now, I'd lied to the Professor. Henry wasn't doing any of his work, and I had kept the gun. *Turn around and go back*, I thought, *tell him the truth about both*. On the corner of the strip and University Ave. I stood as the crosswalk signal cycled through twice. He would understand and guide me to the right path. Then I saw her. Nicole entered the coffee shop and I stopped thinking of anything else as I dodged traffic against the Don't Walk sign.

She waved to me while she stood in line as I crossed the street. When I entered, she gave me a warm hug, then asked what I wanted. "Get a table; I've got time if you do," she said. I found a booth in the back corner and waited as the moments drew out.

She arrived and I reached for my wallet. "Don't be silly, this is my treat." We faced each other alone, she was mine if only for a few moments, and her smile held back nothing. I could barely breathe as she gently brought me out.

"So how did spring practice go? I'll bet you're the star of the team, right?"

She made me blush. "You know that's not true. Do you really understand my role on the team?"

"No, tell me."

"Okay, but only if you tell me about you."

"Maybe," she said. Even her playful coyness affected me.

I'd never been so engaged in small talk, even her laugh was perfect, bubbly, and full of life, but not childish. I told her about Coach Oldham and everything he meant to me, about my friends back home that had moved away, about Jeremy, Eddie, and Tony and how they showed me the ropes the first season. Then Dion, the greatest quarterback that ever played for the Tribe. She made me share details of my life I typically hid from others, but they flowed out as she leaned in and listened to everything.

"What about you?" I said.

She shook her head. "The most boring life in the world, tell me about your brother."

I told her about the Minister, how I taught Henry to kick, she gasped at the story of Henry's discovery by Coach Griffin.

"Do you mean that if that coach would've gone to a different restaurant that night, you wouldn't be here?"

"That's right, but here I am," I said.

She sat back in the booth and folded her arms. Her eyes drifted away as I backtracked the conversation to see if I'd said something wrong. Then she looked back, her face serious. She didn't speak.

"Is everything okay?" I said.

She took her time; I was afraid her coffee was getting cold. "It's scary," she said. "You make a million little decisions in life, and you think none of them are important. Then you look back one day and point to the exact choice that didn't seem important at the time, but it was the one that changed your life. And there's nothing you can do about it."

A waitress stopped by and I shook my head. Nicole seemed lost in thought.

"What decision did you make?"

She looked up. "I saw you the other day," she said. "You were walking on campus near that one intersection. I just left the football offices, I had to pick up something. I wanted to honk my horn but there were too many people. Then someone stopped you and the two of you chatted. It was such a beautiful day and I sat there watching you. The campus is so pretty, I wanted to park and walk the whole campus with you."

I didn't know what to say. Her hands were on the table inches from mine, I wanted to hold them. The silence between us was like a pleasant electric buzz, voiding all other noise. I took my chance.

"Maybe we could get together sometime, just you and me."

A pained smile came across her face and her eyes nearly closed. Then she took a deep breath as if she was closing off fragile access. "God, you're so sweet. But I'm too old for you." I tried to steel myself, but she could see my withdrawal. She reached out and gently took my hand.

"You're not an undergrad." I said. She shook her head. "A grad student?"

She let out a subtle laugh. "Yeah. I do specialized post-grad work. I don't like to talk about it."

"You're not that much older, I mean it seems like—"

"Wally, it won't work, you don't understand," she said.

I was silent and shut off, but I didn't want her to see me pout. "What's wrong, am I not your type?"

She paused a moment. "Oh, my God. No, you're perfect." She let go of my hand and folded her arms. "Look, I know you have a huge crush on me, and it has a big effect, trust me. The men I meet, even the recruits, especially the recruits, talk about themselves non-stop like they really think I'm impressed. Then I met you and right away there was a connection. You are this perfect, innocent guy, good-looking, smart, athletic, and nice." She let out a sigh and dropped her head.

"Then what's wrong, you're not that much older than me. Why can't we get to know each other?"

When she looked up it was like a bitter veil had fallen over her. "Wally, I've had a lot of dark times, things that are my own business. I'm sorry, I don't want to discuss it."

"Is there anything I can do to help?"

She let out a bitter chuckle. "You already do. Sometimes the only thing that gets me through the worst moments is to close my eyes like I'm a little girl and think of something pure and beautiful that I can hang on to. And lately, I think of you. Your face just pops into my head. I think about what it would be like to be your girlfriend, walking on campus, going to parties, watching you at the games, then taking you home and really being with you. When I was your age, I was too cool for my own good and I lost something along the way. Stupid decisions that slide you down a path you can never recover from. I don't know, I get so confused.

I always make the wrong decisions, I hate it. I'm probably making the wrong decision now."

"Just tell me how old you are," I said.

"I should go, I really need to go," she said. "I really value our friendship. Please, let's be friends."

She stood and gathered her purse. I didn't move as she got close. Then, she leaned over and kissed my cheek. I closed my eyes to focus on the sensation of her lips. When I opened them, she was still standing by me. Then she leaned in and kissed me on the lips.

"One thing you should know about me," I said. "I never give up."

She smiled in a sultry way that reached sweet depths, then she drew her finger across my cheek. "Good," she said. "Because I'm only twenty."

As she walked out of the coffee shop, I studied every movement she made, committing it to memory. I'd never felt this way in my life.

▼ ▼ ▼

"Henry, we can do anything, look how far we've come!" Henry lifted his eyes from his phone and stared at me for a moment before turning back. "Like Coach Castritt said, it's all about attitude and nothing's going to stop us. I can't wait for you to meet her, feel free to show excitement at any time."

Henry blinked a few times, but otherwise was motionless. I didn't care, Nicole and I began meeting once a week at the coffee shop.

"Is there someone in your life?" I asked her.

"Yes, there is. It's complex but I'm getting out of it. Please understand."

We kept our meetings secret and I agreed to be just friends. After the coffee shop, she'd drive me back to school and we'd sit in her car behind the parking garage and talk for hours, we craved each other's company. It continued for weeks until she told me she was leaving for the summer, some place in New York called the

Hamptons. "That's okay, I'll wait for you," I said. She closed her eyes and drew in a deep breath. I leaned over and kissed her. Her response was intimate and accepting and long. "I haven't kissed anyone in the longest time," she said. It was some time before I left her car, the feeling between us was authentic and I'd wait forever if I had to.

My focus was unbelievable, Tony and Eddie noticed in the weight room and on the field as we ran patterns for Dion and when I held for Henry's thirty kicks a day. I was earning a 4.0 for the semester, my ability to concentrate surprised even myself.

"What's your secret?" I'd shrug and dismiss the question. I was pure: I barely partied, I always worked out, I did my homework immediately after leaving each unskipped class from where I sat in the front row. My professors knew me and the strength coaches saw me like clockwork.

▼ ▼ ▼

My visits to the Professor used to feel like I was meeting with the school itself, but now, he seemed cut off, more of an individual than a representation of the ideal. He carried the same look he had months ago when we waited for the police at the hospital.

"What's up, Wally? Your grades, hopefully."

"Is this a bad time? I can come back," I said.

He shook his head. "It's fine, I'm admittedly a little on edge. This curriculum issue is driving me to my wit's end; I've never seen such blatant and naked rhetoric. After every meeting I'm amazed they can say these things with a straight face. Anyway, you wanted to talk, what's on your mind?"

"I just wanted to check in. I haven't heard anything about, you know, Mr. Feldman and his daughter."

The Professor plopped in his chair. "It's a disgrace. Apparently, the surveillance videos around the football dorm are kept for thirty days until they're erased. Just amazing. It seems the police some-how weren't able to request the videos until the thirty-first day, what a coincidence."

"What about Julie, how is she doing?" I said.

A pained look came over his face. "That poor girl. Mary has kept in touch with her parents, she's in therapy but she's not doing well, and she won't meet with the police. This is one of the reasons this crime persists, the victim is sometimes traumatized to such a degree that they can't ever go back. Most likely she could identify him but she's not functional. And the campus and city police—I hate to accuse them of anything, but it's quite clear they'd rather not take this any further."

"How can they do that?"

The Professor looked at me with a sad look, almost conde-scending. "Are you kidding? There was another incident a few weeks ago that's been kept under wraps. It boils down to the age old 'he said/she said.' The young woman admitted to voluntarily inviting a player to her apartment, she claimed she was sexually assaulted and the player said she consented. It was swept under the rug. But don't worry, it seems that the new players aren't restricting their crimes to women. There's been an uptick in violent assaults and a few robberies." The Professor seemed to take himself back. "Listen to me, it's like I'm profiling and blaming everything on the new players."

"It's not just the new players." I told him about a few nights before; Eddie and I were on the roof of the dorm looking over the railing. I thought it wasn't that cold and was surprised to see Pokey and another guy I couldn't identify wearing knit caps as they crossed the boulevard towards the student parking garage. Then, just as they crossed the street, they pulled down the knit caps over their faces, they were ski masks. Eddie and I looked at each other, then withdrew inside.

The Professor looked at me like a doctor, realizing the disease was worse than he thought. "I'm afraid this is just the beginning."

"How can they let this happen? Bastille is special, we're not like other schools," I said.

The Professor sighed and repositioned himself in his chair, there was an anger to him that scared me. "This is happening even faster than I would've thought," he said.

"What is?"

He looked at me again, this time it had a piercing effect. "The breakdown of our values, the wild embrace of violence. Sorry, I'm sure you've had enough of my speeches."

"No, I want to know, I've got to know, we can't let this happen to Bastille," I said.

"Okay. You know about tribes, you know that survival is paramount, you know that morality is whatever the tribe chooses to subscribe to. There is no external agency from where morality comes, it's nothing more than the protocol of the Tribe. But what you don't know is what feeds all this: It's in our DNA. In addition to our desire to tribalize, we also have a vicious desire for violence. Embedded in every one of us is this aching desire to survive and success came only to those that bonded into a tribe and used violence to achieve that end. All others perished so we're coded with the desire to be tribal and violent. The joke's on us because the world finally grew up, but did so at such a pace that our tribal instincts are still intact. When do you think the world grew up?"

"I don't know, when philosophy started?"

"Not then, they sentenced Socrates to death for having fresh ideas that weren't in line with his tribe. You've read *The Apology*, haven't you?"

I shook my head.

"You should. Instead of a guessing game, I'll throw one out for you, it's not exact but it makes the point. How about the

Enlightenment? It seems the Dark Ages are an excellent example of the horrors that tribes had to endure to survive, so thanks to Descartes and all who followed, we started to use intellect to figure out a better way. Unfortunately, there hasn't been enough time for our DNA to adjust. Let's say the Enlightenment began about 500 years ago and let's presume that homo sapiens are about 200,000 years old, although the evolutionary forces in our DNA stretch back millions of years. That means that the tribal manners of living—starvation, violence, physical domination, conquest—have only been alleviated by intellectual ideas for a small percentage of time, a very small percentage. In fact, around one quarter of one percent. I would say that all the tribal urges present in each of us are still quite vibrant.

"But here's the problem—we can't live like that anymore. Fighting is illegal, physical domination isn't economic, and scarcity is gone by the standards of our ancestors. In fact, modern society is so complex and well-structured we've kind of taken the fun out of things. How well do you think it falls in line with your primal urges to stare at a spreadsheet all day? That's what I used to do, and it nearly killed me. Our society is so atomized, specific, and specialized that we're wholly unprepared to survive in the manner we've evolved from. Then as the world evolved, it became more complex, but the complexity happened in an instant, relative to evolution's time arc.

"You see, no longer do our tribes fight for survival like they used to. Only the few go off to far-away wars, yet the masses still have an unmet urge to fight, to dominate, to claim victory, to celebrate. It's almost a punishment for them to sit in classrooms or offices and study dull topics, what we need is a little excitement. And since it's too dangerous to really take up arms, let's have someone do it for us. Think of all the people going through life, say, in the corporate world. They stare at spreadsheets for decades on end, and, if all goes well, they keep their job with no victories other than money, which, for most, will never amount to much.

"They need proxies. They can work all week and live with two weeks of vacation per year, they can never get ahead, they can only hope to be okay in the face of perpetually being wrong, but to do so, an outlet is needed. A place where they can identify, a place they can show up wearing the signs of their tribe and be accepted on first sight. When the team wins the feeling is real, it's a feeling they'll get no other place in life. Do you think it's an accident that nearly all team nicknames are based on a violent representation? The Clemson Tigers, the Georgia Bulldogs, the Wisconsin Badgers—a nasty little animal. My favorite is Notre Dame: The *Fighting* Irish. Through their proxies, especially football proxies, a sport closer to war than all others combined, they're able to congregate not only with their tribal colleagues but their ancestral ones as well; they can scream as if they're charging another tribe, they can see violence play out before them, they can drink in the taste of blood through their proxies' domination, they'd kill for it, but instead, we use a much more efficient method: We pay for it."

"I've never thought of it this way. I don't know, it's—"

"Unstoppable. So, let me ask you this. If all these forces are in play—powerful, starving, evolutionary forces whose appetite is sated by beautiful, sweet, and violent victory—how is the welfare of one young woman going to get in the way?"

"But that's immoral, you can't say that; people have virtues."

"That's true, some people have some virtues, but you'd be a fool to believe society is based on virtue—virtues are only adopted if they strengthen the tribe. The minute a virtue gets in the way, it becomes nothing more than a spurious idea that can be questioned a thousand ways. How do you think evil politicians win? They scare people and scream that they're the only path to victory, cursing inconvenient virtues in unwashed rhetoric since victory is all the tribe really wants.

"John Oldham was a great man for one reason: He won without succumbing to the sins of the tribe. He believed in virtues and was fascinated by what I'm telling you now. But with him gone, the path to victory is far too easy if the baggage of virtues is tossed aside. The best players to get the job done don't necessarily line up with the virtues the university espouses in the commercials they run during the third quarter. So now the innocent are raped, criminals roam the campus, academic integrity is trampled, and yet the Tribe, the larger Tribe that supports it all, still believes and they can't wait for the season to start."

▼ ▼ ▼

The Professor's ideas stayed with me, although I didn't completely believe. Yet, when I walked across campus or in town, I noticed with more focus the Bastille-labeled items. Sweatshirts and caps for all ages, license plates on cars, and banners on storefronts. One time back in West Temple I saw a college kid wearing a Harvard sweatshirt and thought, *What's that arrogant asshole doing in rural Georgia?*

During finals week I had time on my hands. The Professor's academic techniques had paid off, so I didn't need to study too much and I found myself wandering the Performance Center, looking for teammates and missing the daily hum of the team in perpetual training. Henry waited for me at the practice field and we went through our thirty kicks.

"Yo, Wally." It was Dion, spinning a ball in the air as he approached us at midfield. "Run some patterns?"

The hard spin of Dion's passes never became routine; his accuracy was pinpoint. I ran through all the routes and the only reason the ball touched the ground was my own hands. After we finished, he lingered on the field, lost to his own thoughts as he spun the ball in the air. He'd be gone after the season; it was like the beginning of a long goodbye.

"Are you staying for the summer?" I said.

"Yeah, I got two classes. Plus, I need to be around here as much as possible."

"Everything okay with you and Castritt?"

The topic registered subtly. "Sometimes I don't get it."

"What do you mean?" I said.

He shook his head and tossed me the ball. "I thought it was supposed to be about us. It's funny, they pay us with an education we don't have time for but at least the game was about us, at least it used to be."

I tossed the ball in the air, trying to mimic Dion's spin. "There's a guy you should meet. He used to be my advisor, he's a professor. You should hear what he has to say."

"Who is it?" Dion said.

"Professor Bertrand, I can introduce you."

Dion pulled out his phone and looked up his course schedule. "No need. I'm taking his class over the summer, some course about the Tribe."

"I don't think it's about Bastille, it's a real class, he's an anthropologist and a philosopher."

He studied his phone. "'The Tribe: Anthropological Dynamics of Tribes.' Shit, I thought it was one of them, you know, appreciation courses about Bastille. Maybe I should drop it."

"Don't, this guy is incredible," I said.

"Is it hard?"

"Just sit in the front row."

Wally

....

iii.

*Tribelifer@Aggiebabe: You so dumb you thought a quar-
terback was a refund. How can you believe for a second
that Dion won't throw for 500 yds against your poor
excuse for a defense.*

*A&MBeast@Tribelifer: I can explain it to you, but I can't
understand it for you. Check last years FSU game, w/o
perfect protection McAres sucks. Garr will eat him and all
your snob fans.*

MY ARM WAS stronger. The ball was still in the air when I
reached over with my left hand to feel my right shoulder, a subtle self-congratulation. But Tony dropped it, the pass glanced off
his hands. I made a mental note: Tell him to look the ball into
his hands before breaking up field, a bad habit due to insecurity
about his speed. The indoor practice facility hummed with air
conditioners as the late July thunderstorm raged outside.

Dion was on the other side of the field throwing to Tarik,
Marcus, and a few other receivers. Even though I'd been through
the playbook with him all summer, Dion still reverted to the patterns he liked. I dropped back as Eddie ran a crossing pattern and
unleashed a pass well in front. But Eddie's speed was better than

my velocity, he reached back and caught it with one hand and the few players on our end whistled and clapped as Eddie returned.

"Pass like that will get me killed, boy," Eddie said. "That's if you get it off, you're holding on too long."

More patterns, my accuracy was improving, then Tony tapped my arm. "Check it out." He pointed over to Dion's end of the short indoor field. All activity had stopped, except for Dion, Coach Dixon, and Sly. They walked to middle of the field for privacy, too close for us to run our patterns. Dion stood with his arms crossed and a football in one hand while Sly spoke. The conversation was audible, but we couldn't make out the words. I tossed the ball to Eddie ten yards away to look preoccupied, but our curiosity made us pause after a catch to steal a glance. At one point, Dion circled away from Sly and slapped the ball in anger, then returned with his hands on his hips. Then, Sly, hands extended with his palms up, must've dropped a verbal bomb. Dion spun and spiked the ball, his body seething.

"You lying motherfuckers!" Dion screamed. "I *am* the Tribe! You hear me? I *am* the goddamn Tribe!"

Coach Dixon stepped between them holding Dion off, the only one at Bastille that could.

"It's a team, Dion," Sly yelled back. "It's not all about you. This is Coach Castritt's decision, and you better get used to it."

Dion's verbal assault didn't stop, Tarik and Marcus helped Coach Dixon hold him back. After a moment Sly turned and quickly walked away, and without instruction or suggestion, all of us left the field.

I didn't bother showering, just a quick change into my street clothes. Instead of leaving, I ran up the backstairs and waited to make sure I didn't cross paths with Dion or Sly. The second floor was quiet. In the players' lounge a few TVs were on with the sound off, nobody was shooting pool or playing ping pong. Through the glass partition I saw the top of Jeremy's head sticking out over a study cubicle. He looked up when I entered, he must've known by the look on my face.

"The news must be getting around," Jeremy said.

"What's going on?"

Jeremy tossed his pencil on the desk and leaned back. "Unbelievable. This week is the conference media day in Orlando. Castritt isn't taking Dion, it's a real slap in the face."

I took a seat. "How can he do that? Why?"

"He's the head coach. It's pretty obvious Dion isn't buying in. Do you know he's the biggest interview request in college football? He's putting Dion in his place."

"Castritt didn't even do it," I said. "Sly told him in front of everyone on the indoor field."

Jeremy chuckled in disgust. "Sly. I guess when you get paid four hundred grand a year, the dirty work comes with the job. My bet is that he wanted to do it in an open space to send a message. Goddamn, I'd do anything for Dion."

Jeremy wasn't alone, we all felt for Dion. At the dining hall that night, conversations were guarded out of respect. I spent the summer helping him with the Professor's class even though I'd never taken it. After the second week of classes, we met to review his first paper, a minimum of a thousand words about the effects of tribalism on the economics of developing countries. I'd read the material and put together an outline he read over with an approving look. He pushed the pages back to me.

"Nice. You mind writing it up?" Dion said.

"You know I can't do that, not with Professor Bertrand. You know how close we are."

He started shaking his head, half laughing. "Being a student must suck," he said.

"The Professor really makes you think."

"Oh, do I know." He took a moment; his mood had changed. Then he looked at me. "Me and the Professor, we've been talking outside of class. I mean some of the stuff he says kind of messes with my head."

"Do you think he's wrong?" I said.

"No, but I don't get it. If he's so right, how come nobody else sees it that way?"

"Because they don't want to."

He leaned back with a look of intrigue in a moment that dragged on. Then he spoke. "I do like him, funny little guy. I'll tell you what, I'll write it myself, but I need help on this other stuff. Philosophy, it's required and I've been dodging it."

The assignment he handed me was familiar. "I took this last fall, yeah, I can help."

"Make sure it's original."

▼ ▼ ▼

I didn't know the date of Nicole's return; I just assumed she'd be back by the start of classes at the end of August. A mental note at first, then a circle around the date. I couldn't help myself, I started to cross out the days and what was once measured in months became weeks. It had to change this time. A weekly rendezvous at the coffee shop wouldn't cut it; I wanted her hand-in-hand on campus and at parties, or quiet nights studying and watching TV with Henry.

I had told each about the other and she wanted to meet him. Henry's response cut into me. "Are you getting married?" I smiled and told him yes, someday we'd get married and the three of us would live together; it sent me off into another spell of daydreams. I couldn't wait until each day was over, I began crossing them off the calendar in the evening then in the late afternoon. It was four o'clock in the afternoon on the last day of July when my phone rang.

"Professor, is that you?" There was noise in the background.

"Wally, my young friend, I wanted to share some terrific news with you. Hold on, let me step outside." His apartment's screen door creaked open then closed. "Sorry for the noise, we're having a bit of a wild party here, at least for us."

"What's happening?"

"I wanted to reach out to let you know some good news. I mean really terrific news, we're all ecstatic." The sound of voices on the other end were picked up by the Professor's phone; a gentle laugh, a voice raised in a toast, I imagined the sound of clinking glasses. "The good guys won, Wally; we actually pulled one off. I'm sure you recall the curriculum issue we've been battling. Earlier this week our committee voted, and we recommended that the administration deny this new curriculum, and today they accepted. For us academic types it's like we've just won the biggest game of the year, you can't imagine how excited we are."

"That's terrific news, Professor. How did it happen?"

"It wasn't easy. They tried to stack the deck with people from non-academic departments I hadn't heard of, but we held firm. The key thing for us was the bylaws; they mandate that all major academic issues must be decided by a committee comprised of sixty percent faculty and they loaded the committee with as many non-academics as they could. Even some of the faculty participants were shams, just folks who had taught at some point in their life but were clearly there to sway the vote. It was pure chicanery and before we knew it, they had the votes."

"What happened then?"

"None other than yours truly. I made an impassioned speech right before the final vote. Now, I certainly don't like to toot my own horn, but it made the difference. I could see it in the eyes of the key voters that were on the fence. I spoke of the larger academic mission that's bestowed on us, the stewards of this great institution. It was important for me to tell you."

"I appreciate it, Professor." I paused for a moment. "I'm not sure why I matter, though."

He replied with a long, drawn-out chuckle. "Wally, my dear friend, you matter more than anyone in that room today and I couldn't wait to tell you. You matter more than any football coach, fan, professor, administrator, or booster. You and everyone like you that attends Bastille and places your trust in us that we'll train your mind. You and I have already been through a lot together, and it's become important to me that you don't lose your deepest beliefs in Bastille. If we don't have institutional integrity, we'll begin to rot from the inside out. This isn't vain pride on my part, Bastille has to mean more than a winning football program."

After I hung up, I looked over to Henry, he was sitting on the couch staring at his phone with the TV on.

"Henry. You should put that down and look at your homework."

"Okay."

I looked back to the calendar to pick up where I'd left off. I loved Bastille. The marker's black ink slowly crossed the day, leaving a thick path.

▼ ▼ ▼

"Shotgun pro slot left, X waggle, rip, 32 option on one." I broke the huddle with a clap and set up five yards behind the center. Sweat seeped into my eyes, I couldn't see where the strong safety was. I pointed to Hunter, number 51, and let everyone know he was the Mike.

"Cone?"

"Pic, pic, pic."

The heat was unrelenting, the humidity draining, I heard the constant buzz of cicadas in my sleep. Chafing on my knuckles from a week of camp seemed like permanent markings, red and cracked and never healing. My legs were constantly tired, my body bruised from facing the first team defense. A quick mental rep: catch the snap, ride the ball in the fullback's belly and give or pull, scrape the line, look for the outside backer to commit to the pitch man or close on me and hope like hell that guard and tackle held their block on the defensive tackle.

"Set, hut!"

The snap was below my knee and off to the left. I collected it, turned right, and didn't even try to fake it to the fullback, he was already past. Just an arm from the defensive tackle is all I saw as I sprinted, then the outside backer kept a mirrored pace with the running back trailing me three yards back and three yards out. A gap opened between the backer and the linemen. I didn't know what was worse: having the outside backer close on me at full speed planting his helmet into my chest as I pitched to the running back, or having him follow the back, forcing me to turn it up into a maze of moving walls. Maybe this worked for Dion, or better yet, Cooper Jones; he had the speed and reaction time to slip into gaps and react to full speed motion like he was dodging shopping carts. For me, it wasn't as sporting.

As soon as I turned up field, Pokey, at his defensive line spot, slipped the last half of the weak combo block and laid his shoulder into me, but he was already extended and didn't wrap up. I should've gone down. Instead, off-balance and turned sideways, I continued a yard past the line of scrimmage. A flash of Hunter's green jersey came towards me. I ducked instinctively and he flew over me, grasping my left arm and the back of my shoulder pads; I was bent over and going down. Then Cyrus hit me—my entire being immediately shifted a couple of feet at a speed I could never generate on my own. For good measure Melvin finished me off, coming from fifteen yards away. He could've killed me, but it was a glancing shot, more to show the coaches he was hustling.

"Holy shit, you're slow," Hunter said to me.

"He's soft, though, like hitting a pillow," said Cyrus.

Melvin extended his arm to help me up and stared as he shook his head. He was either trying to tell me to protect myself, or Hunter and Cyrus were assholes, maybe both.

"Goddammit, Pokey, if you can't split the double team against the scout team Oklahoma is going to roll your fat ass down the field!" The defensive line coach got in his face then called for the two scout team linemen to get in standing position as props while Pokey was taught again how to set position then slip the crack to break the double team. On the other field, where the first team offense faced the scout team defense, I was sure the offensive line coach was screaming the opposite argument.

Next play: a three-step drop back off the shotgun, look left to get the safety to move in that direction, then hit the tight end up the right seam over the hash marks. The safety, Melvin, didn't bite; he knew I couldn't hit the deep receiver on a fly pattern with my arm. Throwing to the tight end with Melvin waiting would be abetting assault. It didn't matter, Pokey and Hunter met at my location. They flayed the ball from my body, and I hoped their attention would follow it. Instead, I had to fight for air underneath them as my bulging eyes focused on the torn sod pressing through my facemask.

When the horn finally sounded to end the segment, the daily feeling of relief washed over me. My favorite part of practice was next, Henry kicking. I was a supporting player in a role only I could play. Instead of sneers hurled at me like I was chattel, I was given the huddle.

"Field goal on first sound," I said. A rote exercise but never boring as Henry's kick arced above the players and dropped through the uprights. Castritt allowed the team to chant Henry's name in stereo again, the highlight of practice. The day before in heavy rain we practiced indoors until it was time for Henry to kick.

"Outside for field goals," Castritt said over his bullhorn.

Gusting winds and slanting rain made it difficult to look up, but Henry stared at the goalposts as water ran down his helmet and face. He looked to me and nodded, and I turned to the center and called for the snap. The kick started wide right from forty-five yards and spun its way through the rain without slowing, then the wind swept it left through the uprights.

"Goddamn, that's beautiful," Castritt said. "Fifty-yarder from the left hash. And get some arms up on defense!"

Castritt looked on from just behind and I caught a glance of him watching like an art lover viewing the *Mona Lisa*. Water dripped off the brim of his cap, drops fell from his nose, he was oblivious to the encroaching moans after he called for kick after kick.

"That's thirty, Coach," the specials teams coach said. It wasn't even close, but Castritt was in a daze and ended practice. But that was the day before.

After field goals we lined up for sprints. All but Henry ran; he stood with Castritt like a favored pet. In between runs I looked over and saw Castritt speaking while staring straight ahead as Henry looked at him. The day before Henry had told me he had to do everything Coach told him to do.

At ten o'clock at night I laid in bed knowing I should get up and review the new scout team plays. I tried, but the bedsheet was stuck to my knee where blood and puss formed scabs. Each day, wounds were reopened and each night they tried to heal. I used the bathroom, then took off my shirt. There were two welts on my left ribs and one on my right, my neck had red marks from the hands of defenders and if I pulled down my shorts, I'd see a large black and blue bruise covering my right hip.

Dion's last philosophy paper was due, something about John Locke versus anarchists. I'd written it the year before but even loosely copying it was more than I could ask myself. I'd do it later.

In a couple of weeks, we'd be in Norman, Oklahoma, at Memorial Stadium, another great college football cathedral. I began to drift off to sleep, thinking about the thrill of running through their tunnel. Then my phone rang.

"What the hell is going on there?" It was Samantha Yardley; I'd thought she had forgotten about me. "You won't believe what the conference media day was like. An offensive lineman? No Dion? You've got to work with me, Wally."

"Coach Castritt is just spreading around the attention. In fact, it might've been Dion's idea."

"That is such bullshit and you know it. The rumors are flying about Bastille, but the place is a fortress. Just give me something, one little nugget."

"Or what? You're going write a story to expose my brother?"

"People are talking. He barely kicked last year so he flew under the radar but if he gets on a roll and handles all the kicking duties the attention is going to be unbelievable. Let me take the lead and I'll shape it whatever way you want. Just give me something on Castritt versus Dion."

Finally, I spoke. "I know, but I can't."

She sighed and it troubled me. There was plenty to tell her, and she'd kill for any of it. I wanted to tell her about Julie Feldman and Hunter. I wanted him exposed; I wanted Mr. Feldman to read it and finally see that it wasn't ignored.

"Wally, this isn't how it works. You can't abstain, you're in it whether you like it or not."

"You're acting like I'll get something out of this. I don't want attention. I don't need a sportswriter hyping Henry so he'll get a look from the NFL. I just want to be left alone."

"I could give you information, maybe you'll play ball then."

"Information about what?"

"Dixon. Haven't you guys wondered why he's still there?"

"What about him?"

"Oldham wanted him to be the head coach. Not just because he deserved it but also because he was protective of you guys. Castritt is the last guy Oldham would've wanted. To make sure of it, Oldham fought with the administration for years and finally got a deal for Dixon to stay on and if he wasn't named the head coach and was fired by the new one, he'd get a buyout."

"How much?"

"Millions, like north of five million. Apparently, Oldham wanted Dixon to stay at least one year after he left to help ease the transition. He tried to get the same deal for the other coaches, but he passed away before any of them were done. When Castritt found out, he lost it and ever since they barely speak. On the one hand, every Black kid in the South loves Dixon, he's great for recruiting. On the other, he's one of the top defensive coordinators in the country, so Castritt let it go, but they don't get along. By the end of the season, they'll be at each other's throats."

"How do you know all this?"

"Come on, you think I'd give up a source? Help me out with something."

The story of the Professor's curriculum battle would be another she'd love. "I'm sorry, I can't. Please don't go after my brother." I waited for her to reply.

"Screw it, you're not ready. I'm not here to hurt you, trust me. To show I'm serious I'll give you another bit of news. You know that four-star recruit out of Fort Myers that had offers from everywhere? He wanted Bastille but couldn't get in because his test scores were atrocious. The rumor is that he somehow miraculously increased his SAT enough and he's just been enrolled. You'll see him soon."

After I hung up, I walked into Henry's room, he was already asleep. I sat on the floor next to his bed watching him as his soft breaths calmed me. I relaxed and dropped my head between my knees. I don't how much time passed. When I looked up, Henry was propped up on his elbow, staring at me.

"Henry?"

"Tony said a bad word."

I didn't see Tony after practice, and he wasn't at films. The four-star recruit was a receiver. "Oh, shit, I've got to go."

I scrambled up and ran down to their floor. Their door was open, Eddie stepped out and faced me.

"I was just about to come get you. He's inside," Eddie said.

Packed bags were on the floor, the room felt deserted even though Eddie wasn't leaving. Tony sat on the couch with his head in his hands. When he looked up, I could see his eyes were puffy. I gave him a hug and felt shudders in his breathing.

"What happened?"

Tony slowly shook his head as he brought his hands to his face.

"Want me to tell him?" Eddie said. "They, uh, told him he ain't on the team no more. Violation of rules; it's bullshit."

"I haven't smoked weed since January," Tony said. "I've tested clean for months."

"It's fucked up," Eddie said. "Them new guys Hunter and Cyrus smoke like chimneys."

"My dad is on his way. He's so pissed, he's going to kill me. They even called him and made it sound like I should go to rehab."

"Who told you?" I said.

"Fucking Sly. He told me I flunked the drug test and I told him the last time I smoked was before our first meeting with Castritt. So, then he says, 'You admit it then, you're a drug user.' God, I hate him, I hate all of them."

"That's bullshit, waiting until halfway through camp. Why would they do that?" Eddie said.

"I can't go home. People said I'd never make it here, my dad's going to kill me."

I didn't know if I should tell him. I must've looked preoccupied.

"You know something?" Eddie said.

I nodded my head. "Just something I heard tonight. You know that kid out of Fort Myers that everyone wanted. He just got admitted, they needed the scholarship."

I couldn't gauge their reactions, they looked at me, then each other, and Tony's anger grew.

"Those motherfuckers, that's some dirty shit. Now I'm going to have to explain myself wherever I go. It's too late for me to find another program this season, Oldham would've never done this."

It was hard to console him; any rationalization would've been a lie. We talked about what he could do—how to find another program, schools in a big conference were probably out of the question. Maybe another Division I school or an FCS team.

"You definitely have to go to a community college to keep your academics alive," Eddie said.

"You guys better go; you don't want to be here when my dad comes." We waited anyway.

"Dixon will be a reference for you, he'll tell any coach what really happened," I said.

"Man, just keep playing. Guys change schools all the time," Eddie said. "Half the NFL comes from outside of the power conferences."

"Fucking spring game, that's when they decided," Tony said. "They were never going to play me after that. Three drops."

We fell silent sitting in the same seats we always did.

"You guys can't be here; I'll text you when I'm gone."

I hugged him and held on for a minute. "Let's keep in touch," I said.

"I'm leaving some stuff for Eddie," Tony said. "I want you to have this." He handed me his Tribe flask; I could tell by weight it was full. "I can't let my old man find this."

▼ ▼ ▼

The ball was slick from my sweat, I could barely hold on. Camp was almost over but Castritt wasn't happy. "Five second clock," he screamed. "Defense gets a point for a sack otherwise it's the offense." Three on three pass blocking with a twist—full, live contact on me, the QB. The team was circled around each respective side, offense behind me, defense on the other side. The winner would only have to run half of the practice ending sprints, an incentive that had grown with different drills throughout camp. Castritt wasn't happy with the pass rush and line play in general. Not violent enough, they hadn't been sharpened to an edge.

The offensive line coach signaled the snap count out of view of the defenders in the drill, either on one or two. After the second play, I could tell the defensive guys not in the drill were tipping the snap count to the players taking part. It wasn't enough for Castritt if the defenders won and tapped a blocking dummy which was standard across every team in America, he wanted the defense to close the deal by tackling me and I wasn't allowed to pass.

"Set, hut." I could only fade back a couple of steps, blocking dummies were laid to enclose my movement. My only hope was to wait for the whistle while I dodged hits. On the first play the defense got through, a linebacker slapped me on the shoulder to indicate he'd made it and Castritt screamed at him, "Tackle the son of a bitch! This isn't touch football, goddammit!"

I stepped back in the pocket as the bodies in front of me collided, spun, hit the ground, grunted, held, fell, got up, and descended on me. Since it was all one-on-one blocking and no threat of a run, they were on me within three seconds. Any one of them on either side could've broken me in half, most weighed over a hundred pounds more than I did but I had to live for two more seconds without going down. I ducked as an arm swung past me and when I looked up, I was pressured from the left. A momentary alley opened, I stepped through and wanted to unleash a pass but instead got to the enclosed border then looked for more space. As I turned a helmet speared me in the chest knocking me over the blocking dummy as the whistle blew and the defense howled in victory.

"That's a fucking late hit, we get the point!"

"Bullshit, his spikes were in the air when the whistle blew!"

Everyone looked to Castritt for his decision. He took a moment staring straight ahead as he fidgeted with his whistle. Then he brought it to his lips and blew. "Point defense." The defense screamed as I bent over trying to let the pain evaporate.

"Four to two, defense ahead."

"Hestia, you okay?" It was Coach Dixon.

I quickly nodded. "I'm fine."

I didn't get much better and the offense lost ten to eight. But something had been building ever since spring practice. It was like my soft outer shell had been battered away and in its place scar tissue arose, the kind of scar tissue that can only surface after repeated beatings and losses that were too much to bear. Maybe this is why kids from tough neighborhoods took to the game. I'd had enough of Hunter Devlin's coronation as the best player on the defense, earned by destroying scout team players like me. Melvin was a better player anyway, a pre-season second team All-American.

Hunter's taunts after each hit burned into me, he piled them on to the point that other players would mention something in support after practice. As much as their words softened the sting in the moment, I'd find myself lying in bed fantasizing about retribution. He'd knock on my door at night to wake me with screams and threats and laughs. My clothes were taken from my locker a couple of times. Instead of lining up and calling out "The Mike is 51, the Mike is 51!" I wanted to yell "The Mike is a rapist, the Mike is a rapist!"

My moods became dark and once I snapped at Henry, then immediately begged for his forgiveness. I couldn't face Nicole when she returned, knowing I'd been bullied by Hunter and Cyrus, too. If we did see each other and spent time in public, he'd see and take wild delight humiliating me. My fantasies darkened, and I dreamt up scenarios using Mr. Feldman's gun.

I breathed to get through the moment until the scout team lined up against the first team defense. On the third play they called option right, a play I'd learned to pitch early, which caused the defense to flow outside every time we ran it. I called the snap and faked to the fullback but then did something unexpected: I faked the pitch to the running back and cut up field. Hunter had flown past to the outside and was caught up by the tight end. He was off balance, and I could've dodged left and waited for Melvin to take me out, but I couldn't help myself. For a split second as Hunter tried to reverse his momentum, he was vulnerable and exposed and a flash of excitement shot through me. I put my head down and aimed for his chest. When I hit him, the solid thud rippled through my body, he reached as he went down but I was past him. Hoots of surprise sounded; I didn't know I had supporters. Melvin appeared quickly and gave me a soft push. "Nice," he said.

I felt it. I felt something deep inside well up, a dominant feeling I'd never had, a victory everyone had seen. Then I turned and Hunter leveled me.

"You cheap shot motherfucker," he screamed as he started punching me with one hand and trying to rip my helmet off with the other. Instead of balling up and minimizing damage I fought back, something he didn't expect. I connected with shots to his gut while he seemed obsessed with tearing my helmet off. The words I screamed were as vile as his; my desire to inflict pain and humiliation equaled his. I squirmed away and started to get up as the rest of the team quickly formed a circle around us then he threw me to the ground. I'm sure Coach Dixon ran in immediately to break it up, but it felt longer than a quick moment. He pulled Hunter off me without resistance.

Coach Dixon laid into us, and I felt momentary relief in his presence. *Hunter's a bully and a rapist*, I thought. *I wasn't done.* A few guys told me to chill out and I faked acknowledgement. The next play: toss sweep to the left, a play that would avoid contact between the two of us. As we lined up Hunter edged in close to the line.

"You're a dead man, asshole," he said.

"Really?" I said. I couldn't hold it in. "The Mike's a dumbass! The Mike's a dumbass!" I said as I looked right at him. "Same play, same fucking play." I called the snap and headed right, while both sides of the ball came to a stop in confusion. I cut between the guard and tackle and ran straight at Hunter as he came at me. I aimed for his knees. I wanted to put the top of my helmet directly on his exposed kneecap and bust it in half. A concussion didn't concern me, I didn't care if I ever played again. But we met helmet-to-helmet, and I dropped to the ground, neutralized. This time he did get my helmet off and began landing punches to my face, but an offensive lineman and Eddie drove Hunter to the ground. Cyrus jumped in, then everyone was involved. Coach Dixon's whistle had no effect as I wiped away blood and looked for my helmet. Then Castritt's amplified voice sounded, bringing the fight to an end. A couple of scout teamers pulled me back to our side—some were pissed, most loved it.

I stood there panting while the coaches gathered to explain the situation to Castritt. I didn't bother to put my helmet back on and after a few minutes Castritt blew his whistle and ordered us to run.

"Everyone except him, send him to the shed," Castritt said. I almost cheered out loud, finally, Hunter was getting called out. As I started to run with the rest of the team Castritt called out again.

"Did you hear me, Hestia? Get your ass to the shed, now."

I slowed to a standstill and turned to him.

"You heard me," Castritt said. "You pull a stunt like that again and you're done."

Sly led me to the shed without saying a word. I'd never been in it, only a few had. The floor was loose dirt, the air unbreathable and sooty, the temperature hotter than the already unbearable weather.

"Don't sit," Sly said. "If I find dirt on your ass, you'll spend the entire practice in here tomorrow."

Then he slammed it shut and I was in complete darkness. Even after a few minutes of keeping my eyes shut to acclimate I couldn't see anything when I opened them. The only sensory input was suffocating heat and the bitter smell of dirt. I could hear practice going on without me. It reminded me of hearing the West Temple games when I was a kid: contact followed by whistles and excited voices yelling words I couldn't make out. It sounded happy. I began to squat to sit down then remembered Sly's instruction and stood back up. Sweat began pouring out of me, far worse than practice which I thought couldn't be surpassed. I was thirsty and with each breath it felt like dirt was accumulating in my throat. I had to focus. Number 51 was sanctioned, he could do whatever he wanted; I mocked my own surprise, he'd done whatever he wanted since he arrived.

Samantha would love this, a newly built shed reportedly for equipment that had an altogether different use. I would explain it to Nicole, and she'd be horrified for me and I'd take in all the sweet sympathy she'd offer. The Professor would be disgusted, I could see Mrs. Bertrand: "I told you Milo, it's dogfighting." If Tony would've been there, he would've been the first one to jump into the fight, just like Eddie had. I didn't know what Dion would say, I didn't want him concerned. I worried about Henry. He had to have seen the fight, then my exile. He was unsupervised for most of practice, he would've followed me and was probably waiting outside the door. Each person I spoke to in my head revolved in conversation like they were on a merry-go-round, spinning by slowly, each conversation picking up where it left off before a new face came into view. The Professor: "This is beyond any level of decency, if you have a single self-respecting bone in—" Tony: "Let's fuck this asshole up, next play we'll—" Nicole: "You can't let them do this, let me—" Samantha: "Do you realize they could be arrested for this? This is perfect, I'm going to—"

The conversations spun and veered, my perspective broke down, my body sagged, then I squatted. With everything shut off I couldn't gauge time. I opened my eyes to blackness and screamed as I tried to see my hand in front of my face, then I stood and screamed louder to feel something beyond darkness, another scream to throw off the dirt I was buried under. The gun: I'm going to shoot Hunter in the head, his sins had to be atoned for. Castritt and his fat belly and grinding jowls—shoot him! My head pounded; I couldn't form enough saliva to spit out the dirt. I screamed again. And again. I waited to hear the sounds of practice. I screamed again. But the sound of practice was gone.

The only sound was a soft thud. I tried to calm myself, I thought of Henry, I loved him so much. I didn't want to scare him; I regretted the screams. Henry asleep under my care. Henry following me under my protection. I wanted him to meet Nicole. *Thud*, it happened again. I slowed my breathing to a crawl and drew out time to its longest strand, just a fine point that floated on a distant horizon. I waited and breathed again. *Thud*. I waited and it happened again. Practice was over, probably long ago. Sly, that bastard, he probably left me to figure it out on my own. *Thud*. I can leave when I figure it out by myself. *Thud*.

Moving forward in the dark wasn't easy, my sense of balance was unaided by sight. I walked with my feet spread apart and my right hand carefully reaching out. *Thud*. I crept forward, afraid to fall, afraid to touch. *Thud.* I wasn't making progress; I slid my cleats through dirt to measure distance. A full foot length felt like a sprinting stride. *Thud.* I started to wobble, but held steady, then slid another length, this time further. *Thud.* The door or wall was near, the metallic scent seemed close, I lifted my hand and touched the wall, it was bare. I reached to my left and felt a vertical metal bar, the doorframe. *Thud.*

With careful steps I made my way over and found the door handle not knowing if it was locked. *Thud.* It turned and the heavy metallic creak of the door was louder than my screams. Light shot in and I had to close my eyes as I pushed the door open, and the ninety-five-degree temperature rolled over me like a cool breeze. Henry wasn't there, then I heard the source of the sound. *Thud.* It was someone kicking a football, but not a field goal. Another breath, I needed water, I could walk normally. I could see.

In the middle of the field, Henry was surrounded by the special teams coach, a ball boy, and Sly. The ball boy set the ball on the tee, the special teams coach nodded then Henry approached and swung his leg into the ball. *Thud.* The ball compressed into the ground directly in front of the tee then bounced high into the air on an arc that went at least ten yards. I jogged over, then slowed to a walk as I got near. The next kick was higher, Sly let out a slow whistle and the special teams coach clapped.

"Fucking beautiful, I've never seen anything like it," Sly said.

"And he's just getting the hang of it," the special teams coach said.

Sly heard me approach and turned to me. "Oh, shit. I forgot all about you." He looked to the special teams coach. "That's enough for today."

I walked with Henry towards the locker room. When we were out of ear shot, I asked Henry about it.

"Coach Castritt wants me to do onside kicks."

I stopped him. "Henry, you can't. You'll get killed."

"Coach said I have to."

▼ ▼ ▼

My helmet hung in my locker, it was dinged and scratched from head-on collisions. I'd taken more hits to the head in camp than all my years of playing football. Tired breath left me, but with new breath I felt the euphoria shared by the rest of the team: Camp was over, and we finished with the intra-squad scrimmage. Ones versus ones, twos versus twos. Except for field goals, I never saw the field, but the elation was real, it infected everyone, and the next day, Saturday, was off.

At the beginning of camp, we couldn't do anything right but by the end of camp nothing could stop us. Screams of disapproval, humiliation, and questions about our character evolved into celebratory screams, exultations of big hits, and sweet affirmation. After the scrimmage, Castritt brought us together in the middle of the field. His pitched speech was met with raised arrows, the "Tribe Forever!" chant took over as coaches looked on in satisfaction. Everyone except Dion.

He was diminishing before us, and it wasn't discussed. "Cooper, get in there!" was a phrase we'd heard too much, and every play Dion ran was met with Castritt's disapproval. Receivers weren't open but he forced the ball anyway and the interceptions piled up. On options he made the wrong choice, the offense was foreign to him. In the middle of audibles Castritt intervened and barked out why the original play shouldn't have been changed. Dion was just a player now.

I pulled off my shoulder pads, debating whether I needed a shower.

"Wally, I need that paper tonight," Dion said. "I already asked for an extension."

He startled me, usually I heard him coming. "I just have to review it," I said even though I hadn't started it.

Eddie had dressed already. "You coming? The place is crawling with all them new freshmen sorority wannabes. They're all having mixers and we got the invites."

"I can't, I've got to finish that paper for Dion," I said.

"He took classes over the summer?"

"Two, and they're both hard. I said I'd help."

"Damn, you going to be his valet when he's in the NFL?" Eddie said.

"If he wants me. I'll meet you out later, don't go too hard before I get there."

"Bring Tony's flask, we'll drink to him."

"Nice catch, today," I said. "You're running with the twos."

"Oh, yeah."

On the walk back to the dorms, signs of the new school year appeared. Students had been arriving all week, lines of cars bottle-necked streets. Parents stared from their cars as they watched us migrate from the Performance Center while TV news vans parked illegally, their on-air personalities staring into cameras as they pre-viewed Castritt's debut season.

John Locke versus anarchy; I could barely remember what I wrote the previous year. Henry pushed the elevator button, and the door was nearly closed when a hand reached in. As the door reopened, Cyrus stepped through. A tremor of fear ran through me. Then Hunter followed.

"Look who we got here," Cyrus said. He pushed the stop button, and the elevator came to an abrupt halt.

"My boys!" Hunter said. "What's up my little fucks?"

We were without the buffer of helmets and pads, without the structure and oversight of coaches. Henry was immune looking at his reflection in the silver elevator door.

"Now's your chance," Cyrus said.

Hunter took a quick step and flashed a fist. It made me flinch and they both laughed as Henry turned to them briefly. It was plausible, since I'd already instigated it once, Castritt would believe them when they said I started another fight. Then Hunter closed in bending down to my level, his eyes inches from mine, his face devoid of emotion. He held the stare; it was like Henry looking at his phone. Then he smiled.

"I fucking love this guy," he said and put me in a headlock. "I love him." I thought he was going to pull my head off, then he released me, I would've fallen if not for the elevator wall. "I'm serious, Cy, he's a tough kid." He turned to me, his face bitter. "I hate pussies, I swear to God I hate useless little homo pussies."

"You can't say that, boy," said Cyrus.

Hunter raised his hands in faux apology. "Sorry, no homo jokes these days. It's bad karma, bro. Seriously, Cy, my boy Wally here took a beating, I was sure he'd be gone by now. And your brother! The Nuber! You are a motherfucking righteous kicker. Dude, you and I can room together in the NFL."

Cyrus, leaning against the elevator wall with his arms folded, started to chuckle. "That *was* some funny shit—'The Mike's a dumbass! The Mike's a dumbass!'" he said in a raised, mocking voice.

Hunter was serious again. "He was talking about you, bitch. My boy would never say that shit to me, he loves me, right Wally?"

"You said that shit about me?" Cyrus said. His smile was gone.

I tried to slowly breathe in. "Neither, the strong safety was creeping."

"And he's smart as fuck, too," Hunter said as he pushed the stop button to release us.

"Seriously, bro, I'm cool with you now. When I see you tonight, we're partying. Fucking Tribe Forever."

After we left the elevator, I stood in front of our door with my eyes closed. The echoes of fear pulsed through me as I waited a moment, letting it expire. Henry was staring at his phone and waiting for me to open the door.

"Does Hunter ever bother you?" I said.

"No. He's the second-best player on the defense after Melvin. They're going to play in the NFL."

"How do you know that?"

"Coach Castritt told me. He said Dion's never going to play for him."

▼ ▼ ▼

Concentration evaded me, I stared at my old paper trying to absorb what I'd written a year ago. Dion not playing, the implications shattered me. *Calm yourself*, I thought, *it was an idle thought by Castritt*. Dion ran most of the plays with the first team, he was only trying to break Dion.

Dion was maturing, he would yield as needed. I saw him carrying a book from the Professor's class, I knew they were forming a bond, a bond that would avail the Professor's wisdom. John Locke, the intellectual lighthouse for Thomas Jefferson. I'd like to know what he'd think about football. I knew what he thought about tribes, he had the same thoughts as the Professor did, the words from my old paper quoted him.

> The key distinction is Locke asserts that living in a
> state is preferable to living outside of one, because
> life is easier, safer, and more enjoyable: "to join
> and unite into a community for their comfortable,
> safe, and peaceable living." (page 59).

I used the line, my quiet way of saluting the Professor under the cover of the great philosopher. The rest was a struggle, it was just after eleven o'clock when I finished and sent it to Dion and was surprised by his immediate acknowledgement. I checked on Henry then headed out.

Eddie didn't answer my texts. As soon as I stepped outside, I could feel the energy on campus and in town. I opened Tony's flask and took a long pull of his whiskey while absorbing the throbbing music from passing cars and music drifting from apartment parties, then the intermittent smell of weed and stale beer from cans littered on the front lawn of a frat. By now Eddie would be at the Parthenon, maybe at the corner table if the fat guy was still alive and partying. I hurried to a jog.

The crowd in front of the Parthenon spilled into the street under small clouds of smoke. Police in yellow control vests herded them onto the sidewalk when the bulge encroached active lanes. I circled around the crowd, hoping to spot oversized silhouettes waiting for special entry but saw only familiar bouncers. One caught my eye and signaled to me.

"Not tonight, bro."

"Why not?"

"You can go in, but there's a dude in there taking names of the all the football players. This new coach of yours must be a real hard-ass."

Finally, a text from Eddie. A party at Zinc, the huge apartment complex with a pool and open courtyard, the flask's contents kept me company on the way over. It took a while to get in, the crowd was dense around the DJ, hopping in rhythm, cups raised, beer spilling. I wandered the edge, stepping on beer cans and red cups. I felt nauseous from the whiskey and drank more, then a hand closed around my arm.

"This place is lit." It was Eddie, he spoke directly into my ear as he handed me a beer.

"What?"

"Upstairs, too crowded here."

Eddie knew somebody on the sixth floor, we were greeted with raised arrows and shots. The music was almost as loud as the DJ downstairs, bros asked if we were going to kick the shit out of Oklahoma. A girl next to me tried to make small talk, but I couldn't hear, she didn't compare to Nicole.

After an hour we left and headed to frat row. From the street I heard competing thumping music from different frat houses as I kicked an empty beer can for half a block and kept taking sips from the flask. A car tore by with little Tribe pennants sticking up from the side windows, forcing me to jump onto the curb. Balconies adorned with painted sheets spelled out crude offers for incoming freshmen girls and were occupied by frat boys eyeing foot traffic.

Eddie led us into a crowded frat, we had to snake our way through the crowd. A few other players were huddled around a tiny worn-out bar, and we waited for ten minutes to get foamy beer.

Eddie yelled into my ear, "Basement, less crowded."

The path down was a trail of people, we passed others ascending as the smell of weed wafted up from the basement. It wasn't as loud and was less crowded, there was space at a small bar.

"My bitches!" It was Hunter.

I turned and saw he and Cyrus sitting on a couch while a group was playing some drinking game behind them. He waved us over.

"You sure about this?" Eddie said.

"I guess he's over it. He's still an asshole; I'll tell you later." The whiskey brought out an edge in me. "Don't worry, they're mellowed out from the weed."

Hunter declared his love for me with a headlock and meaningless punch to my gut. He was unstable and flopped back on the couch as Cyrus gave us fist bumps. Hunter tightened his ponytail then took a hit off a bong as Eddie and I stepped away.

"Tonight is it, man," Hunter said. "No more partying after tonight. Fucking Oklahoma, baby." His eyes were bloodshot and after he exhaled, he stretched out like he was the only person in the room and scratched his crotch. Then he held his breath and winced. I didn't hear it, but Cyrus did, he turned and started waving the air.

"You stinking motherfucker," Cyrus said to him as he stood and made his way to the bar.

Hunter started giggling as he pointed at Cyrus, then threw an empty cup at him. Eddie and I watched from ten feet away as Hunter leaned over the bong for another hit. My whiskey hit full stride; an evil bloom washed over weak barriers. With each breath it was stronger, my thoughts clarified while Hunter's dulled. He probably wanted hugs and pizza, I wanted pain and atonement.

I drained my beer and headed to the bar with Eddie following. I'd had enough. The first incident with Hunter popped into my head when he pinned me against my old locker. I lowered my head and closed my eyes tight as the memory played; he didn't have to do it, he didn't have to humiliate me. The embarrassment was buried deep, covered with distractions and rationalizations: I was surprised, there was nothing I could do, I'm a good guy, I'd never been in a fight. Self-loathing welled up; I could feel it in my throat.

"You okay, man?" Eddie said. "You want a beer?"

I nodded and closed my eyes again. I was their whipping boy, an easy target, just a dopey fool that believed in everything and thought everyone else was the same. The Professor said it, we're not driven by virtue, we're driven by survival, hardcore, razor-sharp impulses honed over millions of years all at our disposal. *I denied my own, I'm such an asshole, such an asshole.*

"Who's an asshole?" Eddie said. "Do I need to get you out of here?"

I raised my head and looked at him and wondered how Eddie did it. "I'm okay," I said as I took another sip from the flask.

"Give me that shit, your head is all fucked up."

I let him take it. "Don't tell me this was full when you started."

"I'm good." The beer was like water, I swallowed half the cup and took a deep breath. "I'm going to talk to my boy, Hunter."

Eddie tried to stop me, but I shook loose and took a seat next to Hunter. His frame was huge, muscle hung from him like baggage. Eddie and Cyrus took seats across from us, both looked on with concern.

"So, Hunter, how do you like Bastille? I mean what's your favorite part besides the team?"

His eyes were closed to slits, his body rocked in a gentle silent laugh. He pointed to me then looked at Cyrus. I was wired hard, he looked like he was in the sweetest part of sleep.

"Is it the girls?"

The question affected him, he let out a gentle moan. "There's so much pussy here, dude. At that juco, we were in the middle of nowhere, man. This place is awesome."

"Are you banging a lot of girls?" I said.

"Get control of your boy," Cyrus said to Eddie.

"I'm cool," I said. "I just want to make sure Hunter is enjoying himself."

"Yeah, dude," Hunter said. "Lighten up, Cy. Yeah, there's so many hot chicks, I can't get enough."

"They all love it, don't they?"

"You bet, dude, the horniest chicks in the world, right here."

"That's right, they all love it." Eddie didn't know, but he sensed it. When I looked at him, he was staring back hard, slowly shaking his head. "Not all, really, just most, right? Some don't want it."

"Yeah, there's a few bitches here. But they still want it, at least from me," Hunter said. His own words triggered another quiet laugh that none of us shared.

"Are you sure?" I said. "Yeah, probably. But I don't know. I mean, there's this one girl I met and I don't think she wanted it."

After a moment Hunter stopped laughing, his face was still, his mouth open. Out of the corner of my eye I sensed tautness in Cyrus and Eddie. "Doesn't matter, she's gone now. Nice girl, maybe you met her?" Hunter stared at me. I could tell he understood.

Eddie stood and took hold of my arm, but I wouldn't budge. "Let's go, we're out of here," he said.

"I think you met her, Hunter. Did you *make love* to her?" Hunter stared at me, and I leaned towards him, inches from his face. He was mesmerized and I spoke in a whisper. "Or was it just sex? Or did you fuck her?"

He blinked but otherwise held his stare.

"Come on, Hunter," I said. "You can tell me. You did it, didn't you?"

His breathing was calm. He was alert but not in control.

"Just nod your head. You raped her, didn't you?"

"Don't you say a thing to this asshole," Cyrus said.

But it was too late, Hunter began nodding his head. The whiskey got the best of me, I launched into him headfirst. Cyrus pulled me off and flung me over the couch, then Eddie wrapped his arms around me and began pulling me out. Everyone in the basement stared, the music was turned off.

"You raped her, you fucking raped her!"

Even in his stoned state Hunter was quick. He lunged at me, landing a punch on my face. Eddie and I were knocked back, we fell, and I broke loose. Cyrus held back Hunter as people scrambled to get a better view. "You're a rapist motherfucker!" I screamed. I'd never felt this way, it was beautiful and righteous. I was taut and exploding, I could kill anyone.

Then someone tackled me, another held me down. I heard Eddie's voice, then others.

"Get him out of here!"

"Kick his ass, Dev!"

"Carry him out."

"He's a fucking rapist," I yelled.

I didn't walk upstairs, I was half carried, half dragged, taken through the front door and deposited on the street. Eddie picked me up and hurried me into a jog, then pulled me along into a full sprint. I screamed a wild howl and we came to a stop as I bent over for air.

"What the fuck is the matter with you?" Eddie said.

I stood panting, not knowing what to say.

"They let him do whatever he wants," Eddie said. "He could beat you to death and they'd make up a reason that would let him play."

I spoke through gasps. "I don't believe it. They're not going to let him touch me."

"How do you know?"

"Henry's too valuable. Let's get something to eat."

▼ ▼ ▼

The text from Sly said ten o'clock but I didn't care. The morning sun seemed to accentuate my hangover and it was quarter after when I arrived at his office. Hunter was already seated, his hair in a man-bun like he was trying to hide it. I didn't knock or ask to be seated.

"You look like shit," Sly said. "Did he do this?"

"No, I fell, Hunter didn't do anything."

Sly looked to his note pad and jotted something down. "Now, Hestia, I understand you accused Hunter of a heinous crime, is that true?"

I leaned forward. "You know what, Sly? It was a pretty crazy night. After me and Hunter and the guys left choir practice, we headed over to the bingo hall to help the old ladies. Those women get crazy, a lot was said that I can't account for."

Sly dropped his pencil and sat back. "Fuck you, Hestia. I don't know what game you think you're playing." He stared but I didn't respond, then he seemed to soften. "Listen, I know you've been through a hard time. You were pretty shaken that night I picked you up. I also know that you had a pretty rough camp and this knucklehead over here was particularly hard on you. I imagine in that straight-A head of yours somewhere a lot of pressure is relieved if you link the two. You have to understand; it was a tragic thing that happened to that poor girl and sometimes it's hard to get your head around the fact that we live in a pretty sick society. But the police have thoroughly investigated the affair, they've talked to me, Coach Castritt, campus security, and even Hunter. They're still actively looking for the assailant and they won't stop. But you should know, they've cleared Hunter, he's not a suspect."

"Seriously, man," Hunter said. "I know I can get pretty crazy but I'd never do anything like that."

"The most important thing is to let the police do their work and for us to be focused on Oklahoma. Are you ready?"

I looked down and gave them a humble nod.

"You've done a great job on the scout team, Coach Castritt has noticed, and you will be rewarded, trust me," Sly said.

"Yeah, he's a tough kid, Sly. I really respect him."

"Agreed. Now let's talk about Oklahoma," Sly said.

Even though Hunter's play through camp showed that he'd be one of the top linebackers in the country, he'd never played in front of a crowd like Oklahoma's. I didn't worry, I knew he'd be fine. Unless he was arrested for rape before the game. After twenty minutes we were free to leave.

"Seriously, bro, I didn't do it," Hunter said as we stood. "I'm not that kind of guy. Let's be together, man, were teammates, we're on the same side."

I shook his hand and agreed but as I left the office, I was grateful he didn't say "Tribe Forever." I stopped by the locker room to use the restroom then looked in the mirror as I washed my hands. My face looked awful, the skin around my left eye was bruised and purple. A vein in my eye was popped, a squiggly red line like a lazy river emptied into a red blur that dipped below my eye lid. *I am Bastille,* I said to myself. *I am Bastille and all that She means.* I put my sunglasses on, it was time to talk to the Professor. He spent Saturday mornings grading papers in his office. I didn't think he'd mind the interruption.

▼ ▼ ▼

The Professor would listen intently as I described the previous night's confrontation. It wasn't an all-out confession, but it was enough. Enthusiasm would build, the Professor's valor would rise. A pleading call to Mr. Feldman would take place and he'd hear how I stood up for his daughter, enough to move the process forward.

I ascended the stairs two steps at a time. The hall lights were off but ambient sunlight reflected off the floor and I could see someone standing in front of the Professor's door. Someone big with a mohawk Afro. Dion. He saw me approach.

"He ain't here. I really have to see him," he said.

"What's wrong?"

"I need my grade. Sly said he'd help but nothing's happening."

"Can you wait until Monday?"

"No way. Sly told me that if I don't get it in the system by Sunday at midnight, I can't play. Nobody's helping, I'm kind of nervous."

"I know where he lives, he won't mind."

"We'll take my car."

Even though I gave specific directions Dion almost passed the Professor's apartment complex. He pulled in slowly and we sat with the car idling.

"You sure he lives here?" Dion said. He looked to the far end of the complex and nodded. "See that end unit, the one boarded up."

I hadn't noticed it before. There was an orange X spray painted on plywood that covered the door. A window screen was torn, the hanging mesh fluttered in the breeze. "I never noticed."

"Some bad shit happens in there. That's where the crack-heads go."

We ascended the outer stairs as I took notice for the first time of the building's decrepit shape. The Professor's door was open, I heard his voice through the screen door. Then Mrs. Bertrand met us at the threshold as she was leaving.

"Wally, I didn't expect you," she said. She looked upset.

"Is the Professor here? I need to—"

"You must be Dion," she said. She wiped her eyes and steeled herself.

"Yes, ma'am. I was hoping we could—"

"Now's not the best time, maybe you two can call him later," she said.

The Professor must've heard my voice. "Wally, is that you? Come in, come in."

Mrs. Bertrand closed her eyes and nodded. "Don't be long," she said, then left.

The screen door creaked, and we stepped in. Milo Jr. sat next to the Professor, they were looking at a page, then the Professor nodded. "Yes, I'll fill it out today," he said. Milo Jr. said hello and Dion introduced himself. I could tell Milo Jr. was struck by Dion's presence, then he hurried out.

"Dion, you, too. Such a surprise, I'm so sorry I haven't gotten back to you. I presume you're here regarding the class."

"Sir, if this is a bad time we can talk later," Dion said.

"No time like the present," the Professor said. He waved his arm for us to sit, spilling the drink in his hand. "Do you want a drink? Heavens no, what am I thinking, you're both in training."

We sat slowly as Dion and I traded glances. "Professor, is there something wrong?" I said.

"Now Dion, about the class, I believe you have an assignment outstanding, is that correct?"

Dion looked at me then responded. "Yeah, I was hoping to maybe get an extension or something. But the problem is I need the grade in the system, kind of like—"

"Not a problem, in fact, let's take care of this presently," the Professor said. "I'll call her at home." The Professor pulled out his phone and called someone and as he waited, he gave Dion a reassuring nod. "Betty, Milo Bertrand here. Yes, yes, I know. None to worry. I understand, thank you, I feel the same. Betty, hold on, Betty. Yes, I agree. Betty, just a moment, I have a very important issue to resolve regarding a student. Can you get online from home? Excellent, yes I'll wait." He covered the phone and looked to us as he waited. "Are you sure you won't take a drink? It's a very special bottle."

I was about to answer when Betty must've come back. "Yes, go into the portal and my account, I believe you know the password. My last class, yes, go to the final grade. Good. The student is McAres, Dion. Yes, that McAres, got it? Okay, for the final grade please input—" He covered the phone and looked to Dion. "What did you think you've earned, a C? No, better than that, you sat in the front row. How about a B? I say we go for the whole shebang." He turned his attention back to the call. "Betty, this student did a spectacular job over the summer. Is there any way we could give him an A plus? No, fair enough, an A will do it then. Yes, Betty, we're reviewing the final paper now, he's really earned it. Excellent, I've got to go."

The Professor hung up and turned to us. "That was easy. How about that drink? Or did you have other business, Wally?" He took a long sip as Dion tried to offer appreciation.

I must've had a troubled look on my face. "Come on, Wally, speak. We've gotten to know each other well enough, tell me what's on your mind."

"It's about the, you know, the attack. I got him to admit it at a party last night. They called me in this morning, they're scared."

The Professor got up and filled his glass. He waved his hand as he flopped on the couch. "It's over, Wally, there's nothing more to be done. Mary talked to Mr. Feldman and got a full description. Then she called the police and threatened to bring pressure, which, of course, we have none. They could easily request a DNA sample and be done with it."

"I don't know what you guys are talking about," Dion said. "But all those drug tests they make us take, can't they get DNA from that? What's going on?"

"What's going on is that one of your star players committed a horrible crime." He let out a slow bitter laugh. "If it wasn't for Mary the police wouldn't have administered the rape kit. She talked to Mr. Feldman that night and convinced him to convince his daughter to go through with it. It happened at the hospital, the DNA is there. They said without a positive ID they won't force someone to submit to a DNA swab, too invasive of a person's rights, they said. It's over, Wally, it's all over."

"What's wrong?" I said. My voice had raised enough to alarm him.

"Have that drink and I'll tell you." He poured Dion and I a drink and sat back down.

"Do you remember that little committee I was on, the one where we thought it was our duty to uphold the integrity of Bastille? Well, it seems as though the result was unsatisfactory to the powers that be. The issue is being revisited, just in time for the new semester."

"Can't you fight it again?" I said.

"No, I'm no longer on the committee. And they've also scared the rest of them, it should meet with unanimous approval."

"I don't understand," I said.

The Professor sat up and took another long sip. "They fired me, Wally. I had just heard about the new committee when they knocked on my door. I'm done, we're all done. How did you get that black eye, by the way? Please don't tell me he beat the confession out of himself by using your face?"

I turned numb, numb and nauseous. It was unforgiveable, they were falling without hope, all because of me.

I heard myself moan, high-pitched and vulnerable. I pressed the heels of my palms into my eyes, I knew why they did it. The Professor touched my arm in comfort.

"Don't tell me it's going to be okay, don't lie," I said.

The Professor shook his head. "No, this, in fact, certainly will not be okay."

"Professor, I'm sorry, sir," said Dion. "I don't know what to say."

The Professor sat back. "Dion, you have no idea the peril you're in. Your livelihood, your future livelihood, may be in just as must danger as mine."

"This is my fault," I said.

"Dion, my son, Milo—" He dropped his head as remorse poured out. He straightened himself and wiped a tear from his eye. "My son is a big fan of yours. Your first two years he knew everything about every game you played. And he's followed what's happened this year, how you played in the spring game, the rumors about you, your battles with this new coach. Christ, I can't even say that bastard's name. Well, it seems you're having some difficulty, but it wasn't my place to say anything before. What you don't get is that the Tribe's desperation for victory far outweighs everything, including how they feel about you. This new coach is ruthless. He will stop at nothing to win, and he isn't interested in sharing the glory. If he wins with you, people will say he won because he inherited a great quarterback. In fact, even worse, he inherited John Oldham's quarterback. Then you made some Twitter statement about how Coach Oldham will always be your greatest coach. He wants you out. He's a narcissist, he'll lie and manufacture reality to his liking and it doesn't include you."

"But he can't, I don't do anything wrong. I don't go out, I don't smoke weed, there's no way he can get rid of me," Dion said.

"What are you going to do?" I said.

"Me? I don't know," the Professor said.

"Can you find another school?"

"Another school? I'm in my early fifties. Do you know how hopeless it's become to be a college professor? It takes at least six years to get tenured, I was hoping to earn tenure at the end of this year. The great Bastille, one of America's top universities, yet less than a quarter of the professors are tenured. In fact, more than half are part-time adjunct professors. Do you know what that means? They get paid by the course. No benefits, no security, no future, all at less than half the rate of a full-time professor. It's amazing how the school lies to prospective students. They see pictures in the brochures of students in labs with test tubes or wearing eye protection as they bring some robotic invention to life, or they stand at a white board with a wise mentor as they decipher indecipherable mathematic equations. The reality is that all of us have no security and too many classes with too many students. My favorite is the latest trend, online courses. They had us make videos which were then available to the hordes of students as they watched from their dorms, a thousand students per class. Do you know what it's like to have multiple classes with a thousand students each? We're no longer teachers, we're data processors.

"As for you, Dion, go into your coach's office the first chance you get and apologize. The first interview you do, rave about the greatness of him like you don't even remember John Oldham. Play the game as best you can then get the hell out of here."

"Professor," I said. "What are you going to do?"

"Well, to start with, when you came in my son handed me this." He held it up, a job application for the local supermarket. "I've always dreamed of working with my son, never this way, however." Then tears rolled down his face. "Oh, God, Milo Jr. A 4.0 student in organic chemistry entering his senior year, he wants to be a doctor." He wiped his eyes. "It'll have to wait. As my son, he had free tuition. Now he has to pay and we can't afford it. He's dropping out."

"What about Mrs. Bertrand, she still has the women's center," I said.

"That's another thing, their final way of exacting revenge. The women's center was funded by the university, the least they could do with all the sexual assaults that take place here. They pulled the funding, Mary just left to inform the staff. The new committee meets this weekend, and you can bet there won't be any opposition."

The Professor finished his drink. "A fine bottle, I was saving it for the celebration of earning tenure. Look at me, I'm drunk at noon, at least I'm fitting into college life."

"This is my fault, it's all my fault," I said. I cradled my head as I slid to the floor, I was a toxin.

"Wally, there are a lot of people I could blame but you're not one of them."

I shook my head through tears as Dion tried to help me up. "It's me, I did it. We'll quit; I'll do it today. They have to give you your job back."

"How is this your fault?" Dion said.

I looked at the Professor. "Because I lied to you, Henry can't do the work," I said. "He's never done any of it. They set up this new curriculum for him."

The Professor's t-shirt was stained and worn, he looked unemployed. "It was bound to happen regardless of Henry. I'm an idealist and I got run over."

"Please, I'll do anything."

"Wally, you need to move on. Face it, I'm roadkill."

▼ ▼ ▼

Dion made me ride back with him even though I wanted to walk. We rode in silence, no music, no conversation. I slumped against the door and ignored the one question he asked.

He asked again when he parked. Instead of answering, I asked him something.

"What are you going to do?" I said.

He looked away and then nodded. "I'm going to listen to the Professor; I'm going to apologize to Castritt. You don't understand, Wally, if I don't play, I won't get drafted. How about you, are you going to answer me?"

"Sure. I'm going to quit," I said.

A harsh look came across his face. "Damn, Wally, you can't do that."

"Why, because Henry's too valuable?"

"Yeah, he is and you brought him here. We need him. Come hang with me, you need to chill. The Professor will figure it out, he'll be okay. Hang out with me tonight."

"I can't, I'm meeting my aunt for dinner. She's the one that pays for me."

▼ ▼ ▼

The maître d' stood at his podium, ignoring my presence with haute bitterness. Nothing offensive was said yet his tone and movement made it clear I didn't belong. I didn't know Bastille had restaurants like this, I didn't know they existed at all. Middle-aged and elderly men wearing suits, sometimes in pairs, sometimes with a woman, were greeted warmly and led inside as if the restaurant had opened just for them. Another glance from the maître d' triggered a response.

"I'm still here," I said.

He looked away. Small wine cabinets on the wall of the foyer, some nearly empty, others stacked full with a half-dozen dusty bottles. It was a badge for rich people; they had the restaurant stow their favorite wine with their name affixed to reveal their exclusive status. I looked at the names, knowing what I'd find. It was on the far end with a new brass plate—Boone Castritt. I looked one locker over—Sly Ellington. Then someone touched my arm.

"Let me look at you," Aunt Janie said, her voice sweet and lilting.

Her warm embrace broke my tension, for a moment I didn't think of the Professor. I took off my sunglasses and her response embarrassed me.

"How did this happen? I thought you wore helmets," she said.

I touched my eye. "It was an accident; my helmet was off. I don't think they're going to let us eat here, I guess I'm not dressed up enough."

Aunt Janie looked at the maître d'. "He's a student and he's with me. And he plays for the Tribe."

Aunt Janie handed the maître d' a twenty with the same disdain he had for me. He turned and snapped his fingers and a sport coat appeared. He even helped put it on, accommodating me with words and gestures as if the previous twenty minutes never happened.

The table was covered in linen, wine glasses, heavy silverware, and funny-looking plates. When I asked Aunt Janie if they served the food directly onto it, she told me it was a charger, just decoration.

"You can't believe how excited we were," she said. "All of us were gathered around our tiny TV, I screamed when I saw you run out onto the field the first time. Were you nervous? I could barely breathe."

"That time I was. I guess every time, but it got easier," I said. My focus wandered. A man with a younger woman at the table next to us, an older couple stared off in different directions like they didn't want to be together. I wondered how they got here, if they were boosters, if they would ever know how Bastille ruined the Professor.

"I can't believe it's been a year since I've seen you, I hope you don't mind my visit."

"Of course I don't."

"I tell everyone that my nephew is at Bastille, I get such a kick out of it. When I tell them you play football here, they're amazed, I mean they really are in awe."

I looked down at the table and closed my eyes. I told Dion I was going to quit; I didn't think of what Henry and I would do. She didn't know me, I didn't know how to tell her. We ordered and I barely spoke. Everything was paid for by Aunt Janie, I owed her everything, but her questions were answered with minimal words, her responses filled in my silence.

"Straight As at a school like Bastille. You can do anything you want. As a matter of fact, a lot of Silicon Valley companies recruit here and—"

I couldn't pay attention. I nodded and tried to eat, but she sensed my mood and her questions slowed to a trickle. Soon, we ate in silence. The waiter came and bussed our table, I'd barely eaten.

"Do you want to take this home?" Aunt Janie said. I responded with a silent shake of my head. "Walter, I realize we don't really know each other, and I'm not offended by your silence. But if there's something wrong, I want you to know you can tell me. Okay? I'm going to use the restroom and give you a minute. I'm only in town for this evening, I would hate to leave not knowing what's wrong."

I sat back and sighed as stale tension left me for a moment. I'd tell her everything. She'd give me advice on where to go and what to do, she'd help, maybe offer to move us out west and start over again. When she returned, I'd tell her everything.

"Well, it looks like Bastille has all the trappings of a big city. I always thought this place was just a quiet Southern town," she said.

"What do you mean?"

"There's a working girl at the bar and by the looks of it, a pretty high-priced one." She nodded behind me. "She's been at the bar ever since we got here but I think she's got her work for the night. I'm not judging her, by the way. Most of them are victims of cruel circumstances."

I didn't fully understand but my curiosity was piqued. I turned around in my chair and looked down the narrow hall that led to the bar. I stood without permission and walked with discretion. When she came into view my heart froze, my feet felt numb. It was Nicole. Her tiny black dress accentuated her cleavage, the short hemline exposed her legs. She wore gold hoop earrings and heavy makeup. I clutched the fronds of the fern tree next to me. Then Sly appeared from the door of the restroom and made his way over to her. She placed her hand on the small of his back while he paid the bill, then he took her by the hand and led her to the door. I couldn't react, I couldn't speak. My grip on the fern must've been too tight, it started to fall before Aunt Janie caught it. Someone gasped when they saw what happened, another person clapped when the accident was averted. The entire time I stood watching Nicole.

The disturbance got her attention when she was halfway out the door. Nicole turned and saw me, her hand came to her mouth and her eyes nearly closed. Sly led her out the door. Aunt Janie stood by me the whole time as I stared at the door waiting for her to come back and explain. But the door remained closed. Aunt Janie led me back to our table like I was an invalid. The waiter stopped and she ordered another drink.

"Walter, is that what's bothering you?" She spoke softly.

I couldn't answer, I began trembling. Aunt Janie asked again. "She lied to me," I said.

"Is she a student?"

"She lied."

"I'm so sorry, this is terrible. Is this why you're upset?"

"Everything's wrong. Last year was so good, it was better than I could've hoped for."

"What's wrong? Can you tell me?"

I told her everything. When the waiter offered dessert, she ordered another drink and gave it to me. It took a while, but my words came out without effort, like someone else was talking.

She learned about Julie Feldman and her father and the horror they'd gone through and the cover up. I described Castritt and Sly, the shed, the brutality of Hunter and Cyrus. I told her what they were doing to Dion. She learned about Tony getting cut to make room for a better player at the last minute, and Samantha Yardley looking for dirt and provoking a fight between Dion and Garr Johnstone. Then the Professor and how he'd been fired. I told her how I lied to everyone about Henry so I could fulfill my dream.

"Maybe it's time to consider other options," Aunt Janie said. A hardness emerged in her face. "I made this offer to you when you were in high school and it still stands: Come live with me in New Mexico, the university isn't that far, or I'll get you an apartment there."

"What about Henry?"

"He can come, too. You can both leave here tonight."

I nodded and felt like collapsing, I didn't want to move.

"I don't mean to push you, but this is unconscionable. It's disgusting what they do to young men. All for a game."

"Coach Oldham wasn't like this. He was special, he took care of us."

I thought about Nicole and winced in pain at the thought of her with Sly. Then worse, she had recruited Hunter and Cyrus, and they'd been with her in ways I'd only dreamt about. I rubbed my face and heard the sound of my own moans.

"You don't have to decide now, or you can. It's up to you."

I began nodding. "Yeah, I'm done. I want to leave."

Aunt Janie seemed relieved, she started making plans.

"I need to pack tomorrow and say goodbye to a few guys. We don't need a flight; Henry and I can take a bus." Emotions welled up in me, I rubbed my eyes and moaned again. "She lied to me."

"What did she say?"

I sat up and looked at her, no longer affected by humiliation. "She said she hadn't been kissed in a long time."

Aunt Janie bowed her head and took a moment, then she looked at me. "She wasn't lying, Walter. It's kind of a thing that—" she hesitated.

"Prostitutes?"

"Yes, prostitutes. They don't kiss their customers."

Wally

....

iv.

Tribe4Ever@A&MCountryboy: If I gave you a penny for your thoughts, I'd get change. Dion has never lost to Dorkansas A&M and he told Bastille how stupid Johnstone is.

AggieMonster@Tribe4Ever: I could eat a bowl of alphabet soup and crap out a smarter comeback than that. I know for a fact Garr hates McAres and is going to end his playing days when they meet.

AS AUNT JANIE drove me back, the town, the campus, and the ideal of Bastille all felt foreign. As I closed her car door I wondered if my resolve would weaken. When she drove away it felt like I was deposited in a ghost town, even though the campus was rich with activity.

Henry was sitting at his desk, watching a video. I approached and looked closer; it was an instructional video for onside kicks. His eyes were inches from the screen, his body still. An onside kick was exhibited in slow motion, the video stopped to show the target area on the ball for the kicker's foot. Another freeze frame showed the ball's compression on the ground immediately in front of the tee after the kicker's foot struck it. Then it bounced high into the air with enough height to allow the kicking team time to invade the receivers.

"Henry, turn it off, we have to talk."

He closed the laptop lid and turned to me. He needed a hair-cut. I hadn't paid him much attention through camp. "We need to discuss some things," I said. He sat with his hands on his lap like an obedient child. "Some bad things have happened, and I don't know if we can stay here." I waited for his response but he didn't move. "Monday morning we're going to leave, there's a better place we can live. Is that okay?"

He stared at me for a moment, I was about to ask again when he replied, "Okay." I closed my eyes in relief and began to sort through the logistics. Too late to pack tonight, if anyone stopped by it would draw suspicion. Not enough time in the morning; films were at ten, our absence would be noticed. Get bus tickets for Albuquerque after films, pack Sunday night, then leave first thing Monday. Aunt Janie gave me enough money, we'd have to leave some things behind. When I opened my eyes, Henry was looking at the video again.

At films the next morning, I could tell that Dion had already begun his long act of contrition. His enthusiasm had returned, and I caught myself expecting Coach Oldham to walk through the door. As I entered the team meeting room, it struck me that he was talking to Hunter and Cyrus, their conversation animated like they were reunited high school teammates. It only stopped when Castritt approached.

"Coach, we're going to get them Sooners!" Dion said.

Castritt gave a quick nod with a smirk on his face as he descended the stairs of the auditorium. I sat through films disin-terested. After the meeting was over, I gathered Henry and slipped away instead of attending the mandatory weight room session.

Hype for the Oklahoma game was bigger than the year before. Castritt's presence was everywhere, there seemed to be a constant stream of television crews eager to help groom his persona and mastery of the program, like Coach Oldham had never existed.

The campus was gearing up like it was a home game; Tribe flags flew and bars advertised the number of TVs they had. Students wore Tribe shirts and hats and everything else that sported the logo. One shirt making the rounds stated "Stay in your wagon" and had an oversized Tribe arrow gashing the Sooner Schooner.

I pulled out our ratty suitcases and emptied my dresser. There was plenty of room; more than half of our clothes had Tribe logos, but I wasn't taking any of it. I was surprised how easy it was to pack, even though I consciously avoided the top corner of my closet. I knew I had to get rid of it. The gun was hidden underneath a blanket and extra pillow, I'd wait until dark to find a dumpster.

It was time to say goodbye, but Eddie wasn't in his room. The campus was quiet at dusk, the main quad empty and pristine. I took a picture of our dorm then made my way over to the Student Center. I stood in the spot where I'd first met Nicole, trying to sweep away ill feelings and remember the moment I first saw her. I took a picture of where she stood to record the background, the rest I could fill in myself. I walked the same path I led her on that day and took more pictures of the places we stopped. The sunset brought out the silhouette of Masters Library, and the interior lights cast a depth through Gothic windows. I wanted to take another photo from the inside, but it was locked. As I made my way around the library, the Professor's building came into view. I stood looking up at his window then I raised my phone and took a picture then looked at the image. It was empty and lonely.

"What are you doing?"

I looked up to the familiar voice, it was Eddie, then I looked back down to my phone. The photo couldn't stay, none of them could. I wanted no reminders. The delete icon, the little garbage can, ate each one as I touched them goodbye.

"I need to tell you something, let's head back to the dorm," I said.

We ended up on the roof as night fell and the stars came out. We filled Tony's flask and Eddie produced a joint. He held it up with a smile. "No drug tests until the bye week." I filled him in and let him know my plan.

"I figured something was up after the other night," he said. A car passed below, honking its horn in celebration as the first parties of the year were underway. "I can't believe you're out of here. A hooker? Damn."

"You can't tell anybody; Dion is the only other person that knows we're leaving."

"You know I won't say a word," Eddie said and I knew he'd keep his promise.

We drank whiskey then Eddie retrieved beer from a stash he had in his room. Eddie left and by one o'clock I floated on a gentle buzz, my thoughts dissolving before I could get anything out of them. I barely remembered stumbling to bed. Sleep would come easy, the next day we'd be free.

▼ ▼ ▼

Three hard knocks woke me. I turned and covered my eyes from light pouring in through the half-opened blinds. Pain throbbed in my head, standing would make it worse. I turned over and pulled a pillow over my head.

Three more knocks but this time they were thuds, like someone was using the bottom of their fist. I yelled for them to go away hoping sleep would come back and it was silent until I heard the jingling of keys. First, metallic clicks, then our door unlocked. I sat up and rubbed my eyes hoping to hold off the coming headache. Then my bedroom door opened and Sly entered.

He glanced at our suitcases. "Going somewhere?" he said.

"What are you doing here? You can't just come in like that," I said.

"Sure, I can. Get up, you have a visitor."

I stepped into the bathroom. My face looked horrible in the mirror, my black eye had turned yellow and red. My shorts from the night before were in the corner, I pulled them on and charged into a t-shirt. Maybe they brought Tony back and I was the first person he wanted to see. Or maybe it was Nicole, they'd explain the situation, something harmless that would prove she wasn't a—

Then I heard his voice, it was unmistakable but impossible. He stepped into my bedroom with the same broad smile he used on his congregation. It was the Minister. He wore a Tribe polo shirt and freshly ironed khakis. When he saw the look on my face his smile deepened.

"Wally, it's good to see you," he said. He hugged me but I didn't respond, I just looked at Sly standing in the doorway with a half-smile on his face.

"Where's Henry?" Sly asked as the Minister released me.

"Probably at breakfast," I said. Then I turned to the Minister. "What are you doing here?"

"Good news, good news indeed. Providence has blessed us; we're going to be a family again." The Minister turned towards Sly. "You want me to tell him?" Sly nodded. "It's unbelievable Wally, I'd grown tired of my old ministry, I knew I needed a change and prayed to God for a new calling. And then, it was like the Lord himself opened a divine new window. Coach Castritt called me. He said the team was in desperate need of spiritual guidance and asked if I would fulfill the role of team chaplain. Now, I know Bastille is a secular school, however, that doesn't mean there isn't a need for God's presence. I couldn't be more excited; I resigned my ministry and I'm selling the house."

"Hestia, there's going to be few changes," Sly said. "Your sophomore year is going to be a little more challenging, academically. We think the best arrangement going forward is for Henry to live with Minister Nubinski. That way you'll be able to concentrate on your studies."

"I'll drive Henry to school and practice every day," the Minister said.

"Actually, all of his courses are online this semester, so just bring him to practice," Sly said. "Reverend, let's go see Henry and take a tour." He led the Minister out, then stepped back into my doorway. "Wally, I trust we'll see you at practice today." Then he nodded to the suitcases. "You can unpack that now."

After they left, I sank onto my bed as the pain in my head grew. I reached over to Tony's flask and slowly unscrewed the cap. The cap hung by a beaded chain as the smell reached my nose. I took a sip and waited for my head to clear.

▼ ▼ ▼

When Eddie asked at practice, I pointed to the Minister standing on the sidelines and explained what happened.

"Damn, how'd they know?" he said.

"It had to be Dion," I said. "I told you, Henry's too important for them to lose."

Every time the Minister spoke, I cringed. He attended practice walking the field like he was an assistant coach. "Nice hit, Hunter!" he said as he clapped like he'd been a part of the team for years. I didn't tell Aunt Janie why I stayed, she was kind and left the offer open.

They took me off the scout team and I didn't ask why. I stood alone off to the side waiting until I was summoned while Henry stood with Castritt on the far sideline. It was the same on Tuesday and Wednesday. My only participation was holding for Henry, my hands were automatic, my voice a recording that spoke the same line on command.

At night I returned to my dorm with food from the dining hall

I wouldn't eat. Henry's bedroom was empty, just a few remnants left behind that I didn't touch. School would start the Monday after the Oklahoma game; I couldn't see applying myself like I did the first year.

After practice on Thursday, I went to Sly's office. He sat with his arms folded waiting to hear the reason for my visit.

"I want to change classes; my course load is too much."

"Okay. What do you want to take?"

"Why don't I just take the same classes as Henry?"

Sly started to laugh. "That's perfect, it really is. It's good that you're here, though, I was about to send you a text. Come with me."

He led me down the hall into Coach Castritt's outer office where Dion was seated, waiting to be called in. Sly entered Castritt's office, then entered the Coach's glassed-in conference room where he took a seat with a few other people.

"What's going on?" I said.

"I don't know," Dion said. He looked worried.

When Castritt entered the conference room Sly came to the other door and told us they were ready. Castritt didn't look at us, he sat at the head of the table reading pages spread out before him. No one spoke as he read. He turned over a page and continued reading, after four pages he looked up and glared at Dion, then nodded to Sly.

Sly looked at us. "Gentlemen, we're here because of a very serious matter. But first, let me introduce everyone."

I didn't catch their names, only their titles. Assistant Athletic Director of Compliance, University Chief Counsel, Head of Campus Security, Associate Dean of Academics, and PR Director.

Then Sly continued. "It's come to our understanding that there's been a violation of the academic honor code that strikes at the very heart of who we are here at Bastille. Hestia, did you in any way assist Mr. McAres in the completion of a philosophy paper for a class that he took over the summer?"

At the far end Castritt glared at me. "No, Sly, I didn't. I didn't even know Dion had a summer class."

"Did he ask to borrow your computer or get access to your university email?"

"No, we just talk football once in a while," I said.

"This is bullshit, Sly, and you know it," Dion said, his voice tense and wavering.

Castritt slammed his hand on the conference table. "That's enough out of you," he said to Dion. "You will not use foul language in my office, and you will show respect to everyone at this table. Continue, Sly."

"Well, it sure seems like something's going on. You see, there's a software program used by the University—most universities, actually—that assess whether plagiarism has occurred. It's an accredited tool that Bastille uses for all students and your paper has red flags all over it."

"Yes," the Associate Dean of Academics said. "The probability of plagiarism, according to the software, is 89%. The key is that there was a direct quote taken from Mr. Hestia's paper that was originally turned in during last year's fall semester. To be frank, if not for that quote, I'm not sure—"

Castritt held up his hand to the Associate Dean without taking his eyes off of Dion. I couldn't absorb anymore, I looked down with my eyes closed recalling what Henry told me: "Dion will never play for Castritt." They reviewed the depth of the infraction, gauging it against precedents and the resulting punishments. It was all staged, I could feel Dion's isolation.

"The implications of this should be assessed in the context of the situation," the Associate Dean said. "We should take into account the offender's perspective and contrition and his desire to adhere to the principles and the spirit of the university." The Chief Counsel nodded in agreement. "I think it would be prudent to give Mr. McAres a chance to speak for himself."

Dion leaned forward and folded his hands. He was unprepared while everyone else had known the meeting was coming. He took his time as he looked around the room at people who bragged about knowing him. He settled on Castritt. "I'm not a cheater," he said. "Ever since I've been here, I've been everything the school wanted me to be. That quote in my essay, I got it off the internet when I was doing research, I didn't get it from Wally, maybe we copied the same source. If you want to expel me from school, then do it. I don't know what you expect from me. I've given everything I have; I love Bastille more than anyone. If there's punishment, then I'll accept it. If it's worse, I need to hear it now."

Everyone looked to Castritt, he took his time before speaking. "Dion, when I was offered this job, I told the Board of Regents that the most important aspect of what I'll do is help young men grow and mature. I told them it's the values and principles of this school that are so meaningful that I was able to regain my spiritual energy to take on the awesome responsibility of this position. As hard as coaching is, the harder part of this job is handing out tough love. Your attitude has improved on the field, let's see if it improves off of it. Six games. You're suspended six games."

▼ ▼ ▼

The news swept through the team, the campus, and the college football world: undisclosed violation of team rules. The Chief Counsel helped Dion with his statement: He thanked Bastille, Coach Castritt, and the Tribe Nation for their support and apologized with the utmost humility.

On the plane to Oklahoma, Henry sat up front with the Minister while I sat in a window seat with headphones on and the music off.

"What happened?" Jeremy tapped my shoulder; I didn't notice he'd pulled Eddie out of the aisle seat. Everything the Professor said resonated like the echoes of unheeded warnings. I was emptied and refilled with a foreign substance I couldn't process. I was becoming inert.

"Everyone wants to know, word has it you were there," Jeremy said.

I nodded. "They said he cheated off me, that he copied a paper I wrote."

"Did he?"

"No, he didn't copy it," I said.

"Did you write it for him?"

"Don't ask. Six games. I thought they expelled you for cheating," I said.

Jeremy looked up to the front of the plane then behind him. "There's not a chance they're letting him out of here, these guys are too smart. If they expel him, he'd either declare for the draft or sit out this year and come back to haunt Castritt next year. I don't think he'll declare for the draft. He should be a top five pick, maybe first overall if Oldham was still coaching. But the NFL doesn't draft quitters in the first round, too many character questions, and Castritt will trash his reputation. He'll drop to at least the third round, maybe further."

"How could he hurt Bastille?"

"If they expel him, they cut his scholarship. It's too late to get on another team this year but next year he can pick wherever he wants to go. What do you think Alabama or Florida State would do to get their hands on Dion? Then he'll roll back into town and run up the score on Castritt. By suspending him six games he's stuck and they know it. He'll set his hopes on finishing the season strong, but you watch, he'll barely play."

"Why?"

"Have you seen Cooper play?" Jeremy said. "He's no Dion, but he can run this option offense. By the time Dion gets back he'll struggle to get a few plays per game. I just don't know why he hates Dion."

"I know. It's Castritt ego. If Dion's the QB, Castritt doesn't get the credit. Besides, like you said, Dion didn't buy into anything. The only way he gets back on the field is by kissing ass," I said.

"How's he taking it?"

"Not good, I don't think we're going to spend any time together," I said. Jeremy patted my arm and told me to hang in there. I stared out the window at passing clouds, but the memory was too strong; Dion banging on my door, screaming at me until I opened it, then guys gathering outside after he entered.

"Do you know what you did to me? I told you, you fucking idiot! They won't play me now, I won't get drafted, I'm damaged goods. You ruined me, you and that dumbass professor of yours."

He wouldn't stop and I couldn't respond, I looked straight ahead while he placed the blame on me and when he was finished, I sat alone staring out the window. The stadium was in the background, I closed the blinds and sat in darkness. Later that evening, Eddie stopped by, he tried to provide comfort but I was past acceptance.

"Don't take this the wrong way, you know I care about you," Eddie said. "Maybe you should split, this shit is too heavy."

"I can't," I said. "I can't leave Henry with the Minister."

After Eddie left, I sat on my bed, staring at the floor with my hands folded. This can't be, I thought. I had no idea what the Minister was doing to him, echoes of pain reverberated off the floor and around the room. He needed me. We'd never been apart.

Game day at Oklahoma was the same as the previous year but in reverse. The network held its pre-game show on campus, tailgaters flooded the parking lots, and the hype was just as thick. But, for me, it was like looking at an old photographic negative: What should've been bright was dark, what should've been unseen was in full bloom, but only to me. The band played and the jets flew, we were booed while Oklahoma was welcomed by a sprinting team of horses pulling a covered wagon.

We won the toss and deferred. Our special teams coach gathered the kicking team together, their intensity stoked to a level that left consideration of personal safety behind. From the opening kickoff I knew it immediately: We were better, better than Oklahoma and better than last year.

They went three and out, then punted, Hunter and Cyrus made all three tackles. Maybe they'd prepared for Dion or maybe they lost too many guys from the year before. Cooper Jones led us on a ten-play drive with only two passes; the rest were options and a couple of backside traps. I didn't see the touchdown, just our guys in front of me jumping and cheering while the Oklahoma crowd deflated. I got Henry and we ran out on the field for the first of four extra points. Final score: Bastille 28, Oklahoma 13.

There weren't any questions from reporters about Dion. I even looked around the locker room trying to find Samantha Yardley. The only negative outcome of the game was Jeremy's concussion in the fourth quarter. None of us saw it happen, just his slumped body lying on the turf after the other players receded from the pile. They brought him to the bench, but it was like he was a television with no reception, just scrambled and incoherent. After a minute they took him to the locker room and I didn't see him after the game.

As soon as the game was over, the media started talking about our game against Florida State, our ninth game of the year. If we were 8–0 it would be the marquee game of the year, at least one of them. Dion would be back by then. It was a brutal schedule: FSU, Alabama, Arkansas A&M, and then Georgia Tech, the reigning national champs. And I didn't care.

I tried to remember the inspiration I used to have but all that was left was adherence to something I'd lost hope in. Yet if I tried to change, take a different path, deviate from the basest routine, I couldn't. I walked the same path to the Performance Center, I stood on the same spot of the practice field, I responded when summoned for a field goal.

Henry stopped talking, worse than when we were in high school. The Minister brought him to practice and took him back to his apartment without a word to me. It was the first time in my life since I'd been adopted that Henry and I didn't live together. Looking at his empty bed triggered only mild nostalgia; I couldn't feel anymore.

But Castritt could. We thought practices would become routine, but instead he found something to tear us apart with every day. We weren't tough enough, too sloppy, too entitled. Jeremy didn't come back, and in our second game against Eastern Illinois, our new long snapper blew it on a field goal at the end of the first half. I called the snap and everyone moved except for him. They moved us back five yards to make it a fifty-six-yard field goal and Henry hit it. We led 31–0 at the half but all we heard during halftime was how stupid mistakes like the center missing the snap count would cost us at some point.

Against Towson it was another lopsided game. In the fourth quarter Towson scored against our second team and Castritt blew a gasket. His target wasn't any player, it was Coach Dixon. The TV crews caught all of it: Dixon standing stoically on the sideline as Castritt screamed at him until his face was red, then returning to repeat it a second, then a third time. Everyone on the team was scared to make a mistake, except me.

Jeremy left school before the Miami game. I sat in my room thinking about it but was unmoved. Castritt pushed him to return to the lineup but he couldn't, I saw him in the study room at the Performance Center looking lost as he stared off in a direction other than his computer. I approached him to see if he'd talk. "I can't study," he said. It was the first time I sensed fear in his voice. "It won't go away. I'm falling behind in class." Two days later, his father flew in and pulled him out of school.

The Miami game down at their place was awful; high winds, hard rain, and they'd figured out Cooper Jones. But Henry's kicks awed even the Miami fans. We led at halftime 9–3 after Henry kicked from thirty-seven, forty-five, and fifty-three yards. The field was torn and muddy, on the last kick I couldn't find a decent blade of grass to focus on, just brown mud and torn roots. But Miami scored late to win it 10–9.

After Duke and Louisville, we were 5–1 and Dion was back. Half the season was gone and I was immune to all of it. I never set my clock, I slept as long as liked. Practice was my only appointment. At night I'd look at the simple online class videos and wait until the last moment to do any work. I watched TV, annoyed at the lack of entertainment. I lit up on the roof and stared at the stars while my brain morphed into its own little dance. Eddie was playing with the second team, too focused to join me. I stopped caring.

▼ ▼ ▼

"Jesus H. Christ, Cooper, get the goddamn snap off on time!" Castritt's screams were the rhythm of practice, we knew they were coming and were the reason to keep focused. "Dion, get in there," Castritt said.

It was near the end of practice, eleven on eleven, full live. If the offense made a play, someone on the defense was excoriated; if the defense stuffed them, we waited for his victim on offense. Eddie was sent in and I watched him hold his block on a cornerback on an option to his side. The corner got loose as the running back went by but didn't make the tackle for another five yards. The outside linebacker was called out for not holding the edge and I saw relief in Eddie as he made his way to the huddle. Dion called the snap, he faked the jet sweep, then looked downfield. Eddie had beaten his man but Dion never saw him. When Eddie got back to the huddle Dion tapped Eddie's helmet in recognition, he'd throw it to him next time.

Tarik was sent in and Eddie started to jog off then Tarik stopped to retie his laces. "Goddamn, Tarik, you will not hold up my practice to tie your goddamn shoes," yelled Castritt. Eddie ran back and I saw the nod from Dion as they broke the huddle. At the snap, Eddie was jammed by the cornerback, but he gave an outside step then slanted across the middle. Dion saw him and threw a dart that Eddie caught with his fingers, cradled it, then pulled it close. That's when Cyrus hit him, helmet-to-helmet. Eddie spun, he must've been dazed, I wanted him to go down without losing the ball. Instead, he wobbled a step as another player stopped his progress then Hunter flew in. Then I saw a defensive back frantically waving to the trainers as Eddie lay twisted, clutching grass.

"Sonofabitch!" Castritt screamed. He approached Eddie and leaned over. After a quick word from the trainer, Castritt yelled into his bullhorn. "Everybody, twenty yards that way." I passed by Castritt on my way to Eddie and heard him talking to himself. "Losing enough fucking time as it is."

It was two days before I saw Eddie in the hospital. I met his family; they'd heard about me and were glad I visited. Eddie's leg was splinted and fully dressed; his thumb clicked the morphine button in vain as the pain of his leg ravaged his face. His mother spoke for him as we sat on opposite sides of the bed. "He's a strong young man, and with the Lord's help, we'll get through this," she said. I bowed my head in prayer with them, I held one of Eddie's hands and felt the tremble in his fingertips. Then his mother gave us time alone. I asked how bad.

Eddie inhaled and spoke through held breath. "All three ligaments, man. Motherfucker didn't have to hit me." He exhaled and began clicking the morphine button.

"You want me to get the nurse?"

Eddie shook his head. "No, they say they're already giving me more than I should have." He let out a pained sigh. "Twelve months. That's what they said, twelve-month recovery."

"You'll be back. You won't lose any speed, either."

He turned to me, his face in anguish but not because of the pain. "I'm done, we both know it. There'll be a whole new crop next year."

His tense arm hung over the railing; it was covered with tattoos. We'd been friends for over a year, but I never really looked at the designs on his arm. Thick veins bulged from his tight skin, veins that carried the blood of thousands of workouts, thousands of pass patterns, all for a single catch against Duke. I didn't argue, I offered to bring his books and laptop, but he just shook his head and closed his eyes. Slowly, he drifted off into an uncomfortable sleep.

▼ ▼ ▼

Rain poured down, forming little streams on my dorm window; it prevented my nightly trip to the roof with my pipe and empty thoughts. When evening came, I thought it would stop, but an hour later I looked again even though I could still hear it. Whiskey was worse but it was my only option. Out of habit I looked to my flask, nodded, and said Tony's name before taking a sip of the bitter liquid. I coughed and thought I heard a knock on my door. Then another knock. "Pizza."

I waited a moment then replied. "I didn't order a pizza."

"It's for you." The voice was odd, like a kid trying to sound older. After the flask was safely hidden, I opened the door. She was dripping wet; her head was covered by a baseball cap and the hood of her raincoat. Nicole held the pizza box spattered with rainwater while I stood mute.

Finally, I spoke. "You can't be here."

I could see the anxiety in her face, she tilted her head slightly, pleading with body language. "I'll never bother you again. Can I please come in? It'll only be a minute." I opened the door and gave her room. "The pizza really is for you."

I was afraid of my own reaction, I needed time. I offered her a chair and sat across from her on the couch. Seconds passed as she looked around, more time as I waited for my emotions to take over. She needed a towel but didn't ask; I got her a clean one from my bedroom and when I returned, I was stunned in sadness.

"I know you hate me. I'm so sorry, I should've never talked to you." I didn't respond. "I'm leaving the area, I wanted to say goodbye."

Water dripped from her coat, and I counted the drops as they pooled into a larger spot on the tile.

"Say something," she said. Her look would've broken me months ago, her beautiful eyes were tear worn and vulnerable. "I know how you felt about me. It was so good, and it hurt so bad. Please say something."

"Where are you going?" I said.

"New York City."

"Better work up there?" I said.

She quickly stood and wrapped her arms around herself, then turned and brought her hands to her face. "That's cruel," she said. With her back to me, she began to nod. I gave her time and she settled back in the chair. "You don't understand," she said. "I came from nothing, I don't have any money, I could never afford to go to a place like this even if I did have the brains." She wiped her nose with her coat sleeve.

"Sorry, I don't have any tissues."

She shook her head. "When we met, I was completely caught off-guard. I started having these little fantasies about being normal and having a boyfriend, not filthy men. It got so sweet and bad, but I couldn't stop. I knew you'd find out."

"Why did you come here?" I said.

She locked away. "I was a different person with you, I've never felt that way. I just wanted to feel it one more time."

Without invitation and with no resistance from me she approached and sat on my lap. I held her tight and let her cry. "Please remember me like you used to," she said. "I want to keep this imaginary life in my head."

I held her and felt the building rush, then whispered in her ear. "Why do you let them do that to your body?"

She wrapped her arms around me, I could feel my affection wake up without remorse. "You're no different," she said. "Look what they do to your body, all of you guys. At least I get paid." Then she stood and wiped her eyes. "I don't know, I guess we all have our prisons."

I stood and retrieved our hug and she responded in kind as we gently swayed. I couldn't help myself, I thought of Aunt Janie's words, her comment that she was probably a victim of cruel circumstances. I wanted to protect her.

"Please stay with me," I said in a soft whisper. "Better yet, come with me and Henry, we're leaving, too."

"I can't, I'm too broken," she said, but she didn't let go.

"I have to tell you how I feel, I—"

She looked up to me and raised a finger to my lips as tears rolled down her cheeks. "Don't say it, just feel it. I need to feel it, too."

"Please run away with me, I don't care about what's happened, please," I said in a whisper into her ear.

She slowly shook her head. "I'm not right for you, I can't."

My mind remembers letting the embrace eventually fall away, I remember walking her to the door and etching her face into memory as she walked away with a final look back. But I had to recall it, I couldn't feel it, I could only feel her as we stood wrapped around each other, swaying and feeling. After replaying the feeling again and again, I began to come to and her words were a final gift: "We all have our prisons."

I shouldn't be in this one, I thought. Henry and I should be in

New Mexico living with Aunt Janie. I'd go to school in peace, far from the hysteria of southern football, I was sick of it, I was sick of Dion. I'd never fully digested it, I looked up to him too much, but he did it to me. He was the only one who knew I was going to quit; he was the only one who could've told Castritt.

I couldn't stand the sight of Castritt, his ego was too big, his toxic presence destroyed sanctity. Eddie pointed it out before the Oklahoma game after I told him how a year ago Coach Oldham tapped me on the helmet as we stood in the tunnel. "Enjoy it, this is a special moment for you," he had said. Eddie loved it, then made a bet. "Guarantee you, Castritt ain't going to be in the back of the tunnel. He'll be right out front, mugging for the camera." As I stood in the back of the tunnel I tried to remember if we bet any money, because I lost.

▼ ▼ ▼

In the days after Nicole's visit my descent was unmitigated. I fell deeper as I watched it happen, commenting to myself about the absurdity of it all. Grown men whipping us into frenzies for gobs of money and false glory that would evaporate as soon as it was over, the only residue would be a banner hung somewhere to proclaim our victories to people that only looked forward to the next one. But I was affected and torn along the way. At least Dion would hear it.

The quarterback's meeting room was dark, the door was open. We hadn't spoken since his suspension, but I knew his routine, he'd be completely engrossed in game film. I took a seat as he watched Vanderbilt's defense in slow motion. He ran through a couple plays before he finally acknowledged me.

"You want something?"

"Just thought I'd watch some film."

"Why don't you watch someplace else."

Castritt's voice erupted down the hall. "Goddammit all, if he can't hold the edge, I'll cut his ass at halftime." Even in the dark I could see Dion slightly wince at the sound of Castritt's voice.

After a few more plays, I turned on the light to get his attention. "You really screwed me over, and Henry, too."

Dion squinted then turned to me with a hard look. "What are you talking about?"

"You told Castritt I was going to quit and take Henry. That's why they called his father. Henry lives with him now, have you noticed that Henry doesn't talk anymore?"

"Nope."

"The Minister's a bully, he takes it out on the weak. I was the only one that could protect Henry but now I'm not allowed to see him outside of practice. You did that."

Tension broke, he dropped his head. "I got a lot of shit going on, now. Don't lay this on me."

I thought I heard Coach Dixon's voice then Castritt yelled again. They were just up the hall and I turned towards the door.

"*K-reem*, if you can't get him to follow his assignment, I'll find someone else and I'll find a new defensive coordinator."

"Coach, their receiver hit him with a crack back, it was the corner's job to hold the edge," Coach Dixon said.

"That's bullshit, and you know it. I'll bet you ten thousand dollars the receiver didn't touch him. I'm pulling the goddamn thing up on video right now," Castritt stepped into the room and Coach Dixon followed. "Dion, pull up the Louisville game, third quarter, second defensive series when they busted one open for twenty-something yards."

Dion opened the file folder on the computer and found the Louisville game. Coach Dixon acknowledged me as he took a seat on the other side of the small room. Castritt ignored me and sat next to Dion, breathing hard out of anger. I nearly panicked and started to leave, but Coach Dixon gave me a nod to let me know I could stay.

"There, right there," Castritt said as he pointed. But it wasn't the right play. Our outside linebacker held the edge and turned the play upfield where he was nailed by Cyrus with Hunter finishing him off. "Nice play," Castritt said to himself.

On the next play the Louisville receiver came in motion and blocked our outside linebacker who was looking at the ball carrier. Our corner whiffed on the tackle, and they ran it for twenty-seven.

"That's not the one I'm talking about. Go to the next series," Castritt said with a sharp voice. I was glad I was out of Castritt's view. He moved his chair forward and stared at the screen as Dion played the video through the next series, but we all knew Louisville didn't have another run over ten yards.

"It was the Duke game, pull that one up," Castritt said.

Dion opened the video file and ran it forward. The play he stopped on was a field goal; he was about to fast-forward but Castritt told him to play it. I saw myself on screen huddling the team, breaking the huddle, picking my spot, and finding my blade of grass. It was a fifty-one-yard kick into the wind. Even during the game, I thought the ball held in the air forever, it was the same on video. Castritt let out a sigh, his tension seemed to ease.

"Pull up the kicking package, all the field goals," Castritt said. Every field goal was edited into a single file: I saw Henry and I taking our positions, each time the same, each kick perfect. The first was against Eastern Illinois then two against Towson. "Watch these next ones, the three against Miami," Castritt said in a low voice. I couldn't tell if he was talking to us or himself. His anger dissipated, his breathing settled, a calm came over him as he watched Henry's kicks navigate harsh weather. "I could watch this all day," he said. Henry kicked four against Duke and three versus Louisville and by the time it was over Castritt's body was completely relaxed.

"You want me to find the play you were looking for, sir?" Dion said.

Castritt didn't respond at first. "No, run the Miami kicks again, but do it in slow motion, the slowest it will go. And zoom it in."

The ball sailed from the center inching slowly across the screen into my hands. Henry approached the ball, his leg swung and for an instant I could see the compression of the ball. Then it sailed from his foot, arching over upraised arms into rain.

"You know what," Castritt said in a near whisper. "I bet if you took his pulse when he runs out on the field it's the same as when he's sitting in class." The next kick slowly unfolded on the screen. Castritt's voice slowed; he was absorbed in the video. "His blood pressure never rises, I know it. And the sound of all those screaming fans means nothing to him, it's like hearing the wind blow." The video showed the ball slowly spinning towards the goalposts. "He doesn't have a nerve in his body that goes off and screws him up." The kick slowly arched its way to the goalpost and fell through. "Goddamn, I'd love to have more players like him."

None of us moved, the only sound was the hum of the laptop. Then Coach Dixon spoke: "Coach, there's a little more to the game than that. We also need guys who can—" Coach Dixon paused, "think on their feet."

"Really?" said Castritt. "Dion, pull up last year's Georgia Tech game and go to the end when Stills fucked up the snap."

I was surprised he knew about Jeremy's bad snap. Dion found it and fast-forwarded to the end. The snap was off, and I saw myself like a different person, chasing after it, picking it up, and getting swallowed by the Georgia Tech defense.

"Freeze it here," Castritt said. "What a mess. Everyone, except for one guy, gives up. The long snapper dropped to his knees and stayed there, the right guard is walking around with his arms raised like a confused kindergartner, and your Academic All-American left tackle is standing there with his dick in his hands while the holder got mauled. Now I know that every team has a fire call when this happens but rerun it and I'll show you something." Dion reran the play in slow motion. "Look at him, look at the Nuber. As soon as the snap is past, he follows his order and runs the pattern. Freeze it here. Now if just a couple of guys were to," Castritt turned to Coach Dixon, "*think on their feet*, then the holder might've had a chance to throw it to him."

Castritt turned back towards the screen to the frozen shot of Henry standing alone fifteen yards downfield. "I'll tell you what, when it comes to the Nuber, I don't have to worry, not one bit."

"What do you mean, Coach?" I said.

He replied without looking, I wasn't sure he knew it was me. "I don't have to worry about him mouthing off or posting some ridiculous comment on social media. I don't have to worry about getting a call in the middle of the night because he's been in a fight or he's drunk."

Coach Dixon cast me a glance, we both knew Sly took those calls.

"I don't have to worry about him raping some co-ed or taking money from boosters. No fear of him getting arrested for robbery or dealing drugs or having a bad game because his girlfriend is breaking his heart. There's no academic issues or threats to leave early to play in the NFL. He doesn't party and I guarantee you he doesn't own a gun." The room was still. "I'd kill for more like him. Shit, you give me a QB and twenty-one retards and I'll win the goddamn conference every year."

Then Castritt turned to Coach Dixon. "I don't care what the film shows, you get your linebackers to hold the goddamn edge or, God help me, I'll destroy them."

Castritt abruptly left the room in the same manner he'd entered. As Coach Dixon followed, I wondered how long his sentence would last. I turned to Dion; he had a vicious look on his face.

"I'm sorry about what I did," he said. "I'll never bother you again. But what you heard right here, 'QB21,' you never repeat that to anybody on this team. You got that?"

I nodded and Dion left, leaving me alone in a cold, bright room.

▼ ▼ ▼

"The New Bastille" was the headline on Sports Inc.'s homepage. It featured a picture of Hunter, the new face of the program. We were ranked seventh in the country; Florida State was number one, while Alabama had already lost two games and Arkansas A&M's offense was pitiful. Georgia Tech lost too many players to the NFL and were struggling, and everyone knew the season would come down to the home game against Florida State.

Dion was barely mentioned in the article; Castritt was lauded as a tough-love coach who won despite having his best player unavailable. "A principled man," they called him. *This isn't Bastille*, I thought, *not* my *Bastille*. I curled up on my bed, opened the flask and said Tony's name. Poisonous vapors filled my nose as I stared at the Tribe logo; a year ago I felt belonging and kinship with anyone who wore it. A year ago, I was nestled under the leadership of Coach Oldham; now we were Castritt's automatons. Everyone except Hunter.

Earlier, at the team meeting, Castritt recognized Hunter's play and his Sports Inc. honor. He even said he expected Hunter to be an All-American and made a playful comment about matching any offer from the NFL. Then he offered Hunter the chance to speak, the spot where Coach Oldham used to stand.

"Fuck, man, I don't know what to say," Hunter said. "This year has been a dream come true. I have to be honest with you guys, if it wasn't for Coach Castritt, I wouldn't be here. I love this guy, the greatest coach I've ever had." Hunter turned and hugged him. "No offense to you guys that have been here but I'm sure you can tell: This is a football coach, a real football coach. It shows in our toughness, it shows in our record, and it shows in everything we do. Shit, I might stick around for another year." He started to walk away, then turned back to the microphone. "Just kidding, one and done, baby."

Everything I'd loved was infected; I didn't know how I'd escape with Henry intact, but we were leaving. I imagined life in New Mexico but then thought about watching Bastille from afar while it rotted from within. I couldn't leave Her in the shape She was in. QB21. I couldn't let Castritt and Sly and Hunter continue, I had to do something. Coach Oldham's advice came to me, "When you find yourself completely powerless, take comfort: At your darkest hour, your character will find power within you." I let the thought roll around in my head, there was a way to save Her, but the damage might be too much.

I touched the name on my phone and the connection began, then second thoughts. I was about to hang up when she answered.

"This is Sam, who's calling?"

I didn't respond. One touch of the red phone icon and the call would end.

"Is this Wally Hestia?"

Her words triggered a response. "I'm sorry, I accidentally hit your number."

"That's all right. How'd you like the article we put up? I didn't write it, it's a real puff piece, not my specialty."

"Yeah, interesting." Neither of us spoke for a moment, she played me out.

"I'm going to take a guess here, Mr. Hestia," she said. "I don't think you accidentally dialed my number. Got something on your mind?"

"I guess, I don't know. I can't tell you, but if you knew—" My voice trailed off. "So much has happened."

"Come on, Wally. You've got the balls, what happened to Mr. Nobody?"

"You don't understand."

"I understand more than you think," she said. "Just give me a hint, just a tiny scrap."

"There's got to be a way I can tell you without—"

"Wally, I'm boarding a flight soon. Just give me the general idea, I'll figure out the rest."

"Maybe I could have someone else call you; they know," I said.

"Does it have to do with the coaches? Is money involved? Is the NCAA aware?" she said. "Just give me the tiniest detail and I'll—"

"Hunter Devlin raped a girl and they're covering it up. I know; he admitted it to me." She was silent, I thought the call dropped. "Are you there?"

"Holy shit. Tell me more."

"I thought you were getting on a plane?"

"I'll get another one, I'm all ears."

We spent more than an hour on the phone and I gave her the story. The only break was when she had to let the airline know she wasn't boarding the flight.

"What else is going on there?" she asked.

"Don't, there's other stuff, isn't this enough? This is still my school." I said. "Even though I'm leaving."

"Do they know that?"

"No, I tried to leave once, but—"

"But what? You can't leave. If you do, they'll blame it all on you, you have no idea how much they'll lie. If you go, they'll say you were the one that attacked her and you're trying to frame a rival. You *have* to stay, at least until it's published."

"When will it come out? Before this week's game?"

"No, not even close. You've got Vandy this week, right?"

"Yes, then NC State, then the FSU game."

"If this holds up, probably the Tuesday before the FSU game. I've got to talk to everyone involved. The good news is I've got a source inside the Bastille City Police who can verify they interviewed him. Jesus, this is big. If this is for real, I won't show my hand until the Monday before, otherwise Castritt and that dirt bag Sly will bury it. In the meantime, don't breathe a word of this to anybody."

"One more thing," I said. "You're not going to use my name, are you?"

"Trust me, I know how to do this. They'll never know it's you."

After she hung up, I sat in silence. *The Tribe, the larger Tribe, all that love Her, will back me. They believe like I do.* The FSU game, I could last until then. And then after the game, Henry and I would escape.

I looked to the spot on the couch where Henry always sat and imagined him looking at his phone playing his numbers game or watching TV. My question was involuntary: "Henry, did I do the right thing?" Silence accentuated my loneliness, even though the answer would've been the same: Nothing.

On Saturday, I stood in the tunnel next to Henry as the crowd raised their arrows. It was like a flush of bodies when we ran out. Castritt was in front when the crowd dropped the arrows and sounded the collective *BOOM*. Vanderbilt was playing the best they had in years, but they were no match. At halftime we were up 17–10, the final was 31–13 and Dion didn't play.

I spent the next week self-medicating even though I knew I had to straighten up. At night my mind collected scenes of revolt against the school, a revolt I triggered. Then the horror turned on me for letting the outside world know our sins, a sin that couldn't be washed away. The Bastille name would be sullied, my name remembered as the one that did it. Whiskey stirred my thoughts until I was too incapacitated to stay awake. In the mornings, the bright fall mornings, I felt hope and shamed myself for the painful state I was in.

We rolled NC State and Dion didn't get in for a single play. He was in his own free fall, powerless to the situation. After an upset weekend with number two Wisconsin losing to Minnesota and USC falling to Colorado, we were ranked fourth. If we beat FSU, we'd climb to at least number two, and possibly the top of the polls. Then we'd have Alabama, and then the hated Aggies of Arkansas A&M.

On Monday of FSU week, Castritt addressed us. "I know there's all this bullshit between us and the Aggies," said Castritt. "Put it aside, for now. McAres, I guarantee you'll get a chance to stuff it in the face of that loudmouth asshole Garr Johnstone. And you better get it done. But until then let's remember our hatred of Florida State." He paused and took a deep breath, his nostrils flaring. "If you think about it, I can't imagine any team I hate more than the Seminoles. I grew up hating them, I hated them when I played against them, and I've hated them my whole coaching career." By the time he was done, hatred for FSU oozed out of everyone's pores.

Back in the dorm I looked up Castritt's playing career; he'd never played against Florida State. A couple of guys were talking as they passed by my door. I used to hear Tony and Eddie approach, but no one stopped by any longer. Jeremy was gone. Henry was isolated. Then my phone rang, and I knew why. I wasn't ready.

"Get your ass over here right now," Sly said, "or I swear to God I'll have you shot."

I hesitated. "Yeah, sure Sly. What's going on?"

"Just get your ass over here!" he screamed. I had to hold the phone away from my ear.

It was after eight o'clock, but it was still eighty-five degrees as I walked to the Performance Center. Sweat poured down my back as if my body knew the depth I'd stepped into while my mind pled ignorance. The police would've written down my name the night we took Julie to the hospital, it was public record and there were a lot of people at the frat house the night I confronted Hunter. Everyone on the team had become aware of Hunter's crime, but it wasn't discussed.

Coaches were always in the office late, but this was different; there were people I didn't recognize, all in suits. They weren't boosters waiting to see Castritt, they carried themselves in haste, talking in whispers, as if they were trying to solve a dreadful puzzle with time running out.

From the lobby I could hear someone in Sly's office, but not Sly himself.

"If he's the source and he refutes then it's dead. They can't run it."

"A lie detector? That's not the point, we need him to recant."

"I wouldn't use those words but sure, if you can crack him."

A man in an expensive suit left Sly's office and entered the conference room as the rest of the group assembled and I was summoned in. The room was full, even the Minister was there. He was against the wall leaning against the Tribe flag. There were no introductions, I was seated at the opposite end of the conference table from Castritt. He sat with his arms folded, all of his power concentrated and aimed at me. Then the man in the suit began.

"Mr. Hestia, are you familiar with a woman named Samantha Yardley?"

I couldn't help looking around. "No, I don't think so. Is she a student? What is this about?"

"You know goddamn well who it is," Castritt said.

The man continued. "We have it on record that you interacted with her after a game last season. She's a journalist from Sports Inc. It's on the internet, you referred to yourself as 'Mr. Nobody.'"

It was a step closer, if anyone had seen me with her in Vic's they'd know. "Oh, her. Yeah, she was needling Dion after we lost a game. I kind of stuck up for him. She was being a—" I fumbled for a polite word, then just said it: "She was being a bitch, I kind of told her off and got in trouble for it."

"Why are you sweating?" Sly said.

"It's ninety degrees out and I ran over here after you called. What am I being accused of?"

The man in the suit began to speak but Castritt cut him off.

"Let's cut the bullshit. We all know what happened. Some lit- tle slut is trying to accuse Hunter Devlin, a fine young man, of a horrific crime. The police have been involved, they've spoken to all parties, they've looked at video tape, and they've completed an exhaustive investigation. There's not a shred of evidence, the whole thing has appeared out of thin air and we thought it was over. But now, this scumbag journalist has written a hit job on Hunter, conveniently timed to cause a distraction before this week's game. There's only one person that could've provided her with the infor- mation, and that's you."

I shook my head. "No, you're wrong, it wasn't me. I don't know why you hate me; I've done everything you've asked me to do. I did find a girl that night and I helped her. I even talked to the police, but there was nothing for me to tell. As far as Hunter goes, he was being obnoxious and he told me he did it, that was in front of a lot of people. Hunter was really stoned—" Castritt held up his hand. "Anyway, Sly called us in the next day and told me what you're telling me now, that the police looked into it and Hunter didn't do it. I dropped it."

Castritt kept staring but the surrounding intensity abated. The man in the suit rubbed his eyes, the issue was still unresolved.

"I don't think this is the right avenue," he said. "If I understand correctly, the woman who ran the women's shelter who took her to the hospital that night is the wife of a former Bastille professor. Is it correct that he was recently terminated?"

"Yeah, performance issues."

"Gentlemen, that's clearly the most obvious source of suspicion here. Have we had any luck finding him?"

"No," another man in a suit said. "His phone has been disconnected and there's no forwarding address. If it was him, and that's what makes the most sense, I don't think he'd recant, anyway."

"What the fuck do we do?" Sly said.

"At this point we deny and leak that a disgruntled former professor manufactured the story," the man said. "In the meantime, we state we are suing this professor for libel—we can have that filed first thing in the morning—and then weather the storm. Of course, the prudent thing to do is withhold Mr. Devlin from this week's game."

"Not a chance, not this week," said Castritt. "If it gets bad, we'll hold him out against Alabama or better yet, wait until A&M. Our second team defense could shut them out."

"Perhaps we should discuss this further, but let's excuse Mr. Hestia first."

Castritt kept his glare on me as I left the conference room, then the Minister followed me out and cornered me alone in the lobby.

"Wally, so help me God, if you're lying you will suffer the wrath of God," he said.

His bloodshot eyes were the same. I hated how his nose hairs seemed to grow into his mustache. He belonged here less than I did, but I still couldn't face up to him. "I'm not lying, sir."

The sweat never evaporated, I let it pour off me as I ran back to the peace of my dorm. Inside, cold air would wick it from my body along with the accumulated fear. But when I sat in my room a sick feeling sank deep within me. I was a liar, no better than them. I shook Tony's flask, but it was empty. It was time to go to the roof.

▼ ▼ ▼

Tuesday morning, I woke in Henry's room, my t-shirt carried the scent of weed and I couldn't remember going to bed the night before. At noon I went down to the dining hall and returned to my room with food. I ate in silence, then made Henry's bed and tried to do homework but it was useless. I couldn't look at Samantha's article.

Finally, I pulled it up and a tiny picture of her appeared in the corner; she didn't look that good in real life. As soon as I started reading, I understood why they blamed me; she included details only I would know. Rainwater on the bushes, my muddy sweatshirt being tossed aside, the desperate, crazed look in Hunter's eyes when we fought. I couldn't leave.

Castritt would have to address the article in our pre-practice meeting, I decided to go early to avoid contact with anyone. Twenty minutes before the start of the meeting the room was empty, then a few players arrived. Usual loud voices were whispers and no one approached me. I felt a little better. Henry arrived and pulled out his phone and I breathed easier sitting next to him.

"Henry?" He didn't respond.

"Henry?" He looked up at me and a wave of relief poured through me.

No one spoke to me or cast an accusing glance. Quiet conversation hummed; the first hurdle was past. I dropped my head and closed my eyes to visualize the next one. My teammates would want to know the source and it would quickly turn to me. I started to pick out the guys that would support me then I noticed the room had fallen quiet. It startled me; no voices, no movement, like the silence was coordinated. When I looked up, everyone was staring at me with a look of concern. Then I heard it behind me, less than an inch from my head: a deep inhale followed by an exhale that was nearly a growl. My skin tingled on the back of my neck; I could feel his breath as I grasped the arms of my seat. Without looking, I knew it was Hunter.

"I swear to God, you little fuck, I'm going to put you through so much pain you'll never recover. You're dead."

"Hunter," Sly yelled out. "Take your seat."

Hunter stared at me as he walked by while the room remained silent, then Castritt took the podium. Even in the worst situations his speaking skills were extraordinary, the only raw material he needed was confusion and angst. He talked about distractions, the price of fame, the noble duty to endure and keep focused. We didn't hit at all during practice; I think he was afraid we'd peak too soon. After practice I left without showering under watchful eyes.

By Tuesday night it was national news. On CNN, half the panel argued about the abuses of big-time college football, while the other half called for due process. Every channel ran clips of Castritt proclaiming the virtues of Hunter and his innocence as established by the police. The university Chief Counsel read a statement indicating that a disgruntled former professor and his wife were the source of the salacious lies and a civil lawsuit had been filed against them, Sports Inc., and Samantha Yardley. I didn't eat that night, too afraid to run into Hunter. Tony, Eddie, and I traded texts, but they couldn't help. Eddie was still immobile and Tony was under lockdown hundreds of miles away.

I woke Wednesday morning to the sounds of a group of women picketing in front of our dorm as a camera crew filmed them. It took campus security over an hour and their best manners to get them to leave; the university was private property and they'd have to take their protest off campus. On the news I saw they'd setup on the sidewalk at the campus entrance with Prisoners' Fountain in the background, the same background used in the university's promotional videos. No one spoke to me during Wednesday's practice, and I left without showering again.

On Thursday morning it broke that I was the source. Sly sent me a text telling me not to leave my room until practice. Food would

302 SINS OF THE TRIBE

be brought and campus security would escort me to the Performance Center. One post on social media referred to me as a brave whistleblower, then an avalanche of posts flooded in: a traitor, a snitch, a mole within the blessed Tribe. Then the conspiracy theories surfaced: I was the culprit and had schemed up an elaborate ruse to avoid prosecution; I was getting paid off by Florida State to sow havoc the week before the game; I was gay and had been rejected by Hunter and made up the story out of spite. The story was still in the news cycle Thursday night with shots of more protestors and questions posed regarding whether Hunter should play.

Normal distractions were unavailable. I shook Tony's flask, knowing it was empty and going to the roof was out of the question; I didn't have any weed left, anyway. My email was full, none of the senders were familiar, none of the messages positive. "Hestia, you evil weasel! You will not live to see the sunrise Sunday morning." It was my favorite death threat due to its correct spelling, concise language, and a specific timeline. Food was delivered and I received it without a word. After I ate, I sat on my bed without purpose, staring at the top shelf of my closet. Then I got up and retrieved Mr. Feldman's jacket, I held it in my lap and unrolled it, exposing the gun. Its metal was cold to the touch.

I couldn't go forward and I couldn't go back to West Temple, I couldn't even make it across town to catch a bus out west. Dread filled me. I didn't want to breathe, but my lungs did anyway. I didn't want to see but my eyes wouldn't close. Time was lost to me in reverse; it wouldn't pass no matter what I did. With the gun in hand, I paced the room, carving a path over tiles that soon became a path impossible to break. Then, I was sitting in the middle of the floor. They'd sue the Professor; they'd break him even further, the thought of it made me cry out. Just one pull of the trigger and it would be over. Maybe there was something else, something beyond, someplace where truth reigned, even hard truth that might take your dreams but wouldn't take your freedom. A place where suffering wasn't a necessary byproduct of tribes.

If there was a place, maybe I'd see Coach Oldham and he'd tap me on the shoulder like he did before our first game and offer kind words. I let myself go in memory, back to the stadium tunnel over a year ago to see his face and feel his reassurance. I could feel the tight chin strap and see the bars of my facemask as he tapped my shoulder pads. I turned and saw his face, but it drove me deeper into despair. It was a look I'd never seen from Coach Oldham—disappointment, bitter disappointment, like he regretted ever meeting me.

"I'm sorry," I said to him, my eyes closed.

"That's an unforgivable sin."

Tears rolled down my face. "I won't, I won't," I kept on saying it, urgently, he had to know I wouldn't as his face drifted away and Henry's came into view. Henry's pureness, his vulnerability, when he looked to me; I needed him more than he needed me, and he needed me more than anyone.

I opened my eyes and looked down at the gun. "Goddamn, I've got to get rid of this thing." I wrapped it up in Mr. Feldman's jacket and returned it to the closet. I don't know when sleep came, the last time I looked at the clock it was after three in the morning.

When I woke Friday morning there was a text from a number I didn't recognize. *Players-only meeting at noon.*

I didn't wait for my escort and arrived early again. The room filled sooner than usual, and at noon the doors were closed. I didn't know who called the meeting or who would lead it; then someone spoke from the back.

"Looks like we got a little problem on our hands." It was Melvin Richardson, not someone I would've expected. He walked down the steps to the front of the auditorium like the moment of rectification was inevitable and waited as our silence confirmed his role. "First, I've got a few questions. Then, if any of y'all got something to say, raise your hand. I'm going to start with Hunter." Melvin took his time. "Hunter, did you rape that girl?"

Hunter looked surprised. "No man, like I told everybody: I didn't do nothing."

Melvin pursed his lips and slowly nodded. "Okay, okay." Then he turned to me. "Wally, did you talk to that reporter?"

I wanted to tell them. I wanted everyone to hear what it was like to find her, to see the horror in her face, to see her broken father, to realize the vulgarity of the cover-up. But if I did, something in the room would've snapped. I could feel it in every eye staring at me; they had to believe. The truth would break a sacred seal and the room would drain of power. The tribe was more important, I denied the truth to save the tribe. "No, I didn't do it."

Melvin gave me the same nod and waited but no one raised their hand. "Now, this is the way I see it. This thing that happened is bad, real bad. Whoever did it should be thrown in jail. But that's not my job to figure out, it's not the job of anyone in this room, we'll let the police do that. So, in this room, if Hunter said he didn't do it, then he didn't do it. Also, if Wally says he didn't talk to that reporter, he didn't talk and that's it. After this meeting, I'm talking to the media—and Dion, you're coming with me—and we're going to tell them what we just decided. Now, I love this school, I always have. We've got a chance to beat the number one team in the country tomorrow and we ain't going to let this get in the way. I know we're better, Bastille is better, everything about it is better. Everybody cool with that?"

A few responded verbally and others began to clap. Melvin kept nodding as a righteous feeling started to grow. It continued until Melvin abruptly stopped it.

"I just got one more thing that's been on my mind. Hunter, we all know you're a great player, I'm sure you'll be playing on

Sundays next year. But this year, you're here. Now, you said you didn't hurt that girl, and as teammates, I've got to accept that. But I've seen some of the shit you been doing around campus, including that dirty shot you laid on Eddie. You're a guest here, like we all are. If you can't show Bastille and all of us the respect we deserve, then you need to go, now. And, if I ever hear you say Coach Oldham wasn't a real coach or disrespect his memory in any way, I'm gonna fuck you up something bad, me and about seventy other guys in this room. You hear me?"

Hunter didn't respond as Melvin held the silence until his point settled on everyone. Then he turned his attention back to FSU and spoke to our deeper selves, like he was an honest preacher cleansing the soul of the Tribe. Before we were done noise erupted, big noise with raised arrows and "Tribe Forever!" chants. Maybe I didn't have to leave. I stood with my teammates, my hands raised in the arrow, chanting "Tribe Forever! Tribe Forever!" The sweet noise lifted me to a place I could never ascend on my own, the exultations a constant climax. *This is why I played,* I thought. It had always been why I played.

▼ ▼ ▼

I knew it was coming. I picked my blade of grass, looked to Henry, and was about to call the snap when the whistle blew. The ref waved his arms and signaled time-out, Florida State. They were trying to ice Henry, a waste of everyone's time. The clock showed three seconds left before the half, we were down 10–0.

"Nu-Ber! Nu-Ber! Nu-Ber!" The chant used to thrill me, I always let the sound settle in my head so I could listen to its echoes later. But now, I was troubled.

It started on the walk from the Performance Center through the yellow-roped alley. The Tribe faithful lined the walk and I waited for the inevitable to occur: protests for Hunter and death threats for me.

My imagination the night before got the worst of me; I visualized poster boards with "rapist" written on them, and I mentally practiced my reaction to someone charging me. The walk was too far and the crowd too large to be effectively policed and the outpouring during the week too great to be ignored. I wanted to see Hunter humiliated, I didn't care what happened to me. I wanted to see him face the signs and hear the taunts, then hang his head in shame. Deeper punishments ran through my head. Screams coming from inches away driving the pressure to react beyond his control, then physical contact as cameras recorded a fight he could never win.

But instead, they applauded. Faces blurred from one to the next, some clapped, others extended their hands, wanting to touch. The suspense was never answered, and I should've been glad. Inside the locker room I sat next to Henry as his twin, voiceless and unmoved. I shook my head and reminded myself, *They're good people, now's not the time.*

The first half was ugly football: offensive miscues, penalties, and cheap shots by us. On our opening drive Cooper got wrestled to the ground and as the whistle blew our tight end decleated an FSU defensive back twenty yards from the ball. Two of their guys jumped our tight end taking it to the edge of disqualification before the refs stepped in. After a late hit on their QB by Pokey, another fight nearly erupted and there was no way to prosecute it. Hands clutched opposing facemasks as the refs tried to break it up, only the threat of more penalties and ejection brought it to an end.

On one play, Cooper was forced out of bounds on their side and he didn't immediately reappear. A cluster of FSU players in garnet and gold swarmed like piranhas triggering our side to rush the field. Only Coach Dixon stopped them and after he got our guys to the bench, he turned to the ref screaming for them to get control of the game. The only response was a yellow flag that offset the mugging of Cooper.

On our last drive before the half Tarik exploited a blown coverage that brought the ball to their thirty-five with less than a minute left. A year ago, Coach Oldham would've told Dion to take his shot. It still pained me to see Dion standing on the sidelines holding large poster boards with ridiculous images signaling the next play. After three plays, Henry and I were sent out for the kick, our first time on the field.

It was different from any game I'd played. I was used to corners flying by at a speed that was easier to hear than see or defensive linemen nearly breaking through with enough energy to flip a car. They'd land in front of us as the kick sailed safely away then ignore us as the focus of their effort was gone. Even against Miami, a team still saddled with a dirty reputation, a defensive back flew by and after he got up, he was standing next to me as the kick sailed through. He had a gold tooth and dreadlocks, and I froze waiting for him to start something. But all he said was, "Damn, your boy can kick." But in this game, our edge had been honed at a different angle.

Our guys thought we'd done nothing wrong, but all our cheap shots turned the game into a different contest. Threats and heated words were exchanged at a well-practiced level, just out of earshot of the refs. When I arrived at the huddle, our linemen were scheming about how to hurt one of their defensive linemen. What scared me the most was during the time-out one of their linebackers said something in the earhole of their edge rusher, number 17, then he pointed to me. The edge rusher nodded and looked at me like I was prey; I didn't think they were discussing my courage as a whistleblower.

The ref blew his whistle to start the play clock and the players tensed up in position, more than two tons of angered organisms trying to survive in their own way. The snap was high and I caught it with my fingertips. Henry wouldn't adjust his timing, I had to place it quickly. I could tell by the sound it was good but didn't see it go through. As their edge rusher flew by his cleat hit my helmet, then he grazed Henry. Out of the corner of my eye I saw a yellow flag in the air and number 17 in Henry's face, unleashing a string of invectives. I should've walked away. Henry was immune to it and the FSU player couldn't take things any further. But I couldn't help myself, I'd been under Castritt's spell too long.

The stadium lights reflected off his visor and I couldn't see his eyes, but I could see his lips moving in anger at Henry. My first thought was to earhole him, but then I'd get ejected. But all those power cleans finally came in handy; I came in from his left side and launched my hands into him and extended my legs, it was probably the most powerful I'd ever been. The shot moved him a couple of yards and he threw his hands up in disbelief as another flag was thrown at my feet. Guys on our team went after him but were quickly neutralized in a scrum. More flags came in then the refs started throwing their hats as adrenaline released. I wanted blood, I wanted to get ahold of a facemask and pull a helmet off. I wanted to land a punch and inflict pain even though there was no one on the field I could dominate. And then I saw Henry, standing a few yards away unaware of the physical danger he was in.

It ended as fast as it happened, it took the refs longer to figure out the enforcement. I stood on the sidelines with Henry as players congratulated me with slaps to the helmet. Finally, the ref broke from his own huddle and announced the penalties: two personal fouls on them, two on us, all offsetting. We were down 10–3 heading into the locker room as the crowd chanted Dion's name.

I was still half-cocked on adrenaline as we waited for Castritt in the locker room when I started to look around. Our equipment manager looked like an airline attendant pushing a cart through the locker room, but instead of coffee and soda, his cart was loaded with ice bags; he stopped at raised hands as trainers quickly affixed bags to players' limbs. Another trainer used a pen light to gauge the dilation of another guy's eyes then he looked up to the position coach and shook his head. Ankles were rewrapped and bandages were applied. Then Castritt came in and the room fell silent.

"That was weakest goddamn football I have ever seen!" His huge voice carried through, vibrating us to the core. "If that's what you call football, we will not win another game this year. Only four first downs! Did you hear me? Four! If I had a goddamn quarterback, we'd run these sons of bitches off the field. Defensively, we're not good, we're lucky. They had over a hundred and fifty yards on offense, a hundred-fucking-fifty! If they had half a Nuber we'd be down by twenty." He paused and scanned the locker room, his breathing heavy as if he played. "Before you go to your position coaches, I want to let you know one thing. On your way out of this locker room each one of you is going to look me in the eye and I better see the fires of hell burning deep or you'll never suit up for me again. Dion, warm up."

I was last in line leaving the locker room, it was like ten lanes of traffic funneling into one. Castritt stood just outside the door with his arms folded and his teeth clenched. Most of the players with clean uniforms were quickly nodded away with a twitch of his head but the guys that played got an extra second. He held up Hunter and wouldn't let him go until Hunter unleashed a scream, then Cyrus did the same. Henry was ahead of me, he edged forward in half-steps and almost got away from me until I pulled him back. Coach Dixon pulled Dion out of the line and told him to wait. When the room was nearly empty, I heard Dion.

"Motherfucking bullshit!" Dion said.

I turned just in time to see him whip his helmet across the room and I knew immediately. Castritt wasn't benching Cooper, he just wanted to scare him. Dion dropped to a stool and clutched his head, slightly rocking in pain as Coach Dixon spoke to him quietly.

"I'm trying to fix this, Dion, you've got to hang in there."

Coach Dixon looked up and saw me staring. He gave me a quick jerk of his head so I'd turn away, and when I did Castritt was in front of me. I guess I'd forgotten my fires-of-hell eyes, because I wasn't allowed to pass. Castritt stepped back into the locker room, closed the door, and pinned me against it with his forearm.

"You little son of a bitch, you cost me fifteen yards with that stunt of yours. We need every yard we can get and all of a sudden you've got to act like you're some kind of badass. You've already done enough damage to my team, you better hope like hell I'm in a good mood after this is over."

Then he let go and I dropped a couple of inches, unaware he'd lifted me up. After Castritt left, I tried to take a deep breath and when I did, I noticed my bottom lip was quivering. Coach Dixon was still kneeling by Dion, but he looked at me.

"You okay, son?" he said.

I nodded quickly and put my helmet on; he had enough to deal with.

Nobody scored in the third quarter, neither team even crossed the fifty. But each play was a series of collisions and deep struggles that bound the crowd's attention. If Florida State got a first down their fans, just a sliver in the top corner of the stadium, sung out their weak version of a war chant. When we made a play, they were punished by raised arrows and became the target of the *BOOMS*.

Then, on the first play of the fourth quarter, football disaster struck. As Cooper called out the signals the FSU strong safety overloaded to our right, he must've been tipped by something. We were deep in our own end and at the snap the strong safety shot the B gap. He must've crushed Cooper; all I saw was the ball popping up in the air and the play breakdown into a scramble. The ball

took a funny bounce as an FSU defender tried to scoop it, then
it rolled across our goal line out of reach of the hands and arms
struggling for it. They were about to fall on it in the end zone and
put the game out of reach when Cooper dove and knocked it out
of bounds for a safety. No one was happy, not even Florida State,
although their fans picked up volume to stick it in our faces.

Cooper's effort was something he should've been proud of;
he was blindsided by a shot that would've knocked me out then
he fought through to limit the damage to a safety. But when he
got to the sideline, Castritt ripped off his headset and, with a finger pointed in Cooper's face, began a thirty second nationwide
instructional moment that seemed a lot longer and deeper to those
of us on the sideline. After they got the ball from the free kick our
sideline was spent. Dion sat on the bench and our guys seemed
more concerned with consoling him than focusing on the game.
Florida State drove down and kicked a field goal to make it 15–3.

We went three and out on our next three possessions and
everyone knew it was over. Then they drove the field with little
resistance and would've scored on two different plays if not for
Melvin tipping a pass at the last second on one play, then running
down a receiver from the opposite side of the field on the next.
But it was first and goal from our five-yard line and the thought of
going down 22–3 felt like a blowout.

I crept towards the sideline to get a better view, pushing in
front of disappointed administrators and big dollar boosters.
From the right hash they ran a dive play through the right-side A
gap and their running back was met by a pile of collapsed linemen and Cyrus shooting over the top to meet him head on. But
he didn't have the ball. Their QB, ball still in hand, did a reverse
pivot and rolled left to find their tight end running a flat route
into the end zone all alone. The QB threw, it would be an easy
touchdown. Except the pass floated.

I didn't see him at first, I didn't think it mattered, but Hunter kept sprinting. Every split second the ball was in the air his odds improved. The crowd stood in anticipation, everyone on the sidelines moved forward for a better look. There's no way, I thought, at best he could knock it away. Then he leapt and with one hand tipped the ball as it tried to sail by. It was the kind of play that drew deep focus, my powers of observation slowed time. The ball spun end over end, I could read the NCAA label as it spun while Hunter fell in a somersault, it wasn't possible. As the ball descended, Hunter regained his feet and reached, tipped it again; then it fell into his palm, and he secured it as his feet tried to break his momentum and not go out of bounds. He cradled the ball and came to a stop on his toes less than an inch from the sideline. Castritt was in front of me, crouched and looking down the line to see if Hunter had stepped out of bounds. When it was clear he hadn't, Castritt leapt with arms extended and his play sheets flailing beside him as the get-back coach pulled the back of his shirt.

Hunter turned to the open field in front of him, the only threat to catch him was their QB since they ran the play with jumbo personnel and no receivers. But their QB was fast and began to close quickly as Hunter ran down the sideline past waving arms in a valley of screams. He was five yards away when Hunter cut sharply and ended all doubt. Their QB was still sprinting and unprepared to catch the top of Hunter's helmet under his chin. The violent shot at high speed knocked him backwards and he hit the field hard, then rolled over and covered his head.

The remaining sixty yards were the loudest I'd ever heard. After Hunter crossed the goal line, he came to a stop by sliding on his knees, both arms extended, the ball held aloft in his right hand. Players who ran after him held off their hugs and slaps, they provided Hunter room to receive. He stood and turned in a slow circle with his arms extended as the shrieks built and the arrows were raised, and I couldn't believe it. After a moment to allow their energy to peak he dropped the ball, brought his hands to his chest and pulled them away to expose his heart. The arrows dropped in his direction and the sweet *BOOM* was delivered in perfect unison. It had to echo out of the stadium, and I turned and walked away.

It was a moment of clarity, a moment that triggered horrible nausea. The last tumbler clicked and opened my eyes for good. If there was any doubt about the Professor's lessons, they had been extinguished by the arrows shot at Hunter.

Henry made the extra point and instead of being down 22–3 the score was 15–10 and the Tribe had life. Momentum belonged to the Tribe and with three time-outs the defense forced a three-and-out without taking much time off the clock. It was Cooper's chance to redeem himself and after two incomplete passes he escaped the rush on third down and ran out of bounds after a twenty-nine-yard run. After they dropped a sure interception, Cooper threw a screen that took the ball to their twenty. Three incompletions later it was fourth and ten with thirty-five seconds left, we had to go for it. Even though we were told to get ready I didn't expect to go in; a field goal would make it 15–13 with no way to stop the clock. The only way to get the ball back was an onside kick and a chill ran through me. They'll kill him, I thought. Henry and I were the weak links and the strength of the team and Florida State knew it. Their guys didn't have much left, but one hard shot to Henry would end it. Then Castritt sent us in.

In the huddle nine sets of eyes looked back at me, their faces worn with sweat and dirt, pained and wanting it over in victory, not prepared for the abyss of defeat, even though we clung to a disappearing ledge. After calling the field goal I told them: "Do not let them touch Henry." It gave them further purpose, another reason to draw deeper from themselves. As soon as the kick sailed over the line, I escorted Henry to the sideline, watching it go through over my shoulder. I took note of the clock, just twenty-nine seconds left. Even though I knew it was coming, I had to stop it.

When I got to the sideline, I screamed at Castritt, "They're going to kill him and you know it."

He didn't acknowledge me as he frantically waved and yelled for the onside kick team to gather during the TV time-out. The special teams coach had his hands on the side of Henry's helmet giving final instructions. There was nothing I could do. It was my fault, I brought Henry here to be the target of violence illegal anywhere else. FSU didn't care about the last field goal, they cared about the next one. I got in front of Henry as the onside kick team took the field.

"Henry, this is different than field goals, it's a live play, they're going to hit you. You've got to protect yourself," I said.

"Coach told us to get the ball."

I wanted to take him by the arm and make him run with me to the locker room, then anywhere—anywhere but here.

"You've never been in a game without me, after you kick don't go after it."

"Coach said we have to."

"He didn't mean you; you'll get hurt!"

The special teams coach got ahold of his arm. "It's time," he said. When he led Henry away, the full pressure of the moment fell on me. Both teams had taken the field, most lined up on the left, directly in front of us. The TV time-out official dropped his arm to let the refs know we were live. I couldn't look, I turned around to see the reason. Tens of thousands, most wearing Tribe green, many with replica jerseys, a few in body paint. A middle-aged woman was in the front row bobbing up and down with her hands clasped in prayer, the beads around her neck bouncing in rhythm on her Tribe jersey. Around the nation, in bars and in homes, millions watched as Henry walked alone to the tee.

I had to watch; it was my punishment. Henry walked slowly past our players assigned to run full speed through the FSU hands team. Henry, my brother, my innocence, was unaware of the Tribe's needs and demands, unaware of the lengths taken to feed them with moments like this. The ref handed the ball to Henry like a sentence.

My childlike naïveté was my sin, believing in something that didn't exist, or existed for reasons I hadn't understood, and supported by means that caused an entire tribe to look away until it was game time. Like a child fascinated by the danger of wild animals and wanting to get close, I'd walked deep into the jungle and brought my brother with me.

After he placed the ball on the tee, he carefully took three steps back and one over. Then he slowly raised his hand waiting for the whistle from the referee to begin play. The whistle blew and Henry lowered his arm. For a brief moment, he didn't move. Then, he approached and swung his leg full-speed into the top of the ball and the play began. Our guys sprinted at full tilt, as did a few of the Florida State players. There was no design, just medieval simplicity full of false rage. Henry's kick compressed the ball to the ground immediately in front of the tee, then bounced high, maybe twenty feet, in a beautiful arcing spin that made it anybody's ball. My eyes didn't follow it, I watched Henry ignore my plea and run after it like he was chasing butterflies. I wasn't the only one ignoring the ball and watching Henry. Number 17 had him locked in at full speed. Henry never saw him coming.

The ball was still in play when Henry was hit—his head snapped backwards and his helmet was dislodged as his feet completed a circular path. I guess we recovered the ball; the expulsion of 90,000 screams of joy concussed the stadium as Henry's helmet rolled to a stop and his body didn't move.

I was on the field before the trainers were, sprinting without my helmet like it was a red-cross symbol; I wasn't there to fight. He was alive, I saw his hands dig into the holy grass, then I heard his cry.

"Henry, I've got you. Can you move?" I had to fight off my own tears.

"Wally, we've got him," the trainer said.

I moved out of the way, then heard the Florida State trainers attending to one of theirs. Up field, where we'd recovered the ball, a Florida State player writhed in pain on the ground. "It's his ankle, maybe broken. Get the cart," the FSU trainer said.

I looked back to Henry and saw our trainer nod in reassurance to Castritt, who was standing a few feet away. When our eyes met, I didn't say a word but my glare, full of hatred, let him know all that was needed. His own hatred for me was gone, he was unaffected. Then he spoke.

"Get him ready."

I couldn't believe it, there was no end. They sat Henry up and blood poured from his nose, soaking his jersey before they could place a towel over it. I pushed my way in and helped him stand.

"I've got him," I said. I wanted everyone to see his pain and hear his cries. A path of blood stained the front of his jersey and his naked cries were pitiful. He didn't cry through the guards of adulthood, he sucked in a breath and expelled it with full force. He cried openly like a child, open wails to exercise pain, but they were more powerful as a message. An alley opened up on our sideline leading to the medical tent, our teammates looking on ruefully, like they were as guilty as me.

The medical tent was too small for me to enter, I looked through the opening as trainers sat him on the table and began examining his face as he continued crying. Then I heard the ref's call:

"Bastille has possession of the ball at their own forty-nine-yard line. Also, unsportsmanlike conduct on Florida State, number 17.

Number 17 is ejected from the game and Florida State is penalized fifteen yards. The ball will be placed on Florida State thirty-six-yard line. Injury time-out."

It would take a few minutes to get the injured FSU player off the field. I pushed my way into the tent and the Minister followed me. "How is he? Can he go?" he said.

"Get out of here, now," I said as Henry continued to howl.

"Henry, you're going to feel a little prick on your face to ease the pain," the trainer said. "Close your eyes and it will be over in a second."

A drop hung from the end of the needle. Henry moaned in terror as they held his arms and head, then inserted the needle into his face.

"You assholes, you're shooting him up to play!" I screamed.

They ignored me as they injected more into his face.

"Leave him alone, he can't play."

Cotton swabs were inserted deep into his nostrils as tears ran down the sides of his bloated cheeks.

"Do we have another jersey?"

"No, just wash out the blood."

"You don't even know what's wrong with him!" I snatched the wet towel out of the assistant trainer's hand. "Get out, get the fuck out now."

"You watch your language, boy," said the Minister.

I placed my hands on the table and looked into Henry's eyes. "I'm sorry, Henry, I'm sorry I ever got you mixed up in this," I said. "Do you want to go home to the dorms? Do you want to leave?"

"Coach wants him ready now!" the Minister said. "They're carting off the injured guy in a minute. There's only nineteen seconds left; you're supposed to get him ready."

It wasn't planned but it was years in the making. Like a snake, my left hand snapped from the table, exploding across the

Minister's face in a backhand. His head whipped to the side and
he covered it with his own hands as he looked at me in disbelief.

"You're a bully," I said. "You've always been a bully. Leave or
I'm taking you out."

"I got this," Castritt said as he pulled the Minister out of the
tent and entered. It was just the three of us, and my adrenaline
fought against fear I couldn't control. He looked over Henry then
raised his index finger. "One kick, that's all I need."

"Fuck you, you fat bastard."

Castritt's large head turned to me, I couldn't tell if he had the
beginnings of a smile or a snarl, I didn't know if he was going to
intimidate or manipulate me. He chose the former. "You listen
to me, you little shit. You've been trying to ruin this program since
day one and I'm done with you. You're going to go out there and
hold and Henry's going to kick or so help me God I'll—"

"You'll what? Ruin me? I'm already ruined."

"Not like I'm going to ruin you. I'll take everything you've
ever had."

"You already have. We play for free while you get millions, we
don't get educated, you've taken my friends, my brother, and every
ounce of dignity."

"You whiny puke, I've turned this program around. Listen to
them, this is what they want. Last year it was luck, but I've got
Bastille back to where it should be."

"Right, we'll be ranked number one, we'll be a school again.
Except we don't have any professors left, you fired the best one.
Instead, we've got hookers, thugs, and rapists. And you covered
it up."

His nostrils flared, he growled through shallow exhales. "You
did it, I know you did. You betrayed me and talked to that reporter."

There was nothing he could do, and I felt the grace of sick
power. "One kick. One kick and we're out of here. And you're
goddamn right, I'm the one that talked."

His ire deepened to a hard red as my evil laughter, uninhib-
ited and free, taunted him. He slammed his fist on the table, then
left. I gathered myself and turned to Henry. "After this kick, we're
through with this. I'm going to take you to a place where there's
no more yelling, no more violence. We'll live in peace and finish
growing up."

Henry slid off the table and stood before me. I couldn't tell
what he was thinking but his crying had stopped. Then he followed me out of the tent.

The ambulance was leaving midfield with the injured FSU player
when Henry and I reappeared out of the tent; somber applause for
the injured turned into loud applause for us. The first time we took
the field more than a year ago against Oklahoma, I'd trembled in
fear; I wanted to be like Dion and run onto it with confidence, with
a special power to which the Tribe pledged their love. Now we
were, but it was a parting gift. The field goal team assembled in the
huddle in front of us and I buckled my chin strap as I approached.
Henry took his position, and I entered the huddle.

"Is the Nuber okay?" one of the linemen asked.

"For this kick he is. Field goal on first sound. San Fran, San
Fran."

The FSU defenders were like hot animals, moving and jumping,
they wouldn't hit us, there'd be no point. I knelt and rubbed the
grass with my palm, my way of saying goodbye. So, who would it
be, my last blade of grass? I picked it out, an average one, just like
me. *An innocent blade planted only to get trampled.* I looked to
Henry, at his bloodstained shirt and his bloated face with cotton
swabs sticking out of his nose, which had turned red. He nodded
and I turned to the center. I wished it was Jeremy snapping, but he
was long gone.

Then a cruel thought hit me: I could blow it, I could call the
snap and let it fly by, ending the game in horror for the Tribe
faithful—they deserved it. I could see it now, an iconic image of

me holding my receiving hand out and not moving as the ball
sailed past. If I didn't move, Henry wouldn't either. It would be
hysterical and macabre as the two of us remained frozen as the
cries erupted and the mad scramble ensued. Both sides would
fight for it, Bastille's effort in vain and yet Henry and I would be
frozen still the whole time. It would make the top ten and when
interviewed, I'll tell the world everything, that my protest was the
only way I could give voice against the sins. "Set." As the ball left
the center's hands my plan was final, I'd let it fly by.

What happened next, I'll never resolve. I had no control; I was
a trained cog in a violent machine, like an odd but critical com-
ponent on a fighter jet. As the ball reached my grasp, my finger
left the blade, and my hands automatically caught the ball. Then
I placed it down, spun the laces out, and Henry's foot struck it,
sending it high and straight into a cloud of tribal screams. Sixteen
to fifteen, the Tribe was ahead. After the kick, instead of escorting
Henry off the field, I stayed in position, oblivious to everything. I
was unaware of the cheers, the celebration, and completely tuned
out from the fight.

It must have started with a couple of linemen, the scrum in
front of me was still moving after the kick had gone through. An
FSU helmet was off, its owner's naked head was obvious: Blood
trickled down his face as he grasped one of our guys amid falling
bodies and swinging arms. Near our sideline, a group of four or
five from each side were in full battle, a few hit the ground as
others were tackled. But still, I didn't move. There were multiple
conflicts and they migrated towards our sideline, where players
from the bench merged into the fight, outnumbering the FSU players. It wasn't just pushing and taunts, I saw an FSU player thrown
to the ground, then cocked arms with elbows high, firing into the
player as it grew like an out-of-control fire.

Then a wave of FSU players sprinted past me as I remained

kneeling on the ground, their entire team abandoning protocol to save their teammates. Then the fight completely engulfed our sideline as coaches from both sides rushed in. It was time to go, no one would notice us leaving. I turned to Henry, but he was gone. Then, through a maze of players running to the half-dozen hot spots, I saw him. He was walking as if it was a trip to the dining hall. I buckled up and sprinted towards him, he was heading for the middle of one of the fights.

Then Henry was knocked over and couldn't get up, lost in a labyrinth of bodies, and someone hit me from the side. I got up, not caring, and began to weave towards our bench through clutched bodies spilt over with anger and blood. Through still more I fought and was clutched but I raised my hands in peace. Then Henry was there, surrounded and lying on the ground fifteen yards away; my feet dug in, driving my charge with precision. Then Castritt fell, and it changed everything. He was on one knee directly past Henry, disheveled and confused.

In the moment I didn't blame myself, Castritt had trained me and we were all brainwashed to overcome obstacles with violence. Someone almost hit me as I took aim and launched into the air. There was no sound like two helmets colliding and I barely felt anything, but it happened. Hitting Castritt's unprotected head was like hitting a bag of flour and the rush I felt came from deep within and tickled my sickness with delight. I pulled Henry over to me and covered him.

"We're leaving right now and never coming back."

The fight raged and I heard someone say police were on the field.

"Henry, did you hear me? We're leaving, look at me."

He stared at the grass hard, like he was holding on to something I couldn't see. "Coach said we have to stay. Coach said we have to stay. Coach said we have to stay."

I yelled into his ear, "Are you a robot? Stop screaming and look at me, we're leaving, now!"

But he repeated it in his monotone voice, "Coach said we have to stay. Coach said we have to stay. Coach said we have to stay."

He kept on repeating it even after I stopped urging him, his eyes never moved, he couldn't see me anymore. I looked over to Castritt lying on the ground motionless, blood seeping from his ears and mouth and nose.

"Coach said we have to stay. Coach said we have to stay."

As I led Henry to the safety of the bench, he kept repeating the words in his monotone voice and he never looked at me. I jogged into the medical tent, unbuckled my helmet, and dropped it on the grass. Then I untucked my jersey, unhooked my shoulder pads, and pulled them off, letting them fall to the ground. I stepped outside the tent and jogged against the stadium wall as the crowd booed over me and called for more at the same time. Police and event security were flowing onto the field from the tunnel and let me pass without question. When I got inside the tunnel someone took hold of my arm.

"Wally, are you okay?" It was Samantha Yardley, and I could tell by the look on her face that I was insane.

I dug the heels of my palms into my eyes and heard a moan come from my chest. She pulled me over to the side.

"I watched you fly in there, what happened?"

I leaned into her ear. "You've got to get me out of here, I fucked up Castritt, bad." I tried to see if there was any sympathy in her face.

"I've got to cover the game," she said.

"It's over, everything is over."

She looked out onto the field at the madness Bastille had become. "I will if you tell me everything, everything you've seen."

"I will, it's a nightmare."

"You're right, the game's over. Get your stuff."

Samantha

....

THE SECURITY GUARD wouldn't let me on the field. I pled, threatened, held my press pass up and shook it until I almost snapped the lanyard. The old codger didn't hear half the words I said, his walkie-talkie squawked with voices and static as police and event security in yellow windbreakers flaked out. None of them wanted to go out on the field to break up the fight if the coaches, the only real authorities on the field, weren't able to stop it.

A sold-out stadium, national TV, a week-long buildup for this week's game of the year; two hallowed programs, ranked one and four, all set for war, a death match, on the idyllic Bastille campus. They really did it this time.

"Get all security around the wall, do not let any civilians jump onto the field." The voice on the other end of the walkie-talkie kept calling out the message as the old coot began directing his people.

"Go, go, go!" Then he looked at me. "You go on the field and you're arrested!"

"Fuck!"

I couldn't tell if the fans were for or against the fight, it was a strange cacophony of boos, screams, and flying cups with fifteen seconds left on the clock. My phone buzzed—it was Brendan, my editor.

"Are you in the box or on the field?" I could barely hear him and retreated deeper into the tunnel.

"I'm in the tunnel, they won't let anyone on the field," I yelled.

Brendan relayed the images and commentary from the broadcast. "You've got to get a quote before they cool down. Do *not* leave the field," he said.

I didn't respond, I lowered my phone as I watched Wally Hestia cross from the bright lights of the stadium into shadows. I barely recognized him, jogging with his helmet off, his jersey and shoulder pads gone, his face full of anguish. He didn't sob, there wasn't a heaving rhythm to his pain, it was frozen at its peak. I reached and got his attention.

"You've got to get me out of here, I fucked up Castritt, bad."

My source was ready.

"Get your stuff."

After he submerged into the locker room I walked back to the edge of the tunnel.

"Sam, are you there? What's going on?" Brendan said.

The fight had stopped. FSU players receded to their sideline while a crowd of Bastille players stood circled around a spot on their side. Someone in a suit and tie waved frantically towards the tunnel like he was calling for me, then a piercing siren behind me lit my ears for a half-second. I jumped out of the way as an ambulance drove past and headed for the Bastille sideline. *I've got to get him out of here*, I thought.

"Brendan, I've got to go."

As I approached the locker room, the door swung open and Wally ran out wearing slacks, an unbuttoned dress shirt, and loafers without socks, exposing his taped ankles. His Tribe backpack, slung over his shoulder, bounced on his back as I tried to keep up with him. When we got outside, he pulled out his phone, broke it in two on the edge of a garbage can, and threw it away. Then he turned and looked out over the thousands of cars, the anguished look still on his face.

"Where to?" I asked.

"Anywhere, anywhere west."

"What about your brother?"

The question hit a nerve; Wally moaned painfully as he sank into a squat with his hands over his head.

"Follow me," I said.

Media parking was close and within minutes my rental car's weak engine whined as we sped out of the parking lot, up the stadium drive, and onto the main thoroughfare of the city as Wally, bent over in the front seat holding his head, rocked and screamed through exhales.

"West, like west of the city or further?" I asked. My phone buzzed; Brendan was calling. I declined the call and tossed it in the back seat. "Wally, talk to me."

He cried through his hands, full throated like he was trying to destroy himself from within. The car, even at full speed, seemed to rock with his movements; his head still covered and bent over, his torso slamming backwards against the seat.

"Wally, don't break the seat!"

"No, no, no!" He picked his head up and repeatedly slammed the bottom of his fists on the dash, popping open the glove compartment. He looked forward with bulging eyes and screamed out like he was trying to shatter the windshield.

"Wally! Stop!"

But he couldn't. We passed a car dealership, a Walmart, a supermarket plaza, apartments, and restaurants as he melted down beside me.

I've seen a lot. I've seen the shells of coaches after their final defeat, reciting post-game phrases drawn from a bankrupt well of clichés, knowing their careers were done and probably wondering if they still had a connection with the families they barely knew anymore. I've seen star players suddenly stripped of their golden auras, rendering them into vulnerable, oversized twenty-year-olds as they realize their greatest achievements had already occurred. I've seen my mother, after my father died, sob in horror as our new reality unfolded every day like a punishment, knowing I was the only reason she held on.

But I'd never seen this. A true believer who used his only power, innocence, to become part of the goddess he worshipped, only to find her center so deeply corrupted that he found himself the only one still looking, until it tore him from his moorings. As we drove past city lights, past suburban commerce and cheap apartments, he came apart. Over time he stopped damaging the car and turned inward. His violent screams and digging clutches intensified into an ongoing pulse until it smoothed out, just a straight line aimed deep within, draining him away. I didn't know where we were going, I couldn't tell how long we'd been on the road that had turned into a dark path with two yellow lines and no streetlights. I could almost hear the bugs in the dense trees on either side of the road.

"Are you hungry? Are you thirsty?" I said. He didn't reply and I had a piece to write. "Wally, please talk to me."

"Do you have anything to drink?" His voice was different. "I'll tell you everything."

"I have water in my backpack," I said.

He sat up and slowly shook his head. "I mean something to drink."

I stopped at the next cluster of lights at a small plaza, a generous use of the term. "Wait here." A truck-grade service center was on the far side but what got my attention was a small set of shacks that offered three staples of the deep South: guns, fried chicken, and liquor.

The medium bottle of Jack I brought to the counter wasn't enough; he needed food so I added a bag of beef jerky from the front of the counter.

"You a journalist or something?" The clerk was obese, his fat arms spilled out of the flannel shirt that had its sleeves cut off.

"I'm sorry?" I said.

He nodded to my press pass; I'd forgotten to take it off. "Can you believe it? The Seminoles pulled it out. They ran the kickoff back after that big fight. Goddamn Tribe."

"What about the coach? I heard he got hurt," I said.

"Took him away in the ambulance. Got his ass kicked in the fight."

It was getting late, near midnight and I had to get in touch with Brendan. A modest-looking motel was ahead; I pulled in and got Wally a room. The room smelled of mildew and the air conditioning kicked on with a loud, deep buzz as we walked in. The bed sagged under the weight of cheap use, there had to be bed bugs, I thought. We sat by the small desk, and he slowly unscrewed the bottle of whiskey as he stared at me. For a minute I thought about my own safety, then shook away the thought.

"I want your backpack," he said.

I looked at his own bag and understood immediately; it had his name and number 16 and was adorned with Tribe logos. "Yeah, sure," I said, and poured the contents of mine on the bed. "Here."

"Where do you want to start?" he said.

"Just let loose, Wally. Now's your chance."

He took a long sip of whiskey then closed his eyes and sighed like an old man who couldn't see retirement. I took a sip, too, and nodded.

Hours later, the bottle was empty and Wally was asleep on the bed. I went to work. I don't know how much time passed before I had a draft I was happy with. It was still rough and vague in spots but I had a first-hand source, the details could be hardened later. Brendan would be happy; with a little work it could be uploaded to the website by eight in the morning. I sent it off then realized

I'd left my phone in the car. I went outside and lit a cigarette, then retrieved my phone from the backseat. Brendan had called five times, the last two hours ago. He needed time to read. I smoked another cigarette, then sat in the rental watching the occasional car pass. Then he called.

"Well, I guess I know who you're with," Brendan said. "He's actually there?"

"Sleeping. He's in rough shape."

"I can tell by your piece. But first, I thought I asked you to stay on the field. And why wouldn't you answer my calls?"

"Just read the piece, Brendan."

"I did, it's useless except for one thing."

"How can you say that? It explains everything that's going on, it's—"

"You were the only one we had there, and every other outlet has the thing covered in detail; we had to write it up after watching it on TV. You screwed up, Sam. You became part of the story by driving that kid out of there, you could get fired for this."

"What about the real story?" I said. "That's more important than a fight and a close game."

"You didn't see the kick return, did you? The most dramatic finish to a game in years and you missed it. What do you think we're paying you for? An investigative piece takes weeks or months or longer, you know that, and you want to publish this now? Even then, big deal."

"Are you kidding?"

"Let's see what you've got. An egomaniac coach, sexual assault, player abuse, hookers, using drug tests to cut marginal players to get the scholarship back, no-show classes, running roughshod over academic types, and a cover up. This stuff describes half the programs in the country; I'd get fired if I posted this story. I heard your name came up at the parent company's board meeting this week. There's a lot of Bastille influence around and they want to know why we're picking on them. If I publish this, they'll come after our heads."

"There's not anything you can use?"

"One thing—if your kid goes on record saying he took out Castritt on purpose, that's news."

"He didn't say it that way." The line fell silent. "What will happen to him if he does?"

"I don't know, probably nothing. Will he do it?"

Probably nothing. Brendan knew and I could tell by the tone of his voice he was lying. It was assault with a deadly weapon. "I don't know, that's a lot to ask."

"It's a big deal and if you have an exclusive with him right after it happened, you'll be all over the place and it'll make up for tonight. Ask him. No, don't ask, make him go on record."

"How is Castritt?"

"Not good, at first the announcers were worried he was dead. He's obviously concussed and his face is busted up; broken jaw, cheekbones, stuff like that. Get him to do it."

"What did it look like on TV?"

"You can't tell who hit him, there was a pile of players. It looks like Hestia got pushed or something, they don't have an angle that shows Castritt getting hurt yet; most of the cameras were focused on a different fight. When everyone got up, Castritt was lying there. Get him on record, Sam."

A cold front was coming through, I could feel relief from the humidity as I walked back to the room. I would explain the risks to him if I could wake him. The words so far were only between him and me. My head was too dizzy to recall exactly how he'd said it. It would be the kind of story that would land me on TV shows, I'd become a brand. He knew what he was doing; he's always known. He was the one who called me about the rape story.

I tapped the door gently then opened it to a crack. "Wally? Are you awake?" There was no sound except for the air conditioner. I opened the door and looked in but my eyes couldn't see in the dark. I found the light switch and turned it on: He was gone. The only evidence he was ever there was his worn and empty Tribe backpack.

As I sat on the bed, a feeling of emptiness deeper than the subtraction of one person came over me. I thought about chasing after him, I knew he was headed west. A chill settled over me, and as I closed my eyes, something left me. They'd chase him down, maybe find him at a bus station as he tried to escape. I'd have to go and watch him get cuffed and hauled away and in the last moment before his head was pushed into a police car, he'd see me.

I called Brendan. "He didn't do it," I said. "He said he saw Castritt laid out already when he went to protect his brother."

Brendan's silence unnerved me. "Give me a thousand words on the whole fiasco. Maybe you can go back into Bastille and scare up some quotes, even if it's from a fan."

I laid back on the bed waiting for my crash to sound. Back to Bastille for a thousand words with a building headache, no food, and my feet killing me. My source fled and I missed my assignment, the kind of night that should make me cry if I could.

Samantha

....

RESTON, VIRGINIA
A YEAR AND A HALF LATER

BOOKS OF FABRIC swatches covered the table and Abbey leafed through each one, pausing on the samples she liked and asking my opinion. A light red mesh pattern, then green foliage with yellow flowers. I swallowed my last sip of beer before answering.

"To be honest, they all look the same," I said.

"You sound like Jerry."

A baby's cry came over the monitor and Abbey looked. The cry turned into a yawn then sleep resumed.

"How old is he now?" I asked.

"Six months. My doctor said I could have a half glass of wine. Can I pour you some?"

"A half glass? I'm going to spill more than that."

Their new house felt sparse; walls painted with off-white builder's paint and rooms filled with apartment furniture that barely filled the space. I loved that she was excited. I took a seat on the couch as she handed me a glass of wine. Her figure was on its way back from childbirth but she pinched her tummy in disgust.

"Fifteen pounds, I've still got fifteen pounds to lose and it's so hard," she said.

"You look great. I'm twenty pounds overweight and I didn't create another person, all I've created is—" My voice trailed off.

"What? You love your job, don't you?" She waited but I didn't respond. "Jerry had poker night here last week and all his buddies know who you are. I listened from the other room while he told your stories like he lived them himself, it was so cute. Is there something wrong?"

I shook my head and stared at the TV. Sports Inc.'s TV show was on with the sound muted. "I love this time of year," I said. "I get to relax a little. The conference media days are next month and that's when the grind starts again."

"You mean the fun grind," she said. "You should see Jerry and his friends talk about it; they can't wait for the season to start. His one friend is a huge Bastille fan, by the way. Jerry likes them, too, but he needled this guy something terrible when your story came out about the sexual assault a while back. Are you sick of the travel?"

She leaned forward and wouldn't let it be. It bothered me that we rarely got together.

"I like that I can tell you anything," I said. "I don't like that you *make* me tell you everything."

"You love it."

She made me smile for a moment, I was thankful for our connection.

"I don't know anymore, it's just the same thing over and over. You either write puff pieces to build them up or hit jobs to take them down. That's my specialty."

"More wine?"

"I'll get the bottle." It was nearly empty. "This is the deal, sometimes I wonder if the hassle is worth it. The travel is a bitch, the stories are the same—you could just swap out names and a few details and it's always the same. And female reporters have to put up with an element that men don't."

"What do you mean?"

"Access is everything. Male sportswriters trade info, but women are asked to trade something else."

"How bad is it?"

"A subtle offer here, an innuendo there. I get my ass grabbed once in a while."

"Can't you report them?"

"Sure, you'll never work again if you do. It's terrible and humiliating; some women, the smart ones, get out of the business because of it. I can deal with the travel, I can deal with the repetitiveness, I can deal with the fact that I've got to feed the beast every week with original stories that are the same every year."

"Then what's the problem?"

"I can't take the narcissistic bullies anymore spouting out hypocrisy year in and year out. No matter what I write, nothing makes a difference."

"That's not true," Abbey said. "What about the story I just mentioned, the rape at Bastille? That made a difference."

I let out a bitter half-chuckle. "That was the tip of the iceberg, at least until I was told all the other shit was commonplace." I took a sip of wine as Wally's face appeared in my mind. "I wonder what ever happened to him."

"Who?"

"My source. I just loved this kid and, boy, did they fuck him over. He was ruined by the time they were done with him and then he disappeared. The thing is—do you remember that game, FSU at Bastille a few years ago?"

"The one with the huge fight? Jerry told me about it. Were you there?"

"Yeah, I was there." My thoughts drifted away, the feeling of entering that empty hotel room and knowing he was gone fell over me. Something was lost that night.

"Well, tell me."

I folded my legs underneath me. "He was my source for the rape story. If it weren't for him, nothing would've happened. He found the girl and got her help. He even told me how the girl's father came looking to get revenge and he talked him out of it."

"Did anyone ever find out he was your source?"

"Yeah, they did. I think it was a pretty rough time for him. He was really something. This kid believed in his school like no one I've ever seen. He wasn't a good athlete; he was only there because his brother—that's another story—was this wunderkind kicker. But he believed in all the great aspirational values these schools drape themselves in. Under the old coach, it was all true, too. But when the new coach showed up, it all changed and he paid the price. He held on hard to what he thought was right, but the ship left the dock and tore him in two." Abbey was silent, she knew I had more.

"Those bastards, Castritt and Sly Ellington, he's the one that likes to grab my ass. Anyway, the kid snapped, he was the one that took out his own coach on the sideline during this huge fight and then took off. I almost got fired for it but I took him away and he told me everything; it was the one article I wrote that got to the heart of it and showed who these bullies were, but they never printed it."

"Why not?"

"A bunch of reasons. It doesn't matter. All that matters is Castritt and Sly Ellington are still there, still collecting a king's ransom. I hate them, I can't tell you how much I hate them."

Abbey set her wine glass on the coffee table and stared at me with her mouth slightly open in a bitter way.

"What's wrong?" I said.

"What about the kid?"

"I don't know, he disappeared. My God, he snapped right in

front of me, I mean he really snapped. He's got to be damaged goods now."

Abbey shook her head and went into the kitchen. I heard her open another bottle of wine and when she returned, she filled my glass and then sat with an air of dismay.

"You're wrong," she said. "You're wrong and obsessed. For someone so worldly I thought you'd be smarter than this."

"What are you talking about?"

"There will always be bullies, and you're playing this weary role like I should feel sorry for you. What about your source, the kid?"

"What about him?"

"Remember years ago, when my mom was dating that jerk and he picked on me during that game? You stood up to him and changed everything."

"Yeah, then he came back the next year and rubbed it in my face."

"I'm not talking about him, you changed everything for me."

She waited for my response, but I couldn't speak. A hole opened inside of me, something that had been building for some time.

"What about the letter you wrote?" she said. "The effect it had on your father and me was incredible. There will always be hypocrites and bullies but you saved us at that moment by pointing it out. And if you do it enough times people start to believe again."

"And what good will that do?"

"They'll feel safe. They'll know that what's right matters, but it can't be false. Everything you do won't be real unless the people that get abused aren't forgotten. You used that kid for your career and to get that blowhard coach. You're as bad as the rest of them. If that kid is ruined forever, your work is meaningless."

"I'm a journalist, not a social worker."

"You're a person first, find him on your own time and see if he's okay, let him know he matters. And if he is messed up, tell him to get help. You used him and that's what's killing you."

"He's gone, Abbey. Don't do this to me. I didn't ruin him."

"You're a journalist. Find him."

Samantha

....

AUBURN, ALABAMA

IN THE GLARE of the morning, public garbage bins overflowed with beer cans and Solo cups as anonymous men pierced trampled grass with spiked poles to collect and deposit stray refuse into the bags dragging behind them. Remnants of toilet paper hung from sparse trees as I waited at the light in my rental at the corner of College and Magnolia; it was a nice season-opening win for Auburn on a Thursday night. The drive to UCF in Orlando was almost seven hours, and, if I kept pace, I'd get there by three, plenty of time for the interviews at five. The QB, a defensive lineman, and the entire offensive line were scheduled. How cute, the offensive linemen only agreed to be interviewed as a group.

Against my better judgment, I looked at Abbey's text: *If you don't have a heart, you're a pussy.* Bastille's season opener was in twelve hours, a Friday night game. I hadn't been assigned to one of their games since it happened, but it was on the way and there was enough time to pay a visit to an old acquaintance. The car behind me honked its horn, the light had turned. I couldn't do it, I thought, nothing good would come of it.

Three hours later, I was in Bastille. The Fountain Apartment complex was a couple of miles from campus, it probably looked cheap when it was new. I drove slowly past the entrance looking to see if there was more than one exit. The far end of the parking lot was open, I picked a spot and backed my car in. Apartment 126, right in the middle.

Thirty minutes passed as I waited in the car; I wanted to see the flow of people and traffic, I wanted to know what station in life they'd found themselves in to live in a place like this. An elderly man pulled into the lot and spent a good minute parking, a maneuver that should've taken seconds. His door opened, a cane appeared, and then the real work started. It took ten minutes for him to get out, retrieve a single grocery bag, and make his way in through the gate. He passed a youngish woman whose ethnicity I couldn't discern, she was trailed by three children and neither the old man nor her party acknowledged the other. The door to apartment 126 remained inert, maybe the address was old, maybe he was inside. I took a breath, opened my door, and hurried to the gate before it closed.

"Excuse me ma'am, can you hold the gate for me?" I said.

She was leaving but let it close anyway. "Don't worry, it don't lock," she said.

The heavy meshed gate seemed like the sturdiest part of the complex. It creaked loudly when opened like a warning, the only security it could offer. Then I stood in front of apartment 126 unsure of what I was going to say, unsure if he'd even talk to me. I pushed the doorbell but didn't hear a corresponding ring inside, I gave it a moment anyway.

Then I knocked. An undecipherable voice called out that wouldn't have been him. It would be easier to explain I had the wrong address to a stranger and apologize and leave. The sound of slow footsteps approached from inside. Then the deadbolt clicked and the door opened. It was him and I couldn't walk away.

"Henry, do you remember me? I'm Samantha Yardley."

He didn't respond, he stood looking down like I hadn't struck the right input.

"Who is it, Henry?" The voice was from inside the apartment, then I heard the rustle of someone rising.

"Henry, do you remember me?" I said, my voice pleading.

"Goddammit, Henry, who the hell is it?"

"Henry, do you know where Wally is?" I said.

He looked up and I nearly stepped back. His gaunt face was bruised on the right cheek, a faded yellow that drew my attention away from his eyes. Then I noticed red marks on his arms—they were fresh.

"Wally's not here," he said.

"Who is it?" the man said. I recognized him from my research—it was Henry's father, Minister Nubinski. He pushed Henry out of the way, and I noticed his own signs of disrepair.

"I'm Samantha Yardley, I'm a journalist for Sports Inc. I'm trying to track down an old friend, Wally Hestia."

He turned and snapped at Henry. "Get back in there." Then he folded his arms and looked me over. "I know who you are, you're the one that tried to ruin this place a few years ago. I should be asking you where that embarrassment is, you were the last one to see him."

"I'm not looking for any trouble and I'm not on assignment. I just wanted to check in on him, that's it," I said.

"I bet you are. I should give Sly a call and let him know you're poking around. No one wants you here. Get off my property."

The Minister slammed the door and I stood motionless as I heard him retreat into the apartment. Then, through a small window a few feet from the door, I saw Henry looking at me. I stepped over to it, wedging in between the window and a bush that had lost most of its growth. The back of the Minister's head was visible from the next room, Henry stood alone in the kitchen. I held my hand flat against the window trying to get a response, but he just stood there. I could tell he didn't want me to leave, but I couldn't provide what he wanted. All I could do was mouth the words he wanted to hear.

"I'll bring Wally back."

In the background I saw the Minister get up and I scurried out, tearing my jeans on the bush. I didn't turn to see if he opened the apartment door again until I got in the car. When I looked, the door was closed but I looked around anyway to see if he followed. Wally had mentioned his adoptive father briefly, he didn't talk of his childhood except for the fact that he and Henry hadn't spent a night apart since he was adopted. I shouldn't have come; it wasn't my business. I texted Abbey: *I'm not a pussy, this is a mess.*

As I drove around the complex, I figured out it was a large square building and there seemed to be a courtyard with a non-functioning pool in the middle. On the next side of the building was a sign for the office. I parked, closed my eyes and, with my hand on the door handle, considered my position. If I missed the interviews and Brendan found out why, I'd be fired.

My very best. *What did I do when I was at my very best?* I knew the signs of my own mediocrity, they were marked with late night rationalizations, complaints about the life, and dreams of finding peace. The sound of the car door popping open felt like relief, I headed to the apartment's office with purpose.

"Hi, my name is Sam and I'm just moving into town. Do you have any apartments available?"

The apartment manager seemed uninterested until he looked at me. I expressed vague needs as he walked us through three apartments, all on the second floor. Wretched places full of mildew and linoleum, residences of last resort.

"No, these won't work. I need to be on the east side," I said. "The morning sun is my alarm clock."

He grunted and led us over to Henry's side of the building, apartment 228. The door wouldn't open after he turned the key, he had to put his shoulder into it. Inside the carpet was rolled up and the kitchen faucet was missing.

"This one isn't ready, obviously," he said.

"But I love the view. How long will it take?"

He peered through the windows with a strange look. The only visible sights were Spanish moss and a self-storage building.

"Probably two or three weeks, how soon do you need it?"

"Perfect, not for another month."

"Okay, I guess. Do you want to see the lease? We'll need a deposit if you—"

"Wait, there's one thing that's a must. I need to sit and take the place in for a little while. I'm really into feng shui and I need to feel the vibe. You understand, don't you?"

He shrugged and seemed okay with it. "Sure, I can give you a half hour or so. Will that do?"

"I kind of need it a little longer, maybe for the night. I'm really into yoga, I sleep with my legs crossed."

"I'm sorry, I can't. That's out of the question."

I turned around and closed my eyes. It was a move I hadn't done in years; it was beneath me but was all I had. Fling the hair, tilt my head. Slowly I undid the top two buttons on my blouse. Then I took a deep breath, stuck them out, and turned around, speaking in a voice that used to make Abbey laugh.

"Are you a Pisces? You're a Pisces, aren't you?"

It always amazes me how men of any age lose their objectivity under the spell of a single gesture. I told him by eleven I'd have my vibe and probably a few more and he should stop by with a twelve pack to make sure I wasn't being a naughty girl.

The UCF PR director said his guys would be disappointed when I called to tell him I wouldn't make it by five. I sensed a trace of inferiority in his voice and could guess the words in his head: *She'd never do this to Ohio State or Bastille.* One thing I've learned from football coaches: the bigger the lie, the more they believe.

"I know you're disappointed and I shouldn't tell you this but the reason I can't make it is because a couple of NFL directors of college scouting want to meet me for dinner. They want some intel on off-the-field behavior of a couple players from—I can't say."

"Is it—"

"Don't mention names. What I will do is tell them about your guys, I'll rave about them. Then, I'll interview your guys in the morning."

"Coach doesn't allow game-day interviews. Besides, you're known for asking some pretty tough questions."

"Come on, you don't play until seven o'clock tomorrow night. I'll make it early and by the time I'm done your guys are going to feel like All-Americans, this isn't going to be a hit job. Trust me, when they read it on the web it'll be worth it."

He paused a moment. "Okay, I'll make it work."

Then I waited. The back of the apartment had a small balcony that looked down on the courtyard, its mesh screen was torn but I kept the glass door open in hopes of hearing something. The kitchen counter had mold in the corners, I didn't want to touch anything. But after an hour passed, I found myself sitting on it staring out the front window to see if they left.

What am I doing? I thought. The air conditioner was too loud, I had to turn it off. Within an hour the apartment was the same as outside; ninety-five degrees and ninety percent humidity. Sweat dripped down my back and stained the underarms of my blouse as I sat on the counter with my head on my knees. Drowsiness came over me, I found myself daydreaming about the comfortable air-conditioned hotel room waiting for me in Orlando. I should be there, getting ready for the interviews; big, jocular guys whose demeanor always changed as soon as I walked into the room. Either poorly constructed pretentiousness or obsequious fawning.

A door slammed on the level below and I lifted my head. I thought I was still daydreaming. The Minister walked to his car and Henry followed in a full Bastille uniform, he looked like a kid going to a Pop Warner game. I made a note of the car and license plate, then waited for them to pull away. Following them wasn't hard, I knew where they were going. It was already five thirty and game time was at eight. They pulled into an administrative lot by the stadium as I drove to the media lot, then an attendant waved for me to stop at the gate. "Media only, ma'am, please turn around."

"Shit." I didn't have a pass and didn't think about it. I circled the stadium, but all parking was pre-paid and required a pass. Ten minutes later I found a twenty-dollar lot a half-mile away. The crowd began to build even though the heat was oppressive; frat parties in full swing, pre-game events for boosters under large tents, and tailgaters forming a tent city that ringed the stadium. I had no idea how to find him, there was no way to get in the stadium, and I couldn't figure out what Henry would be doing fully dressed in football gear. I calmed myself and began walking through the outer ring of tailgaters.

A river of people began to form and flow towards their practice facility. Not everyone, just enough of a pattern to sense that something was happening. I followed suit and listened for clues.

"The band plays the fight song an hour before, you've got to see it."

"The chicks with the batons do this thing, it's awesome."

"You can get a picture with the Nuber."

I picked my pace up to a jog for the last hundred yards and squeezed my way in through the gate. The band was warming up on the far end and people took seats on the small sets of bleachers or ringed the field. Then I saw him.

Henry was on the near side standing with his back to the stadium. His helmet was on and even from a distance I could see a sheen of sweat on his neck. A line had formed, it started near a placard that was too far to read. I pulled my running hat out of my purse and wore it low in disguise, there was enough activity to blend in without Henry's father spotting me. I avoided the line and approached the placard.

Henry 'The Nuber' Nubinski

NCAA record holder for kick %

Never Missed! 100%!

Pictures $10 or $5 with your One Tribe Booster Club ID

Henry posed with people as the line moved at a quick pace. The Minister collected money while a student staffer took the customer's phone and recorded the image. I couldn't get in line; I'd be face-to-face with the Minister.

Then I saw my chance. The Minister was engaged in conversation and the flow was held up for a moment. I stepped behind the student staffer and held my phone up for a picture of Henry and people I didn't want to know. Four images were recorded and I looked at them as I walked away, hoping they were clear. I took another look at Henry before leaving, then at the line of people. Bastille hats and jerseys, some of them waving fans to keep cool and talking as they soaked up excited energy and contributed to it in kind.

The scene struck me: people, good people, enjoying the celebration of their team, of themselves, wanting intimate proximity to the Tribe's greatness, willing to hand over a few dollars that would never be missed. They'd send the picture to friends or post it on social media. "That's me, that's us," they'd say. "That's us with the Nuber. The greatest kicker in Tribe history." When I walked away, I was pretty sure no one called him Henry. I knew I wasn't done.

It was eight thirty when they came back, I was confident the Minister wouldn't stay for the game. I opened the sliding glass door again and perched by the balcony, waiting to hear something. An hour passed; the only sound was the game broadcast from their TV. When darkness fell, I stepped out onto the balcony and leaned over the railing trying to see below and one apartment over. A cheap lawn chair was on their patio, a stained cooler was next to it. I sat on the balcony with my back against the railing waiting to hear.

I'd have to leave before eleven or face the apartment manager's clandestine visit. I didn't know what I was waiting for, I wasn't a real investigative reporter and this wasn't something I could file. I looked at my phone to see the time—10:30, I needed to leave. My legs were stiff and my back ached as I rose. Then I heard their sliding glass door open, it froze me.

"Goddammit all, Henry, you backed up the toilet, didn't you? Didn't you?" I could tell he was drunk.

The Minister stepped out onto the patio. I heard his zipper, then the sound of him relieving himself onto the grass below me. The smell of urine rose and I wanted to throw up.

"I've told you a million times, use the goddamn plunger. I'm not fixing it; you'd better get your ass in there."

I couldn't hear Henry's reply.

"What? You didn't do it? Are you saying *I* did it? Are you calling me a liar? Get that goddamn look off your face, just like at the field tonight. You stand there with that droopy look and people are going to want their money back. Look at me, goddammit." The Minister went back into the apartment without closing the door.

Then I heard a slap. I slung my purse strap over my head and shoulder, quickly checked to see if I'd left anything, then lifted my leg over the railing, then the other leg, then I slid my hands down the vertical posts and was about to drop to the ground. I didn't check to see if the apartment below was occupied, but I had no choice, and let go.

The fall wasn't far, but in the dark, I didn't have any reference. After hitting the ground on my feet, I stumbled over a yard onto my rear end. Horror welled up as I felt dampness creep into my jeans, then underwear, then skin. Then the smell of urine surrounded me and my mouth opened in horror.

"It's always you, Henry. Everyone wants to see you. Nobody says a damn word to me about what I have to go through to take care of you." Another slap.

I got up and quickly stepped to the edge of the sliding glass door holding my phone in front of me. If someone were to see me, I'd look like an intruder holding a gun. The camera icon was inches from my face, I opened it and switched to video.

"Listen to me, I've had enough! We barely made any money tonight because you have that goddamn look on your face. Look at me."

Then it was a different noise, more than a slap and Henry cried out in a howl. His voice was awful, he cried out as loud as his pain. I stepped in the doorway and began recording. The Minister, with his back to me, held a belt and waited for an open spot as Henry tried to cover himself, then he whipped.

"It's too much this time. You complain that it's too hot, how'd you like to be me? I'm the one carrying the load around here."

He unleashed another whip as Henry writhed on the ground and screamed. An outdoor light three apartments over came on and a sliding glass door opened. I held the phone steady as the lashings continued. Someone called out from across the courtyard, I only had a few moments before I could escape. If the Minister saw me, he'd tell Sly, and Sly would tell Sports Inc.

Another lash, then yells from the neighbor, I had thirty seconds recorded. The light in the apartment I'd jumped from came on, it was the apartment manager. A man approached from the far side and began asking me what I was doing. I had to leave but I couldn't let Henry's whipping continue. I picked up the lawn chair, turned and threw it into the apartment then darted away through a far gate.

As I drove away, my travel plans changed. After UCF, I wouldn't fly home to Virginia. I had to go to Buffalo.

Dion

....

MY OLD STADIUM looked tiny as the plane circled Bastille, but I could still make out the *"The Tribe"* in one end zone and *"Bastille"* in the other. It felt like the jet was attached to the stadium by an imaginary string guiding us in a lazy circle. The field was just a patch of turf, a grass rectangle I'd sprinted all over for years and the only window through which the outside world saw the university. People thought they knew Bastille through that window, they thought they knew us.

I tried to remember what it felt like when Coach Oldham coached us—we were heroes and I was in the lead role. Everything was perfect, especially the fans, and the world was right without a worry from me. I risked my body, but my heart was always full. The only thing I ever learned under Castritt on that field was a sad lesson that had nothing to do with football. He wasn't the Tribe and still isn't. I wondered if Wally would actually show up.

That night was long ago but it dug a small cavity in me and it's been growing ever since. Coach Oldham tried to teach me and I thought I understood but my actions were meaningless, I was just checking off boxes. The fight was bullshit, just a handful of hotheads that dragged the rest of us into it. What people never knew is half of the FSU team were guys I knew pretty well and we were the ones that ended it. Not the coaches, not the refs, not the event staff; we did and I was real proud of myself. Until I saw Wally run off the field.

After it was over, it was all about their kick return and all about the fight. Damn, for the first time in my life I was glad I hadn't played. I was standing in front of Wally's locker when an equipment manager tossed his shoulder pads and helmet into it and that gear landed with a thud like it was a carcass. His Tribe blazer just hung there, and below were his spikes and unstained football pants. I reached out and touched the blazer and I knew as sure as anything that he was gone. I really tried, a lot of us tried, but every effort to find him began with this nagging thought that it was hopeless from the beginning. Then we didn't talk about it. Coach Dixon felt it, too, but he got me focused again and thank God he did, even though it was Wally that made it possible.

After I left Bastille, I kept searching the internet, it was a nightly effort typing his name into a search engine even though I knew the results before they appeared. His picture from the Bastille football archives; articles about Bastille's mysterious kicker, Henry Nubinski, and his adopted brother, Wally Hestia; made-up conspiracy theories preaching knowledge of his links to FSU and how he sabotaged the game by inventing the sexual assault story My favorite was a story titled "Free Wally." This woman sportswriter took up his whistleblower cause, explaining how his courage to confront the rape when the powerful covered it up should inspire us all. I wasn't inspired, I felt worse, even worse than the comments left for the writer calling her a whore.

I lost hope; it was going to be a part of me forever. Time would pass and the memory would recede but the hole in me would grow. Then a note was handed to me, right out of the blue. I was watching film of the Raiders' defense at my new home away from home when a PR assistant gave it to me. *I need to see you regarding Wally and Henry, it's urgent. Samantha Yardley.* I didn't know what surprised me more, the topic or the source.

"When did you get this?" I asked.

"Just now, she's in the lobby."

I didn't wait for the elevator; I took the stairs down two flights then calmed myself to make sure I didn't look too excited. Samantha was looking at her phone when I entered the lobby and it dawned on me that she could be setting me up for some cruel trick. But the rumor was, she drove him away that night and she never denied it. I could tell she was all business when I saw her in the lobby, that hard face and aggressive stance like she was some badass looking to pick a fight. She had to know I was still pissed off.

"Congratulations," she said. "Starting quarterback for the Buffalo Bills."

I couldn't talk to her, I wasn't going to let her hear my voice, I just stood and stared down at her and had to remind myself that this was about Wally and Henry. She got the point and I was amazed at how she refused to get rattled.

"How do you like Buffalo? A lot different than Florida."

Then I finally spoke. "The only reason I'm talking to you is because of Wally and Henry. And, yeah, I love it here, this is my new home."

"So, you got my note?"

I could feel myself softening. "What's going on? You seen Wally?"

"No, but we have to find him," she said.

She explained how she'd been looking for him for a couple of months without success, then came across Henry down in Bastille. She showed me the video, but I couldn't watch the whole thing.

"We've got to find him," she said.

"How am I going to if you can't? No one from the team has ever heard from him, if they did, we'd all know it immediately."

"You have access that I don't. Access to people at Bastille."

"Like Castritt or Sly? They aren't the real Tribe."

She didn't look convinced. "Maybe, but I've been thinking. He was a walk-on, right? Somebody had to pay his way. Somewhere at Bastille there's got to be an address or a phone number or an email for the person who knows him. It wasn't Henry's father, I already checked. Use your charm, you're the only person that can pull this off."

Access is everything and after a few calls I had a dozen emails and a few phone numbers. I looked at each email address thinking it was the one, but only two replied asking if I was really Dion McAres. After another set of phone calls, an admin in the financial aid office sent me another email address. It was my last hope.

When I got Wally's reply I nearly jumped out of my chair. I let out a yell like we'd won a playoff game and told Garr all about it. He just laughed in that low voice of his and I knew he was happy for me. I counted down the days, it would be my first time back.

By the time I made it to the hotel I was nearly worn out, but I loved my people. Tribe fans at the airport shook my hand, wished me well and some asked for my autograph. The hotel check-in was the same: people were pouring in for the Kentucky game and you would've thought I still played for the Tribe. Samantha was in the lobby but didn't approach, she sent me a text asking me to reply with my room number.

Have you seen him? I texted.

Not yet.

The attention was too much, even for me, and Samantha agreed to wait in the lobby. I texted the number Wally gave me letting him know my room number and the room I had waiting for him. I called that number dozens of times, but he never answered. After a while, Samantha came up and joined me.

"So, this is how the other half lives," she said.

"Don't give me a hard time. I didn't ask for a suite, they upgraded me," I said.

"I'm not, you deserve it. You're finally getting paid. Take a look at this."

Samantha handed me her phone. It was an ad for the One Tribe Booster Club pre-game activities: It noted the time of the marching band's warm-up on the practice field, the location of three different sponsored tailgate parties, and the Nuber. For a hundred dollars you get a replica Tribe jersey, you get to wear a Tribe helmet and you get to hold while Henry kicked. Photographs and a video would be taken as you enjoyed a once in a lifetime opportunity to hold for the Tribe's and the NCAA's all-time greatest kicker.

"It's a nice way to keep him involved," I said.

"It's sickening."

She took a seat on the couch, and I was surprised by her silence, even more surprised we were in the same room together; I'd spent way too much time thinking up ways to humiliate her. Then she spoke.

"I'd like to make a formal apology about the whole Garr Johnstone issue, it was inappropriate and immoral. I've got my own issues, but I'm truly sorry."

I took my time answering, I looked at my phone, then out the window. My own words sounded odd coming out of my mouth, but Coach O made too big of an impact on me. "Apology accepted, it's over." I let the topic hang in the air until its use had been served but it did feel good, like heartburn that had been relieved. Then I smiled and got her attention, it felt good being on the same team. "You're a reporter, aren't you going to ask me anything about Bastille or the NFL? It's kind of odd sitting with you in silence."

She shook her head. "Not now, we're here for something else." She gave a pained smile and let it go. "Strange, though. What a strange situation we're in."

"It is. I know why I'm here, I'm not sure why you are."

She bit her lip and let my comment linger. "Let's just say I've been part of the problem long enough. I wasn't sure you'd jump on board, I got lucky."

I laughed a little, maybe it sounded sarcastic. "Don't know about that, I think I'm the luckiest man in the world."

"What do you mean? Because you can play? You know I've always wondered about you. I've seen you play, what makes you so different?"

I leaned forward in my seat and took my time answering. "No one gets it. They all talk about height and weight, arm strength and accuracy. Those are important, but it's something else."

"What?"

"I just know, I always have. Don't get me wrong, I work out harder than most people can imagine. But I just know, or better yet, I just feel it. I know if my receiver has a step on his guy out of the corner of my eye. I can feel the defense's flow and know where the soft spots are without thinking about it. I can sense a blitz without even looking, I don't really get it myself. The best way to explain it is, for me, it's like sticking my hand in my pocket and knowing I've got three coins and one's a quarter. But when someone else tries, it's like they're wearing mittens. But that's not the real reason I'm so fortunate."

"What's the reason?"

"It's simple, I'm one of the best in the world at something tribes desperately need."

"Tribes? Are you talking about Bastille?" she said.

"No, tribes with a little 't.'"

"I'm not following you."

I tried to explain as best I could, but told her she needed to talk to the Professor to really understand. "The important thing is, this tribe, the *Tribe*, is different."

"Are you sure about that?"

"Yes, I am. This thing with Henry's father ain't right, but he's not the Tribe."

Hours passed, it was approaching nine thirty and it felt like we both knew he wouldn't show. I stood at the window looking at the modest Bastille skyline highlighted by the stadium lights a mile away, wondering if he was out there.

"I'm going back to my room," she said. "I've got some work to do."

I acknowledged and kept on staring as I heard the door open. Even if Wally didn't show, something had to be done to help Henry.

"Dion, did you order a pizza?" said Samantha.

"No, wrong room or someone trying to—"

"Dion, I think the pizza is for us."

I turned and saw the delivery guy: long hair and straggly beard. He gave Samantha the pizza and slowly removed his hat.

"I'm here," Wally said. I didn't recognize his voice, it was flat and tired, like every breath was an effort. "The pizza cost twenty bucks."

Maybe we were too late, I barely recognized his face through his beard. His long hair looked like it hadn't been washed in days and his thin face was that of a man who had lost hope. I peeled off a twenty, then another and gave it to him. The look on my face must've said everything. I offered him a seat at the table and sat across from him.

"I'm really hungry," he said. "Can I have a piece?"

"Wally, I can't believe it," I said. "I kind of lost hope. You've changed."

He ate like an alley cat and we didn't interrupt him at first. Samantha retrieved a soda from the minibar while I tried to make small talk. His answers were brief and vague, the personality I remembered was gone. Finally, he asked.

"What's happening to Henry? The Minister is abusing him, isn't he?"

Samantha nodded and described what she'd seen. He was stoic at first but I could see anger begin to rise.

"Why did you go there?" he asked.

"I was looking for you," she said.

"We've all been looking for you," I said.

"Why?"

"Because we let you down," I said. "Especially me." I apologized for blaming him years ago but he didn't seem moved.

"Tell me about Henry."

Samantha opened her laptop and brought up the video. "Wally, this might be hard to watch." She played it and he watched without turning away. After it was over, he sat looking down at his hands as Samantha and I were silent.

"That's what we grew up with," he said. Then he looked up. "I'm taking him with me, I want to get him now."

"Just wait, there's someone I want to bring into the conversation," I said. I dialed the number and put it on speaker. As it rang, I could tell Wally's attention was fading, his mind focused elsewhere.

"Samantha, what's the address," Wally said as he stood.

Then the Professor's voice came over the phone. "Dion, is he there?"

"Yeah, he's here. You're on speaker by the way."

The sound of the Professor's voice reversed something in Wally. He slowly sat back down, and his look of anger turned into anguish. He put a hand to his head and leaned towards the phone.

"Wally, this is exciting, let me hear your voice," the Professor said.

He didn't respond until Samantha pushed the phone towards him.

"Professor, it's me, Wally. How are you?"

"Never better, Wally. The question is, how are you? You're a hard man to track down."

"Are you teaching?"

"Yes, as a matter of fact I am, things are great. Milo Jr. graduated from Florida State and he's getting his PhD in Organic Chemistry up north. He's so smart, takes after his mother. Mary works at a women's shelter here in Tallahassee and is back to saving the world."

"Are you a professor at Florida State?"

"Not exactly. I'm teaching a couple of classes there this semester and one over at TCC."

"What's TCC?"

"Tallahassee Community College. It's good stuff, the kids keep me young."

"But what about, you know, tenure?"

"Hold on, I've got to step outside," the Professor said. Then he spoke to someone with him. "No, that order gets three shots of decaf espresso, and hurry the customer's waiting." A door closed in the background. "Sorry, I'm still at work. It's my day job but it's actually at night. It's an upside-down world these days."

"Professor, you're not teaching full time, you're—" Wally's voice trailed off, he dropped his head into his hands.

"It's not what you think, Wally. Actually, it kind of is but it certainly isn't your fault. I was afraid of this moment. Listen to me, I may have been too idealistic, but I wasn't wrong and neither were you and that's enough for me to live on. Yes, I'll never get tenured and that's sad. But I'm happy enough. Milo Jr. is doing fantastic; Mary is still full of passion, and I like my job. I'm the night manager at a coffee shop right across campus and I'm at peace. I love the students that come in, I've even got a bit of a rep as a tutor for the humanities if they order food with their drink. I'm no longer torn by the conflicts and seedy politics. I'm at peace and I'm hoping you are, too." Wally stared at the phone and didn't reply. "Wally, are you there?"

"He's here, Professor. He's a little shocked," I said.

"Come on, Wally. I understand we've got a situation with your brother that needs resolution. I've seen the video. What's the plan?"

"I'm going to get him; I'm taking him with me."

"Does his father approve of this?"

"I don't care what he thinks. I'll take him out if he gets in my way."

"Wait a second, Wally," the Professor said. "We need to think this through. First, let's recognize that your brother has certain intellectual and social challenges, and he probably wouldn't be viewed as a functional adult able to make his own choices. If you take him without approval, it could be considered kidnapping. I think the better course of action is to make the appropriate authorities aware of the situation and work it through the legal system."

"This is Bastille, Professor," Wally said as his agitation built. "The Minister is part of the program; he can do whatever he wants. He'll lie and I'll be arrested for just being here."

"That's not true," I said. "No one's coming after you."

"Actually, there is an issue," Samantha said. She took her time. "I checked with some contacts here. There's a standing order with the police: If Wally's seen, he's to be arrested for the assault of Castritt. Also, Wally, when they cleaned out your dorm room a gun was found. They think you're a danger to the community."

"Jesus, Samantha, why the hell didn't you tell me that?" I said. Wally got up and started pacing, I was afraid he was going to leave.

"Take it easy, I just found out today," Samantha said. "The pizza delivery ruse was pretty smart."

"I think we need to get Wally out of town right now," the Professor said.

"The assault charge will never stand," Samantha said. "Neither will the gun issue. They just want their pound of flesh."

"So, if the Minister sees me, he just has to call the police and I'm done."

"It's not going to happen," I said.

"It will! You just heard her say it," Wally said. "I never should've come back, I knew it! And he's beating Henry and there's nothing I can do about it."

"Wally, does Henry have a blood relative?" said the Professor. "Anyone who could step in and care for him?"

"Blood relative?" Wally said. He had the look of someone who'd never been understood. "*I'm* his blood relative! He's my brother, the Minister is my father."

The Professor, Samantha and I stopped talking as if our voices had been revoked. A casual conversation passed in the hall; a car's horn sounded on the street below. Finally, the Professor spoke.

"Let me get this straight. The Minister is actually your biological father?"

"Yes."

"Why have you always called him your adoptive father?"

Wally sat down, he seemed spent. "Do you have anything to drink?" he said.

"The last time I bought alcohol you took off on me," Samantha said. "There's some in the minibar, I'll get it."

He took a sip of whiskey and tried to relax. "I thought I was adopted, that's what I was always told. The true story is he got my late mother pregnant while Henry's mother was already pregnant. I was his greatest sin, and by the time I became aware of it, I hated him. He used to beat us so much, I was the only one that protected Henry. Coming to Bastille was our way of escaping. But look at us now, it only made it worse. Think about it—he's a 'man of the cloth,' as he used to say. He used it like it was his free pass to do whatever he wanted. All he ever wanted to do was judge people and survive off of their guilt. And beat the weak. He's my father and I did everything I could to not be like him. The only way I could survive my self-hatred was to be pure. That's why I loved Bastille so much, it was pure."

Samantha and I traded glances. "Goddamn, Wally. I'm so sorry."

"That's unbelievable," the Professor said. "But now, we have to get serious." There was a hint of aggression in his voice.

"Maybe Wally's right," I said. "Let's just go get him."

"Too messy," the Professor said. "We need to create separation."

"How we going to do that?" I said. "We've got tomorrow and that's it."

"I need time to think," the Professor said. "Since he's your blood relative, that's enough to go on to save an abused person. But we've got to get you both out of town safely."

"You guys brought me all the way here and there isn't a plan?" Wally said as he stood.

"We had to see you first," Samantha said. "I've got an idea, but we all have to be in this together, and I mean really together. Dion, you're going to have to lie your ass off and you'll probably need a lawyer."

My hesitation surprised me; I don't think I inspired confidence. "I can do that." I said. "Wally, sit down, brother, you're making me nervous."

"Okay, hear me out," Samantha said. "I say we let Reverend Nubinski's greed and ego do the work for us. Tomorrow during the pre-game festivities, Dion, you meet with the Minister and buddy up to him. Tell him now that you're a big star in the NFL you've got a way to make a lot of money off Henry's skill. Tell him you want to make a series of instructional videos to share with all the aspiring kickers in the world. People will want to watch and learn. Tell him you could host a kickers camp together, all sponsored by the shoe companies, of course, who would kill to get Henry's endorsement. He'll be so excited he won't let you leave town without a commitment. But then you ask him if Henry can make his own decisions, otherwise, you're not doing it. Of course, he'll say yes, which is very important. Then you tell him that he and Henry need to meet you here. Don't even wait until the game is over, do it right away. When you arrive, text me and I'll knock on the door. You'll say an old teammate is up the hall and he'd like Henry to stop by. Then I'll bring him to Wally's room."

"If he doesn't want to leave with me, I won't force him," Wally said. He lowered his head and closed his eyes in despair. "That night, the night of the fight, I begged him to leave with me but he wouldn't."

"Or couldn't," the Professor said. "But it's a good point, Henry should give some indication of his preference in case this ends up in a legal battle."

"Fine," Samantha said. "Believe me, he wants to be with you, Wally. Then, after Henry is safe you say to the Minister there's one little problem. Show him the video and make him answer to it. Then tell him Henry is gone and you're lawyering up on behalf of Wally and Henry to make it official and you've already got the media on your side."

"That's some sneaky shit," I said. I looked to Wally. "What do you think?"

He nodded and I could see a trace of vengeance in him.

"Professor? Is this still too risky?"

He took his time replying. "Let me get this straight—we're going to lie, correct?"

"That's right," Samantha said.

"How old is Henry?"

"He's twenty-one," Wally said.

"And he's never been diagnosed by a medical professional?"

"Correct."

The Professor softly hummed like he was mulling it over, I got the sense he was pacing. "Dion, if you think you can pull it off, I think it will work. I'm coming up tomorrow, I'll be your witness at the reunion."

▼ ▼ ▼

It was late but I didn't care. Samantha had left and I convinced Wally to stay and watch a late college game. Bastille was playing at three thirty the next day, we were in no hurry.

"We're going to get him, Wally. One way or another," I said.

He slowly nodded without looking at me. I muted the television and looked at him, still surprised by what he'd turned into.

"Where did you go that night?" I said.

He didn't react, his slow movements and hard stare at the TV unsettled me. Maybe the alcohol affected him, he swirled the ice cubes in his drink like it was the only thing worth his thoughts.

"What did you think about all the stuff that happened afterwards?" I said. He shrugged his shoulders. "You had to like the way some of it turned out."

"I don't know what happened," he said.

"None of it? Some of it was all over the news. What you did changed my life."

Then he looked at me. "I threw out my phone, I never came back for my laptop. I've been in another world ever since it happened."

"You really don't know?"

"I don't know anything. No computer, no TV, no phone. The number you have for me is for a phone I bought at a convenience store the day before I started driving here. My aunt made me get it and she emailed you the number. The first time I turned it on is when I got into town tonight."

I tried to grasp what life off the grid would be like and felt a little envy. "Everything happened, all because of you. Don't give up on the Tribe and pass me the bottle."

"Don't you play on Sundays or something?"

"Not this week. We have a bye and a good one, too. We're six and one, already beat New England at their place." I settled in trying to think of where to start.

"I don't believe in the Tribe anymore," he said. "I almost didn't come because you put 'Tribe Forever' in your email."

"It's not the Tribe's fault. The Tribe is more than Castritt and Sly. I'll admit, there were some things that bothered me," I said.

"Like what?"

"Hunter getting the arrow after that pic six."

"That's exactly what I mean," Wally said. "I can understand people cheering for the touchdown, but to give him the arrow? You have to think about that, not everyone gets the arrow."

"I know but it was just a moment. You can't throw out everything the Tribe means just based on that."

"Now I am curious. What happened?"

"First of all, after somebody took out Castritt—"

"It was me," Wally said. "The only hit I ever made in a game."

"I love it," I said laughing even though he didn't react. "Anyway, he was out bad. Face all busted up, his skull cracked. They even induced a coma while they figured out how to drain something out of his head. When he was out Coach Dixon took over, it was in his contract. I remember the team meeting on Sunday when Sly gets up there talking about you and if anybody saw you, they were supposed to call the police. That's when Coach Dixon walked in and told Sly to get his wrinkled old ass out of his meeting and go administrate our bus schedule or something. Man, we just loved that. After the meeting Dixon pulled me aside and said he was trashing the offense, benching Cooper, and putting me in. Cooper was relieved and excited for me, he kept on apologizing and offering to do anything he could to get me ready for Alabama. Now, you can't turnover a new offense in a week, but we adapted, ran max protect and any patterns I wanted. Tarik and Marcus were all pumped up, they couldn't wait."

"What ever happened to them?"

"Tarik got drafted in the seventh round by Denver but was cut during preseason. Never learned to block and couldn't make a tackle on special teams. Marcus got invited to the Cowboys' minicamp as a free agent, but didn't get signed. Anyway, we got Alabama and with Castritt gone everyone thought we were going to get killed. Didn't happen that way. I threw four touchdowns and no pics for more than five hundred yards. It was like all that football was stored up in me and I let it loose all at once. We won 45–24, upset of the year they called it even though we were ranked ahead of them. Damn, that locker room after the game was something else. Coach Dixon quieted us down and he nearly had tears in his eyes. God, I love him. So, after he got everyone's attention, he makes this short speech about me and gives me the game ball. Everyone went crazy. Then I got them quiet again, held the ball up, and said this is for Wally. The place went berserk." Wally looked down in humility and I gave him a moment.

"Did Henry kick?"

"That's another thing. In practice that week when it was time for field goals, he wouldn't do it. He lined up, bent over slightly, and then when they snapped it, he just stood there. Then your father—"

"The Minister."

"Sorry, the Minister. He came out on the field and started bitching up a storm at Henry until Coach Dixon got ahold of the back of his shirt and ran him off the field. Pokey thought it was the funniest thing he'd ever seen, and Coach Dixon let him laugh as long as he wanted."

"Whatever happened to Pokey?"

"Not good, man. He hooked up with Malibu out in California. Got themselves in a little legal trouble, they should be out in about five years. The next game was against Arkansas A&M, won that one, too, 49–31."

That finally got his attention, a little like the old Wally. "How did they score thirty-one? Their offense was terrible."

"Not when our starting linebackers were gone," I said. "You really don't know, do you?"

"Nothing."

"Damn, this is tripping me out. You probably get it by now that taking out Castritt changed my life, right? Dixon started me those two games and everybody could see I still had it. Well, you also changed some other lives." I sat up and made sure I had his attention. "You see, the day after the FSU game you were the talk of the football world and the surprising thing was the press got wind of how happy the team was without Castritt. You know that girl that was attacked? The Professor could probably tell this better, he got called by the girl's father. Apparently, the father—"

"Mr. Feldman, I met him the night it happened. That gun Samantha mentioned, it was his, I talked him out of going after Hunter."

"You're kidding me. Damn, brother, we should've talked more back then. Anyway, this Mr. Feldman saw what you did, and I guess it inspired him in some way. Instead of letting it eat him up inside he started to work the system. Lawyers got involved and some pretty influential people jumped on board immediately. It only took a week because on the Monday after the Alabama game Coach Dixon got a visit from a whole bunch of people from the Governor's office. I guess they were gearing up for a fight and Dixon cut them off with one sentence. Something like: "Ladies and gentlemen, the entire team will be drug tested today, you're free to look at the results." We didn't know what was going on, instead of a urine test they used swabs to get saliva samples and it took so long we didn't have time for practice that day. Well, the week goes on and it's Friday night's big pre-game dinner with all kinds of people there. We were still ranked in the top ten and every booster that could, sat in the dining room with us chomping away. Then I look up and there's a half dozen police at the door with a bunch of guys in suits. Dixon got up from his table and slowly made his way over while we all just stared. Then he led them over to Hunter and this guy in a suit starts reading Hunter his Miranda rights. All those drug tests, Castritt's way of weeding out guys he didn't want, well, Coach Dixon used it to collect DNA. I'll never forget Hunter crying his eyes out while the cops held his head down on the table and his arms behind his back as they cuffed him up."

"You said both linebackers, what happened to Cyrus?"

"They cuffed him up, too. Both of them raped that girl. And this is what bothers me: All the boosters had this horrified look on their faces, just scared to death. I saw that and had to do something. So, I stood up and starting clapping, and before Hunter and Cyrus had left, the whole damn team was standing and applauding the arrest while the boosters just sat there."

"The boosters were worried about the game, right?" Wally said.

"I don't know, maybe they thought it wasn't their place, maybe they were horrified to see who they'd been cheering for."

"What happened to Hunter and Cyrus?"

"Both in jail, now. By the time they get out, their playing days will be long gone. My only regret is that you weren't there to see it." I gave him a moment to let it sink in.

Finally, he spoke. "What about Arkansas A&M? What happened when you faced Garr?"

"This is another thing that really bothered me. Even after Samantha retracted her story the fans just kept on feeding the fire between us, Garr wouldn't even talk to me. Remember Randy, our old DFO under Coach Oldham? Well, he's at A&M and after the arrests and the boosters sitting there scared we were going to lose, it got me thinking. So, I go over to A&M's hotel and Randy got us a place where we could talk and told I Garr my plan. He wanted to see me as bad as I wanted to see him, I mean it was crazy. We grew up together and were best friends our whole life until that mess."

"What was your plan?"

"Pure beauty, the Professor loved it, said it was great theater. I told Coach Dixon I wanted to be the only captain for the coin toss and Garr did the same with his coach. On the way out onto the field for the coin toss I told the camera man to keep real close after it was over. I met Garr at midfield and everyone is watching to see what we're going to do; I mean the hatred was peaking. We shake, he wins the toss, I pick the north end of the field. Then the refs started to walk away and me and Garr were left standing there by ourselves. I took off my helmet and set it on the grass and Garr did the same. Then we approached and hugged each other, and my emotions just exploded. I love Garr so much and he loves me, too, man. We just held on as the camera guy got views of the tears coming down our faces and I even heard our voices over the PA system.

"Then the strangest thing happened, something I didn't expect. The crowd started to boo us. Just a little at first, but then it grew until it felt like the entire stadium was shaming us for being friends. The refs didn't know what to do. But then we gave them what they wanted; it was part of our plan. We broke the hug, put our helmets back on, and buckled up tight. Then we got a hold of each other's jersey and started a war scream. Facemask to facemask, I can still see his eyes bulging out and the little red veins starting to appear. Actually scared the shit out of me but I didn't stop. We just kept on screaming and all those boos turned into wild cheers and the whole damn stadium was fired up more than I'd ever seen it. They wanted to see us kill each other and the refs had to break it up."

"They booed? The Professor was right about all this stuff," Wally said.

"I don't know, it was just a moment when they didn't know what they were doing. I still believe in the Tribe."

"Really?" Wally said. "I'm sick of tribes. What happened during the game?"

"Garr chased me all over the field but I was on, I threw for over 450 yards. Then Coach Dixon pulled his own little trick. After we scored to go up by eighteen there were only five minutes left in the game. I came off the field, he comes over and tells me I'm done. He said I'd done enough in those two games to get back up the draft board where I belonged and on the next series, he told me to run it out of bounds and pull up like I tweaked my hamstring. I asked him why and he said that even though Castritt wasn't going to be on the field for the rest of the year he was out of the hospital and was going to call the shots. Apparently, Castritt was so pissed off at the two of us he was going to undo everything I'd done in those two games. The next day I packed up my stuff and left Bastille."

"Didn't people go crazy? You can't just leave."

"You did. Coach Dixon told the media I was injured and out for the year. He wanted me as far away from Castritt as possible."

"Didn't Coach Dixon catch hell for starting you?"

"I'm sure he did, and I was worried for him. But then he told me something that made it all okay. That long-time coach at FSU was retiring at the end of that season, it was a big secret. Through back channels they offered him the job."

"Did he take it?"

"Been the coach there for the past two years. They're a top five team, from what I hear it's like Bastille used to be."

"Imagine that, Kareem Dixon," Wally said. "A Black man with a Muslim first name getting named head coach in the Deep South. Whatever happened to Jeremy?"

"He's in law school. You know how they say offensive linemen are the smartest guys on the team? I guess it's true."

"What about Garr? Are you guys close again?"

"Oh, yeah. Last season, my rookie year in Buffalo, our starting QB goes down, an all-pro guy. Then I stepped in and lit it up. After the season our GM traded that QB away, right in the prime of his career. We got a first and a second for him then our GM takes those picks and adds a few more draft choices and trades it all to Baltimore for the first overall pick. We got ourselves Garr Johnstone with the first pick in the draft. He moved in with me, I don't even make him pay rent. We're finally on the same team after all these years."

"Do you remember Tony and Eddie?"

"Yeah, but I haven't talked to them in years. You need to look them up."

"What about Melvin Richardson? I'll never forget how he stood up for me in that meeting."

"It's funny, all those players and all those games. Everyone that ever played for the Tribe thought for sure the minute they stepped on campus that they had a long career waiting for them in the NFL. Just me and Melvin. We're the only ones. He's a rookie this year, the starting free safety for the Pittsburgh Steelers. But it's not about the NFL, don't give up on the Tribe, Wally."

"The Tribe gave up on me. It gave up on all of us, if it ever really existed in the first place."

▼ ▼ ▼

Morning light filled my room when I drew back the heavy curtains. I sat by the window and rubbed my eyes as the last clouds of sleep floated off. A couple of blocks away a hydraulic lift on the back of a beer truck slowly descended as the delivery man stood beside the kegs. He loaded the first one onto a dolly and wheeled it towards a frat house, a place I'd been many times. The vibe was building for game day and I was unprepared. Little Tribe flags sticking above car doors seemed to be everywhere, the dominant color was Tribe green except for a few folks in Kentucky blue. Then it dawned on me, I'd never in my life seen a game from the outside.

Samantha brought breakfast up for Wally, they were talking in his room when I stopped by.

"You don't want to go down there, the place is packed," she said.

"Wally, you got to stay in the room all day," I said.

"He will. You should head over to the pre-game events around one. Are you ready?" Samantha sat beside him as he ate, she looked like a nurse.

"I think so," I said. My hesitation bothered me.

The noisy dining room was filled to capacity but fell to whispers when I entered. A path was cleared to an empty table, even though I offered to wait in line, but I knew the price; I had to sign autographs in between bites. The love and pampering get to be a habit, something money can't buy. Back in the room I tried to study video of the Giants' defense but couldn't concentrate. Anxiety was building but I couldn't pinpoint the issue. I closed my laptop and turned on the college pre-game show hosted from somewhere in the Midwest.

At noon I flipped between three different early games but couldn't find any reason to be interested and soon found myself watching the scene on the street below. Off in the distance I saw wooden barricades blocking off traffic at the square. All morning a flow of people headed towards it but now the foot traffic shifted towards the stadium. I always thought they just showed up to the game, maybe had a beer beforehand in the parking lot.

At one o'clock Samantha texted me: *Good luck, send updates.* At two o'clock she called.

"What's it like? Have you seen Henry?"

"I'm just leaving now," I said.

"Dion, is there something wrong? Can you pull this off?"

"I'm fine."

I knew I wasn't. The last thing I wanted to do was leave the room and I didn't know why. My legs felt heavy and a sadness settled over me like I had to deliver bad news. Everything was easy up until now. I pulled on my shoes and headed out the door.

"Mr. McAres, the van is ready whenever you are," said the young hotel staffer.

It took a few minutes to get through the lobby as I signed autographs and shook hands with a weak smile.

"It's great to see you back, Dion. Can we get a picture?"

"Sure, but I'm running late," I said.

I breathed easier inside the hotel van. A few people waved and a young woman took my picture through the window as the van waited for people to clear the entrance. A man tapped her shoulder, and I could tell he was asking her who it was. *Dion McAres.* The guy was about thirty or so and he approached the van, cupped his hands against the window to see me and then screamed my name through the window. I waved and asked the driver to get me out of there.

"We can only get you to Tribe Way, but we called ahead and there'll be a golf cart waiting to take you the rest of the way," said the driver.

Then there was a knock on the door and the driver stopped. The door opened and someone got in the front passenger seat. When he turned around, I almost died.

"Nice to see you, Dion," Sly said. "You should've let us know you were coming so we could give you a hero's welcome. Unless, of course, you're here for another reason."

I must've been slow on the draw. Before I could respond he got to the point.

"I always knew it would be you. Where is he?" Sly's look was familiar, like he owned me, the same as when he owned all of us.

"Who you talking about?"

"Come on. You're not the kind of guy that travels alone. Unless you're up to something."

I looked out the window and waved back to another Tribe fan. "I'm hooking up with Tarik and Marcus, not sure they made it into town yet."

"Sure, you are. At least you didn't say you're waiting for Pokey."

"You wouldn't be around if Pokey was here. The way you and Castritt talked shit about him in the press right before his sentencing was real class. Motherfucker."

"Ouch. And I was hoping for a happy reunion. Driver, I've changed my mind, I've got my own transportation. You can let me out here." Then he turned to me. "I'll be seeing you later."

After Sly got out, the driver turned to me with a concerned look. "Everything okay, brother?"

"Yeah, we good."

At the corner of Tribe Way, a big golf cart, a dude in a yellow windbreaker, and a young woman with a walkie-talkie were waiting for me.

"Can you take me to the practice field? I heard the band's warming up," I said.

I sat in the back of the golf cart while the young athletic department staffer gave me an overview like it was a tour of a historical site. Some people recognized me and called out my name as they held their beer up in my honor. We waited at an intersection while the crowd passed in front of us. The traffic cop held out his fist as we crossed, and I responded with a fist bump. It was a sea of tents surrounding the stadium, most adorned with some version of the Tribe arrow large and small. Smoke from grills rose in wisps in the beautiful afternoon sun like it was the most pleasant refugee camp on earth. My name was called out and it began to feel like they were telling me who I was in case I forgot. One group was tossing small bean bags and erupted when one of the bags disappeared into a hole, another was playing some drinking game. A beer was stabbed with something and then the guy popped the tab and sucked it down. When he was done, he threw the can and screamed: "Saturdays are for—" I didn't hear the rest, we passed into an alley of Winnebagos.

The practice field was ahead and the driver turned on a beeping noise like you hear at the airport to part the crowd. A security guard waved us in with one hand as he held up the crowd with the other. When I got out, I was twenty feet from the front of the band, the sound was incredible and I almost had to put my fingers to my ears. Green sequined baton twirlers were in front, I had to squint into the sun to see the path of a baton as it spun high then came down with precision into a girl's hand. Then the band turned in unison and marched backwards opening a semi-circle for the team of green sequined baton twirlers and their male counterparts.

The pace of the music picked up as the sequined team assembled. A row of five guys got in line on one knee as four girls did flips as they approached then they jumped onto the waiting shoulders of the guys. When the guys stood, they held the ankles of the girls standing on their shoulders and the crowd let out a huge applause.

Then, the music stopped and a drumroll began as a petite little thing ran full speed down an alley of the band. I didn't see anyone place it, but there was a small circular trampoline just before the cheer team and I couldn't believe she was going to use it. She bounced off the trampoline, flipped once, and landed in a standing position on the shoulders of the two middle girls. Then the band kicked into the finale as the crowd went wild and batons were tossed up to free hands to be spun in celebration. I turned to my tour guide.

"They do this every week?" I said.

"They're really good."

When they dismounted, I noticed a crowd of people at the other end of the field and a line of them up the sideline.

"What's going on over there?" I said.

"It's your old teammate, the Nuber. Do you want to say hi?"

The line stretched for twenty yards, two and three people thick. We had to wait for the band to march past us towards the stadium and when they cleared, I saw Henry in full Tribe uniform with a mirrored visor on his helmet. He waited as a middle-aged woman with a Tribe jersey struggled to put on a helmet. We started walking towards them. A young male staffer seemed to give her instructions as someone in a Tribe football uniform, playing the part of the long snapper, waited to see if the woman was ready. She must've declined the snap because the long snapper stepped out of the way and the woman was handed a football and listened for final instructions while a man with a large camera on the left waited for his cue.

The woman held the ball upright and I could tell she was tentative by the way she tilted away from the ball. The photographer waved his hand, encouraging her to kneel straight while Henry waited. Finally, she fixed her position as the cameraman snapped a few pictures. Then I saw the Minister, he said something to the woman, and she froze in position; I could feel the tension. Then, the Minister barked something to Henry, who approached the ball.

The kick was good, but it was a poor imitation of Henry at his peak. The ball floated end over end; the height not great, the distance only twenty-five yards. Then a quick group picture was taken of Henry, the woman, and her companions as the Minister prepped the next customer.

As I passed by the line, my name was called out and I gave a friendly wave to my people but stayed far enough away to avoid getting trapped. Some approached but my tour guide led the way and let them know I couldn't sign autographs just then. People that had watched the band made their way over to watch Henry. By the time we got close, the crowd stretched around the event in a huge semi-circle, held off by a yellow rope.

"Dion, great to see you," the Minister said. He shook my hand and held the yellow rope up for me to pass under. "Thanks for stopping by." Then he turned to the crowd. "Dion McAres, everybody!"

he yelled as he put his arm around my back. The crowd applauded, some yelled, and others raised the arrow. "This is a big honor, Dion."

"Just wanted to say hello to Henry," I said.

I was directly behind Henry, ten yards away when the crowd began to chant my name and the Minister handed me a football.

"Just one pass, Dion. They'll love it, you owe it to them," the Minister said. He turned to the line of people and called out to a teenager. "Run a fly pattern, son. Dion's itching to complete one."

The kid tore up the field and without thinking I turned, set my feet, and arced an easy ball to him. After he caught it, the kid turned towards his family and pumped an arm as the crowd erupted in applause.

The Minister whispered in my ear, "Dion, we've got a little time before the game. How about twenty-five bucks per pass? It all goes to a good cause."

"Not now. I'm just here to see Henry," I said.

The crowd chanted my name as Henry's next customer got ready. The kick wobbled wide of the goalposts then they set up the next customer. Henry kicked it through, but the ball spun in a funny way.

"Come on, Henry, nail it," I said. I don't know if my presence affected him or maybe the ball was held correctly. The sound of the kick was familiar and it flew like Wally was holding.

"Finally," the Minister said. He turned to me. "Sometimes he acts like he doesn't care." Then he stepped away to get a better angle to speak to the crowd. "Let's hear it for the Nuber! You know the call."

The Minister directed the crowd to chant like they used to. The people on the left side chanted "Nu" and the right side "Ber." He pointed from side to side until the crowd found its rhythm and took off on its own. Another kick, then another as the crowd continued to chant. The line didn't seem to get shorter even though it was approaching three o'clock. I didn't chant, I watched Henry as he was taking more time to approach the ball after the Minister barked at him.

"Nu-Ber! Nu-Ber! Nu-Ber!"

Some men and women in business clothes were at the far end, I knew one was a Dean of something and the other was in charge of alumni relations. They chanted and clapped along with the crowd.

"Nu-Ber! Nu-Ber! Nu-Ber!"

Another fan was waiting to kick but Henry didn't move. The Minister approached him and spoke through the earhole of Henry's helmet. I saw a flash of anger on the Minister's face then he turned to the crowd with a smile as he lifted his arms in rhythm with the chants.

Henry kicked and it bounced off the left post only midway up and the Minister quickly approached him and began yelling in his ear.

"Nu-Ber! Nu-Ber! Nu-Ber!"

Another kick and I could tell Henry was weak. He had to stop.

"Nu-Ber! Nu-Ber! Nu-Ber!"

The next kick wouldn't have cleared the line if there'd been one; it never rose above ten feet.

"Nu-Ber! Nu-Ber! Nu-Ber!"

The next customer waited as the chants grew louder, but Henry didn't move. The Minister approached and I could see his hands tighten.

"Nu-Ber! Nu-Ber! Nu-Ber!"

The Minister yelled into his ear like he was trying to speak above the crowd, but I was tuned in to his anger. The Minister clutched Henry's arm and yanked, while his lips nearly touched the helmet as he spoke. Then Henry wobbled, then he slowly sank to the ground. He put his head between his knees and curled up in a ball as his body subtly rocked. I quickly jogged over to him.

"Henry, you okay?" I said as I bent over.

The Minister yelled to the crowd. "He's fine, just needs to stretch his back." Then the Minister spoke into my ear. "He's fine, he just acts like a baby sometimes. Help me get him up."

"Henry, talk to me. It's me, Dion." I knelt down, placed my arm around his shoulder pads, and whispered through the ear-hole of his helmet. "There's someone waiting for you at my hotel, someone you haven't seen in a while." I wanted to tell him, but the Minister was too close.

"Get him up, Dion," the Minister said. "This is embarrassing."

The crowd had stopped chanting and the silence amid all those people was unnerving. I got in front of him to unbuckle his chin strap and began to lift his helmet off, but the Minister tried to stop me. I gave him a sharp look and told him to back off. The helmet wouldn't come off at first, I had to coax it. Then he finally lifted his head and I saw my reflection in his mirrored visor. That's what they want, I thought, the Tribe wants to see themselves in his reflection. The bottom of his face was without expression, but I could tell it was drawn like he wasn't fed properly. He seemed dirty and there was a mix of peach fuzz and stubble on his chin. I lifted the helmet off and saw a bruise around one eye and scuff marks on the other side.

"How many kicks, Henry?" I said. "How many balls have you kicked today?"

"Ninety-three," Henry said.

"He falls all the time," the Minister said. "He's fine, trust me."

I dropped my head and closed my eyes as an awful feeling gutted me. It was like I'd found Henry at the bottom of a garbage chute and there was no way to get either of us out. This is what Coach Oldham was afraid of, something he could no longer fend off. I felt like a child, helpless with no one to guide us. When I looked up to the crowd, it had taken on an ugly new image. It wasn't a group of people anymore, it was a single entity, a monster with hundreds of eyes and a single mind, a mind without the ability to reason. It was time.

The Minister was looking over my shoulder and I snapped at him loud enough for people close by to hear. "You're ruining him, do you know that? Thirty kicks a day, that's his max."

"But, he's—"

I held my hand up to the Minister as I stood and the crowd waited for me to speak.

"He's done," I yelled. "Henry's overworked, the show's over."

Groans and complaints rose.

"We already paid!"

"That's not fair!"

"You can't do this," the Minister said. "I've got customers, we can't let them down."

The look on my face must've scared him, he backed off with his hands upraised. I wanted to deliver the same punishment he gave to Henry but do it in public in front of the Tribe. I wanted to walk Henry in front of everyone and show them his bruises, show them their desires had gone too far. The Professor was right, Wally was right. I tried to channel the Professor's words, there had to be a way out.

Tribes are the source of all human power.

Tribes can achieve anything and destroy everything.

Tribes are impenetrable, immune to everything in their way, except one thing: lies.

"I have a better idea and it's why I'm here," I said to the Minister. "We can make a lot of money together off of Henry's skills, are you interested?"

He didn't react until I told him he was killing the golden goose, it seemed to trip something in his mind. The fear on his face subsided as he realized the opportunity I described in broad terms. Instructional videos, a camp for kickers, shoe company endorsements.

"I love it. But we have to talk this through before you leave," he said.

"The only time is now. Let's go back to my hotel and we'll sketch it out. There's only one catch. Henry has to agree; he has to choose what he wants to do."

"Absolutely, he's just having a bad day. This was his idea, in fact."

The Minister ended Henry's session and didn't seem to care about the complaints. He told the staff they were done for the day and collected the money box. I stayed with Henry as the crowd dissolved like cotton candy.

As we walked through the Performance Center I was lost in thought. *We're not different*, I thought. We say we are but the purity and virtue we'd dressed ourselves in for decades was a sloganeer's trick. Exploitation was in plain sight and documented by receipts for tickets, parking passes, booster donations, and fees to hold for Henry. The Tribe, the larger Tribe, was no different than any other. I had to save Henry and go home to Buffalo. I couldn't face the Minister anymore and I didn't want to be seen with him.

"How about you meet us there," I said. "Henry and I are going to walk around a bit."

"There's a ride waiting for us out front," the Minister said. "Besides, he can't walk around in his football uniform."

A white Cadillac Escalade was idling in front of the Performance Center. I got in back with Henry and didn't notice who the driver was as the Minister got in the front.

"I told you I'd see you later," Sly said from behind the wheel.

I was stunned and fumbled for a response. "This is a private meeting, Sly."

He gave me a half-smirk as he spun the wheel. "Not to me, this is going to be fun." We drove past fans walking to the stadium like rivers flowing towards a larger body and I was going against them. At a red light I thought about opening the door and dragging Henry out with me. Or maybe popping Sly, the old bastard, and throwing him out.

"You'll never believe the opportunity Dion is proposing," the Minister said to Sly. "This is what I've been waiting for."

"Really," said Sly. "Fill me in and then I'll let you in on a little secret."

As the Minister explained it to Sly, I tried to figure out what to do. Henry was staring out the window completely unaware of his role. The Minister was almost done and then Sly would tell him. He knew, Sly always knew.

"Reverend," I said, "don't forget to tell him about the shoe company endorsements, my agent has already talked to them."

Sly turned back to me. "You've got to be kidding me, you're really taking this thing pretty far."

The Minister kept talking and I texted Samantha: *Trouble, Sly driving us, he knows, he's coming, what do?*

The hotel was ahead, all Sly had to do was mention Wally's name. I began to feel sweat on my forehead and my mind followed the worst path: Wally exposed and arrested, the Minister leaving with Henry and taking out his angst on him, Sly leaking it out that I was involved in a plan to abduct Henry.

My phone buzzed. Samantha had responded: *Bring Sly to me*

We pulled into the hotel drive and the Minister was still talking. He interpreted Sly's smiles and sarcastic laughs as enthusiasm. I had to come up with something.

"Sly, you remember Samantha Yardley?" I said.

He parked in front. "Oh, do I. Don't tell me she's in on this, too?"

"That name's familiar," the Minister said.

"She's here and she'd like to see you. I'll drop Henry and Reverend Nubinski off in my room and you and me can go see her. She's with the person you're looking for."

The valet waited for Sly but he was staring at me trying to figure out the plan I was unaware of. Then he raised a finger. "Up there, he's up there right now?"

I nodded. "I'm not getting in the way of this shit. I'll take you to him," I said.

"Hot damn," Sly said as he slapped the steering wheel. "My job just gets easier and easier."

The Minister looked at me and I shook my head with a look like it wasn't any of his business. The four of us took the elevator up to the top floor and I could barely breathe as we walked the hall. I couldn't feel my feet, the card key trembled in my hand.

"I'll be right back, Reverend. You and Henry make yourself at home, use the minibar if you want."

When the door closed and it was just me and Sly, he looked at me with grave satisfaction. "You're a pussy. A real tough guy on the field, but off it you fold right up. As soon as I verify he's there, I'm calling the cops then you can go and carry on this charade with that goofball. Let's go."

Wally's room was five doors down, the door was cracked open by the security bar. I opened it and walked in. Samantha, Wally, and the Professor were waiting. Then Sly walked in and stood with his hands on his hips.

"Holy shit. This is like the hall of fame for Bastille losers," Sly said. He pointed to Samantha. "I thought we banned you." Then he pointed to the Professor. "I thought we fired you." Then he looked at Wally. "And I've been waiting to get my hands on you for two years."

He pulled his phone out and was about to dial when Samantha spoke up.

"Thanks for coming, Sly. Before you call the police, you should check your email. You'll be glad you did," she said with a condescending smile.

Sly hesitated then tapped his phone. As he began reading his confidence turned to concern. His body language shifted as he read the email, then he turned and brought a finger to his mouth. I looked to Samantha and she slowly shook her head as she held up her hand. I traded glances with Wally, then the Professor shrugged like he didn't know what was going on. Another minute passed as we waited in silence. Then Sly turned to Samantha.

"You fucking bitch."

"Enough with the potty mouth, Sly. Did you see how many there are?"

"This is bullshit, they can't prove anything. What do you want?"

"They're journalists, they're very skilled at writing down pertinent details. Now, I suggest you excuse yourself immediately and if you do, I'll drop the whole thing." Then she turned to the Professor. "Professor Bertrand, would you mind escorting Sly out of the building?"

"I'd love to," the Professor said. "In fact, I'll buy him coffee. Sly, do you know anything about coffee? I know a lot about coffee."

"None of this is true," Sly said.

Samantha brought her hands to her face for a moment, then stood. "You can't lie your way through this, I'm one of them. Are you going to tell me I fabricated all the times you touched me? You're the only DFO in the country who's done that. Same for the other women."

Sly held up a finger but didn't speak. He looked at his phone again then turned around. Samantha gave him time as she stood with folded arms. I was in awe of her. Then Sly turned to Wally.

"You're not worth it, you little shit." Then he flung the door open and walked out with the Professor trailing him.

After they left, I turned to Samantha. "What the hell was that about?"

"Do you think I'd come here without a plan for Sly? Men aren't the only ones that know how to form tribes, this could be its own story. Now go see the Minister, I'll be there in few minutes to get Henry."

"Are you really going to let Sly off the hook? That's some serious shit you called him on."

"Yeah, I am," she said. "Don't worry, I told all the other women what was going on. They're going to nail him without me."

It made me pause, she was going to pass on finally bringing down someone that deserved it.

"You've got to hurry, Dion," Wally said. He had a hopeful look on his face, like it was the old Wally.

I hesitated. "Why don't I bring him down myself, I'll get him now."

"Stick to the plan, you have to distract the Minister or he'll get suspicious," she said.

"But—"

"But *what* Dion?" she said.

I took a deep breath knowing she was right. "I want to see the reunion. I want to see the brothers, my brothers, together again."

"Another time, Dion," Samantha said. "Go."

As I headed back to my room, I tried to steel myself for another session with the Minister. When I entered, he was propped up on the couch with a drink like it was his room. I didn't have a chance to say anything before he launched into his ideas. I almost felt sorry for him.

"Dion, this is fantastic, I can't believe we're going to work together." He held his hands up like he was framing a video shot. "We'll have footage of the Nuber making some of his best kicks and then freeze the moment and have his shoe zoom up to full frame—'The Nuber, the NCAA's greatest kicker wants to show you how!'—What do you think?"

With a quick smile and a nod, I told him it was awesome and to keep them coming. As he prattled on, I didn't hear a word he said, half the time he wasn't even looking at me. He started pacing the floor making grand gestures like he was in front of a congregation. Then Samantha knocked.

"I'll get it," he said.

"No, I'm expecting someone." I hurried over to the door and stepped out into the hall.

"If it's good," she whispered, "I'll come back and give you the nod. Wally's really worried Henry won't want to leave."

"Why is that?"

"Did you forget what he said last night? How he tried to take him when he left after the FSU game but Henry wouldn't go? The poor guy is on pins and needles. If Henry doesn't want to leave with Wally, I'll bring Henry back with me. If he wants to leave with Wally, I'll come back and give you the nod and we'll finish this off," she said. "Give me your room key."

I stepped back inside and shut the door. "Henry, an old team-mate is here and wants to see you."

Henry stood and approached, he looked silly wearing his full uniform.

"Anyone I know?" said the Minister.

"No, you don't really know him at all, Reverend."

Henry stepped out of the room and Samantha took him by the hand. I closed the door and returned to my seat. "Now, where were we?" I said.

"A shoe line for kickers only."

"That will never sell, there aren't that many kickers in the world," I said.

"Good point. Next idea: a multi-city traveling road show and kickers camp. We could go nearly year-round from city to city, hosting kicking tutorials. Did you ever notice how the Sports Inc.

website has something about football on it every day? It's truly a year-round sport. I'm thinking we're going to need some other kickers, maybe some retired NFL guys. Do you know any?"

The Minister's ideas were endless and distracting as I tried to imagine what was happening down the hall. I was afraid Henry would want the obvious thing, to go back to his childhood and to stay with his father and have Wally remain with him. He couldn't understand there were other ways to live, that he could be free. If it happened, Wally would be crushed and never make it back to the place from where he came; he would drink and hide and hole up somewhere until he didn't exist anymore. The last of the Tribe I believed in would be gone and all that would remain would be something base and grubby, fighting to survive by exploits and carnival barks.

"What do you think about adding punters to the mix?" the Minister said.

"Never trust a punter," I said. "They give the ball away."

I dropped my head into my hands. Too much time had passed, if it was a happy reunion, Samantha would've returned or called or texted by now. Anger started to grow, I wanted to lash out, but the sources of my hate were selfishness and ignorance and apathy, the sins of a tribe gone wrong. The only physical target available was the Minister and I'd save him for Wally. I looked at him as he spoke without hearing a word. His lips moved and his exuberance buoyed like we were afloat the most magical ride ever. If Henry declined, I'd get Wally and let him have his day.

Why not tell him now, I thought. Why not bring everything out into the open and let it play out. If Henry wanted to stay, I was going to the police. If Henry wanted to leave, then the Minister should suffer the pain of seeing it happen. Why make it so complicated, I thought.

"Hey, Rev," I said. "You want to hear something really interesting?"

Then the door slowly opened, and Samantha entered with her back to me as she quietly closed it. I would see it in her face the second she turned, she always had a hard look, I wanted to see it softened and humanized. But when she turned around, her face was harder than ever. Then I saw tears rolling down her cheek as she began to nod, the tears carved a path like sweet water over hard ground and I realized they were the tears of life that could only be triggered by witnessing something beautiful and sacred. She brought her hand to her heart, exhaled, and gave me the most beautiful smile I'd ever seen. I leaned back in my seat and brought my hands to my face to control my own emotions. I wanted to hug her and run down the hall to see my brothers but I couldn't take my eyes off of her.

"What's the matter?" the Minister said.

I gathered myself as Samantha sat next to me and wiped her eyes.

"Do you know my colleague, Samantha Yardley?"

The Minister recognized her, and his confusion might have been the most profound thing he'd ever felt. I only remember snippets of the conversation, because, once again, Samantha took the lead.

"No, your other biological son."

"Please take a look at this video."

"Henry has made a choice; he's going with Wally."

I peppered the conversation with disgust, it was a rout. The Minister threatened, then broke down, then begged for mercy when Samantha said she could have the video displayed on Sports Inc.'s website within the hour. Only the threat of calling the police got him to leave and he left with nowhere to go.

When we were alone, I picked up Samantha and hugged her as she described what had happened. Then I paced the room with excitement.

"I want to see them, I want to see Wally and Henry together again," I said.

Samantha was by the window looking down. "I'm sorry, Dion, they're gone. They wanted to get out as soon as they could. Look, there they are."

I hurried to the window and saw them walking together, Henry in street clothes.

"I bought them this morning," she said.

The Professor was with them, and they approached an old truck parked on the street. I started banging on the hotel room window but knew they'd never hear me.

"Wally! Henry!" I kept pounding the window with the bottom of my fists as Wally opened the passenger door for Henry. I still had the email, but didn't know if he'd ever respond. The Professor hugged them both, then Henry got in the truck as I kept banging the window. Then Wally stopped and looked up. He saw me, I knew he did, and I stopped banging. He pulled Henry out of the truck and pointed up at me. They stared for a moment and then Wally did something that shocked me. He raised his hands and arms into the arrow and held it high while Henry stood looking. I screamed in joy and raised the arrow in response. Wally kept it raised for a moment then he slowly dropped the arrow until it was pointed at me. *This ain't right,* I thought, *it should be the other way around.* I didn't move, I didn't deserve it, but he waited until I had no choice. Finally, I brought my hands to my chest and ripped them away to expose my heart. Then, Wally fired away.

I watched as they drove away, their taillights disappeared under leafy trees. They were free and Wally believed again. And so do I.

Wally

....

ALBUQUERQUE, NEW MEXICO
SEVERAL MONTHS LATER

WHEN I OPEN my eyes and let the beauty overtake me, I become stunned in silence feeling every living goodness play its part in taking me forward. Like Aunt Janie said, turn each moment into a gift because you'll never get it back. A gift to be enjoyed, a gift to solve a problem, a gift to move forward.

I began my ascent up the hill, hoping I wouldn't be too late; dusk had begun the transformation that always struck me with awe from the spot up above. Yearning, I'd always been yearning for something pure to take hold and lift me out of pain. But now I know, it's only with each step up that I will be able to become who I want to be. I stopped looking deep within to find my true self; I started looking high above to see who I wanted to be, that's the true me that I will become. I continued to climb.

My phone sounded a text alert, someone added to the group chat. Dion had responded. I halted my climb and scrolled back to the beginning and reread the latest thread that had started earlier in the day.

Samantha: *OMG, you can't believe what I just heard!!! Castritt is stepping down!*

Professor Bertrand: *That is news, do you know the reason? I hate to openly display schadenfreude, but in this case I think it's warranted.*

Samantha: *I can smell a scandal. It was way way too low key. I'll do some digging and get back to you. Good luck with the playoff game, Dion.*

Dion: *WTF, is he really gone?*

Professor Bertrand: *Yes, good luck, Dion. Mary and I will be watching!!!*

Me: *Professor you're making me look up words again.*

Dion: *Just checked, the mofo had to go!!! Glad you said that Wally, I thought the same thing.*

Dion: *Tribe forever!!! Need to hear it Wally!*

Me: *TRIBE FOREVER!!!!*

Samantha: *How's school Wally?*

Me: *Sitting in the front row, bro.*

Professor Bertrand: *Now that's what I like to hear!*

Me: *Good luck Dion.*

Dion: *Thanks guys. I'll text you after the game.*

My tribe, I thought. The four of us would be bound together, forever.

My climb continued up the hill. Soon, the mountains to the west would lose their detailed luster with the fading sun, becoming a silhouette that was ready for sleep. The city and the campus would transform with a shimmering quality that would soon become points of light.

Therapy was helping, my thoughts had been organic demons that forced self-medication, which I no longer did. The trauma was unpacked and tamed into inert memories that could no longer harm me. I was done looking at the future through the broken lens of the past. But I had to keep on climbing to get there. It wasn't much further.

When I crested the hill, I had to catch my breath in awe. It was more than a sunset; it was a vision of joy and my future. Henry and Aunt Janie sitting side by side, framed inside the half-submerged setting sun. I didn't mind the diagnosis, mine or his, but I loved the prescription: stay together, always. And no more sins. No more sins.

ACKNOWLEDGMENTS

MY DEEPEST APPRECIATION to my wife, Courtney, and our children, Mac, Carley, and Caity for their love and support over the years. This novel wouldn't have happened if not for their encouragement.

Many thanks to Bill Brannen, Alexander Cocron, Scott Disher, Todd and Tammy Eide, and Tom Notar; they all gladly read early versions of the manuscript and provided valuable feedback. Also, many thanks to Beth Havlicek for her support.

A special thanks to Chuck Neumann, for pointing out the three sources of the truth, and to Bert Gambini, Nick Quarantillo, and Shelly Dinan, for their invaluable insights and thoughts.

I would also like to express gratitude to the incredible Greenleaf Book Group team; their excitement, expertise, and support throughout the process has been more than I could've hoped for.

Finally, and most of all, I would like to acknowledge and thank you, the reader.

ABOUT THE AUTHOR

MARK SALTER grew up in Western New York. He graduated from Canisius College where he played college football and
was later inducted into the Canisius College Sports Hall of Fame.
He was signed by an NFL team but didn't make the final roster.
Mark received his master's degree from Carnegie Mellon University. He currently lives with his family in Jupiter, Florida.